T0367931

Dr. J. Norberto Saracco
Pastor of Buenas Nuevas Evangelical Church, Buenos Aires
Founder and Rector Emeritus of FIET Theological Institute
Former Director for Latin America of the Lausanne Movement
Founder and Co-Coordinator of the Council of Pastors of the City of
Buenos Aires

To honor and serve God is the dream of everyone who loves Jesus. How can we do this? This is the big question. Some, the least, embark on the adventure of ministry. Others live their lives, professions, and occupations with the guilt of not having put priorities in the right order. In both cases, good intentions confront the reality of life as it is. Ministry is not always the idyllic place to serve God, nor does a profession or occupation in itself displace God from center stage. Life decisions are full of contradictions. "Pastor, Pastor" shows us, in a warm and engaging way, the struggle of its characters to find their own destiny amid life's contradictions. Above the right or wrong decisions, it teaches us that God always gives us another chance.

Lic. Ruben Del Ré
General Director of the Argentine Bible Society
Member of the World Council and Executive Board of United Bible Societies

Through a particularly good narrative, we meet characters who represent the ideals, the heart, the greatness, the mistakes and the miseries of many who long to serve God and people. Those of us who have been in the world of evangelical churches and "ministry" for several decades will feel that we are reliving stories that happened to us, of which we were part (or suffered) in one way or another. The critical look at certain emphases and practices of recent years can help us to open our eyes to some imbalances, but with a constructive spirit, seeking to clear the way to recover the essence of life in community of the people of God.

PASTOR PASTOR

FEED MY SHEEP

ALEJANDRO FIELD

WESTBOW
PRESS®
A DIVISION OF THOMAS NELSON
& ZONDERVAN

WestBow Press books may be ordered through booksellers or by contacting:

WestBow Press
A Division of Thomas Nelson & Zondervan
1663 Liberty Drive
Bloomington, IN 47403
www.westbowpress.com
844-714-3454

ISBN: 978-1-6642-0426-3 (sc)
ISBN: 978-1-6642-0427-0 (hc)
ISBN: 978-1-6642-0425-6 (e)

Library of Congress Control Number: 2020916958

Print information available on the last page.

WestBow Press rev. date: 10/19/2020

CONTENTS

HERE
(2000)

FROM THERE TO HERE
(1978 - 2000)

FROM HERE TO THERE
(2000-2003)

FROM THERE ON
(2003)

HERE

(2000)

1

PEDRO: IN SEARCH OF A FRIEND

We search for them, for one, for any
And find we've lost them all already

"Hallelujah!"
"Praise the Lord!"
"Tell the person next to you, 'God loves you!'"
"Louder!"
"A hand for the Lord! Hallelujah!"

Pedro knew the routine too well. That intoxicating back and forth from the stage to the audience. Since that youth congress in Mendoza, barely eighteen years old, and for the last fifteen years in charge of his church. How he had touched the sky with his hands when he first got on the platform! And how he had felt so palpably the power of being in front of so many people who obeyed him blindly, seeking, almost wishing that he would tell them what to do at every moment. That feeling was embedded in his memory, like the indelible smells of some places and moments, and it was still as real today as that night in February 1972, as warm as tonight.

He also remembered how an inner voice, an almost imperceptible red light, had warned him that this power would be bad for him. Like wine for the alcoholic, it would be something he couldn't control. But he had ignored it, a little because of the importance of the event and a lot because of that sense of duty he had carried since he was a

1

boy. "Challenges and problems are meant to be overcome, Pedrito, not avoided," his father had told him hundreds of times, in that intimidating six-feet-high voice. To refuse the challenge, to get off that platform that night, would have been to dodge the problem, to quit. He didn't. He wondered at that moment if the young man in charge of shouting the slogans tonight had gone through the same process.

He looked to his right, from whence an unfamiliar face was shouting at him at the top of his voice, "God loves you, brother!" He mechanically answered something neutral that could have meant anything. Still, it didn't matter because no one listened amid the shouting and the hackneyed phrases that everyone knew by heart and repeated without thinking.

Ah, the routine. Doing the same thing over and over again. On one side of the pulpit and on the other. Up and down the platform, like dance couples. If only he had reflected, if only he had stopped the ball in time, of his own free will, before being forced to do so. He had had at least two clear opportunities, and he had ignored them both: the incident with Sara and the scene in front of the crowd. The memory of both situations still hurt. How much time and how much bitterness could have been saved. And now, the third warning: the mysterious man with intense blue eyes who appeared and disappeared out of nowhere saying strangely significant words. As he looked for a handkerchief to wipe his forehead, a used sugar packet fell from his pocket. He picked it up from the floor and remembered why he had kept it. It was from the coffee he had drunk the night before with Virginia. It said, "Life always gives you a second chance, but rarely a third." Could God speak to him through a sugar packet?

Someone tapped him on the shoulder from behind, and suddenly he found himself lifted from his seat and hugged to the point of suffocation by a gigantic, sweaty man he had never seen in his life. As he tried to break free in the best possible way without offending this effusive brother, he felt that this hug symbolized the oppression of that point in his life, but also an excruciating need for affection and contention.

At that moment he felt as if everything around him was talking directly to him about his own life and needs. The sugar packet. The embrace of the stranger. The strident lights and music that fell on the audience from the multicolored stage spoke to him of the life of appearances he had sought and achieved, a show put on for others. The neat rows of chairs facing the stage mimicked the type of church and the relationship between pastor and congregation—and perhaps even the relationship with his family and friends—that he had managed to build: orderly, predictable, one-way, top to bottom, with him always in control.

In the front and above, a group of young people, microphones in hand, sang the songs while moving back and forth, too sensually for the place. Pedro had once wondered if this wasn't another mechanism borrowed from the secular world to maintain the interest of the audience. The lad, having finished his part of the show, had left his place to another slightly older and better-dressed young man, Pastor Carlos, who lashed out with renewed enthusiasm. He seemed happy to receive a primed audience.

"How many want to be happy tonight?" Lots of hands were raised. "How many are sad tonight?" No hands. "Tell the person next to you, with a huge smile, 'You can't be sad tonight because the Lord is here.'" Huge commotion. "Now say it to the brother or sister in front of you." With a hint of a smile and shaking his head, Pedro thought, *How could no one have realized the logical impossibility of this maneuver? How can I talk to the one in front of me if he in turn is talking to the one in front of him?* But he knew it didn't matter much. The point was to keep people moving, always telling them what to do and say. Standing, sitting, greeting, singing, repeating, giving... A kind of church gymnastics to spare them the work and the danger of thinking. The obsession with noise and joy reminded him bitterly of the time he had used a similar routine to lift people's spirits and later learned that there was a man in the audience who had just lost his wife. He never saw him in church again. He hardly would have gone to another one, he thought.

He had sat in the last row up on the balcony where he was least likely to be recognized. Besides, he always arrived half an hour after the meeting had started, so it would be harder to cross paths with an acquaintance. In any case, his appearance was so changed that it would take a miracle for someone to identify that grizzled, overweight man with the former brightest star of the evangelical circuit in recent years, Pastor Pedro Terrero. For those who focused more on the eyes than on the outward appearance, it would be even harder. The sure and penetrating gaze, full of contagious life and optimism, had disappeared, and in its place was a vague, imprecise, jaded, and cynical contemplation.

Why had he come today, and the last three Sundays to this church in a precarious neighborhood in Barracas? He wasn't sure. The senior pastor of the Faith and Love Church, Nacho Leiva, had studied with him at the seminary twenty years ago, but he never found him at the meeting; he was at a conference, traveling, in a daughter church, or doing something else. It reminded him of his life of the past few years: always busy, always active, hardly available for those who needed him. But Pedro needed to meet with Nacho, if only for a few minutes. He didn't know why, but he felt that Nacho was the only one right now who could help him. They had only seen each other a couple of times since they had graduated, at a conference and at a pastors' meeting where they had exchanged a few words of circumstance. He remembered Virginia had mentioned he had called several times asking how they were, but he had never returned those calls. Nacho had always conveyed something different to him: a warmth and authenticity that he desperately needed now. So, even though he couldn't find him and almost everything he saw in his church was negative, Pedro kept coming back.

"God wants to do great things tonight! Come on! Repeat after me: 'God wants to do great things tonight!'"

The audience repeated obediently.

"God keeps his promises. Is it true?"

"Yes."

"Louder!"

"*Yesssssss!*"

4

"Repeat after me: 'God keeps all his promises.'"

Pastor Carlos had gone on autopilot.

"God keeps his promises! Amen?"

"I can't hear you! Do you really believe it? Come on!"

"God keeps his promises every day of the week!"

In meetings where he had been in the audience and had to repeat this routine, Pedro had sometimes toyed with the idea of what would happen if this pedagogical method were used in college. For example, he imagined a physics professor saying to his class:

"For each force acting on a body, it performs an equal but opposite force on the body that produced it. Do you believe it?"

"Yes," the students would reply.

"Do you really believe it? If you believe it, I want to hear a louder 'yes'."

"*Yesssss!*"

"Tell the person next to you, 'For each force acting on a body, it performs an equal but opposite force on the body that produced it…'"

Pedro found it very amusing to imagine this situation, and he himself had always resisted the temptation to use it. He considered himself to be in another category— spiritual, but without neglecting the mind. Like the crutch "Amen, brothers?" "Amen!" that was repeated incessantly, reflecting the insecurity of the preacher, in what he said or in his ability to maintain the interest of his audience. And the chaos that would occur if faced with an "Amen, brothers?" someone answered with a *no*?

The fledgling pastor who was taking his first steps with his suit and tie that looked ridiculous in the forty-plus degrees on the stage was coming to one of the most important moments of the service: the offering. Pedro could foresee with almost mathematical accuracy what would happen. He would first begin with some indirect reference to the importance of giving, then take some Bible passage out of context that he would use to corner the undecided faithful, and end with a brief harangue on the importance of giving and how God rewards the giver with an implicit suggestion of the dire consequences of not giving. Then the baskets would be passed to the rhythm of an allusive song. He wasn't mistaken, except for the addition of a couple of testimonies from people who had given offerings the week before and had been generously rewarded by the Lord.

So, when this moment came, he stood up abruptly and looked for the exit, elbowing his way out through the ushers who approached him with their plastic smiles and brochures. He took another look and noticed that Nacho wasn't sitting on any of the chairs on the stage or in the front rows. As soon as he came out, he felt the fresh air of the street and a certain relief. From the brightly lit sidewalk with the signs that said, "Night of Miracles and Healing," he could look in and out. The contrast seemed enormous to him. Inside, a bath of happiness and unreality; outside, street kids, scavengers, dirt, darkness, danger. Attempting to find images, the door of the church hall looked like a time tunnel, transforming people as they went through it in both directions.

He crossed the street and entered the bar La Encrucijada,[1] a name that sounded prophetic to him today. He chose a low-light, tucked-away table, too close to the kitchen and bathroom odors, and asked for a café latte. He needed time to reconsider before returning home.

After a while, he realized that several of the people in the place had come, like him, from the church across the street, including the bear hugger. Some carried their Bibles, and some men wore suits, but in general they had that indefinable quality of evangelicals (or "evangelists," as everyone called them) that he recognized at once. It was the typical group of those who attended, but didn't stay in the church, finding more satisfaction in chatting with others on the sidewalk or in the bar than in the impersonal, predictable, and repetitive ritual offered inside. If he had to define them, they were a mixture of people who were not in their best relationship with the Lord and others who were overwhelmed by an excess of activity and responsibility. Pedro remembered a similar group in his church, when he was a youth, who would sneak out of the service to go for coffee with *facturas*.[2] The only difference was that they hadn't dared

---

[1] In Spanish, The Crossroad
[2] Typical local Danish pastry

to choose a place so close to the church then. Their escape point had been about three blocks from the temple, at the Café Osiris.

The waiter brought him back to the present.

"Your order, sir."

"Thank you. Who's winning?" gesturing nonchalantly towards the switched-on TV. Boca was fighting for the top.

"Gimnasia, two-nil."

"No way!" Even at that, he was doing badly.

His eyes wandered around the room as he absent-mindedly stirred the coffee. Suddenly, they landed on a couple in their forties, like him. They were sitting two tables away and weren't believers, because they both smoked and peppered their conversation with swear words. His face looked familiar, and that way of cocking his head after making a joke, as if waiting for an answer. But it was a phrase he said that brought it to mind. At one point he heard the characteristic "You'll have to believe me..." and thought, "Hugo Carvajal, from the SeBiPa!" and lowered his head at once. What if he recognized him? How had his life continued after what happened with—what was her name? —yes, Verónica? Because that wasn't Verónica with him. What a bad way to handle the matter! And he had never even called him...

Suddenly he heard a shout:

"Pedro! Pedrito Terrero!!" Hugo was shouting at him from his table and had started walking towards him.

"Hugo! What are you doing here?" Pedro stood up, feigning surprise, and they gave each other a strong and loud hug.

"Hanging around... Hey, you're changed... on the outside. I'm sure you're the same old scamp from the seminary... Those were the days."

"Don't be too sure...," he answered him, without much strength and avoiding his gaze. "If you see me changed on the outside, you have to see me on the inside..."

"No way! What happened to you? Don't scare me!" He waited for an answer, a joke, in vain... "Let me introduce you to Mía, who was about to leave."

Hugo took Pedro by the shoulder to his table, made the

introductions, and after saying goodbye to his partner and leaving a note for the bill, he sat down at Pedro's table.

"Do you have time? I'll ask for something... Waiter, two lattes!... You're a mess. What happened? Did someone die?"

Hugo had always been talkative and affectionate, a simple and straightforward guy. Pedro would have thought that he had reasons to be angry with him after what had happened, but all he could feel was the sincere joy of meeting him and the concern for his condition.

"Someone died... Ha, maybe...," said Pedro slowly, with an empty, sad smile.

"Hey, don't scare me. Your dad? Someone I know?"

"No.....it's just that I'm thinking a lot in images lately. Don't worry, no one you know died. What died is my ministry, Hugo. I'm finished. Twenty years down the drain..."

Hugo said nothing this time, but his frank and interested face was the best invitation for Pedro to open up in confidence.

Pedro told him everything, or almost everything. It was difficult to talk about certain things with someone who had been out of the picture for so long. But, on the other hand, he felt that he was talking to his old study partner, with whom he had shared so many dreams and such a beautiful time. And with that Hugo he felt comfortable. It was true that their lives had taken quite different paths, but they had started from the same point and now, on a whim of fate—of fate? — they had met again.

"... so the church decided to give me a year's leave, to sort out my things. But it seems to me that this is the end of a stage. Things aren't the same anymore, and I have a lot to sort out with Virginia. And the kids are teenagers, young, and they need me to be okay."

"Virginia... So you married her? How many kids do you have?"

"We have three. Roque is 12, Luciana is 10 and Valeria is 8... no 9. What image am I giving them? Okay, enough of me. Tell me about you."

Hugo told him that after what had happened at the Seminary, he had cut loose from everything that had to do with the church. He felt disillusioned and bitter. He went into construction and, after struggling hard and setting up a small company that was doing very well, he was hit by president Alfonsín's crisis in 1989, and lost everything. He had married, and things weren't going well. They say that crises unite or separate couples, depending on how they find them, and they went their separate ways. Noelia stayed with their three-year-old son, Santiago, who was now thirteen, and he tried various unimportant relationships until he met Mía. They were a couple, and he was now helping her in her clothing business.

The question was in the air, and Hugo saved Pedro from it.

"Do you know I had nothing to do with Verónica?"

"Really! Then why did you leave?"

"Because I was so angry about how they tried to saddle me with something that wasn't mine. It was the opposite of what they were supposed to teach us, and that we were to go out and teach. Nobody cared about the truth, nor about people. All they cared about was the image of the Seminary, what people would say. They wanted me out, so I left..." The subject was already closed for Hugo. "Hey, I didn't ask you. What are you doing here?"

"I was at the church across the street. I wanted to talk to Nacho."

"Nacho... Nacho Leiva?"

"Yes, he's the pastor of the church."

"You're kidding me! What a great guy! If you see him, send him my regards."

"Done!"

2

JUAN: IN SEARCH OF A PLACE

We wander through life's hundred paths
Stumbling, groping, falling apart

Juan walked the dusty road alone. It was a way of getting to know the town, and he could use the extra time to continue thinking about what he had experienced the last few months. There was a hint of self-imposed penance too. He needed to purge the thoughts of anger and frustration he had brought with him from Buenos Aires. The midday heat and the weight of the luggage would help him forget the spiritual burden he was carrying. Inside him, silent voices suggested action after action he should have followed to take revenge on those who had hurt him so badly—him and Mariela. Weren't there the famous imprecatory psalms in the Bible, which called for the destruction of enemies? But how could a pastor hate? Wasn't that a contradiction? Shouldn't he have forgiven them by now?

There was no one waiting for him from the church when he arrived at the bus terminal. A bad sign. After walking a couple of blocks mechanically, he found an empty stone bench and dropped heavily on it. It was still not clear to him why he had accepted to come to the mission of the Church of the Open Word in Pueblo Manso, 300 kilometers southwest of Buenos Aires, in the middle of the Pampa, after the dismal experience in the central church in the capital. But he had learned to listen to that little inner voice, and to obey it. Until now it had guided him, getting him out in time from places where time had run out—the first church, the "cult," the family church... and now the structured church. In each place they had lost something, but they had also taken away something good. Each had enriched them in some way. It was true that today it was difficult for him to find something good from the last experience, but surely time would reveal it to him. Ah, the wisdom of Ecclesiastes, "...a time to plant and a time to uproot...[3] a time to tear down and a time to build...[4] a time to weep and a time to laugh..."[5] Surely this was a time to weep. But they had planted, they had built, they had laughed. And those times would return, no doubt. You bet they would!

"Pastor Cristante?" A blue-green truck had stopped abruptly across the street and a man was calling him from the open window. "Pastor Juan Cristante!" he repeated louder. Juan was so absorbed in his thoughts that he only heard him the third time.

"Yes, it's me."

The man got out of the truck and ran across the empty street. He shook his hand and grabbed the heaviest bag in one move.

"I'm Saverio Montes, from the church. So sorry for not arriving on time to pick you up! The truck simply refused to start!"

"No problem. It's good for me to rest a bit after such a long trip." Juan liked the tall, skinny man right away. The clean, spotless F100 pickup truck, with plenty of shiny chrome spoke of a tidy man who took care of his things.

"I really can't understand how this happened to me, pastor. I get up early, get the truck out first thing, to make sure everything was okay, and when I'm leaving for the terminal it refuses to start. It looks like the devil's work." He was visibly sorry for not having arrived on time.

"Please, Saverio! Don't worry at all. There are worse things in life."

"Yes... they told us something about what happened at the central church. Let me tell you from the start, so you can relax, that here we

---

[3] Ecc 3:2
[4] Ecc 3:3
[5] Ecc 3:4

are quite different from those in Buenos Aires. You'll see. Come on up, I'll show you the town."

Saverio was an excellent tour guide. The few points of interest came alive with his historical description, full of dates and names. The watchtower where an Indian attack had been stopped in 1882, the fresh water spring that had only stopped running once, the day Mayor Garcilaso took office, a violent and corrupt character who had to resign after a month, back in 1930. There was also "the meteorite," a block of stone about three meters in diameter, vaguely spherical and very dark, which appeared an indefinite night in the field of the Costas Navas's. What concerned Saverio was that each of these places had become centers of pilgrimage over time, with their popular worship, candles, stamps, and trade around them.

"Instead of worshipping the God who made the heavens, the earth, man... everything, they worship the things he created. If that's not idolatry, tell me what is, pastor."

"Yes, history repeats itself, since the time of the Israelites." Juan said something mechanically, in "pastor" mode.

Idolatry, he thought. It was so easy to see it in others, or in the most evident forms—an image, an object. But it was much more difficult to recognize it in attitudes or practices. Wasn't it the idolatry of tradition that had caused his work to fail in the last church?

"Pastor, we want you to take a break, think things over. You are exhausted. You are wanting to do too much, and we aren't accompanying you as you need. Why don't you let the Council replace you while you go to the beach for a few days with your family," Antonio had told him the day after the hectic assembly. Good intentions, on the surface.

Pastor, we don't want you here. You're doing too much, too soon. You're changing things we don't want to see changed. We prefer the Council to run the church again while it finds a pastor more in tune with our ways. We want you to leave, was the actual interpretation of the message. The same, but different; in fact, the opposite.

He still carried that awful, indescribable feeling inside him, as if he were sinking in a swamp. A *déjà vu* of what he had felt when he was fired from his first job, at the screw factory, in an orchestrated maneuver, a very dirty pulling the rug from under him. But of course, that had been "in the world." How could he ever feel the same way in the church, his church, from his "sheep," for whom he had done so much, and from whom he had asked nothing in return? He had wanted to cry and scream at the same time. Rejoinder and run away. He had felt violated in his trust, betrayed. Something inside him wanted to say to them, "You are making a mistake! The problem is not with the pastors you bring in year after year and who are gone in no time! It is you, who don't give them time, who want to control them, who don't want to change." But he realized that there was no point. "Meaningless! Meaningless!" another phrase from Ecclesiastes, came automatically to his mind.

He had refused. He wasn't going to take a break, nor was he going to think things over. He preferred to start again, somewhere else, far away. He wanted a second chance as a pastor in this church. It was a way to regain his dignity and initiative, to be himself again. He was surprised by how quickly things were arranged and the possibility of Pueblo Manso appeared on the horizon, a church of the denomination that had been without a pastor for three years. In a matter of days everything was settled. He would travel at once to see the place and the church, and to make arrangements for his family to accompany him before the end of the month.

"Pueblo Manso[6] is like its name," Saverio continued explaining, "a peaceful place. People here value friendship and family gatherings highly. They are tremendously loyal. The worst offense you can do is to fail someone. To be disloyal. The second thing that is not tolerated is lying"— The pastor's surprise gesture was to be expected— "When we tell people this, they don't believe us. But there is like a silent pact between all those who live here, not to lie. Those who arrive at the beginning are amazed, but then they have the option to adapt or leave. That's why it's a small town, because many come here and can't bear to live without lying."

---

[6] In Spanish, Placid Town

"But what happens when one person fails another... or lies?"

"Very simple. You start to feel that people ignore you."

"Just like that? I mean, does it happen automatically?"

"Yes, just like that. It's as if it were in the collective unconscious of Pueblo Manso. Psychologists and sociologists have come to study us. Lawyers and politicians didn't dare to come!" It was the first time he saw him laughing and laughing hard.

"A disloyalty, a lie and... out? I find it hard to believe..."

"Actually, it's even more interesting. The system works with a second chance."

"A second chance? And who keeps track of the first offense?" *Could this be a joke they play on the* porteños[7] *to get back at those we play to those of the interior when they go there?* Juan thought to himself.

"Nobody. It's like an evolution of the collective unconscious to preserve a minimum number of inhabitants." The explanation seemed to Juan too convoluted for somebody like Saverio, but maybe it had become ingrained out of repetition.

"And what did the psychologists and sociologists say? Did they find the mechanism?"

"No. The only thing they were able to measure was the level of rejection of disloyal actions and lies. It's funny, because the first thing they did when they arrived, without realizing it, was to make up the university where they came from, thinking that nobody would notice. Typical contempt of the *porteños* towards those from the interior. They said they were coming by an agreement with the University of Toronto, instead of saying it was a project of the University of Buenos Aires. They immediately felt "a chill"—textual words, not very technical, from the report—a very strong rejection, which made them rectify the information immediately. From then on, they took care."

"Let me guess," Juan began to use the informal address—"tu" instead of "usted"— much more comfortable and natural for him, "after a while they exhausted their second chance."

---

[7] The name given to people who live in Buenos Aires.

"You said it! Despite the fact that the group had promised not to alter the 'factual balance'—as the scholars called it— again, so as not to affect the experiment, one of the psychologists messed up when they wanted to pass her a phone call while she was eating and the phrase "Tell him I'm not here" slipped out. They say there was a silence that is still remembered today. The team wanted to kill her, because after the incident they were unable to continue with the experiment and had to leave."

Juan remained thinking for a while, between doubting and wanting to believe him. It didn't seem like a joke because of the way Saverio had told it. Maybe it was a legend. He mused aloud:

"It should be easy to build a church here..."

"I wouldn't say so. He would need to be a special pastor." Saverio also said it immersed in his own thoughts. *Would this pastor be the one for this town and this church?*

They had already crossed the whole town along the main street and its fifteen half-paved blocks. The half-dozen shops were all closed even though it was Monday, true to the normal schedule in the interior of the country, with their two to three-hour siesta break. Saverio told him that the church was about ten minutes away through a potholed street. Along the way he had seen two small Pentecostal churches, another church that could be Evangelical and the traditional Catholic church in the town square where they turned to the right. He was struck by the number of young people in front of this church at that time of the day. Surely, he would have the opportunity to meet the pastors of those churches and the Catholic priest. He wished they could get along. What would the mayor of a town that didn't allow lies be like?

As they drove along the nondescript road in silence, Juan heard in his mind again his wife weeping when he told her of the Council's decision. Mariela had found the whole situation very unfair, and she wanted only the best for him and the kids. Typical of her, always worrying about others. To think that she had been right, in the end, when she had told him not to insist with those people because they were evil, ungrateful. They'd never really loved them. Behind the façade they showed they were no different from the people of the world, at least in their personal dealing. He made a mental note to pay more attention to her opinions in the future. He didn't know if it was female intuition, common sense, or simply that she could see things with more distance and depth. Perhaps the difference between them was that they both tried to know people in different ways. They used different tools. Mariela did it with a glance, an impression, which translated into a "I think she's a good person" or a fateful "Um... I don't know... there's something I don't like," which usually produced an argument between them. Mariela's hit rate using this technique was quite high, around eighty percent, though not perfect.

Juan, on the other hand, tried to get to know the person by analyzing them as a detective would. The way they dressed, the way they spoke. What came up in the conversation, the things they liked and the things that bothered them. It was a little slower than Mercedes' method, but more "scientific." For example, from the brief time he had been with Saverio he knew he was an orderly, meticulous, respectful person. Also, by his way of speaking he showed some preparation, although some phrases and turns of speech gave away his social condition. Perhaps he was self-taught. He later learned that he was a voracious reader of everything that passed through his hands. He loved his people, but he knew how to recognize their mistakes; this showed a balanced person in his opinions and affections. Juan had to confirm whether he tended to exaggerate, because of the story he had told him about lying. He also showed a restrained, cerebral type of humor. Sometimes it was the most effective because people didn't see it coming.

They finally arrived at the mission of the Church of the Open Word, with the pastoral house next door. It was love at first sight for Juan. Something inside him—that voice? —told him that it would be a place of refuge, of restoration for him and his family. Nothing in the building suggested this feeling, quite the opposite. The need for repairs, painting and refurbishment was more than evident. The uneven and neglected garden pointed to a deeper abandonment. Two broken windows spoke of financial difficulties, something he had been told about in Buenos Aires. Of course, his salary would be considerably lower.

Saverio stopped the truck and headed to the pastoral house with the luggage. Juan accompanied him, but when he saw some boys playing soccer in the backyard, he changed course without thinking, and went to the group as if attracted by a magnet. Something indefinable in the way the boys played, what the game transmitted to him in life and energy, confirmed his first impression: "This is the place." He opened the gate to the corridor that led to the back and walked the five meters with a faster and lighter pace. In that short stretch he felt again things he thought he had lost. Vocation. Love for people. Purpose. Life. Desire to fight.

"Hi," he said to a little boy who was watching the game sitting on a log.

"Hi. Are you the new pastor?"

"So it seems. What's your name?"

The instant he started talking to that boy he felt like the pastor of that church and that town. He had always preferred people to books, life situations to stories of the past, personal encounters of Jesus to his theological discourses.

"Marcos, but they call me Wobbly," letting Juan see the shorter leg.

"Marquitos, then. What's your team?"

"Boca. Who else? The best."

"Then we'll get along fine. I'm from the best too," and took him firmly by the shoulder. There would be time to clarify later that for him "the best" was River, his favorite team. He seemed to feel a current of affection, a mixture of sadness and need, at that moment. Ah, if being a pastor were only this, knowing and helping people...

FROM THERE TO HERE

(1978 - 2000)

3

From where we started, dreams are all
Untainted, untested, immaculate, tall

"Pedro Terrero!" said the announcer, finally. He was number fourteen on the list of graduates of the Seminario Bíblico Pastoral (Pastoral Bible Seminary), SeBiPa popularly, of Buenos Aires, a traditional Bible institute in an old building in the Flores neighborhood. When Pedro jumped out of his chair and almost ran up to the platform, he felt that he had reached the top of the world. As he glanced at his parents and sisters sitting in the second row, he knew they had to be proud at what he had achieved and what lay before him.

"God is going to do great things with you," said the Dean, José Berdisso, as he gave him his diploma and a hug.

"Don't neglect your gift," said Hector Zaldívar, shaking his hand tightly.

"Be strong and courageous," was the other Bible verse left by Christina Klooft, the Professor of Greek. Pedro had chosen her to hand him the leather-bound Bible.

Juan had been the second in the list. His entry was much less dramatic, because he knew his family were perplexed, to say the least, with this last stage of his life with the "evangelists." But they were there, with his sister, happy for him, for his passion to reach people and help them wherever they were.

21

Berdisso said, "You've come a long way already. Don't stop" with the diploma and the hug, but then said something in his ear that made Juan smile. Zaldívar's words were, "Choose life." The Bible was handed to him by Alejandro Mateos, the Professor of Missiology.

That Saturday, December 20, 1980 marked the end of three intense years shared by a wonderful group of fifteen students from all over the country.

Juan Cristante was my cousin. He was two years older than me, and he had been in the Tucumán jungle with the army in the anti-subversive war in 1975 and 1976. He had made the draft a year before and, once finished, he decided to stay on as a regular soldier. When they asked who wanted to go to Tucumán he volunteered right away, partly because of his desire for adventure and partly because he was convinced of the army's mission to cleanse the country of the subversive threat. When he returned, he never wanted to tell more than a few details of what he saw there. From what others say, it was indescribable. It was not an adventure, nor did it have the lyrical and patriotic content that had dazzled him. The Juan who returned had another look. He had lost his glow, and his bright, candid face had become that of a man in his forties. His proverbial good humor had had been replaced by monosyllables and sarcastic and even hurtful phrases. "Really? What do you know? Don't be delusional. The only thing that matters is that you take care of yourself. It's all a big lie. It's always the same people who win." Although at first everyone had been patient with him because of what he had experienced—including the death of a friend he had made in the army—over time they began to leave him alone, because one became infected with the pessimism and bitterness he exuded.

We had met Pedro at a couple of family meetings, as he became friends with Juan, during his time in the Seminary. He was an attractive guy, charming, a good joke teller, the center of every meeting. We met him as a boyfriend with Virginia. Both were from third generation Christian families, a topic they mentioned more often than we thought necessary. But Pedro and Virginia were forgiven everything, because they had a bright future ahead of them in the Lord's work. They were hardworking and dutiful, always ready to help anyone in need. Moreover, it was evident that his contact with Pedro had done Juan a lot of good, and this was worth gold to the family.

With Mercedes, my girlfriend, we knew that we wanted to start something new with either Juan or Pedro. They had so much potential! When they decided to go their own ways, we chose Pedro, in part because of the family relationship with Juan and especially because we instinctively assumed that Juan's *milico*[8] background and way of thinking would make him more authoritarian, more structured. On the other hand, Pedro came from a Christian family, like me, and had a certain idealism that suggested freedom, broadness of mind, creativity. The reality proved to be quite different. This is also our story, that of Raúl and Mercedes, intertwined with that of these two pastor friends who graduated from the same seminary.

Monday, March 13, 1978. This was the customary presentation class. Fifteen students from different parts of the country—eleven men, four women—listened attentively in the first-floor classroom to the welcoming words from a bald, chubby and somewhat scruffy man who was repeating a familiar routine.

"Good morning. My name is Luis Chiavetto. I am the Professor of Church History, and I will be your mentor for the first year of the Seminary. I'd like each of you to introduce yourself with your name, place of origin and denomination. Who wants to start?"

"Hi, I'm Marcelo Rosales, I come from Resistencia, Chaco, and I am a Baptist." A man of initiative, thought Juan, and he wasn't wrong.

"Well... it seems it's my turn. I'm Rosa Hoyts, from La Plata. Ah, yes, I'm from the Nazarenes."

"My name is Juan Cristante, from Buenos Aires. From Núñez, close to the Monumental.[9] Looking for a church."

---

[8] Derogatory term referring to people associated with the military.
[9] Name of the River Plate soccer team stadium.

"What a place to live in! I'm Nacho Leiva, from Avellaneda, just across the glorious Bombonera.[10] We are an independent church."

The ice had already been broken. Marcos Suárez, Trelew, Methodist and Leo Nuccetelli, also from Trelew, of the Assemblies of God. They didn't know each other before the Seminary but became great friends during their time there. Nora Maluf, Tucumán, Free Brethren. Zacarías Pimentel, Esquina, Corrientes, Pentecostal... There was a bit of everything, and each one seemed to be very defined in what they were except Juan.

"...Hugo Carvajal, Santiago del Estero, Pentecostal... Ernesto Saccardi, La Rioja, also Pentecostal... Mabel Duverges, Mendoza, Reformed... Julio Maciel, Alliance, San Justo, Buenos Aires... Santiago Vilches, Formosa, Assemblies of God... Verónica Schmidt, Alta Gracia, *cordobesa*—everybody laughed as she used the typical tune of her province—, Anglican." The presentations followed one another in an orderly fashion and were almost over.

"There's one missing," noted Chiavetto, looking at a tall, blond guy sitting at the back of the room, who kept making jokes about each of the places and names.

"Pedro Terrero, from Zárate, Jehovah's Witness." Since he said it so seriously, and we didn't know him yet, an awkward silence ensued that he broke with a loud laugh. "No, really. I'm from the United Church."

Quite a letter of introduction, Juan thought. During his time in the army he had realized the crucial importance of knowing who those people were with whom he shared so much and who could mean death or life in battle situations. Let's see, what did he already know about Pedro? When he left his presentation until the end, he was either very shy or very calculating, seeking to stand out. He had to discard shyness, so it was clear that he had wanted to be the last one on purpose to make the greatest impact. He had used humor, and well. This means he was accustomed to using this resource perhaps as a defense mechanism. He didn't mind upsetting perfect strangers, including the professor, to achieve his goal. His good handling of the

---

[10] Name of the Boca Juniors soccer team stadium.

body was a powerful resource, especially because he stood out from the rest of the group. And he knew how to take advantage of it. Some would say that this was splitting hairs, but Juan had become an expert in this technique, and he was making fewer and fewer mistakes.

"Thank you. Only three *porteños,* from what I see. That looks great, since I'm from Mar del Plata, from the interior. Today you begin three years of theological and spiritual formation that will allow you to serve the Lord better..."

Juan unplugged his mind automatically, as he did every time a part of him detected that what followed was just a filler. He was interested in people, especially interesting people. Chiavetto was the first to fail in this group. His classifier of people placed him in the category "he is at the Seminary but could easily be at another institute or teaching at home." Marcelo: a good guy, with a worker's face; Rosa: the face of an *inglesita,*[11] her glasses and hairstyle gave her away as a nerd; Marcos and Nora, for some reason they sat together. What were Free Brethren? Would they be among the most liberal, the most open? What was the Alliance?

"...so let us end with a prayer that the Lord will guide us all in this exciting adventure. Let us pray."

They all bowed their heads and followed the professor's litany the best they could. Juan was eager to start but didn't feel as enthusiastic as when he had entered the military service. Then he had felt the sergeant during the instruction stage challenging him to get the most out of himself, to push himself to the limit, to the point where he couldn't take it anymore. "I'm going to turn this group of ladies into soldiers, even if I have to die trying! One, two threeee... One, two... What are you smiling at, soldier boy? You'll see! Fifty pushups for everybody!... Five more laps..." Everyone had hated Sergeant Sánchez then, but he ended up bringing out the best in that group of men. Juan never told him, but he would always be grateful to him. Here, things seemed easier, and he, like Pedro, needed to feel challenged.

---

[11] Friendly way to indicate somebody with an English look.

Pedro's grandfather had founded, back in 1900, the United Church of Zárate. It had begun as a little place on the street and had become a literacy center using the Bible as a textbook. Don Antonio Terrero had led the congregation for over fifty years and now "was with the Lord." His two sons, Jorge and Samuel, had continued his work, but "they weren't the same as Don Antonio," as everyone who had known him said. The church split up, and some went with Samuel, "more open to the things of the Spirit," to the other side of the city and the rest stayed on the premises with Jorge, the Bible teacher. Pedro grew up as the son of Pastor Jorge Terrero, along with his two sisters, Silvia and Nora, and everyone, from the time he started running around the hall as a child during the Sunday sermons, assumed that he would follow in the footsteps of his ancestors. So, when he finished high school and announced that he was going to Buenos Aires, to the Seminario Bíblico Pastoral, no one was surprised. It was written in the stars.

When Pedro arrived at the building that would be his home for the next three years, he felt nothing special. For him it simply meant the next step in his church activity. He had gone through all the Sunday School classes, from six to twelve years old, followed by the teen class and the youth meeting. Then, as expected, he became a teacher of teenagers and then a youth leader. Everything followed its predictable course. Plenty of Bible, lots of "Bible sword fights" (contests to see who could find a Bible passage first) and many memory recitations of the names of the sixty-six books of the Bible by heart: "Genesis, Exodus, Leviticus... Ezra, Nehemiah... Judas, Revelation." He never understood why it was so important to know the index of this fascinating book by heart, but it seemed critical. Nor why there were wonderful stories or parts of the Bible he had heard to his heart's content (creation, Joseph and his brothers, David and Goliath, Daniel in the lion's den, the miracles and stories of Jesus) and others that were never mentioned. But he supposed that those who prepared the manuals for teachers and students of different ages knew their stuff.

When he saw who his fellow students would be, he couldn't help but feel a step above them. Only a couple of them had gone through the whole Sunday School, like him. None of them were the son and grandson of a pastor. Of the rest, those with church years came from denominations with little attachment to Bible study. Pentecostals didn't count because they could only sing, shout, and speak in tongues. But when you considered the Bible, very little. And that guy Juan, a recent convert, what was he even doing here? How hard it would be for him to learn everything he knew so well! Pedro had everything it took to be the best in the class and stand out clearly. Besides, he would have a good time and meet important people in the field: pastors, teachers, leaders... maybe even a trip abroad.

"I hope they're not all like the mentor, right?" It was Juan's deep voice, seeking conversation as soon as the prayer finished, and they dispersed. Pedro found it too blunt, too unpolitical to say something like that on the first day. Although he, too, had found Chiavetto quite boring. Of course, this kid lacked the "evangelical touch" that allowed him to put up with people like this.

"Maybe it's the first impression. But if he's here, he must be good. After all, it's the SeBiPa, right?" He had to defend the system. He had been part of it all his life. What right did this newcomer have to question it just like that?

"If they're all like that, I prefer the Catholics."

This guy has zero sensitivity, minus ten spirituality, thought Pedro.

"Are you serious? The Catholics?" He had touched one of the most sensitive fibers for a pure-blooded evangelical. "They only talk about the pope, the Virgin, the saints. Besides, they tell them what they must believe, what they must think. Nothing to do with the Seminary. Here's Pacero, Smith, Miranda..." He realized that the recitation of the selected eminences hadn't made any impression on this stranger. Of course, how could he understand that Pacero had come to his church to give a series of lectures on the mission of the church last year and had stayed at his house? And that Pedro was on a first-name basis with Carlos, a phenomenal guy. And Michael Smith, "Mike," was an American he had met at the Mar del Plata youth congress, when he was on the committee. He had all the books of Wilfredo Miranda,

27

and he was a total fan of this Peruvian theologian who was the rage among young people and needed to expand his ministry in the rest of Latin America (a possible future position, Pedro had thought several times, if he managed to stand out in the Seminary).

"Maybe, maybe... but we can't generalize. Let's give it time. Shall we have a coffee?" said Juan when he saw the cafeteria. Without waiting for an answer, he turned down the corridor and Pedro followed him.

They chatted until lunchtime, while the rest of the students went around the place, the library, the garden, the neighborhood. The talk would be repeated countless times throughout the Seminary. Early in the morning, after classes, on weekends. There was something between them, in their great differences, that led them to seek each other. Physically they were quite different, almost opposites. Juan was short, brawny, and dark, somewhere between robust and fat. The son of a Spaniard and a Frenchwoman, his frank gaze invited dialogue and exuded trust. He was an excellent counselor, especially because he knew how to listen to others. And because he knew this, he took advantage of the opportunity to make comments and ask questions that were more incisive than usual; hardly anyone took what he said the wrong way. He was an excellent center player in soccer. And, according to one of his theories—you can tell people by the way they play—this indicated balance, sacrifice, vision, teamwork. Instead, Pedro played as center forward, in the goal area. He was a scorer, not so much because of conditions but because of the leading role he played, with the selfish but necessary individualism of the one who must put the ball in the net to score. Every group needs a Pedro, and every group, at one point, gets tired of its Pedro. And it needs its Juan to restore the balance. Pedro knew this, unconsciously, and perhaps that is why he was attracted to Juan. He perceived that the relationship had given him greater stability and had helped him to relate to people and groups. No doubt the same was true of Juan. He needed his complement, and he had found it in Pedro.

Unfortunately, their differences over time not only persisted, but intensified. No longer due to differences in character and formation but because of their basic attitudes toward life. If Juan was an Arminian, Pedro was a Calvinist. Pedro was in favor of large churches; Juan preferred small communities. Vertical or horizontal authority. Institution or relationship. Church or individual. Efficiency or patience. And it wasn't that one assumed a position and the other took the opposite one, but that they naturally occupied opposite sides. The rest of their companions, and even the professors, had become accustomed to considering both as the extremes of any doctrinal or practical position. This was very convenient, for it was then a matter of standing somewhere between Pedro and Juan to be near the truth.

The first storm was in the Systematic Theology class. The discussion seemed to be one more to which everyone was already accustomed, and which usually ended amicably amid jokes and digs. But this time it was different.

"Today we will study the five points of Calvinism: 1) the total depravity of man, 2) unconditional election, 3) limited atonement, 4) irresistible grace, and 5) the perseverance of the saints.

The person writing the titles on the blackboard, in a hurry and with barely legible handwriting, was Vicente Usandivaras, a pastor and lawyer in his fifties, always in impeccable suit, a university professor and an excellent person. According to the students, he was one who wasn't easily deluded, was in touch with reality, and was always very open to the exchange of ideas which, in fact, he often encouraged. The church he led, in the Caballito neighborhood, reflected that open and investigative spirit he promoted. He exuded coherence. A point in favor, both for Juan and Pedro.

"I think it's very nice, very neat... very didactic. But where is this doctrine found in the Bible?" It was the unmistakable voice of Juan. A promise of action from minute one.

"Nobody says it's in the Bible, as such," explained Usandivaras. "But since we are in Systematic Theology"—making the gesture of looking at the folder to see if it was the correct subject—"we know that we are dealing with a human effort to systematize ideas that are found throughout the Bible in a somewhat artificial but useful way. Something like the creeds. Useful tools, but not the ultimate truth. Is that understood?"

"Yes, but if this doctrine were true, no one would do anything. If everything is predestined, why preach, or evangelize? What's the point of praying?" It wasn't the first time that Juan objected to theories that he called "fatalistic" or "deterministic." He considered them alien to the very spirit of the Bible and of Christ. He said they took away his freedom.

"But you can't deny that the Bible speaks of God predestining us for salvation". Pedro quickly looked up a passage in his Bible and read, stressing the parts that supported his position: "Praise be to the God and Father of our Lord Jesus Christ, who has blessed us in the heavenly realms with every spiritual blessing in Christ. For he *chose* us in him *before* the creation of the world to be holy and blameless in his sight. In love he *predestined* us for adoption to sonship through Jesus Christ. Ephesians 1:3 to 5," he ended, solemnly, showing his mastery of the book.

"Look, for every verse that talks about predestination I can read you two or three that talk about human responsibility. They say that we can choose, that we must choose. If everything is already determined, let us stay at home and wait for the end of the world," Juan replied.

"The problem is that you don't know the Bible and you just say what you think. Why don't you read the whole Bible? You'll see that it says that God knows the past, the present and the future. And not only that he knows, but he predetermined it." Pedro had raised his voice, although the subject under discussion didn't seem to justify it.

"Maybe I don't know the Bible as you do, to repeat it like a parrot, without thinking. The thing is that you who grew up in the church bring a lot of ideas that got into your head that have no substance, that are wrong. At most, they were good for another time. The real world has nothing to do with the little glass box where you grew up... You need more street life..."

"It seems to me that there is a bit of both..." said the ever-settler Rosa, "God knows everything, he predestines everything, but he gives us the possibility to choose."

"You're not making any sense. Either one or the other," insisted Juan.

"One moment! Let's get one thing clear, before continuing with this topic." Pedro had stood at the back of the room and everyone had turned around to look at him. "Just because some people have spent their lives doing this and that before coming here doesn't mean they are better than those of us who have been serving the Lord and doing what he says since we were children. And much less that they can come and teach us. Let's see, *milico*, what did you do to serve the Lord before coming here?"

Usandivaras did nothing. He failed to realize in time the gravity of the situation. He mistook dissent for resentment and allowed the controversy to continue.

"What do you mean by *milico*? At least we did something, and we didn't stay singing songs of love and peace or doing coffee politics while others risked their lives..." replied Juan, also standing, from the other end of the room.

The class and the teacher were petrified, unable to believe what they were witnessing. Two great friends who often disagreed, but always within a framework of mutual respect, were beginning to attack each other in a spiral that they didn't seem to be able to control. Because, in reality, this discussion was the continuation of a strong and unresolved exchange from the previous week in the cafeteria about subversion and military repression.

1978 would be remembered by all as the year of the soccer World Cup. The year of the wild celebrations in the streets of the country for Argentina's first world title in its most popular and passionate sport. But it would also be remembered by many for the manipulation of information and massive propaganda by the military junta that made the majority of Argentines think that the country was the victim of a gigantic international smear campaign. The official slogan "Argentines are human and right"—playing clumsily on the term "human rights"— appeared on posters everywhere and even attached to private cars. The news handled by the foreign media that managed to filter through in droplets didn't match the idyllic image that the military regime intended to transmit. The constant terrorist attacks during the fragile democratic government of Juan Domingo Perón's widow had been responded to with unheard of ferocity by the military government that displaced her with a coup. Terrorists were killed or kidnapped, suspects and family members alike, without any right to defense. It was there that the figure of the "missing" arose, according to the sadly famous phrase of the ultra-Catholic dictator Rafael Videla who frustratingly declared before television cameras, when a journalist asked him about people detained or who had disappeared without a judicial process "they are neither dead nor alive, they are missing, they have no entity." In the collective conscience of the country, the question will remain forever floating: How many of these beings without entity were being tortured by other beings with much less entity while the soccer party flooded every corner and conversation of the country? And how many Christians (Catholics, evangelicals) unconsciously participated in that disinformation campaign while a few companions, also Christians, protested in solitude?

This had been the topic of that previous coffee talk, after a rather challenging class on Church History, where the issue of the commitment or lack of commitment of Christians in critical and dangerous situations, where their own lives could be at stake, emerged.

"So you were in the Tucumán jungle?" The question came from Nora, who was from that province. "Where were you?"

"Famaillá, Tafí..."

"Were there as many terrorists as they say?"

"It's difficult to know. And not all of them were terrorists. There were young kids who only had the ideal of wanting to change the world. Like us, or am I wrong?" Juan replied.

"And don't you think they were right about a lot of what they were saying? Isn't everything rotten? I'll never agree to kill someone in the back to take his gun, but their questioning of society is quite correct," Pedro said. A brother from his church who was doing the conscription at the Federal Police in 1974 had been cowardly murdered by terrorists, like so many others, while standing guard on a street corner. Only to have his gun taken away, and without giving him time to defend himself. Many other conscripts had suffered the same fate over the years.

"Look, it's one thing for those who risked their own lives and comfort for their convictions, but it's quite another for those who led the groups for their own benefit," Juan argued.

"They are saying that there are tortures, hundreds or thousands of dead, missing people. A couple of my classmates from high school were kidnapped at night. They say that it was because they were involved in subversion. Maybe they did something... or not... but at least say where they are, have a trial. Something. Is it true, or is it a campaign from abroad, as the government says?" Pedro continued.

"It's probably true, but it's one thing to give your opinion from a coffee table, and quite another to risk your life. On one side or the other." Juan had become serious and looked at Pedro with a fixed gaze.

The phrase stung Pedro, and he jumped up from his chair.

"At least I don't go around killing and torturing people who did nothing!"

"I didn't torture anyone, and if I killed anyone it was to defend the country from Communist infiltration! I can be proud as an Argentine soldier," Juan said, almost shouting.

"I will never be a useful idiot," replied Pedro.

"And I will never wash my hands when it comes to following my convictions," ended Juan, rising from the table abruptly.

The talk stopped there, but it continued in everyone's mind, waiting for another opportunity to prolong it. It simply hid and expressed the contained frustrations, and the questions that a large part of society hadn't been able to answer about its role in that painful period of Argentine history.

33

The second explosion, a week later, in the Systematic Theology class, was predictable. And then the relationship between the two friends changed. Perhaps not on the outside, because they continued to study together, participating from opposite ends in the debates, both excellent students in their own way. Pedro, with his lucidity to interpret themes and find a practical way out of them, to organize a proposal, to overcome obstacles and difficulties. Someone who went ahead, despite everything, and often in spite of people. Juan, much more reflexive, looking for the details, the minutiae, the inflections. For him it was more important to move forward together, even if it took longer, than to move forward alone. The combination of both, if they had got along, would have been perfect. But they were in a setting—the evangelical world—that didn't know how to handle differences. The options have been and continue to be two: either we agree in everything and stay together, or we split up and separate. Consensus, dialogue, listening to the other, healthy negotiation were as unknown as the fission of the atom for pastors and lay people alike. They had grown up in the uniformity of monolithic thought or top-down authoritarianism, and if at any time you found yourself outside the plumb line, your luck was cast. "If you don't like it, leave" was the silent message that was always heard in this environment. The second phrase, often spoken out loud and with much relief by those who remained was, "It is the Lord's will that they leave. He is cleaning up his church. It will surely be a blessing."

Pedro had suffered from this intolerant spirit all his life. He still remembered his father's late arrivals after meetings with church leaders, followed by whispers and mysterious conversations with his mother, until the split occurred when he was fourteen. If it hadn't been traumatic enough to stop seeing each other every Sunday, at camps and picnics with his longtime friends and two of his cousins, much worse was the cloak of silence that was thrown over them, except for the inevitable family gatherings. "That's not talked about" was the other silent message that was strictly adhered to.

The reason for the sharp split of the church had been spiritual, ironic as it may seem. One group had had new experiences of the Holy

Spirit. They spoke in tongues, wanted a more spontaneous worship, a church life more like that of early Christianity, back in the first century, devoid of rigid traditions, structures, and doctrines. The other group didn't see the need for change and didn't understand why renewal couldn't come from doing more of the same, or better of the same. The result of the endless discussions and proposals was the "amicable" division. The traditionalists stayed, the reformers left, to start something new elsewhere.

I had grown up in a church that had no pastors. Instead of having one or more pastors, it was run by a group of elders. Ideally chosen from among the fittest, they most often ended up in rigid, often familial, lifelong structures that prevented the church from growing beyond one hundred or one hundred and fifty members. Unlike hired pastors, the elders were self-supporting and dedicated time after work or on weekends to visiting members, preparing materials, or helping in various ways, without expecting anything in return. In this sense, they followed the example of the Apostle Paul, who had his own manual profession—tent repair—and enjoyed the freedom that came from not having to depend on anyone for their livelihood.

This was my area of growth. Somewhat like Pedro's story, although in a much smaller church and without the prospect of a pastoral career. Saturdays and Sundays at church, Sunday school, Bible contests, "happy hours," evangelization campaigns, youth meetings, camps. The church was the center of everything, providing a reason for life. It was there that we learned to serve, and where we were supposed to serve. Knowing the Bible stories meant knowing God, knowing Jesus. The more you knew, the more spiritual you were. The closer you got to "sound doctrine," the better for everyone—for the person and for the congregation.

Outside were the other churches of the denomination. Further out were the churches of other denominations, from the "social" ones, like the Methodists, and the "ritual" ones, like the Anglicans, to the dreaded Pentecostals, with their noisy worship and search for spectacular experiences. The consensus within our church was that no one knew the Bible like we did, except perhaps the Baptists, but they had their pastors, which was not biblical.

Further outside were the Catholics, with their worship of the Virgin and transubstantiation at Mass... and the pope. And, a little further out, almost falling out of the universe, was "the world," a hostile, dark place that needed to be redeemed by believers.

Contact with that world hadn't been easy. How could one meet the very particular condition of "being in the world, but not of the world" that Jesus had established, especially in school, where being evangelical often meant a certain isolation?

My cousin Juan was never fond of the church my parents and I went to. Beyond participating in soccer games in the back yard or attending special meetings, such as Christmas and Easter, he preferred his neighborhood friends to "the church bores." Besides, he said he wasn't going to a place where he was told what to think, what was right and wrong, what could be done and what couldn't be done. My uncle Osvaldo and aunt Priscilla were faithful Catholics and sent him and his sister Nadia to the best parish schools in the area. Juan said that the Bible was a man-made book, but in his eagerness to challenge what the priests said, he had read it so many times and studied some parts so carefully that he had nothing to envy in biblical knowledge to many believers, Catholic and evangelical.

Until one day he had a profound experience of conversion. It happened at a youth camp organized by the church, in Chascomús. I believe that what happened to him there was that he saw, up close and personally, the best side of evangelicals, sharing a time of freedom in the open air, with their individual and group devotions in the morning, their practical and in-depth Bible studies, sports, team competitions, campfires and, above all, people like Manuel (Manolo) Czyzewski, one of the leaders of the camp. Manolo took him under his wings, followed him unnoticed, and on the last day asked him if he wanted to "receive Christ into his heart," the standard phrase used for conversion. When Juan said yes and they prayed together, he felt that his whole life made sense and that he could suddenly see the God in whom he had always believed with different eyes.

During the three years at the Seminary, Juan and Pedro, along with their fellow students, spent time studying the Bible, theology, elements of psychology, church organization, and church history. They studied psychology, but not sociology, perhaps as a reflection of the considerable American influence, with the philosophy of life centered on the individual and his personal fulfillment. To the class hours were added the morning and evening devotions, the rounds of *maté*,[12] the spontaneous dialogues in exciting after-dinner sessions. There was also the tension of the exams, the satisfaction of the subjects approved, the desire to improve, aware that they had a high mission to accomplish. On weekends they all went out to serve in different churches or service centers in the suburbs.

Pedro's place of service was a slum. The small Pentecostal Light and Love mission was led by Pastor Ramiro Argüello and his wife, María. He left the Seminary on Fridays at 7:00 p.m., in a bus that left him ten blocks from a rustic 5 x 5 meter shed at the back of the pastor's family home in Lanús Oeste. On one side, they had built a small room with a bathroom, where the seminarians stayed on weekends. The time he spent there wasn't too difficult for him. He felt useful and perceived the gratitude and the need of these people so abandoned by society. But deep down, so deep down that even he didn't dare to think about it, he knew that "he was made for something else (more)." He had been marked as a leader since he was a boy, and he had the word "leader" stuck in his head and written on his forehead. It was his destiny to follow that mission in life, using all his experience and charisma to lead larger works, within the denomination, the

---

[12] Tea-like drink traditional in Southern South America, drunk from a gourd and drinking straw.

country, and later, outside the country. He had already helped in disadvantaged places when they had gone with the church's youth group to build the school in the poor neighborhood in the south side of the city. Also, on the mission trips that the church made each year, they got to know very harsh realities and worked hard to help people in the interior. So, he was "conscious," and that was good, because it allowed him to have a more complete perspective of the reality of the country. He admired these "little pastors" who, without expecting anything in return and sacrificing everything, spent hours helping in places that were doomed to failure, to be honest. But he felt much more comfortable and useful in other environments, where his talents and his formation—especially once he had finished the Seminary—could be fully expressed.

He recalled one of the discussions in Missiology:

"What do you think of the culture shock that occurs when missionaries from one country enter another? Is it avoidable?" asked Professor Mateos, a missionary who had spent several years in Malaysia.

"It is something that always happens when two cultures meet. The Spanish and the indigenous, the Europeans in Africa and Asia. I wouldn't call the work of missionaries so much a culture shock, since they were only interested in bringing the Gospel, not imposing their culture," replied Julio, whose dream was to follow in the footsteps of the professor in some Muslim country.

"But in reality, along with the gospel, they brought the good and the bad of their culture, and many times they imposed them by force, whether military or economic," Pedro said.

"In addition to venereal diseases and CIA agents," added Juan.

"Yes, but what would have become of some countries without the Christian message, with its pluses and minuses? Were there not many cultures that made human sacrifices, practiced slavery and subjected or destroyed enemy tribes without any consideration?" Julio would always defend missionary work.

"As you can see, the issue of mission is a complex one. On the one hand, the Christian church has the command of our Lord, 'Go, make disciples of all nations,'[13] but on the other hand we can't impose this message by force, because we would be going against the essence of the gospel, don't you think?" Alejandro Mateos was also a supporter of open discussion.

"Of course, but why didn't it always happen like that? Were those who wanted to evangelize the indigenous people of America by force true Christians? I have my great doubts," was Nacho's contribution.

The discussion went on, and it wouldn't be the last one they would have in the Seminary or outside. The two positions would always appear: evangelization or domination. Interest in people or economic interests. Undoubtedly, there were many instances where behind a well-intentioned missionary there was a political or economic use of their effort. At other times, it would work the other way around: a political breakthrough would open doors for missionaries. But in that world of preparation for the work there was no doubt about the purity of the desires and ideals of those seminarians. To hear Julio Maciel speak passionately of his desire to leave the comfort of his wealthy family to serve in abandoned places of the world as soon as he finished the Seminary was moving. We later learned that he married Roxana, a girl from his church, and they went as missionaries to Rwanda. They spent five years there, had two children and then returned to Argentina. When they returned, they suffered the general fate of missionaries all over the world when they return to their country: they felt strange among their own country. They had experienced things that they couldn't transmit, and they had an unfinished task in the place of service. However, if they returned to Africa, they would have to consider the education of their children. So they stayed, and had serious difficulties in their reintegration. They never stopped dreaming of returning, perhaps once the children were older...

---

[13] Mt 28:19

Juan, as a practical part of his preparation, had to serve on weekends with the young people of the Church of Fellowship, in La Plata, some 60 kilometers from Buenos Aires. He got permission to leave a little earlier, at 5 p.m., so that he would be on time for the Friday night youth meeting. Although at the beginning he didn't feel comfortable within a somewhat rigid structure, where everything was scheduled and the youth activity seemed a carbon copy of that of the adults, he soon learned to adapt and to place the emphasis of his work on individual talks, in one to one chats over coffee, where he really got to know the person. At twenty-six years old, he wasn't too far from the age of kids coming out of high school and into a life of work or study. It was the age of big decisions: career, job, partner. And he was desperate to try to help these young people not to make mistakes, not to rush, but without delaying things. To put the Lord above all, especially when choosing their partner. He knew, and had seen, how a bad choice in this matter could ruin a pastor's prospects. He had before him the image of Pastor Claudio Reyes, who had had to leave the pastorate when his wife turned away from the faith and wanted nothing to do with the church. Given a choice between the church and his vocation and his family, he painfully chose the latter, and although at first Juan knew he had suffered greatly, lately he had seen him smile, as never before, at his job delivering drinks. He had also seen the two of them embracing and very much in love, strolling through the plaza. He wondered what he would do in a similar situation. Of course, he would choose a faithful servant of the Lord, someone who would accompany and support him in his service. A "suitable companion," like Adam's Eve. Suddenly he realized that, of the three important decisions in life, one was defined—his career—the other was on the right track—he had his profession as a mechanical technician and a pastor, once he graduated—but there was one still pending, and he felt an uneasy anxiety.

"Hi. What are you thinking about?" Mariela was staring at him. The young people had left, and they were both alone.

Juan was startled. He immediately felt the heat on his face. How he hated when he blushed at a girl! Where had she come from? Had she been watching him with those intense eyes a long time?

"Nothing. The future."

"What things?" Mariela insisted.

He knew he wouldn't be able to escape Mariela's inquisitive questions, but deep down he didn't want to either. She had such a captivating way of being interested in what he was thinking, what he was feeling, what was happening to him, that it was a torturous pleasure for him to submit to her interrogation.

"The inquisition again?" The mutual code generated complicit smiles.

"Yes. Does it bother you?"

"No, not at all. You know what I was thinking? In these kids. It seems so unfair that they must make such important decisions when they're so young. And almost all of them together."

"What decisions?", asked Mariela.

"Career, job... spouse."

"And how are things with you?"

"Two out of three. Pretty good, right?"

"The most important one is missing."

"And you?" retorted Juan.

"More or less the same."

Mariela had come with three other friends from a nearby church to help in the youth group. Their chats continued week after week, each time they were at work in the church, and he soon realized that he was hopelessly in love with that beautiful brunette, pure joy and vitality, but also with a spiritual and human depth that he admired and needed. He looked forward to weekends, not only to serve in the church, but to share that precious time with her. By January they were dating, and Juan was touching the sky with his hands. Studying to be a pastor, serving in a practical way, realizing that he liked it, and "added unto him"—using biblical terminology—dating Mariela. God was great! Hallelujah!

Mariela's family adopted him as their son. The Luppo's were wonderful *tanos*,[14] always arguing, fighting, and reconciling. At first,

---

[14] The popular way of calling Italians.

he was frightened by this contrast with his home, the Cristante's, which was more austere and silent. Then he would end up adapting, arguing like the best with Pierino, the father, and Silvia, Cristina and Toto, Mariela's siblings, while Constanza, the mother, usually watched in silence. It was with Mariela and her family that he learned that the best way to deal with problems and differences was to talk about them, not hide them. It was better to fight and reconcile than to not say things and keep feelings bottled in. He learned to say the things that needed to be said and to listen to what the other person had to say, however unpleasant or unfair it was. Of course, the latter was harder for him, but he took it as a pending task. What he never mastered was following multiple and simultaneous conversations with interrupted arguments that constantly went off the rails to return at some point to their course and be resolved in unexpected ways.

Pedro, on the other hand, didn't find his suitable companion while serving in mission, but rather among the multiple connections he had established throughout his church life. He was always known to be surrounded by girls, and any father would have considered him a good match for his daughter. He was good-looking, athletic, friendly, funny. Always the center of attention, the joy of any gathering or party. He had been with several girls since he was fourteen years old: Sandra, from school—despite his parents' opposition, because she wasn't a believer—, Alejandra, Natalia, Corina, Mónica. All beautiful and fun. But none of them was the counterbalance that Pedro needed, someone who could provide calm. Or who would give him the self-confidence that he was chasing with his constant need to be in the limelight. When he started dating Virginia in a more stable relationship, his friends thought "more of the same." She was a tall, athletic, dynamic blonde who attracted all eyes in any meeting, and she didn't seem to mind that leading role either.

Virginia's family was of "evangelical lineage," like Pedro's. When Pedro would go to the González Ríos's, he loved to talk to Carlos, a huge man who was president of the denomination's church board, about all the latest activities and meetings, and projects. The talks at and off the table were constantly peppered with name-dropping.

"What a good talk Gerardo had at the business dinner; don't you think?"

"Yes, although it seemed a bit long to me." Don Carlos always wanted to have the last word.

"Yes, me too. I was discussing it with Víctor this morning. We met for coffee."

"Gerardo" was Gerardo Fidanza, a wealthy and generous Christian businessman. "Víctor" was Víctor Valosky, a young evangelist who was making a name for himself on the circuit.

"Do you know if the support of the board of directors was obtained for the August conference? What does Ramiro say?"

"Look, Carlos, there's something I don't like. Damián is always objecting to everything..."

And that's how the talks went at Virginia's house. Always talking about others, about important things and people. One would say that either of them would feel equally comfortable at a political table, simply by changing some topics and names for others.

However, when Virginia went to the Terrero's house, she didn't have such a good time. She could feel the gazes and the pressure on her. She knew she was loved, in their own way, but she never felt she was more important than the chain of friends and girlfriends that had preceded her. Perhaps she had the advantage that they sensed that she would be the last one, the one who would marry "the baby," but she still realized that, like in no other social environment, Pedro's family was the one that generated the most tension for her. She often ended the Sunday visits with a headache, unable to attribute it to anything specific they had said or done.

Nicolás Peretti was a well-known and respected cult researcher. He had appeared on several television programs in police cases involving cults, both at home and abroad. His boyish face, which he tried to conceal with a thinned beard, was quite well-known, as was his shrill voice, which became shriller when he wanted to explain a point or refute an argument. He had a magazine and a weekly radio show. From his Freedom in Religion Foundation he promoted, by all means and with the scarce human and economic resources he managed, freedom within all religions, especially the freedom to enter and leave different religious groups, and financial accountability. Although he called himself a Catholic, in none of his presentations did he demonstrate a faith or belief to counteract the *chantas*[15] and *verseros*[16] that he unmasked.

We had been classmates in high school, so not only did I know all his arguments well, but I was one of the few who knew why he was so averse to what he indiscriminately called "cults," among which he arbitrarily included what he called "evangelical cults." I remember perfectly that cold Monday in August, when he came to me at the break with signs of having not slept and with a haggard look.

"Raúl, I am desperate."

"What's the matter, Nico? You're a wreck."

"Susana's disappeared. She didn't come back last night. She didn't call. We know nothing. My parents are desperate."

"Where did she go?"

"I'm sure it's with that bunch of hippies. She hangs out with them all the time, especially with that old guy, Jerónimo. They've brainwashed her."

"Stop, stop... Are you sure? Didn't she leave a note?"

"She left nothing, but she's been threatening for a while that she'll leave, that they understand her, that we're all bourgeois hypocrites... I don't know."

"We have to go to the police. I'm sure they know something."

It ended up being a simple scare. Susana returned in the afternoon, regretful and a bit shaken. The family felt the impact and joined to give her the love and understanding that she seemed to be lacking.

---

[15] Swindlers
[16] Sweet-talkers

But Nicolás, that same day, promised himself to devote his life to unmasking every swindler and trickster that existed, especially those related to cults. He read all the material that was available, in Spanish and in English that he perfected for this purpose. He even read in French, Italian, and Portuguese, trying to interpret the meaning of the texts. Then he studied Psychology, not to practice it, but to understand the minds of those who were absorbed by these groups, and the minds of the perverse individuals who directed them. It never occurred to him to think about the financial aspect, which ended up being a brake on further progress in his research.

We had endless talks and discussions during high school, especially after the incident with his sister. I was especially frustrated because I couldn't get him to understand that we, my church, weren't a cult. But he insisted that it was.

"How can it be that they're in the church all the time, that all they're interested in is proselytizing?"

"It's not like that. Cults try to isolate you from the world, but we study, we work, we move about in the world. And it's not true that we are only interested in proselytizing, what we call evangelizing. We really are convinced that we have the truth and we believe that the truth is good for people. How will they know it if someone doesn't show it to them?"

"But how can you say that you have the truth, and not the others? That's a sectarian thought, and you can only think that because somehow you have been brainwashed. I saw it in Susana. Suddenly, you couldn't argue with her. There was like a wall between us, and the more I tried to tear it down or go over it, the stronger and higher it became."

"Let's go by parts," I had told him. "If there is truth, a truth, and it is possible to know it, then it isn't sectarian to say that one has it and wants to share it. You are starting from the premise that there is no single truth, that we all have a bit of truth. How can you say that this isn't a sectarian thought that you want to put into me?"

I learned a lot with Nicolás. On the one hand, I learned to know him, especially out of respect. Because he was a sincere seeker of truth, and if I purported to be one too, in some points we should find ourselves on the same side. And it happened several times. When we despaired over the lack of personality of those who let themselves be led by what others were saying, in religion, but also in politics. When we were outraged by the manipulation of leaders, also in both environments. When we saw those who profit from unsuspecting people, especially the poorest. And I think he also respected and valued our talks. We came from two different worlds that were attracted to each other. Two swords that sharpened when they collided, and then could fight the common enemy together.

He helped me to think outside the comfortable glass box in which I had grown up and unknowingly strengthened and refined my faith. Many things that were secondary fell to the ground when the branches were shaken, but the fruits that endured became stronger and more unshakable in me. That's how science works. When posing a theory, the scientist expects and needs other scientists to try to shoot it down with the heaviest artillery at hand. Why? Because, if it falls, it means it wasn't that strong, and it's better for everyone that it doesn't remain. But if it doesn't fall, it will have shown its strength in the face of the best arguments. I learned that the Christian faith is of the same kind. After all, it gave birth to the scientific method. You must submit what you believe to the severest questioning, for if it resists, you will come out stronger; if not, you should revise what you think. Both are good. The opposite attitude, to protect what you believe among cotton wool or in a box, as in a closed community, leads to error and sectarianism, as well as isolation and pride. But to expose what you think can be dangerous, especially under the dissecting knife of someone like Nicolás, and much more without warning and in front of a lot of strangers. I still remember the bad time he put me through, although today I can't help but accompany the memory with a smile. It was back in 1985, when we had just returned from our honeymoon.

"Good afternoon, this is Nicolás Peretti from 'Chantas y Encantados.'[17] Today we're going to talk about the evangelical cults, and we have a great friend of mine, Raúl Encinas, as our guest."

Nicolás' weekly program on Radio Veinte, with an estimated audience of between four and five thousand people, was starting on Thursday at 8 p.m. sharp.

"Hi, Raúl."

"Hi, Nicolás. It's a pleasure to be on your show for the first time."

"Let's hope it's not the last one. But let's get down to business. No beating around the bush. Like we always do. Raúl, what would you answer those who say that evangelical pastors swindle people because they force them to give tithes? Besides, they handle it the way they want, usually for their own benefit, don't they?"

"Let's go by parts. Tithing is something that is established in the Bible. Ten percent of what we earn has to be for the Lord, for His work..."

"But not for the pastor..." Nicolás interrupted.

"Well, it's understood that someone has to be in charge and, as the Bible says, 'the worker deserves his wages.'"[18]

"But, tell me if I'm wrong, you go to an evangelical church and they don't have a pastor. So the leaders, I don't remember their names..."

"Elders."

"Yes, elders, they work in something secular and then collaborate, without charging a single peso. Is that right?"

"Yes, some evangelical groups work this way. Others prefer to have people who work full time, or part time, and pay them. Usually because they have a lot of work, or because the congregation is large." I had no idea which direction the next question would take. I felt like I was on trial before the prosecutor.

"Then you accept that it isn't indispensable to have a paid person at the head of an evangelical church."

"Not indispensable, no, but each case is unique."

---

[17] Swindlers and Enchanted

[18] 1Ti 5:18

"And you also accept that the Apostle Paul worked in something secular, so as not to be a hindrance or have to depend on anyone."

"Right."

"So why is there so much emphasis on tithing, on the pastor's salary, on the blessings that come from putting in more money? Doesn't it correspond to a sectarian behavior?"

"There are good pastors and not so good ones..."

"And some corrupt ones. I remind you of the case of Pastor Nemesio Carmona, newspaper front page last week. How did it get to that level?"

"There's corruption everywhere... And in many cases, it's people who start well and end badly." I still didn't know where the next blow would come from. Obviously, the issue was money.

"What methods of control do you have? I understand that anyone can say he or she is a pastor, found a church, and start collecting these tithes. Let's see if I did the math right. With ten people who tithe, I get a full salary, right?"

"Mathematically, yes, but that's not how churches think of things."

"What if I told you that tithing isn't biblical?"

"How could it not be biblical? It's all over the Bible..."

"But it's not a New Testament requirement, I understand." Nicolás had several aces up his sleeve, and he was starting to pull them out. The worst thing was that, knowing him well, he had undoubtedly studied the issue in depth. He never played by ear. "If I understand correctly, it was a tax for the nation of Israel, dedicated to the Levites, orphans, foreigners and widows."

"Look... I didn't know you were going to discuss this today, so I would have to check it out."

"Besides, you have to recognize that the ten percent of a person who has all their needs met isn't the same as one who can barely feed his family. The first one is deprived of luxuries, the second one is plunging their family into poverty. It would be like a tax that benefits the rich."

"I get what you're saying, but things in the kingdom of God don't work the same way as in the world, but I would like to investigate it further," I answered more firmly. I sensed that he there was some truth in what he said, but not entirely.

"OK, let's have a break and we can continue with this fascinating subject."

I remember I was really furious.

"You made me look stupid! Why didn't you tell me you were going to bring up the subject of tithing?" As soon as the block was over, I faced him head on, thinking not only of the unknown listeners but also of the known friends and believers who would have listened and been disappointed by my poor performance.

"You know we don't beat around the bush in this show. You aren't the first to sweat with the questions we ask. It's what gives us credibility. If you answered everything perfectly, they would think we arranged the questions, like everybody does. When we had the orientalist healer, you called to congratulate me. People want to know; they don't want to be conned. We've discussed it so many times. If it holds up, so much the better. If it doesn't hold up, that's good too. Don't worry, in the last block I'll give you the opportunity to get off right."

Sure enough, Nicolás handled the second part elegantly, with a complicit wink to his listeners.

"I think we threw too many questions at my friend Raúl in the last block, so I'm going to give him time to explain, without interruptions, how his church is run and leave it to others to explain how theirs works. Go ahead, Raúl."

Grateful and relieved, I was able to explain at length and demonstrate the transparency of my group's handling of money, the concept of tithing, and why we tithe. I believe I was able to separate good use from bad use, making it clear that each person was responsible to verify what the Bible said personally and to control the use of every cent.

But I promised myself that I would never again find myself in such an uncomfortable situation, that I would research topics like these that were of interest to people and that neither I nor many in the church had studied. The funny thing was that, when I researched the subject of tithing, I found that Nicolás—or the person who had given him the information—was much closer to the truth than was mechanically repeated in the churches: that everyone was required to give ten percent of their income, and that this income should go entirely to the church they attended.

At that time I saw the lack of interest of the evangelical world— with few exceptions—in facing hard issues, in discussing, in preparing to answer the difficult questions of life, a trend that would increase in the coming years, replaced by the search for immediate experiences, the simplification of the religious message and living, and the blurring of differences in identity in search of a supposed "unity" that was nothing more than a complacent uniformity.

There was an incident that marked very strongly the entire 1980 SeBiPa class. It was during their second year, in July 1979. Verónica Schmidt, the girl from Alta Gracia, became pregnant. Amid the general unbelief, the news spread like wildfire and stunned everybody. In the idealism of those young people, it was inconceivable that something like this would happen in a group preparing to serve the Lord and help others. Even worse when it became known that it had occurred inside the Seminary, with another student! For Pedro it was the first of several personal disappointments he would have during his church life. Until then, the worst thing he had known about the dark side of life among believers was some church friends who smoked or drank, but in general he lived with the illusion that the happy world within the church was inherently different from that of the world. For Juan, however, the lack of church background helped him to assume that such a thing could be more normal. While he aspired to the best for himself and everyone, he had known too much about the fragile human mind in extremely harsh conditions to be surprised that things like this would happen, even in a seminary for future pastors.

If the event was a blow in itself, the way the Seminary authorities treated it shook them even more and showed those fledgling pastors many things that shouldn't be done. First, the secrecy, the lack of clarity. Suddenly they were told that Verónica had to travel urgently to Alta Gracia, a week before the finals! When they asked Mabel Duverges, her best friend, she responded evasively, and even with some fear. At the same time, Hugo Carvajal, from Santiago, stopped attending classes and was "called to his church." It was a matter of putting two and two together to realize what had happened. Juan was struck by the stealth and the uncomfortable silences, and he couldn't stand it anymore:

"Tell me, Professor, what's going on with Verónica and Hugo? Are you hiding anything?" The question was aimed like a missile at the heart of Chiavetto, the group's mentor, at the worst possible moment, and without warning—in the middle of a class.

"They have both had personal problems and have had to return to their places of origin."

"What kind of personal problems? Why didn't they share them with us and leave without saying goodbye?"

"I'm not in a position to answer that question." A government official would have said, "no comments."

"Come on, Chiavetto, we're not stupid. We are supposed to deal with the truth here, with the light. Not with lies."

"Excuse me, student, are you accusing me of being a liar?"

"Hide the truth, disguise it, distort it... It's all the same. Give it any name you like. But the name isn't important, it's the fact."

"Is it true that Verónica is pregnant?" then Nora asked.

"And that Hugo is the father?" Marcelo completed the suspicion.

Chiavetto looked around desperately, waiting for the rapture of the church or the rain of sulfur of Sodom and Gomorrah, the biblical equivalent of "somebody shoot me." Then he looked frantically at the clock on the back wall.

"Look, students, I suggest that you consult with Dean Berdisso, since it's a subject outside my competence and we want to avoid gossip. Nor do we want to affect the good name of the Seminary."

If he had said, "Yes, what they say is true" it wouldn't have been as emphatic as that roundabout phrase. With the aggravating circumstance that it highlighted what was the priority in this thorny issue—not the life of the students, but the good name of the institution.

"So it's true. And why is everything being handled this way? Is this how we're supposed to deal with difficult issues when we leave here?" Juan insisted.

"It's not like that. What happens is that we didn't want to affect the functioning of the institution. Besides, there are issues that must be handled at a certain level, in a proper sphere..." Each time worse, but increasingly illustrative of the attitude that was being taken.

"I don't think it's the best way. The best thing is to speak clearly, to avoid murmuring, gossip, rumors," said Santiago.

Pedro, normally talkative, didn't know what to do or what to say. Something unusual in him, always leading, always with the initiative. He had been compared to the impulsive apostle Simon Peter, a comparison he hadn't disliked. After all, with all the criticism that impulsive people received, "someone had to do things, someone has to take the initiative," a phrase he often repeated. He was one of those doers. Others watched and others criticized. Of course, he made mistakes, but only those who do something make mistakes. Or, to put it another way, the best way not to make mistakes was to do nothing. So why didn't he say something? Why did he let others take center stage? It seemed to him that everyone's eyes were on him, waiting for his input. But he couldn't. In his mind came memories of how uncomfortable situations were handled in his family and in his church. So he ended up saying something political.

"Look, guys, why don't we let the Seminary do what they need to do here, and we can pray for Verónica and Hugo? For Verónica, especially those who are closer friends, like Mabel. I can call Hugo. I know he was going through a difficult time in his life. I know a pastor in his town, and I can connect him. I'm sure the Lord will have a reason in all this, and he knows better than anyone what's best. Let's not judge or try to solve things that are out of our reach."

Everyone was left with the same feeling: a lot of words to say and do nothing, to fill a void, just like the mentor. So that everything stays the same. Kick the ball out of the field, show personal interest without doing anything, slightly muddy the image, put the Lord and his mysterious will, appeal to the positive, use prayer as a wild card. The similarity with the speeches of the politicians was remarkable. The worst thing was that it acted as a sedative, a sleeping pill for everyone. And it gave Chiavetto an elegant way out.

"I think Pedro is right. More than the past, we must be interested in the future, in the kids and in the institution. If we stay in the past or in the present, we get stuck."

Everyone seemed to breathe a sigh of relief, and the class went on for the remaining ten minutes. Juan found this way of handling a difficult subject strange, but he didn't insist, realizing that the others settled so quickly into the new suggestion.

Verónica and Hugo were never seen again. They learned from her, through Mabel, that she had a son and soon after married a boy from her church in Cordoba. With Hugo, they lost track completely. No one called him or connected him with any pastor, not even Pedro, and the general assumption was that he would leave the ministry and the church. To be honest, he didn't seem to be a strong person spiritually. Perhaps he had made a mistake in his vocation. God had his reasons. It would all be for the best, in the end.

After the graduation ceremony, there was a small reception in the elegant hall of the Seminary. The fifteen graduates, with their girlfriends, boyfriends, wives, husbands, parents, and friends, took pictures and chatted animatedly. On one side, the group of professors, together with the Dean and the Rector, talked about plans for the next year, about the holidays or of some "holy gossip" ("Do you know who died yesterday?," "You won't believe what Pastor Núñez preached!," "I met Oviedo yesterday and he told me that he is closing the Reformed Institute..."). There were Pedro and Virginia, Juan and Mariela, and me with Mercedes, accompanying them. The satisfaction of a finished stage could be felt in the air. There was also that fear mixed with uncertainty that surrounds every graduation ceremony. What would happen now? Where would they go? Would they continue seeing each other? Would they succeed as pastors, or at least be able to put into practice what they had learned and lived these three years? Would any of them fail? Was this really the vocation of all these young people, or would some realize that their place in the world was different? Suddenly, the voice of the Dean was heard, who had approached the microphone.

"Brothers and friends, your attention please."

There was a growing silence as all eyes turned toward the voice.

"I don't want to let this moment pass without making a toast to our new graduates. Does everyone have their glasses for the toast?"

He waited a few minutes while people filled their glasses with what was there: juice, soda, and even some bottles of champagne that had appeared at the last moment.

"My toast is not that you can remember what you have studied here. My toast is not that you will represent this Seminary with honor. Nor is my toast that you become successful pastors of large churches or ministries." People were beginning to feel a little uncomfortable, and some began to look at each other. But Juan knew where José Berdisso, a man he had learned to respect and admire, was heading. Especially since he had such a strong spiritual experience, what he called "face-to-face encounter with the Lord" which had transformed him from a brilliant and rather conceited professor into a much more accessible and humble, and certainly happier, man. After that experience, not even the accident he suffered on a trip to Mar del Plata, which had cost him the amputation of a leg, had succeeded in extinguishing the fire that had been lit in his life. Juan had shared with him since then lengthy talks and times of prayer around the Bible. He was going to miss him.

"My toast is that you reflect the life of Christ in everything you do, in every relationship you establish, in every problem you face." His face had taken on a special glow. He was conveying more than just words. "My toast is that you transmit the life of the Spirit from the time you wake up to the time you go to bed… and even while you're asleep!" Some laughed heartily.

A loud and prolonged applause accompanied the Dean's emotional farewell. The group dispersed amidst greetings and hugs, but the more united group of students, together with their partners, prolonged the farewell.

"Why don't we go to the *gallego's*[19] bar... for the last time?" Leo suggested.

"Come on, the last one pays."

They left quickly and crossed the street diagonally for the last time, to the place of so many encounters and disagreements during these three years. Here they had also had lunch when they had a little more money and were tired of the food of Panchita, the cook in the Seminary dining room. *Milanesa*[20] sandwiches, ham and cheese toast, banana shakes, coffee—alone or with *facturas*—, soft drinks. But, above all, shared lives and dreams, along with the inevitable frustrations and wounds.

"I'm going to miss you guys."

"Me, too, but let's keep in touch."

"I'm getting married in April, so I look forward to see you all."

"I'll write to you from Santiago."

"One for all, and all for one."

...

For many, one of the best stages of their life had come to an end.

---

[19] The way Spaniards are called colloquially
[20] Typical breaded steak

4

THE THINGS WE STARTED

Building with others looking ahead
Unstoppable, unflinching toward the end

The first years were beautiful for Pedro and Virginia, from that first talk with Raúl, Juan's cousin, and Mercedes, when they decided to start a work together in the northern area of Buenos Aires. Pedro vividly remembered the times of prayer, the deep search for the Lord's will, the revelations that appeared every time they opened the Word. The first meetings in the living room of his second-floor apartment in San Fernando, first the four of them, then with Marisa, a woman of tremendous faith, two brothers from the province of Santa Fe who had heard about them, the Gervasio family, the grocer and his wife, who were converted when she was healed from a serious problem in her leg caused by diabetes that almost cost her an amputation. In a short time, there were twenty, and then thirty, and they had their first baptism by immersion, in the Free Brethren church in the plaza, because they had a baptistry. What an awesome meeting! Right there ten more people were added, and Raúl's warehouse close to the river, that they had started to use for their meetings, was already small for them.

These were times of struggle, yes, but of much victory. Pedro worked at Virginia's father's car dealership during the day, but as soon as he finished, he went to visit the brothers and sisters, at home, in the hospital, wherever they were. Although it wasn't easy for him, especially when he came very tired from work, they were the best times of the day, because he met people with their real problems and joys, and he felt useful. His "secular" work was important because it put food on their table and helped provide financial support for the church. That was where he really felt his mission was. People appreciated them very much. And that was priceless. Just as the answers to prayers. God was alive today!

Pedro and Virginia got along wonderfully with Raúl and Mercedes. Much of it had to do with their shared stories of growing up in the church. Raúl was a skinny, scrawny-looking man with enviable health and stamina. He had had to wear very thick glasses since he was a child. This disadvantage didn't prevent him from being a voracious reader of everything that came his way, from sports to literature. Mercedes Orozco was his counterpart. Not only physically—shorter and "plumper"— but in the way she faced life, much more relaxed and carefree than her boyfriend. Although initially she gave the impression of someone superficial, when she faced something that challenged her, or if she had to help someone she loved, she was completely transformed, and was able to give herself without reservation. She had been raised by a single mother since her father had abandoned them when she was three years old. This created a solid and affectionate bond between them that helped them overcome a series of misfortunes during her childhood and adolescence. They lost their home to a fire, her mother caught TB and lost her job as a receptionist. Mercedes suffered a hit and run car accident that left her with a slight limp due to a faulty operation. But you would find it hard to deduce any of this by being with Mercedes and Doña Lola. They were constantly joking when in company, mostly with secret codes they shared. Their conversion came through multiple talks they had with their grocer, Martita, who shared the Gospel with them with such an enthusiasm that they accepted to go to church with her and eventually accepted the Lord, were baptized and joined the Love and Hope church in Morón where they had moved. Raúl met her in the

Juventud 77 youth rally in the Luna Park stadium, when they were at the same gate handing out programs.

The group hadn't yet decided on the name of the new church, but they had played with the names Community of Love, Maranatha or simply Evangelical Church, with the name of the city, i.e. Evangelical Church of San Fernando.

Then the Church Growth Workshop brochure arrived. At first, Pedro didn't pay attention to it, because he had already determined in the Seminary to ignore "Christian marketing," which he had known very well as a child. But then he got the phone call:

"Hello? Is this Pastor Terrero?" The accent disconcerted him.

"Yes, who is this?"

"Nice to meet you, Pastor. This is Pastor Tony Vidal. You probably don't know me, but I would like to know if you received our *brochure* on the Church Growth Workshop" The use of that word in English suggested a Puerto Rican, or a Central American.

"Yes, I got it last week. But you'll excuse me because I was about to leave for work."

"Then I won't bother you anymore, pastor. Could we make an appointment when it's more convenient for you?"

"No, I really don't have time and I'm not interested in doing any workshops at the moment." He was struggling to get rid of the cobweb of a professional salesman.

"Sure. I understand perfectly. But it is precisely this workshop that will help you have more time for what you really like to do, your vocation. Why don't you allow me only ten minutes to meet with you and show you the benefits of this growth tool?" Something told him that he should reject the offer, even if it was rude, but another part of him, the one that would cause him so many problems and troubles during the next years, said to him, *What if this is the way to grow, and the Lord is sending it to you?* For a brief moment he thought he saw the same red light he had seen at the youth congress. Probably a problem with his eyesight.

"But what is it about?" He knew he had fallen into the trap. He had let the salesman put his foot in the door. It was the same thing he had been taught in the sales courses at work! Never let the customer say "no." As long as he didn't, there was always hope. And the more time the salesman had, the harder it was for the customer to walk away without buying something, if only to get rid of the salesman.

"It's a system that is showing amazing results in several countries in Central America and Latin America. Created in the United States, with the best management techniques, combined with Latin American brothers who have put our own stamp on it. I would very much like to show it to you in person. What days are you free this week? How about this Thursday afternoon?" He was already moving like a fish in water, sure of the prey.

"Well... Better on Friday, 10 a.m. What do you say?"

"Done! I had another interview at that time, but I'd rather see you. You won't regret it." The mechanical phrasing of the closing sentence should have confirmed that it wasn't something from the Lord, but a simple sale. But it was too late. Friday's talk would do the rest, and soon his small, simple New Testament community would be on its way to megachurch success.

Juan had also set out to avoid Christian marketing at all costs. In these matters he had always been on the same side as Pedro in the discussions at the Seminary. Like the young people of that time, with all their ideals, they too felt that they would completely change the way of being pastors. They wouldn't fall into the mistakes of their predecessors, even though they respected them and recognized the legacy they had left them. So, in their talks over *matés* in the patio with the eucalyptus fragrance, ideas always came up to do things in the "new" way, to "win Argentina for Christ," to "bring the kingdom of God to the earth" and other grandiose phrases. To achieve this, Juan advocated discipline, method, and order, and was invariably labeled as a *milico*. For, as unpleasant as his military experience had been in the latter part in the Tucumán jungle, he had always recognized how much his time of instruction had brought him. Having to accept orders, submit to the group and achieve things not as individuals but as a team seemed wonderful to him and something he hadn't experienced previously. And it seemed natural to him to transfer that valuable learning to the spiritual life. After all, didn't Jesus stay up all night praying many times? Didn't the Bible talk about fasting? Didn't Paul compare the Christian to an athlete preparing for a competition, or to a soldier? Wasn't that discipline?

That's why, when he left the Seminary, he set as an aim to continue and even intensify his disciplines of prayer and Bible study: thirty minutes to read and study the Bible and thirty minutes of prayer, starting at five in the morning. He felt at that point in his career as a pastor that this organization of his devotional life would give him more freedom for the rest of the day. The first thing he wanted to do was to be part of a church where he could learn the ropes and meet people who would guide him in his first steps. He chose to continue serving in the Church of Fellowship, in the city of La Plata, where he had already been going for the last two years as part of his practical service in the Seminary.

Once a flourishing church with some two hundred members and an attendance of over three hundred, it had been reduced to no more than fifty people by a nasty division a couple of years earlier. As Pastor Diego Flores and the people who were left in charge had explained to him, the members who had left didn't submit to authority and were rebellious, so in the long run it would be a good thing for the church. Juan had never taken in that explanation, but he had no interest in the details of what had happened in the past. So he continued to work with Mariela among the young people, organizing the Saturday activity and a couple of camps on long weekends or in the summer.

Once he visited with Mariela the Apostolic Church in the Saavedra neighborhood in Buenos Aires. It was a huge church compared to the Church of Fellowship and everything he had ever known. When they arrived, among the usual introductions and greetings, he was struck by the great contrast between the church's pastor, Luis Guevara, who was about 45 years old, and his wife, Elena, who seemed to be ten years older. He was full of charm, dynamism, and vitality, the opposite of her wife. Her physical and emotional fatigue marked her as an anonymous and unhappy woman, despite the "evangelical smile" she offered mechanically to anyone who approached her. Juan imagined her crying in solitude, burdened by her five children—a number he guessed, but which turned out to be correct—while her star husband traveled and preached, ministered and counseled, and arrived home with a tiredness of a category far superior to hers. He instinctively looked at Mariela's lively face and a chill ran down his back.

He remembered then old Pastor Marchi, the person who most resembled what Jesus would be like if he lived today, according to Juan. He was generous, attentive to people's needs, with a spiritual depth that attracted him deeply. He exuded "something different," something beyond human. Something like Jesus must have had, which made people respect and admire him. Even those who wanted to kill him. If you spoke with Germán Marchi, even on the phone, you didn't speak to just anyone. Even in the things in which they didn't agree—participation in politics, for example—he felt drawn to chat and exchange ideas with him. He conveyed authority. Juan remembered one of the phrases he had collected when they discussed authority in the Pastoral Practice class at the Seminary: "Being authoritarian is the surest way to lose all authority." How many examples of authority and authoritarianism he would see in the years to come! Pastor Marchi had given a talk during one of the classes and Juan found himself hooked immediately to this amazing man.

He decided to give him a call.

"Hi, I'm Juan Cristante. Do you remember me?"

"How can I not remember! There aren't many 'spiritual *milicos*' today. How can I help you, Juancito?"

"I need to talk with you, pastor. When will you have a moment?"

"Come now, son. I was just praying for you."

Juan knew two things. First, that he wasn't saying this out of courtesy. He had really been praying for him. Second, that receiving him would most likely involve moving some other engagement, being late for an appointment, or a meeting. But Don Germán didn't care about that. Nor did he care if he was labeled as unpunctual or informal. For him, people came first, especially those with needs. Actually, God first, people second... and people third. *Like Jesus*, Juan thought to himself.

"I'm going there now. I'll take some *facturas* and you can heat the water for the *maté*. OK?" His heart gave a leap and he felt excited. He knew he wouldn't come out of the talk the same way. He'd see everything clearer and in greater depth.

When that man of God opened the door for him, a blanket of familiarity received him. The abundant and disheveled gray hair, the uncertain gait, and the stooped body spoke of an old man. But the look, the hug, and the words betrayed a vitality that could only come from the God he loved so much. Juan recognized the living room, with its two green armchairs, the wicker table and chairs, the painting with the Bible text in Gothic characters, the family photos. The kitchen, austere but cordial. There was an atmosphere of... he was looking for the best word... holiness. Yes, an authentic, pleasant, even powerful holiness. He felt that he was enjoying in that place and that moment years of prayer of that holy man, of tears of joy and sadness shed for others, of advice that had changed lives. The phrase, "If these walls could speak..." came to his mind. He was also aware of the harsh reality this man had gone through. His wife had been bedridden for years with a very strange disease in her joints and bones that proved immune to the prayers and fasting of her husband or that of dozens of pastors and friends who had interceded for her together with their congregation. Like Jesus on the cross, he would have heard the imaginary voices of many, and his own inner voices telling him, "He saved others, but he can't save himself!"[21]

"That's a nice smell from the *facturas*. Where are they from?" said the pastor, as he unwrapped the package and placed them on a white china plate.

---

[21] Mt 27:42

"Yes, freshly made. From La Ideal, around the block from home... How many memories this kitchen brings back to me, pastor! The talks about vocation, calling, the seminary. Genoveva's pesto noodles. What a great woman!"

"For me she's still alive, practically. And I still argue with the Lord, and question why he took her. She had so much to give, we had so much to live together, even when she was bedridden, believe it or not. I'll tell you a secret, Juan, time doesn't erase anything. Or very little. At least, in my case."

"It's not what you usually hear."

"It's true. People like to hear what they like to hear. And many like to say what people want to be told. But we're not called to be political. At least, in my case"—a catchphrase that was very characteristic of him, a mixture of independence of judgement and respect for what others did. "I remember when she died, and even during her illness, the pressure I felt from the people, who needed me to be well, with all the faith in the world, always smiling... As if they couldn't tolerate the suffering, the weakness of another person, especially from their pastor."

"Would you have liked to have had more freedom to express what you really felt?" suggested Juan.

"Exactly. And now it's too late..." Suddenly he changed his gaze. "What's with the *maté*?"

"See if it's not too hot."

With the *maté* going from hand to hand, the talk continued on the topic that had brought Juan.

"A bit. What brings you here? I'm sure it has something to do with the girl you told me about. Mariela, right?"

"Yes, I don't want to make a mistake. For her, for the pastorate."

"What are you afraid of?"

"What it means to be a pastor's wife. I don't like what I've seen so far."

"Including Genoveva?" Don Germán replied, too quickly. Juan had put his foot in it. But Pastor Marchi always said he preferred not to beat around the bush. "Time is too short," in his words.

"Maybe, a little bit." There was a long silence which, funny enough, was not uncomfortable. "Do you think she was happy, really happy, pastor?"

"Well..."

"What I mean, was she really the person she wanted to be, or was she just 'the pastor's wife'?"

Don Germán was left thinking, looking back at the past, and it seemed to Juan that a shadow of sadness passed over him. He dared to tell him these things because he was like a father to him. In fact, more than a father, because he would never have questioned his own father.

"A bit of everything... yes..."

"But, if you could revive your life with Genoveva, would you change anything?"

"Of course!" The emphasis surprised them both.

"What things? Take care, it's somewhat hot," asked Juan, resuming the *maté* circuit.

"I would take more notice of her, as a person. I wouldn't outshine her so much. I would have more time for both of us, more time for the family, less time for other people's problems..." The last sentence came out of his mouth with great effort, but it was sincere. "I'm telling this to you alone, Juan. I never talked about this with anyone." He didn't care that I saw his eyes were brightening with tears.

Juan was surprised by this confession, because unlike many other pastors he had known, he had a beautiful family, with an engineer son married to a faithful believer and two grandchildren, and a daughter who was doctor, married to a businessman, who couldn't have children of her own, but had adopted a little girl from the church's orphanage. Don Germán was the senior pastor of a beautiful, widely respected congregation. Perhaps the sadness came from all the time he dedicated to so many people, at the expense of his family, and which was later rewarded with rebuffs and betrayals. Like the Sosa's, who left with a group of church people, after all he had done for them. People who didn't deserve such a pastor. Surely he must have wondered if all the time spent with these people was worth it.

"And what do you advise me, then?"

"Talk a lot. Get to know each other. Spend time together and alone. Walk hand in hand, hugging. Show yourselves and show others how you love each other. And above all, have friends who aren't from the church. Even from the world."

The "world" ... What a loaded word! When he was converted, Juan had to learn a whole new evangelical jargon to understand not only the messages but the very conversations between people in the church. Convert or converted: a person who was converted, that is, who accepted Christ as his Savior; unconverted: a person who hadn't yet been converted. After this initial division, came the division between believers (which only included the evangelicals), basically divided among those who regularly attended church—the ones who "assembled"—, the ones who "didn't assemble," and the ones who had "strayed." The "world" summarized everything that was bad and dangerous that the believer should avoid. He was not to have fellowship with the world, he was not to marry someone from the world, and he was to avoid all possible contamination with the world. And here he had an old pastor, his greatest reference point, advising him to have couples who were friends "from the world." What did he want to tell him? Why this change in what he had heard him advise so many times?

"From the world?" he repeated, surprised.

"Yes, regular people, not so nutty as some in the church"—with a knowing wink. "Come, let's pray."

He read him a biblical passage that fitted as a ring, where Jesus was criticized because he ate with "sinners" (tax collectors and prostitutes) and, taking him by the shoulder, he began: "Father, you who know all things, help us to follow your will..." They both prayed, taking turns naturally. An observer would say that, once they warmed up, they moved like fish in water. There were many "flying hours" there, especially the older one. Many kneeling hours, tear hours, comfort hours. It wasn't the traditional list of requests and thanks, but something different. It was a pas de deux in the presence of God, enjoying each other's company and the company of someone they didn't see, but who was as real as the chair, the table, the air.

When they realized, it was dark outside, and a full hour had passed. The pastor dismissed him with a strong fatherly hug at the door, and although Juan knew he had no concrete answer to his concern, he felt much more able to face it than before.

"Pastor Pedro Terrero? You can't imagine how pleased I am to shake your hand. Pastor Tony Vidal, of Fullness and Growth." *Did you say "pastor" or "salesman"?* Pedro thought to himself.

"Hello", he said, trying to distance himself with a minimal greeting. "You'll have to excuse me, but I have very little time." Another vain attempt, especially when he let him give his sales pitch.

"Of course, I don't want to waste your time, pastor." Tony hurried over to the table, took out two identical orange folders from his briefcase, handed one to Pedro, and the other remained in his hands. "Please have a seat."

Pedro sat down. He knew he had lost the initiative; this man was inviting him to sit in his own study.

"I have prepared a special folder for you with different proposals so that your church can grow in one year, two years, five years and ten years at different rates. We believe that no one better than the pastor to determine how his church should grow, but we agree that it should grow, right?" The hand resting on his arm showed who was in control of the situation.

"Of course, though it's not what matters most to me, but to grow healthily and thinking about people."

"We agree a hundred percent! Look at our third principle, the one we call the Golden Principle: Grow Healthy. It's like you read my mind!" He already had the full-color brochure open in front of him. Salesman 3: Pedro 0.

....

"Well, it's been a tremendous pleasure, pastor. I hope you will keep us informed of the results of your inquiries. We will send you information on follow-up workshops and other activities for the next year." Pedro greeted him holding on to his folder. When he returned from the door, he had a gleam in his eye. Five hundred members in two years! Wouldn't this be the revival he had prayed so hard for? In his imagination he went from the modest house in which he lived to the modern living room and office of the pastor who stared at him from the brochure. He tried to rebuke the thought—that annoyingly persistent red light—but it was too late.

November 25, 1983. The church meeting had been called urgently. Pedro had phoned us all, one by one, very excited. He had something important he wanted to share with us. "Friday, OK? Eight o'clock, in the hall."

When we arrived, there were about twenty-five of us, in spite of the heavy rain that had flooded several surrounding streets. The chairs were in a circle and Pedro and Virginia had prepared food and drinks. He looked somewhat anxious, like someone who has a secret to share and can't wait to do it.

"Hi, Raúl. How good you could make it!"

"What's this about? Why all the mystery?"

"You'll see. I hope Guillermo can come. He had patients until late. Hi, Néstor! Berta..."

When almost all the chairs were occupied, Pedro went to his place and, standing up, began the meeting.

"Good evening. Thank you for coming on such short notice. I think you won't regret it. Shall we start with a prayer? Néstor, would you like to lead us?"

The prayer of the oldest deacon in the church helped take our minds off earthly things and focus them on the issues of the Kingdom. It was also a good time to remember a couple of sick people. They all closed their eyes and bowed their heads mechanically.

"...for Rosa and Dionisio, may your will be done in their lives. We ask you to accompany us in every moment of our lives. Give wisdom to Pastor Pedro and his wife. We ask all of this in the name of Christ. Amen."

The expectation was created. While Virginia served coffee and *facturas* to those who didn't have any yet, Pedro took one of Pastor Vidal's orange folders from the Fullness and Growth Ministry and showed it to the group.

"Brothers, this material, which came to me the other day, can change us from a small church in this shed to a church of five hundred members, in a large and modern hall, like many churches in Latin America and the world. And in only two years! Don't you think this meeting is justified? Circulate this, please. I have another one here."

As they received the brochure, people looked at it with curiosity. When it came into my hands and we looked at it with Mercedes, the impression I got was similar to the hundreds of brochures I saw every day at the advertising agency. Lots of color, lots of testimonies, "hook" phrases, smiling photos, promises. Everything in the right place, using the right techniques. It was hard to know if it was something good or something that just looked good.

"It's well done. Don't you think so, Raúl?" He needed my approval, although I didn't look too excited. At least, not as much as he was.

"Yes, the material is top-notch. It's from a Chilean agency. I don't know much about it."

When the first brochure finished circulating, Pedro didn't wait for the second one and wanted to know the impression of the others.

"What do you think? Wouldn't you like us to appear in the testimonies of the next brochure?"

"I don't know, it sounds very *yankee*[22] to me. Where do these people get the money?", Víctor's predictable opinion, suspicious of anything smelling of money or of America, especially inside the church. He was a union leader at the Ford factory in Pacheco.

"I think it's a very good idea, and if the pastor agrees..." The favorable opinion of María Flores was also predictable.

"How did you get the material? Did they come to visit you?" asked Víctor.

---

[22] Popular way of talking of Americans in general

"Yes, I'd better tell you. I understand your concern, Víctor, but I think the point here is to take advantage of the best the world has to offer, its knowledge, its tactics, its experience, and use it for the Kingdom. It doesn't matter where it comes from. Remember the sermon on Sunday, the one about the four animals? 'Sheep among wolves... shrewd as snakes... innocent as doves.' That's what Jesus wants us to be, what he expects from each one of us."

Then he told them about the meeting with Tony Vidal, the impression he had got, his initial doubts and mistrust, and his time of prayer after that. He had also spoken with the pastors that Vidal had given as a reference—Veloso, Querejeta, Soler. All successful since they began to apply the principles of the system. Guillermo Veloso, for example, had gone from a small group of sixty members, mostly people over fifty, to over two hundred, with many young people, in just one year. And he was willing to meet with him at any time. He had even invited him to preach at his church, in San Antonio de Padua. Félix Querejeta was away on a trip, but when Pedro spoke to his wife over the phone she was over her head in praises of Fullness and Growth. Alejandro Soler—a pastor who Pedro didn't like very much because of his constant trips abroad and his somewhat pedantic style—had gone from an old rented shed next to his house in a very simple neighborhood to a hall of his own in a central place in Avellaneda. He already had a newspaper that was circulating in the neighborhood, which was earning money too, precisely because they had used principle number two of the method: "Money isn't bad, only the love of money."

I saw him so convinced that I hesitated to ruin this moment and this momentum with requests for more information, as we did in any business meeting. I imagined a similar situation at the agency, with someone coming in with a brochure and promotional material from an interview with a salesman. He wouldn't get off lightly! We would subject him to a severe interrogation, with crossfire from all sides. Because the prestige and the future of the company was at stake. But here, I don't know why, it seemed different to me. Perhaps because I felt that I would be questioning the pastor, or the figure of the pastor. Besides, Pedro said that he had prayed, something that I didn't do much and that pastors do all the time, right? They are closer to God, in a sense, so they must have a clearer picture. That's what most people think, and that's what we thought then.

The discussion continued, losing strength by the minute, a little because of the late hour and a little because people had come across something that was difficult to understand and digest in such a short time. Pedro, on the other hand, was well acquainted with the material and was telling us, in short, that he warmly recommended it. The illusion of being a big church, with resources, with greater comforts and power, was like an invisible carrot placed before them. After all, people prefer belonging to something big and not to something small. We all like to be with the winners.

"I suggest something. It's late, and many will be tired and eager to go home. Let's pray about it and discuss it next week. In the meantime, I'm fully available to you at any time to talk about this project. Although it isn't approved, I came up with a name: "1984 x 10." What do you think? During the next year, each of us must pray for ten more people for the church. Sounds crazy, doesn't it? But the kingdom of God is for the brave, the dreamers, those who dare to go beyond the mind..." The success-oriented spirit of the program had already begun to take effect in Pedro.

Of course, there was no other meeting. Partly, because Pedro didn't call it and partly, because the implicit consensus was that if the pastor had proposed it, it had to be right. Before long, the small congregation of thirty to fifty members was on its way to becoming a significant church. The poster "1984 x 10" with gold letters on a blue and white background dominated the room and each member received a Statement of Purpose with a summary explanation of the 5 Points for Growth and a blank list of ten people they would pray for and try to add to the church. From a family and informal structure, we moved to an organization with a business model, with an organization chart, written goals, communication materials—we even had a logo now! The dove symbolized the Holy Spirit; the wheat spike, growth; people holding hands, the sense of cooperation and unity that was necessary to achieve the growth objective. Everything followed the guidelines of the Manual for Level One (Bronze) that arrived by express mail the following week against the delivery of a voluntary donation of 200 US dollars, or 2,000,000 Argentinean pesos. A lot, if one looked at it with the eyes of the present; peanuts, looking to the future.

Juan's work among the young people of the Church of Fellowship was hard, but it gave him much satisfaction. He and Mariela felt they were useful and appreciated. The kids had much to share, and many lacked answers to their concerns and problems. So that part of their idea of what pastoral work meant was covered. But he felt that something was missing. Both the Bible and his studies of church history told Juan that there was a life in the Spirit that he hadn't yet attained. He wasn't content with an intellectual, or social, Christianity. Every time he read some parts of the Acts of the Apostles, his inner self cried out to him, "I want that! I need that! I won't settle for anything less!" And another part of him promised, "I'm going to get it! I'm not going to give up until I get it!" So when he heard that there was a group that was meeting in a home, following the simplicity of the early Christians, where spiritual gifts were being manifested and there were signs and miracles, he didn't think twice. He found out where it was, at what time, and on Tuesday at 8 p.m. he was at the home of Jorge and Nilda Varela, in the peaceful neighborhood of Belgrano.

Entering that house of exposed bricks and a gabled roof seemed like an instant confirmation that the undefinable thing he so longed for was here and now. When he went through the door, he breathed an atmosphere of peace and serenity that he had never before associated with a church. Rather, he had become used to the noise, the activity, the schedule, the programs. Jorge's simple and sincere welcome, the natural arrangement of the chairs in the spacious living room of the house, the lack of an apparent leader, all told him, " This is it!" After a while, when there were already eight or nine people, and without prior notice, somebody began to sing, very softly, "Hallelujah, Hallelujah, Hallelujah..." several times, in a repetitive and simple melody. One by one, the others joined in the singing, some with eyes closed, others looking up. No one seemed to notice the others. After a few minutes, another spontaneous song followed, accompanied by a guitar that had appeared out of nowhere. Another soft and powerful song followed:

> Jesus, Jesus of Nazareth,
> Your very image I want to have,
> Just as you are, I long to be,
> Jesus, Jesus of Nazareth.[23]

and then another song, whose lyrics Juan recognized as taken directly from one of Paul's letters:

> With faces unveiled, contemplating the Lord
> As in a mirror, the glory of the Lord
> I am being transformed, I am being transformed
> Into the very image of our Savior
> By the Holy Spirit of God[24]

The image of Jesus! That's what he needed. What he lacked. To be like Jesus. Juan was ecstatic. No one had spoken to him about this in the Seminary, at least not in such a powerful, direct way. He only remembered his talks with José Berdisso, the Dean, after his accident, and his insistence that there was something else he hadn't known before. He also remembered his words when he graduated from the Seminary, that we should reflect the life of Christ. Nor had he seen it in any of the churches he had been to. There always seemed to be something between him and the Lord: noise, ritual, a person, duty,

---

[23] Author's translation. Original: Jesús, Jesús de Nazaret / Tu misma imagen quiero tener / Cual eres tú, anhelo ser / Jesús, Jesús de Nazaret.

[24] Author's translation. Original: Con la cara descubierta / mirando al Señor. / Como en un espejo / la gloria del Señor. / Transformado soy / Transformado soy / A la misma imagen / De nuestro Redentor / Por el Espíritu Santo de Dios.

something. Only in his time alone with God had he been able to feel that closeness occasionally. But to experience it in the company of others, to feel the freedom to act naturally, without worrying about what others thought, was something new. He felt that he was already beginning to be part of that body of brothers, even without knowing them.

After some more songs, and after a time of total silence, to the point of making him uncomfortable, he heard the deep voice of a woman, on his right who said something with the sense that the Lord loved them all deeply.

"Amen... Praise the Lord... Hallelujah..." several responded.

"This is what the Sovereign Lord says to these bones, 'I will make breath enter you, and you will come to life. I will attach tendons to you and make flesh come upon you and cover you with skin; I will put breath in you, and you will come to life. Then you will know that I am the Lord.'"[25] He looked discreetly and saw that it was Jorge who was reading the well-known passage from the valley of dry bones, in Ezekiel.

"Amen!" said a man who had just arrived, with a loud voice.

Another round of singing followed, again with no apparent direction. They all seemed to have all the time in the world. There was no hurry here.

"I will do great things among you. Just have faith and follow my ways." The man who said this, sitting next to Juan, wasn't reading. It appeared to come from within him. Or he knew it by heart. But it fit the spirit of the moment perfectly.

Suddenly, an older man who had been silent until now burst forth in a language he didn't know and couldn't reproduce. The others seemed to attend as if they understood. When he finished, after a brief silence, the first woman seemed to interpret the message:

"Seek not the things of the world, but the things of heaven. Spend time with me, set aside time to be with me."

At one point, Jorge—who appeared to be the natural leader, as

---

[25] Eze 37:5-6

well as the homeowner— read the story of the Prodigal Son, in Luke 15, and gave a simple and powerful interpretation of this well-known parable.

"Here we have a love triangle, with three sides. The father with the prodigal son: rejection, love, forgiveness; The father with the older son: trust, invitation, sadness; The older son with the younger son: contempt, envy, rejection. The story doesn't speak of things or even of people—money, prostitutes, carob bean, party, ring, dress—but of *relationships* between people. God isn't so much interested in things as in relationships— with Him and among us." Jorge's voice was calm and confident; his gaze, direct and frank.

So that's what it was all about. Relationships. And he couldn't help but agree. For Juan, there were always people, with their real problems in real life. With their doubts and fears. With their sins and mistakes. Everything else—institutions, customs—had to be at the service of people. And not the other way around. Would this be what he was looking for? And if so, what did it mean? Should they leave the church where they were and gather here?

The next week he went with Mariela, who was delighted too. Both of them quickly integrated into the style of the meeting, and they couldn't help but think that something like this would have happened in the early years of Christianity, without the structures that man put in place, without the Greek way of thinking, without what came after Constantine, money and power, clergy and laity.

He recognized the voice of the woman from the first meeting who again said something that appeared to be inviting them to seek the Lord with more zeal and devotion. He would later find out that her name was Violeta, and that she had the gift of prophecy.

"We are your people, Lord," said another.

Mariela held his hand tightly. Juan realized that something was happening to her. When he looked at her, he saw tears streaming down her face, bathing her with a glow that made her even more beautiful. But she wasn't sad. She was being treated by the Spirit of the Lord. When they arrived home, she told him about the experience.

"I felt that someone was holding me very tightly, that something like a fire was running through me. I wanted to stay forever. It was Jesus. It was beautiful. Juan, I want the same for you, I want him to take away all the bitterness you bring from the war. It was for real! It was for real!"

They hugged and kissed tenderly. As never before, Juan felt that this experience had brought them closer together, on a deeper level. Jesus was no longer something or someone external, nor was he something or someone individual. He was among them, with them, bringing them together.

They continued to attend on Tuesdays each week. At first, they didn't want to say anything to Pastor Flores. They thought he would take it as a betrayal. With all that had happened, with the people that had left, and with everything that needed to be done, they thought that if he had known they were participating in meetings elsewhere, even if it wasn't "competition," he wouldn't take it well. Nor would he understand what they had experienced. Deep down, they didn't want anyone to ruin the experience they were having by telling them it was wrong, speaking critically of the group or some of the people attending those meetings. Neither did they want, with a certain selfishness, for others to find out about these small meetings, this spiritual oasis, and turn it into something bigger, more massive, and less intimate. So it remained their little secret for several months, until Pastor Flores—or Diego, as they called him—asked them to move the weekly prayer meeting to Tuesday, instead of Wednesday, because it was more convenient for several people.

"Look, Diego, we won't be able to go on Tuesdays," Juan told him.

"Why not? What commitment do you have? I'm sure you can change it. After all, the Lord's things come first." The pressure had been applied right at the beginning.

"Well, it's just that... with Mariela... we're going to some meetings..."—he never thought it would be so hard for him to tell his pastor something that good— "at the Varela's."

"At the Varela's? But it's a bunch of people who come from different churches. Besides, they told me that strange things happen there... Are you really going there? With Mariela too? You didn't tell me anything..."

It was the first time that Juan saw, felt, suffered the zeal of a pastor. It occurred to him that the word "zeal" must have more than one meaning or connotation. He had the impression that it was something good and something bad at the same time. The dictionary said, "fervor for a person, cause, or object; eager desire or endeavor; enthusiastic diligence; ardor." What if this passionate feeling for something good ended up dragging and ruining affections and relationships in its wake? This was what they were feeling about their pastor! A sickly, selfish zeal. He wasn't interested so much in his or Mariela's spiritual life, but in whether it affected his church, his field of action, his interests. What he continued saying helped them decide to look elsewhere, although they didn't feel it at the time and didn't tell Diego. But something deep was broken in the relationship at that moment that would never be recovered.

"You can't mix with that kind of people. They're not even a church. Besides, I understand that the Morales' are going, who were here and didn't contribute anything. And I know Jorge. A wonderful guy, but he never adapted to any church, very idealistic. Here you have everything to grow and develop. There is so much to do, and in a serious church. Besides, you must think about the problems we've had, the people who left, the devil's attack... I don't know, think about it. You're young, and I'm sure there are many things we can improve. I'll be the first to recognize mistakes and start changing things, but we need time and patience, and unity..."

Juan said a few words of circumstance and they said goodbye to the pastor, after the inevitable prayer, with its many uses, including subliminal pressure and hidden messages.

"...and Lord, thy will be done, and thy will alone. You know how much I love Juancito —he had never used the diminutive before, and it felt quite different than when pastor Marchi used it—and Mariela, how we have fought together. Guard us from error, from haste...

Bless their plans... Don't let the enemy get away with it... I humbly acknowledge my mistakes and ask for forgiveness..."

After that meeting, Juan and Mariela alternated on Tuesdays between the activity of their church and the new group they had met, a little because of the guilt the pastor had placed on them and a little because of a sense of false loyalty they felt, but eventually they began to distance themselves affectively from their church, until the time came to part ways. It was their first break with a church, their first pain at having to stop seeing people they had seen week after week, sharing their moments of joy and sadness. While they continued to be in touch with the young people they had pastored, it would no longer be the same. They had left. They belonged to another church. Soon others would come to replace them.

Nicolás's parents were both atheists. According to them, with good reason. His father, Enrique, had gone to a renowned Catholic school, where they had tried to force religion on him through masses, "Our Fathers," and threats of punishment. The catechism materials, which had seemed so interesting to him at the beginning, ceased to be of interest as he grew up and the answers he received to his questions didn't satisfy him.

"Why does God allow evil, suffering, injustice? How can it be that there are children born with malformations or die of hunger, rapes, injustice?"

"That's a mystery of faith. Someday God will give us the answer. Until then, it isn't for us to ask 'why' but 'what for'"—a typical answer that left him intellectually unsatisfied.

Nicolás's father had never found this attitude of not confronting doubts and answering questions with evasions honest. While he was willing to accept that some questions would go unanswered, given the complexity of life and the superiority of God—if he existed— what he had heard smacked of intellectual laziness and cowardice. On the other hand, Marga, his mother, a renowned gynecologist, had clung to science as the only answer to all life's questions. For her, what didn't fall within the domain of science, or what science couldn't yet explain, didn't exist, or didn't interest her. God, the miraculous, faith, were outside of the verifiable. More agnostic than atheist, she said that if he existed then he would be a cruel God.

Parents and children—Nicolás and his younger sister, Susana, years after the incident with the cult—often used mealtimes to discuss these issues, each from their own perspective. Although time shaped them into different positions and roles within the family debates, they all shared a rationalistic and anticlerical bias.

"I'm fed up with priests. Always complaining about the government, but not only are they to blame for much of what is happening, but they do nothing concrete to solve the problems. They are typical Argentinians, coffee socialists, armchair revolutionaries." Enrique had no qualms in showing his agenda.

"I don't know, Dad, what happens is that you look at the hierarchy, the structure. In any human organization, power corrupts. Who was it that said something like "power corrupts..." It was Susana, with her view from below.

"'Power tends to corrupt, and absolute power corrupts absolutely,' Lord Acton," corrected the father with pleasure, "but what does that have to do with our subject?"

"Yes, that's the whole phrase. What I mean is that one shouldn't confuse what the hierarchy says or does with what the rank and file do. How many humble priests work quietly in the slums and with the poor, and no one knows it?" said Susana.

"Except when it's convenient to use them, for a picture or for statistics. There are also a lot of lay people who help and aren't interested in appearing anywhere." It was typical of Nicolás to take the opposite position, especially if it was his father who had raised it.

"It's also true that the church structure always tends to try to make a good impression on the powers-that-be, be it Hitler or Videla, leaving those who play by Christian principles in a no-man's-land between two fires," said Marga, who had lost three friends during the subversive struggle: two doctors with leftist

79

ideals and a catechist and completely apolitical teacher who only wanted to help the poor.

"I'll ask you a question: Do you think that organizations like the Christian church were maintained during so many centuries and circumstances by structures or in spite of structures?" said Susana.

"I don't think you can separate the structure from the rest, in any organization," answered Enrique.

"Let's me put it differently. How can it be that authentic Christians continue to exist despite the corrupt popes, the Inquisition, the Crusades or all the scoundrels we know from these two thousand years? Could it be that 'what is essential is invisible to the eye,' as the Little Prince would say?" Susana added.

"Do you mean to say that there is a visible Christianity and an invisible one, and that it is the invisible one that counts and not the visible one?" The mother asked, by way of a scientific hypothesis.

"Exactly! The fact of its existence in the grassroots proves to me that they are what kept it alive," said the daughter.

The doorbell rang. It was Raúl, who came to get some books.

"We were just talking about your religion," said Nicolás, knowing how much the word irritated him.

"Mine isn't a religion. It's about an experience with God," he answered automatically.

"Well, whatever."

"And what conclusion did this debating family come to?" Raúl admired them in this, because they were serious and knew how to carry on a discussion that was often productive. He could never do this at home, not even talking about church issues. They only got along when they agreed on some issues or chose to ignore the difficult ones.

"That Christianity could only endure because of the grassroots, despite the structures. It isn't a conclusion, but a hypothesis," explained Enrique, who respected Raúl, because he had a different attitude towards the tough questions they threw at him. Either he tried to answer, or he promised to look for the answers; and he always complied.

"Look, Enrique, that's pretty much what I think. Remember that I come from a church with little structure. But I've often thought about that. People look at what's above, at the foam. But below is the foundation, like icebergs. It's the little old lady who spends her day praying for her grandson. The neighbor who gets a plate of food for the one who's sick or lost his job. It's the sister or brother who listens silently to the sorrows and problems of another brother, often without being able to do much more than pray and empathize with the situation. Those who visit hospitals or prisons. Or give money without their left hand knowing what their right hand is doing, in the words of Jesus.[26] And all this anonymously, without asking for anything in return."

"So you would agree to a church without a structure? Would you get rid of the pastors, the priests, the bishops?" Nicolás asked. It was the solution he had often proposed to avoid the manipulation and the sectarian spirit he saw in most Christian and non-Christian churches he knew.

"I don't know. One thing is the ideal, another is practice. Having a leader isn't a bad thing. People like to have someone in charge... What happens is that that person, or that minimal structure, can't go against the very essence of the Christian message. Look at Jesus. He went mad at religious leaders because of the way they told people what to do and they were no examples of anything. On the contrary. He called them a "generation of vipers," "whitewashed graves," and many other strong things. In front of everyone. No wonder they wanted to get rid of him!"

.....

This was one more of many conversations about this and other similar topics that Raúl had with Nicolás and the Peretti's. Strangely enough, although none of them were believers or showed any interest in becoming one, and even though they strongly questioned his faith, he always came out encouraged by these talks. It was as if he was reaffirming the essence of his faith, but he saw the areas around him

---

[26] Mt 6:3

that needed further investigation or readjustment. He felt his faith was tested and came out stronger.

Pedro was excited about the "1984 x 10" project. He felt it was just what his church needed, and what he needed. He had always been more at home with plans, goals, programs, and projects. He knew he was good in these areas, and no one could say he couldn't get things done and bring about change. Accustomed to big events, handling commissions and the challenges of large organizations, he felt outside his scope when he was told to meet to "pray and wait for the Lord's will," for example. They would never hear him speak against prayer and its importance, but he believed that prayer should accompany activity, not wait for it. How would the 1977 Youth Congress in San Nicolás have been held during the military dictatorship if he and the *colorado*[27] Vitelio hadn't moved as they did, among the churches and with the government?

He also found that it was something he could do together with Virginia, also a born entrepreneur. The plan even led them to postpone their marriage, which they had originally planned for August 1984, for the following year. After all, if they were busy with the details of the marriage and, worse still, if they were absent during the honeymoon, who could take responsibility for following the plan? Virgilio? Too... old. Good guy, good believer, but a different generation. Carlos and Silvia? They were young, and he was a successful construction entrepreneur, used to working with people and projects. Yes, maybe... but were they reliable? Better to wait, see what kind of people they were. Guillermo, the doctor? Too disorganized. Not to mention Víctor, the unionist, with his revolutionary ideas, although he respected him as a person. He knew he could count on Raúl and Mercedes to accompany him in this, but not to lead something of which they were clearly not one hundred percent convinced. No, it

---

[27] Redhead

had to be the two of them. At least, at this stage of the church. Later, they would see.

So, before the end of the year, they had all the materials and the structure ready for the campaign. A big blue and white flag—the national flag colors— with gold letters, read: "1984 x 10." He asked Raúl to do it because he worked in advertising. Although he didn't find it the best of phrases, he agreed and did a professional job, with good colors and typography. Pedro had a problem with the biblical text that dominated the back wall of the room until that moment—John 3:16, the evangelizing text par excellence—which he moved to the side wall. "It looks perfect, even better, because it's not so lost on such a big wall," he rationalized. He also produced all the support material for the plan: follow-up sheet, prayer promises, and growth promise verses, such as Isaiah 54:2: "Enlarge the place of your tent, stretch your tent curtains wide, do not hold back; lengthen your cords, strengthen your stakes." He also had several one-on-one meetings with key individuals and couples and a special meeting just before Christmas to launch the plan.

And it worked! The church grew in 1984. Not ten times, but considerably. They went from being a somewhat fickle group of about thirty to fifty people to having meetings of one hundred and fifty or more in one year! In fact, these were the numbers that the Fullness and Growth (F&G) material handled, so this was proof that they knew what they were doing, and that Pedro hadn't made a mistake in hiring their services (the last sentence didn't sound very spiritual to him, but it was the reality). By June they had already had to look for another meeting place and found a bigger and better located shed only two blocks away from the previous one, but closer to the center of San Fernando. It was much easier to access and had heating and air conditioning that worked very well. The rent was much higher, but the increased offerings would more than cover it, to the point that it allowed Pedro to leave his job with Virginia's father to go full-time. Invitations were spreading by word of mouth. It had started with the Veglio family, which in turn brought the Sánchez Miranda family, who were relatives. They came from the Church of the Renewal and weren't too happy there. Later he learned that they hadn't been in that church for too long either, nor in the one before that, and that they had had problems with everyone. "Surely they are people of personality and action, and they found no place in those more traditional churches. They'll be comfortable here; they'll have things to do. Besides, they are an answer to the prayers for the project, so it isn't right to doubt or to put sticks in the spokes of growth," Pedro rationalized again, when Virgilio told him what he knew about these two families.

People—especially his colleagues—heard about the phenomenon. They began calling to find out what had happened and how he had achieved it, to invite him to preach in their churches, and to speak at their pastors' meetings.

"Pedro? How are you doing? Do you remember me? Adrián Vitelio, the *colorado*, from the 1977 Youth Congress!" Another phone call, in the middle of all the activity he had.

"Ah... Hi, Adrián. I'm a little busy. How are you?!"

"Good. I'm fine. Sorry to interrupt you, but I heard from Nacho about your church. Attendance tripled in a single year..."

"Yes, we're very happy, and we continue on. We don't want to interrupt the blessing," following the guidelines of the program, of never settling for what has been achieved, not even in words.

"Listen to me, wouldn't you have half an hour to chat? I don't know if you know that we started a work in Gerli with Silvina, and we're having trouble getting people together. There are the Pentecostals, the Catholics... we didn't succeed in motivating people. We tried a lot of things: Bible study, prayer retreats, vigil, community service..."

"Yes, yes, I understand," he cut him off. *I can't be on the phone for half an hour with everyone who calls,* he thought. "Let me see my schedule and ask Sara."

"Who's Sara?"

"My secretary."

"Secretary? You're kidding me!" When he realized it was true, he looked for an elegant way out. "You must be really busy. What does Virginia say?" He didn't know why he asked the question and wondered if he'd put his foot in his mouth.

"She agrees, of course. Monday, from 7 to 7.30 in the morning. Here at the church. Ok? Do you have the address?"

"7 o'clock? Well... yes, of course. I'll bring some *facturas* and you put the coffee."

"No, thanks. Well, bring some for yourself, but I'm watching my health. I'll explain when you get here, but the image, what we convey, is as important as what we have to share. Otherwise, people won't believe us."

"Sure, of course. I understand you perfectly. Monday, at 7... in the morning, right?"

"All I ask for is punctuality. Thank you."

Pedro put the phone down, wrote something in his diary and called Sara in.

"Sara, put me down in an interview with Pastor Adrián Vitelio, this Monday, from 7 to 7.30 in the morning. And don't put any more calls through to me in the next two hours, please."

"Yes, pastor," heading for the door.

"Thank you, Sara."

He thought he saw the persistent red light again when he followed her on the way out with an absentminded gaze. It must have been only an illusion. He had so much to do.

Juan and Mariela already belonged to the Varela group. The Tuesday meetings had grown to more than thirty people and they no longer fit in the large living room of their house. So they looked for a venue where they all met every Sunday morning. During the week, smaller home groups of up to ten people allowed them to share the joys and concerns of life in an atmosphere of intimacy and practical love. The idea was to cultivate these groups during the week and to leave for Sundays a larger meeting—or "gathering" as they called it—where everyone could share in praise and hear a general message that would give a sense of unity to the group.

The Sunday gathering was a larger version of the Tuesday

meetings at the Varela's. Juan always said, even with what happened later, that it was in those gatherings that he learned to worship the Lord. The songs were instruments to bring them closer to the Lord, or perhaps to bring him closer to them—he didn't care much about doctrinal terminology in these matters. The point was that he could feel the presence of Jesus and the breath of the Spirit in their midst. The person leading the time of praise and worship didn't interfere or impose anything but was a mere aid for each one to express themselves as they preferred. Some closed their eyes. Others raised their arms. Or remained silent, absorbed in a deep experience. In some livelier songs, the congregation clapped their hands, showing their joy, but without disturbing the spirit of reverence and respect that always prevailed.

The messages were short, deep, and practical. The idea that was constantly repeated from the platform was that if the Christianity we had, the life of Christ, didn't produce changes in our daily life, then it wasn't true life. It was just religion. Like the Pharisees, like the religious leaders of other groups. Indirectly, the other concept that was subtly conveyed, was that this group didn't have those defects and would never have them. And, after the gathering, the time of fellowship, of greeting each other and talking with brothers and sisters, was also a delight. To the point that Juan and Mariela were often among the last to leave, helping to close the place. They seemed to be a different kind of people, much simpler and more open than the ones they had met in the Seminary or in the previous church. They had a thirst for God and a search for the Spirit and for other brothers that they had never seen before.

Mariela was the first to perceive something that disturbed her. In fact, it had happened the first time she had heard Sister Violeta, in the Varela's home, but such was the desire to find something good and so great was the enthusiasm she saw in Juan for all the new things they were experiencing, that it took her quite a while to share her doubts about this woman.

"What a beautiful meeting, today! What an anointing! I really didn't want it to end. What did you think of it?" Juan was ecstatic.

"Yes, I liked it very much and it did me a lot of good. The only thing..." Juan was afraid to ask.

"The only thing... what?"

"There's something about that woman, Violeta, that I don't like."

"But she always brings a powerful word. And the pastors support her. Look today, when she spoke of the doubters. I felt touched, and maybe that's what's happening to you."

"Maybe... But there's something about the way she talks, her look. Besides, they're giving her more and more space. Do you know who she is, where she comes from?"

"No, but I can find out. I don't think it matters too much provided she has the Lord's anointing. What else bothers you about her?"

Mariela thought for a few seconds. She didn't want to say anything that she would regret later, nor did she want to disappoint Juan.

"For example, is she married? Does she have a boyfriend? She's always among men. I don't see that she has any friends. And she has... a kind of... I don't know, it seems strange to say it in her. She has a... sensuality in the way she moves and talks that I don't like."

"Sensuality? Violeta? You're kidding me. You're not going to tell me she's a pretty girl, woman..."

"Not in the traditional sense, but that's precisely the danger. No one sees her as a woman, and they might let their guard down... Look, don't listen to me. Maybe I'm thinking badly, and she's an excellent person." She said this without conviction, just to close the subject. They agreed to change the subject. Until the next gathering.

"Sister Violeta has a word for all of us. Let us listen carefully." It was Brother Klingman, one of the four leaders of the larger group. The woman, in her indefinite thirties, was tall and thin, with a whitish complexion, long black hair and languid eyes. Her makeup was very scarce, and always wore long skirts or dresses, to which she managed to give a special movement when she walked that gave her an unexplainable magnetism. From her seat in the first row she slowly climbed the steps to the platform, all too aware of the glances that were fixed on her and the message she would bring that morning. Before picking up the microphone and addressing the congregation, she cast a broad look at the three leaders sitting on the platform, together with the worship leader. Brother Germán avoided her look as he settled in his seat, or so it seemed to Mariela. The woman paused, closed her eyes, looked toward the horizon, and began to speak in her deep contralto voice.

"Brothers and sisters... I have a word that God gave me during our time of praise. When I heard it, I tried to reject it, because I thought it was from the enemy. But it came again. I tried to keep singing, but I couldn't. It was the Lord. His word was clear. He wanted me to tell you that he wants us to move on to the next stage... that we can't continue in the world... that we must come out of what is known... go to what is new... to a new place..." The voice was rising, in intensity and in timbre. "He wants us all together, with him, without distractions! Like in the time of the apostles!'" almost screaming.

After saying this, she went back the way she had come with the same ceremoniousness and scene control she had used a few moments before and sat down. The deadly silence that followed the prophecy matched the perplexed looks of the congregation below and the leaders above. The only one with a different expression was Klingman, still standing in the center of the platform, whose face lit up as he clung avidly to the microphone.

"Praise the Lord! Glory! Hallelujah! Brothers, this is a historic, special... unique day. God has spoken! He has spoken to us!"

The contrast between everyone's stupefaction and Klingman's overflowing joy couldn't be greater. He took it upon himself to give the necessary explanation.

"It's incredible, but what Sister Violeta just said is exactly the subject of my message this morning. And we haven't talked to each other today. She didn't know what I was going to say, and I didn't know what she was going to say. Isn't that amazing?"

The mood of the congregation changed completely. Between gestures of surprise and expectation, they prepared to hear the message of the exultant Kurt Klingman. With the previous seal of approval, they hung on every word. He told them about a vision he had had a few years ago, when he lived in Germany, and which he hadn't considered, until it was repeated to him this week. In this vision, he saw the entire congregation in a beautiful village, with a white temple in the middle. There they lived in community, and the Lord performed miracles and signs. There were healings, words, and revelations constantly, day and night. The very presence of the Lord was there, not only in the temple but in every house, on the roads. Just like the Shekinah glory that fell on the tabernacle, or on the temple of Solomon. People who passed by saw the glory of the Lord and were drawn to it, came to see it and stayed. And the community grew day by day...

The congregation was transfigured, unable to react. When Klingman finished speaking, the time of singing afterwards was completely different. They were holding each other's hands, crying, and laughing. Things would never be the same.

Pedro and Virginia were married in March 1985. Juan and Mariela, the following month. We were the last ones, in August of that year. Each was invited to and attended the weddings of the others, and during that year the bond of friendship was still intact. Within a year, Roque, Pedro and Virginia's first child, was born. Juan and Mariela had twin boys, Mateo and Marcos, the next year. Our first daughter, Melisa, played hard to get, and arrived only in our fourth year of marriage. Partly because of the distance, and partly because of the activities in our churches, we stopped seeing each other little by little. I'm sure that if we had been able to maintain the bond many things wouldn't have happened, many mistakes would have been avoided, and many tears wouldn't have been shed. Looking back, I think we didn't know how to handle the differences, the different stories we were living.

I still remember the last time we were all together, at Christmas 1984. Pedro and Virginia kept talking about their new project, about their dreams, about what they hoped for next year. Juan and Mariela commented on the new group they had found, but we hardly listened to them. They had always seemed somewhat strange to us in their spiritual pursuits. They had even gone to some meetings with charismatic Catholics. With the Catholics!

We had met in our home. As always, what first brought us together was the past, the beautiful times we had shared.

"I still remember the first time I saw you, Juan. You were so serious. You hardly laughed." Mercedes had always considered Juan as the brother she hadn't had.

"Yes, maybe. I was just out of the army, and I remember having this feeling that how could I laugh and have fun with so many kids who had died? And for nothing. For a stupid ideal."

"I don't know if it was so stupid. They wanted to improve things. It went wrong, but at least they tried," answered Mercedes.

"It's the same feeling I had when we were in the middle of the Malvinas War in the south and here everything was still the same... thinking about the World Cup in Spain," said Juan.

"Well, well, let's not get serious and melodramatic, today of all days. I think that if we are here, all together, it is because the Lord brought us here and wants something good for us in the future." Pedro had begun to get uncomfortable with sad situations. In this new phase he looked for "good vibes" and to not waste time on the past, which could never be changed. Sometimes his attitude was good; at other times, it was untimely.

Mercedes and Pedro always clashed. She accused him of being insensitive; he said that she was always splitting hairs.

"Well, the important thing is that Juan has smiled again, and he's a great guy." Virginia shared Pedro's positive attitude, but with better tact and grace than her husband.

"Yes, let's toast for the next fifteen years." I don't know why I came up with that period of time. "So that we aren't only be happy but also can face the difficult moments with strength, with the strength of the Lord... and that we can make happy and help many people who come to us or who are close to us to endure the difficulties," raising the glass that I had in my hand.

"Wait, wait, some have empty glasses."

The six friends raised our glasses, hugged each other, drank coffee and ate cookies. Something told us that this was not just another moment, but a magical one that would last only the length of that meeting. Perhaps that was why we prolonged it longer than usual, delaying the farewell with one round after another of coffee. Even Mariela, always the first to retire to sleep or to go on "automatic pilot," was still fresh and cheerful when the clock read three in the morning.

We said farewell with a round of spontaneous prayer, holding hands.

"*Chau*! Blessings!"

"Happy New Year!"

"Let's keep in touch..."

5

THE CHANGES WE SAW

Our thoughts and perceptions never stable
No limits or boundaries upon our table

Pueblo Santo[28] was built in record time, and was inaugurated on Sunday, March 1, 1988. Kurt Klingman had found a sizeable undeveloped lot of land close to Quilmes, south of Buenos Aires, thanks to contacts from his real estate company. The distance and isolation would be more than compensated by what the Lord would do in the following years with them and their families. Less than two years passed from Sister Violeta's prophecy to the completion of the temple and the last of the ten initial houses. The original idea was not to get away from the world completely, nor to make a closed community, but something in between. They would all live around the temple, which would allow for closer fellowship and more time spent in prayer and worship together. They would work and have their normal activity outside but, in the spirit of Acts, to receive blessings like Pentecost they would have to be together as long as possible. It said there, "All the believers were together and had everything in common. They sold property and possessions to give to anyone who had need."[29] And this was where someone—in fact, later they learned it was the increasingly influential Sister Violeta—suggested

---

[28] In Spanish, Holy Town
[29] Ac 2:44-45

going deeper into the search for God's presence, selling and sharing everything they had, so as not to be tied to the economic system of this world. The proposal met with some initial resistance.

"And end up like the Guyana cult?" Andrés Humada was referring to the massacre of a cult that had ended in the death of more than 900 people ten years earlier.

"How can you compare a cult to what the Bible says, brother?" This was Daniel Valladares, one of the leaders and one of the most enthusiastic advocates of the Pueblo Santo project.

"I don't know, I guess that's not how it started. Wasn't Jim Jones a pastor?" insisted Andrés, referring to the leader of the Peoples Temple cult.

"Yes, maybe, but they probably got into some strange doctrines, interpreting the Bible as they saw fit. I can't imagine that could ever happen here, do you, brothers?"

"But what would we gain by selling everything and living like in a kibbutz?" said Waldemar.

"We would be more like the primitive church, more ready to receive the Spirit," answered Valladares.

"I'd say we think it over and consult everyone before taking such an important step," suggested Andrés.

"Look, brother, this isn't a democracy, where everyone has an opinion and we decide by voting. Those are methods that the world uses, and dead churches, or those that have gone astray. We deal in revelation, in the word of God... in prophecy. Of course, comparing everything to the Bible, it's not that we accept just anything. That's the way we've handled ourselves up to now, and the Lord has blessed our obedience, don't you think?"

"But do you all agree here? Do you know what that means?" Andrés Humada looked around at the thirty or so members who had been summoned to discuss this topic in the temple. They responded with silence and evasive looks. Andrés was sure that several thought like him. He was positive that Jorge, Waldemar, Sergio and Miguel didn't agree with this madness, because they had once talked about it, in a study on Acts. But, as in any human group, there are very few who dare to give their opinion, at least publicly, and much less if it is against the official one. The majority simply go along with what the leaders say. The curious thing was Violeta's silence, when she had been the one behind the idea. She had learned that sometimes it better to let others participate and give their opinion than to compromise one's own opinion and be exposed to rejection.

The idea of selling properties and sharing everything ended up being approved, so two of the leaders, Lucas Vaca and Germán Morales, were appointed to coordinate this stage. When Juan heard the word "coordination," he found it strange, considering that the biblical example was completely voluntary; that is, no coordinator appeared in the Bible. But he didn't ask the question in time, which led to the famous "fait accompli." And the Vaca and Morales brothers, invested with this responsibility, understood it in their own way, which involved having individual interviews with each of the members, asking what goods they had and which they were going to sell for the Lord. The information was then written down, so that Mariano González, who was a lawyer, would take care of the legal details. The Pueblo Santo Foundation had been created to manage the community's assets, so that they belonged to everyone and not to any one person in particular. The foundation's board of directors was made up of six people, the four leaders—Klingman, Morales, Valladares and Vaca—and two brothers from the community, one of whom was González. They had the vision of the project and would keep it alive, following the word of the Lord at all times. When Andrés was called, the interview didn't start well, and ended worse.

"Good morning, brother. You know the reason for the meeting, don't you?" To hear Lucas Vaca in this role of property delivery coordinator seemed unusual to Andrés. He had always been captivated by his spirit of prayer, his simplicity, his warm and friendly manner. What was he doing here, interrogating him? What was going on? Besides, he perceived an artificial approach, as if he wanted to look good before Morales, a completely different man, executive and less spiritual, according to Andrés's impression.

"No, why don't you explain it to me?" He wasn't going to make it easy for him.

"Well, brother Andrés, God has shown us that he has deeper blessings for us, more of his Spirit, if we are only willing to take a step of faith. Do you remember the passage from Acts 2, verses 44 to 47?"

Vaca's patronizing attitude was unnerving.

"Vaguely... What does it say?"

"Well, brother," mellifluous, cloying, "it says here that they all sold everything they had, laid it at the feet of the leaders, and then the Lord blessed them with miracles and signs."

"Let's see, may I?" Andrés took his Bible, looked for the passage, read it and faced them with determination.

"It seems to me that we have different versions. First, it doesn't say that they laid everything at the feet of the leaders. Second, I don't see anywhere that says they all did it. Third, the miracles and signs happened before they sold the things. And fourth, there was no committee in charge of this. It seems to me to be something voluntary, spontaneous, done with joy. Not an imposition, like this."

"Brother Andrés..." Morales intervened.

"Enough of 'brother this' and 'brother that.' I'm Andrés Humada, you're Lucas Vaca and you're Marito Morales. What's wrong with you all? And you, Germán, what's come over you?"

"All right, Andrés, nobody's going to force you to do anything. You have a reading of the Word, but we have another. You pay too much attention to detail, not the spirit. Remember how Jesus criticized the legalists, the Pharisees..." Morales was convinced of what he was saying, or he had been convinced.

Andrés had no choice but to leave the community. Along with the sadness of the separation, he was left with the strange feeling of the sudden metamorphosis he had seen, in people and in the community. Beautiful, simple, humble, and spiritual people had become characters, bosses, officials of a system. Using spirituality not to break down barriers but to create them, differentiating between the most spiritual—always them, of course—and the rest, the second-class people, those who would one day, perhaps, reach their spiritual level. That simple community that he had known in the Varela house was now a vertical group, with leaders and prophets.

But the worst thing was that these people didn't realize the change that they and the community had experienced. They considered Pueblo Santo to be the height of what was biblical, the perfect revelation, where God had chosen to work at this time. Outside the corrupt or dead structures, choosing simple and spiritual people like them, who were willing to leave everything for him, and who didn't listen to the voices of those who opposed them—according to them—out of ignorance or carnality.

It also hurt that all the beautiful relationships that they had established over the years, among hugs, prayer meetings and retreats, suddenly came to nothing. Even worse. He had become practically an enemy. Although everyone said they would keep in touch when they said farewell, he had a feeling inside that this wouldn't happen. He tried a couple of times to talk on the phone and meet up for coffee, as they had done so many times over the years, but all he got was excuses or evasions. "We have a meeting that day." "We're preparing for a retreat." "This is the month of anointing, so we're going to be spending a lot of time in meetings and retreats. Brother Jackson is coming from Florida. I don't know if you remember him."

Only after he left did Andrés realize how much the situation had affected him. He stopped going to church, any church. He longed for the beautiful thing he had known, which no longer existed. For him, the church had become a cold monster that crushed friendships and relationships. The organism had been transformed into an organization. Sundays, once so full of expectation, became ordinary days. Even Bible reading and prayer, often in tears, failed to fill the huge gap inside. At first, he was under the illusion that someone would call him, perhaps one of the leaders, if only to see how he was doing. To take an interest in his spiritual life, or to help him find another church. Nothing. Nothing at all. It was as if he had never existed for those people. Like Videla's "beings without entity." A part of him could be hurt by all the money he gave generously, by the hours of work devoted with so much effort and joy to build the temple, but he knew it was the least of it. In any case, the Lord knew why he had done it and would see to it that it was put to the best use. But his deepest, most human part was telling him, almost shouting, "And these were your best friends, your brothers?"

Nicolás had just published a book. It wasn't from a major publisher, nor was it an attractive edition. But it was a dream come true, and he hoped that these five hundred copies would generate resources and give him the exposure he would need for a second, much better book. The title was suggestive: "Controllers and Controlled — An Unhealthy Relationship." His main hypothesis was quite easy to understand and appeared in the title itself. According to him, the person who controls can only exist if there is another who not only allows themselves to be controlled, but who wants to be controlled, even if they don't say so or recognize it. The most immediate scope of application was the recent military experience, not only of the period 1976-1983, but of all the military governments Argentina had suffered during the 20th century, with some examples taken from Latin American countries, such as Brazil, Peru and Paraguay, which Nicolás had visited and where he had made good contacts. As a researcher, he was interested in seeing whether democracy would change this relationship, making people who were used to an attitude of resignation and acceptance of authority, however illegitimate and corrupt it might be, react, mature and assume the commitment of becoming masters of their own destiny. In 1988, like many, he still had high expectations in democracy, unconsciously blaming many of the ills of the past on the absence of this form of government. And he was convinced that many of the benefits enjoyed by more advanced nations came automatically from being democratic.

The presentation had been made in the sales room of the Primicia publishing house, which specialized in publishing and promoting new authors, at 6.30 p.m., after the opening hours. A desk with a copy of the book separated the author from about twenty chairs, occupied in part by acquaintances, family, and guests.

His book had been presented by an agent of the publishing house, and Nicolás had talked about the writing process, with some anecdotes and curiosities. Now came the Q&A time.

"Nicolás, don't you think your hypothesis is a bit simplistic, that people are dominated because deep down they want to be dominated? What about the imperialisms and oppressions we have talked about so much here before?" This was a student of journalism and social communication, an acquaintance of Nicolás.

"No, Pepe, I'm not saying that. Actually, in my book I describe voluntary controller-controlled conditions. I say that these are conditions in which the controlled have the real possibility of getting out of the condition in a short time. I say real possibility, seen objectively, by an external observer, because the conditioning can be so strong in the controlled that they either don't think they can get out of the situation or haven't even considered the possibility."

"But would you say that at some point the controlled has voluntarily relinquished control to the controller?" Nita Vázquez, the editorial manager, a philosophy professor in the faculty, who had joined at the last minute, intervened.

"Yes, although the fact that it's voluntary doesn't mean it's conscious. In fact, most of the time it's unconscious," answered Nicolás.

"Could you give us some examples?" Typical of a teacher, Nita wanted something concrete.

"Yes, of course. They appear in the book, if you haven't bought it yet..."—laughs— Countries like Cuba, many beginnings of military dictatorships in Latin America, cults, situations of physical family abuse. Look at the negative side. If this attitude of acceptance of control didn't exist, this type of situation would hardly occur."

"And do you think that knowing this reality helps to find a way out of oppressive situations, at least those of the voluntary type?" I had arrived late and had sat at the back. I asked the question, knowing the answer almost by heart. How many times had we talked and agreed on this!

"That's exactly what I'm proposing. When you think you are in a much more difficult situation than you are, you do nothing, or you just keep criticizing the situation or the one who is dominating, usually in completely unproductive settings, such as in a café or meetings with friends. It feels good because you detached yourself from the responsibility of the situation and also you don't feel you have to do anything specific to change it, since it is very complicated, impossible."

"You are at peace with your conscience and with others..." I added.

"Worse still, one even feels superior to those who don't participate in the criticism... Look, I could even be part of that... hypocrisy, right here today. If I think that just by writing a book I have done something to actually change a situation, I am deluding myself. The diagnosis must be verified in the real world, it must 'become action,' as the philosophers would say," looking at Nita.

"A question, please." It was a priest dressed in casual clothes, but with the collar that identified him, who had been sitting in front from the beginning. "Would you say that democracy is going to change this attitude of Argentines, of criticizing the government and not going beyond criticism, with the comfort of having someone to blame?"

"It's something I raise in the book as a concrete possibility," Nicolás answered.

"And why should people change? Don't you think that, except in situations of crisis, such as war, political or economic upheaval, people never change?" said the priest.

"Something like 'Meaningless! Meaningless!... Everything is meaningless?'[30] said Nicolás, trying to show his biblical knowledge.

"Or 'there is nothing new under the sun,'[31] continued the priest.

"The Bible, Ecclesiastes, a cynical or realistic view of life? I believe that this time of democracy will give us an answer. It would be good to be able to meet in ten, fifteen years, and see if people really changed, if society changed, if you and I changed. The way we think, but also if we have done something concrete with what we think."

[30] Ecc 1:2
[31] Ecc 1:9

The time assigned for this part had come to an end, and Nita signaled Nicolás.

"What an excellent audience! I congratulate you for the people who come to this bookstore, Nita," said Nicolás with a smile to the manager, who had approached the group. "Here there's material for a second book, or a debate."

"Why don't we have a debate on the issue of faith?" Nita suggested. "We could set up a table with Nicolás, a priest and a pastor, or a rabbi. This book would be a reference point, but not necessarily. We could even record the debate, and if it's good enough, publish it. What do you think?" Nita was always on the lookout for opportunities.

A few minutes later the book presentation ended. Only about fifteen copies were sold right there, and we found ourselves talking in a group, Nicolás, the priest and I, while the rest were divided into groups of three or four, enjoying the coffee, soda and sandwiches that the publisher had prepared.

"Did you read the book, Father?" asked Nicolás.

"Yes, this week. Let me introduce myself: Nicanor Tosca, 57 years old, priest, seminarian, professor of logic and philosophy."

"What did you think: good, bad, fair?"

"It depends. I found the analysis of human mentality and the functioning of the groups within society excellent. It coincides with many things I've seen at this point in life."

"But...?"

"My impression is that, in the case of religious communities, it doesn't take into account a very important aspect, which is faith."

"But I have a whole chapter dedicated to the theme of faith..." He took a copy and began to search.

"No, no need to look it up. I remember it perfectly: 'Faith or credulity.' But you take faith as an aspect of man that is prone to manipulation, almost as a weakness of the species. Something more like naivety."

"That's what I've seen in practically all the cases I've studied."

"All right. Let me ask you a question."

"Yes, of course."

"Are you a believer? What do you believe in?"

Nicolás hesitated for a few seconds. He didn't know what the priest was aiming at. On the one hand, it was logical that he took an interest in the aspect of faith and questioned it, but at that moment a similar feeling came over him as when he was taking oral exams at school and realized that there was a subject he hadn't studied.

"It depends on what we're talking about. I believe in a kind of superior, transcendent force, not so much in the Christian God."

"Let me explain. My doubt is this. While I believe that you are capable of detecting fraud and manipulation in the name of faith, and I congratulate you on the work of… illumination that you have been doing, I wonder how you will be able to detect authentic faith when you find it. How will you know if you are facing a true healing, a miracle, a genuine religious experience, if you've never been in contact with these things? Unless you don't even believe they exist."

"I don't rule out completely miracles or true faith, but my personal experience is quite negative, and I have done a lot of research and met a lot of people. At the most, I would concede that there is a strong power of persuasion, of transference between a patient and the doctor, the priest, the pastor, or the healer. I don't know whether to call this faith," explained Nicolás.

"May I?" I felt that I could shed some light on the subject. "I would like to pursue the line of Father Nicanor. One of the things that constant exposure to falsehood achieves in people is skepticism, to the point that when they see something authentic, they're unable to appreciate it as such, and it ends up bunched up with all false things. This is the greatest success of untruth, to numb our capacity for discrimination."

"Yes, like when people say we are all corrupt, or we were all guilty of the missing or the Malvinas. Putting everyone or everything in the same bag produces a great average where the person who stole millions of dollars and the chicken thief who needs to feed his family are the same, or the torturer of pregnant women and those of us who didn't even know the concentration camps existed." It was Pepe speaking, while Nicolás listened attentively.

The informal talk continued until 9 p.m. when the store had to be closed, but some continued chatting outside. I knew Nicolás would be quite satisfied.

The New Church of Blessing had a new name, logo, and location, and its size reflected the success of the third consecutive year of growth. The objectives also had grown year by year: "1984 x 10" (1984) "1985 x 20" (1985) and "86!" (1986). Pastor Pedro Terrero had an office that, in size and decoration, transmitted the message of success and growth that he preached Sunday after Sunday from the pulpit, and that was studied during the week in the "islands," the groups of ten people that met weekly in the spacious church facilities. The original idea was that they would meet in homes, as the original Christians, but F&G discouraged this because of some bad experiences in churches where these groups became too independent for the overall vision. The location of the pastor's office, at the back of the first floor, and its restricted access, was a clear indication that the members had trained people who could attend to their most immediate needs, allowing Pedro to devote himself to the most important organizational activities, leadership and relations with other churches and evangelical institutions. It was putting into practice the advice given by his father-in-law to Moses in the desert, when he saw the leader of Israel too busy with the problems of the people and suggested he delegate responsibilities to suitable people. This was a message that he had preached several times, and it had been studied in the islands, in order to make it clear that it wasn't that Pedro neglected his pastoral role or wasn't interested in the people, but that it was a way that God commanded to take care of him in his mission to lead a sometimes difficult people, like that of Israel.

Pedro had traveled a couple of times to the United States, as part of the follow-up to the Fullness and Growth plan, with expenses fully covered, staying in four-star hotels and with visits to successful churches that had implemented the plan in Miami and Houston.

Level Two, which guaranteed to reach three hundred members in three years, had been accomplished by the church in just two years, which earned them a mention and a visit from F&G President John Bassingly, who gave a series of talks and a workshop attended also by several pastors from other churches. The thousand dollars a year for Level Two (Silver) turned out to be an excellent investment in the Kingdom's business, and Pedro had no problem getting the approval of Level Three (Gold), with its five thousand dollars a year, payable in three installments, from his Pastoral Council.

This group of brothers, chosen personally by him after much prayer and fasting, was a true blessing, because they kept him from wasting time in arguments or excessive questioning, as happened in other denominations or churches. They were people "according to his own heart," loyal and trustworthy, who would never speak against him and keep him abreast of what the congregation thought of him and of the church's projects. In this way, they protected him and maintained pastoral authority, something that had been lost in many churches. They functioned as interfaces between the people and the pastor, so that he only saw the critical cases, or the people who, because of their importance, couldn't be served adequately by the Council. Like, for example, Dr. Luis Bendiverde, an important heart surgeon who had recently started attending Sunday meetings. When he showed interest in participating with his wife, Mirta, in one of the islands, Osvaldo Nievas, the island leader took his data and gave it to the island coordinator, Mario Carranza. When he detected that he was an important professional, he handed the form directly to Pedro's secretary, Sara Oviedo, who coordinated an interview with the pastor. This was a special case.

"Good morning, doctor. It's a pleasure to meet you and your wife. May I call you Luis and Mirta?"

"Of course, pastor. And thank you for seeing us. On Sunday we filled out the form to start participating in one of the... islands. That's what they call the groups, isn't it?"

"Yes, we call them islands, but others call these groups, cells, or home groups. The concept is the same, and it comes from the Bible itself. As you know, the early Christians didn't meet in large and comfortable temples like this one." From the mirrored window of the pastor's office they had an excellent view of the main hall.

"And what is done in the islands? Is there Bible study, prayer?" asked the doctor.

"Good question. Actually, we believe that there is a need to completely renew the concept of what Bible study is. Of course, we support everything that is study of the Word, and you will have seen that in my messages I constantly quote passages from the Bible. But it seems to us that today, with the short time we have and the complexity of modern life, there is clearly a need to reapply it, if I may say so. And that is what we, and the islands, and the island leaders are for," explained Pedro.

"So you don't do the classic Bible studies, I think they were called inductive, right?" said Luis.

"Yes, inductive," said his wife.

"Sure, I know them perfectly well. The thing is that they were other times, when people had more time, a simpler life. They were also smaller churches. What church did you go to?"

"The First Baptist Church of Chivilcoy," answered Luis.

"Of course, and I'm sure they had those administrative meetings, with discussions, fights, votes..." said Pedro, with a gesture of annoyance.

"Yes, did you suffer them too?" asked Luis.

"Quite a lot, but here we have eliminated all that. Here the important thing is to do things, to follow the vision. Support the leaders."

Luis and Mirta exchanged worried glances. Pedro noticed it immediately and tried to repair the damage.

"But don't worry. Here I can't do what I want. I have a Pastoral Council that follows me closely, and all the members have an annual financial report."

"No, sorry, Pastor. What happens is that we learned of a case, some friends of ours, who had a very bad experience this year in a church where the leader became increasingly authoritarian, to the point that they had to leave, after almost twenty years. And they told us how he repeated constantly that the important thing was to 'follow the vision,' precisely the phrase you just used," said Luis.

"Just a coincidence because the concept of vision here is something shared by the whole church. And I have the difficult responsibility of ensuring that it is fulfilled. Now, if someone doesn't like it, or opposes it... well, the Lord will show them what to do. We don't retain anyone here by force."

"Back to the subject of the Bible, pastor..." Mirta was not one to overlook pending issues.

"Yes... Mirta." He had written down the names on a 10 x 20 card, as the Manual recommended. There he remembered to look them both in the eyes with a wide smile.

"One thing that always differentiated us from the Catholics was that we read and studied the Bible, and this allowed us to evaluate what anyone said in the light of the Word. In other words, it was a kind of control, within everyone's reach. The great legacy of the Reformation, in fact. My question is: if this important conquest is lost, what guarantee do we have that we won't go astray, or... that you won't?"

"Impossible!" *How dare this woman insinuate this? Doesn't she know who I am? In the end it was a mistake to give them this interview. They should have started with the leader of the island, so that he could screen them,* he thought to himself. "You say that because you come with prejudices and you don't know us, or you haven't listened to my sermons in the last year. I think maybe they have to do with the issue of spiritual authority, which is theme 14 in the Principles for Growth series. It's all explained there." Pedro had lost his composure.

The interview ended quickly, and the couple were left with many other questions, but they were told to ask the island leader. They left with the feeling that they had committed what seemed to be the unforgivable sin: to question the pastor.

With Mercedes, we participated actively in the impressive growth of the New Church of Blessing (NCB). As members of the pioneer group, we felt a healthy pride in what we had achieved. Together, with effort and prayer, and using counseling and human techniques, we had grown from a small group that went unnoticed in society to a congregation "with a voice." Pedro began to be known, both among the churches and in the community. We were leaving behind the defeatist and mean-spirited mentality that we evangelicals had had for so many years and that got us so few results. It was time to be seen, to be heard, especially in places of authority and influence. After all, Jesus came to save the poor, but also the rich; the weak, but also the powerful.

I remember the day we first went to the office of Mayor Mejías. Clearly it was God's doing, because we had submitted the request to enlarge the temple and in no time, Pedro got a call from the mayor's secretary saying he wanted to meet him. It was quite unexpected, and Pedro asked me to accompany him, along with Silvio Carroza, the treasurer. We were both part of the Pastoral Council, together with Amancio Miguens, Martín Poch and Daniel Gobbi, as well as Pedro and Virginia, the pastors. Seven in all, the perfect number. We bought a luxury Bible from the Bible Society, prayed before leaving and showed up on the first floor of the town hall.

"This way, please, pastor. The mayor will receive you right away. Would you like a drink?"

"No, thanks. You're very kind." The waiting room was quite striking, with photos or images of places and personalities of the municipality of San Fernando. Pedro made use of the moment to look through the photos while they waited. There was Tiburcio Gómez, hero of Treinta y Tres Orientales, that only remotely rang a bell. The stunning Sans Souci and Otamendi palaces. He could drop these names as people and places to be proud of. He had been taught in the last course of F&G that he had to make the most of every moment, and these names could be useful in the conversation that was about to begin. He didn't want the mayor to think he was ignorant of the history of the municipality. Anyway, there was always the resource of bringing up the subject of soccer, which he loved and mastered so much. And if he didn't like soccer, he would mention that his grandfather had arrived from Spain exactly in 1900.

"Pastor Terrero... It's wonderful to finally meet you! Have a seat. I've heard a lot about you and your successful church." The mayor, with the looks of a lawyer, perfectly dressed and no doubt used to dealing with all kinds of people, greeted the pastor warmly by shaking his hand and holding his arm with the other hand, and then greeted Silvio and me. He was accompanied by a man with a suspicious face, who turned out to be the Head of Government. When he said his name, Sabadez, I seemed to remember some scandal in which he had been involved. But perhaps it was my prejudice against politicians in general.

"Dr. Mejías, it is a great honor to meet you and we thank you for this attention. We wanted to give you this Bible as a testimony of this interview," said Pedro.

The mayor received the book and almost without looking at it mechanically put it aside.

"Thank you very much. It's a great book. Very inspiring. Look, pastor, I know you must be a very busy man, as are your colleagues, so I don't want to take up too much of your time." He opened a folder that Sabadez gave him and took out a sheet. "I received this request for a permit to enlarge your building and I personally checked to see if there was a problem. So that the beautiful work that you are doing in the community isn't delayed, I want you to leave here today with the permission in your hands," after which he proceeded to sign the sheet with a flourish and handed it to Pedro.

For a few seconds, Pedro froze. He didn't know if he was more surprised to have the permission so quickly or by the personal interest and the efficiency of this man he didn't even know. Could it be they were so important now? Was he so important? Finally, he pulled himself together, took the sheet, saw the stamp "Authorized," and put it in his briefcase.

"Well, I had a different image of what public service was. I had been told that there was a lot of red tape, that it would take forever."

"That was before, pastor. We are changing the way of doing politics, at least from our municipality."

"We agree on that, then. In our church we are trying to renew the structures, without changing the essence of the message, of course. Doctor, I thank you for your gesture and your interest and, of course, if there is anything we can do to help you, don't hesitate to contact me directly." Pedro handed him his personal card.

"No doubt we will be able to do many things together for our community in the future now that we know each other. By the way, do you know Pastor Quijada?"

So that was the contact, Pedro thought. Bernardo Quijada had been at the meeting last Sunday and Pedro had shared their need to expand the hall, and that they expected the permit to take some time. He remembered that Bernardo had said "I'll see what I can do."

"Not much. Why?"

"With Bernardo we've known each other since high school. We drove the "evangelists" crazy, poor things. But now we're great friends. He told me he was president of the United Argentine Evangelical Association. You know he lives around the corner from my house?"

"Yes, I've heard of that organization." Pedro made a mental note to find out what that association was. He might find it useful.

That was only the first time of many that we would visit the town hall. Everything seemed to be going smoothly, much faster than we had expected.

Three days later Sara gave him a neat and detailed report of Bernardo Quijada. He was 35 years old, married to Tamara Gracilazo, from a traditional evangelical family in southern Buenos Aires. They had two children, 5 and 3 years old, Sebastián and Daniel. She worked as an assistant to her father, Pastor Justo Gracilazo, at the Agape Church in Villa Serena. Bernardo had been a bookstore salesman until he married Tamara, whom he met at church. After they married, thanks to his father-in-law's contacts, he became the Argentine representative of WCSM (Worldwide Christian Students Ministry). She would call him on the phone.

"With Bernardo Quijada, please."

"Who's calling him?"

"This is Pastor Terrero's secretary, from the New Church of Blessing."

"One second, please."

The talk was brief but useful. He began to understand how politics worked, inside and outside the church. It was a question of networks. One became part of the network of contacts of others who found that you could be useful to them. In turn, you had to have your own network of contacts by virtue of what they could bring to you. In fact, it was something Pedro had handled very well since he was young, but within the evangelical environment and specifically within his denomination. What was new and particularly useful to him was the possibility of extending these contacts to the world, to people in politics. Or that a mixed network could be set up, where believers and unbelievers could help each other. It was exciting! Especially after the interview with the mayor—a politician— generated by this man, Quijada—a pastor.

Pedro realized that the incident offered two readings. On the one hand, he could think as a believer, and say that it was a door that the Lord had opened for the preaching of the gospel and the extension of the Kingdom. From now on, it would be much easier to get permissions for events organized by the church, and he even felt free to invite city officials to attend church activities. But on the other hand, if he wore the newly acquired politician's hat, this person saw in him someone of political value... someone who could give him something. What could a pastor, Pedro Terrero, offer a mayor and a seasoned politician? Votes? Money? Support? He wasn't displeased with the position he was in. The only thing that was beginning to bother him was that red light that was appearing more often, especially in his dreams.

Ricardo and Irene were on duty this week, and the kids were impossible. They got up late, didn't clean up as they should and were distracted during the devotions and praise. They tried first to treat them kindly and then to stand firm. But it was useless. They knew they would get a reprimand from the leaders for not exercising their authority. They would probably be passed over to another sector, but with a bad record.

So they decided to talk to them, once again. They took them to the yard outside the large orange multipurpose room. It had a beautiful view of the garden and connected on the inside to the rooms and bedrooms for the "community parents" on duty and the children, divided by sex and age. Each one had their own seat assigned, from the boisterous little Febe, one and a half years old, to the oldest, Marcos, seven years old, with his difficulty in reading and relating to others.

"Kids, what is wrong with you that you aren't obeying orders? Don't you know that it's best for you to as you're told? Do you remember the story we told you yesterday, how God punished those who didn't do his will?" Ricardo tried to sound kind but firm.

"We behave well, but we want to play." It was Raquelita, Klingman's four-year-old granddaughter and the leader of the group, even at her age.

"Play has its place, but only after you've done your homework and had your devotions. And if you obey. You know very well," Ricardo insisted.

"I want to be with Mommy... and with Daddy," again Raquelita, between sobs.

"This week Ricardo and I are your mom and dad. Don't you think it's better to have a lot of brothers and sisters, so that your mom and dad can spend more time praying and serving the Lord? Do you think it's good that they know you're aren't obeying, or that you're making trouble? I think it would make them very sad. And we don't want that, do we?"

"Noooo..." Several automatically responded, though not all.

"Why don't we do something about it? If you guys try to make things better, not fight so much and obey us, we'll see if we can get you more play time." Irene used the old method of negotiation.

"I want to spend more time with my mom and dad." It was Josecito, the hardest one in the group.

"Ah, well, Josecito, but then you have to earn it. Do you think God likes the way you've been acting these days?" said Ricardo.

Juan watched the scene from the window overlooking the yard, stunned. Until that moment he had never been interested in the children's ward, which was in a secluded area of Pueblo Santo. But today he had gone for a walk and something led him beyond the white wall the parents and children crossed regularly. He never agreed with the idea of separating the children from their parents after a year and a half. But it was one more link in a chain of things that happened in the community slowly and surely, from the original idea of simply being together and sharing things. Looking back, he couldn't say whether the plan was hatched in its entirety to be implemented later in a studied sequence, or whether the events were happening one after another, without any previous order. Or if under the guise of loose events, someone—who always seeks to twist and destroy God's plans—was pulling the strings according to his own plan.

First were the prophecies directed at people, especially youth and adolescents, telling them that God had called them to the ministry, to be pastors, prophets, evangelists or missionaries, and that they should give their lives to him. This meant, for starters, abandoning any idea of a secular training—sometimes leaving high school, and always avoiding going to college or higher education—to enter the Bible Institute, which operated within Pueblo Santo. Then came the prophecies about who should marry each other. Thus, several couples were formed among the young people of the community, four of them marrying within a year. Two of those who married were dating other people and had to break off those relationships when they received the "prophetic word." The separation of the children from their parents was the third and most profound stage, but no one opposed it, because the idea had already been installed, through various messages and prophecies, that the true or "spiritual" family was the entire community, that the children were the Lord's and that the parents, like everyone else, should submit to the authority of the leaders.

Looking at the sad faces of the children and the hardened attitude of the couple in charge, Juan recognized that if he had known about this before he would have tried to do something, but he admitted with shame that he hadn't reacted to the other changes because they didn't affect him and Mariela yet, because the twins were still young. He shuddered at the idea that one day they would be part of that group of kids.

The other reality was that, as in the Holocaust, or the Military Process,[32] if reality exceeds what you can handle, what you want to believe about people you respect, you tend to deny it. How could it be that people who had such a high spiritual life, with such intimate and constant contact with the Lord, were the same ones who had implemented this quasi-military regime for infants and children? And how far would the changes in this community go? Would they end up like the Guyana cult, as Andrés had suggested, so criticized by the leaders when he left? Had he been right after all? Was it too late now?

But Juan wasn't going to accompany this general passivity. Just as one day he left the army he loved when he realized the terrible things that were going on, even though he wasn't doing them, everything indicated that he should do the same with this group. He would have to talk to Mariela first.

"Mari, I saw something terrible today," he said, at a moment when they were alone.

"What? In here? Where?"

"I went to the children's ward across the street."

"But they told us we shouldn't go there, that we were going to interfere with the spiritual preparation they were being given."

"Yes, but something told me I should go see. And I don't regret it. That inner voice has saved me many times before... and will continue to save me."

"Tell me what you saw." Without realizing it, they had gone to a bench away from the main building and both looked around before sitting down.

---

[32] The official name of the 1976-1982 military government

"They have kids like in the army... There are kids of two, five... the oldest must be seven... and they were asking for their parents. And they were telling them that they should obey, work," Juan told her.

"I wonder if the parents know," said Mariela, after a few moments of reflection, looking for a practical way out.

"I don't think so. They should be told... But I wonder how we could have come to this. And where we will end up. Do you remember what Andrés said, and how he had to leave the next day? Could it be that he knew something else, or did he foresee what could happen?" said Juan.

"But..." Mariela tried to say something, but Juan guessed the thought immediately.

"You think about what we would lose, about the spiritual blessing, the presence of the Lord... the friends."

"Friends? No. Brothers and sisters, maybe. Yes, I was thinking of the blessings we would miss. All those prophecies that said that God had chosen us, that this was the Lord's time... What if we were disobeying God's will? What about the covering?" said Mariela, anxiously.

The covering! One of the most subtle and powerful tools of domination created by some pastors and used in groups where there is no overly formal authority structure. Without any biblical support, "spiritual covering" is a method that demands absolute submission to the leaders, under the hypothesis that they are mediators between God and his followers. The idea behind this concept is that leaders are much more spiritual than people and therefore more capable of receiving from God what is best for their followers. Clearly the idea of having to answer to these leaders went against the biblical concept that everyone is directly accountable to God and only to God for their life. It ends up replacing faith and submission to Christ with fear of and submission to the leaders.

What did this system imply in practice? To be under the covering of a pastor or a group of pastors meant protection, security, not only from one's own mistakes but from the attacks of the devil. Conversely, leaving the covering, or not having it, left a believer at the mercy of the enemy's attacks. This system of manipulation was very well exploited by these leaders, when someone left the community and had any mishap, accident, illness, or job loss. Somehow, it was hinted that this had happened to him because he or she had left the (in)famous covering.

"The covering... Tell me, did we ever study the subject openly, looking at what it says in the Bible? No. It's something mysterious, like the ether in the 19th century, which you don't see, but supposedly exists. And it's not disputed," said Juan.

"But look what happened to Marina when she left. Her father died of cancer," argued Mariela. It was a case that had been mentioned repeatedly by the leaders.

"And Paco, the leader of the institute, who had that accident on the road? Didn't he have the covering?" said Juan.

"Yes, but the Lord saved him from dying," Mariela said.

"And Olga, the cook, who burned herself with oil in the kitchen in the temple?" insisted Juan.

"They said it was an attack by the devil, and that's why they asked for prayer and fasting," replied Mariela.

"Manuel left a year ago and nothing bad happened to him, as far as I know," said Juan.

"But the other day they said they had had a vision that he was drying up spiritually."

"So we can always find an explanation that is favorable to what the leaders are saying. Couldn't they have brainwashed us too?" said Juan, with a desperate gesture.

"Juan! What are you saying?" The look of fear on his wife's face was all that he needed to make the decision to leave. Today, tomorrow, a month from now, but he couldn't accept that the Christian life includes fear. On top of that, from other Christians. His instincts told him that the picture was crooked. He didn't know if he wanted to straighten it out or throw it out because the beautiful had become grotesque, like an unpleasant taste or smell.

"Jesus always said, 'Do not fear,' and that was Jesus. I can't see you in fear, my dear. We're afraid to think, afraid to be ourselves. Look at us, sitting here afraid to be seen or heard. Besides, those kids are our responsibility too, and they're turning them into monsters."

Pedro's ministry was going very well. The New Church of Blessing was the hot topic among pastors. Pastors Pedro and Virginia were famous, and the carefully constructed image of the couple appeared in Gospel Today, the most widely distributed gospel news magazine, on posters, in book advertisements. Pedro asked me to help him with the advertising aspect of the church and its ministry—although he didn't call it "publicity" but "outreach"—but something led me to say no. So he turned to an American company that had extensive experience in promoting ministries and churches, a contact of Fullness & Growth. From there came the photograph of Pedro with the leather Bible open in his left hand and his right hand raised, looking into infinity, a clear reminiscence of the well-known Billy Graham. The second photograph, used especially for the church, was with Virginia, the perfect image of a happy marriage dedicated to the Lord. After all, that was what the photos were asked to convey: attachment to the Word, in the first one; marital unity, in the second.

Pedro had convinced Virginia to take on the role of women's leader. At first, she was able to continue with her part-time job teaching English, which she loved, but the increase of responsibilities and activities in the church led her to devote herself entirely to the latter. When she mentioned that they would lose the income from the English classes, he told her not to worry, that he would discuss it at the Council meeting. The response was quick and encouraging. They had agreed to give her a salary, with the only condition that she would assume the title of pastor (*pastora*), so they could justify it, in the remote possibility that someone would question the decision. Virginia refused emphatically. She saw that she would become too absorbed in church affairs in general, and not just among women, where she felt useful and respected. They all recognized the spark and enthusiasm she put into everything she did and enjoyed her more "mundane" and "normal" perspective on things than her husband, who always spiritualized everything and made them feel inferior. With "la Virgi" you could be yourself and could laugh at everything. She was one more of them. If she were promoted to pastor, she would lose her independence and the same distance she saw between Pedro and his old friends would appear. But a conversation with Pedro was enough to make her change her mind, reluctantly:

"Virgi, I need you closer to me. You can't imagine the pressures I have and all that lies ahead."

"We've talked this over a thousand times, Pedro, since the time of the Seminary. Don't you remember? Neither you nor I are sexist, but it seems to me that men have one function, and women another. How many times do we criticize the concept of the pastor and the wife pastor, as if they wanted to monopolize everything for them? And Roquecito? I don't want him to be a typical pastor's son, like the children of Chávez, your friend Sergio... Victoria. We discussed that, too."

"Look, I know all that, and don't think I forgot, but what we have is different. It has nothing to do with those stories. I'm asking you for a limited time, a year. Then you can decide freely. The truth is that I don't trust anyone in the church when I'm not there."

"What about Néstor? And Víctor? Aren't you preparing them for pastors? How can they get experience if you don't delegate tasks to them?"

"Yes, they can be useful for some things. But they're not mature yet. Probably later. There are always people questioning what we do, and I don't know if they can handle criticism well."

Pedro had become somewhat paranoid. His circle of trust had become smaller and smaller, to the point that, for some things, for example replacing him when he was away, he didn't even trust the Pastoral Council, a group of people he himself had chosen a year earlier. He preferred to bring in guest pastors to cover his absences. He was less and less able to bear opposing views and left less time for the exchange of opinions. This was a technique he had learned to use well and often. When he perceived that a project of his would be questioned and he wasn't willing to submit it to the scrutiny of others, he tried to spend as much of the meeting time in prayer, Bible reflection and other things, which no one could object to. Finally, he would leave a small part of it late at night for others to have their say. Of course, the limited time, the natural tiredness of the day and the desire to avoid antagonizing others who also wanted to return home, in practice conspired against the right to speak. Then, when somebody wanted to give an opinion, either it was impossible to find a time when Pedro was free, or he would answer: "The subject has already been discussed and no one said anything. I don't have time to go over it again."

In the end he managed to beat everyone out of exhaustion, since people had enough personal or work worries to add problems or arguments in the church. He knew that he had the advantage of more time, more information, and he played home all the time. Also, those who were most opposed to some things ended up leaving, which strengthened his position even more.

What I observed was a remarkable change in his whole personality. The funny, cheerful, witty Pedro, with time for his friends, had become a serious person, always busy and worried, although he made great efforts to be kind and warm when dealing with people during worship services. The friends he had since his youth in the denomination and in other churches began to avoid him, tired of trying to talk to him and receiving as an answer: "Pastor Terrero is on a trip, he is in a meeting, he is in a conference... he'll be back late... I'll take note of your name... I already told him that you called..."

His sermons also changed. We had always recognized his ability to speak from everyday life, with commonly used words, everyday situations. For example, he loved to illustrate his sermons with soccer, one of his passions.

"If I had to put the apostle Peter on a soccer team, I would put him as a striker. He wanted to finish, and fast."

"Our life is like a soccer game. Sometimes we can turn the score around in the last minutes of the game. Never give up."

"Yesterday I read in the newspaper the story of Marquinho, the striker of the Brazilian national team. From a life of total poverty, with the support of his parents and much self-help, he became a star. But he forgot his origins, he quarreled with his family, with his manager, surrounded himself with bad influences, got into drugs and lost everything he had. Today he was converted and lives for the gospel, he repented, and God forgave him. He's going to be with us in heaven. But do you think he can get back everything he lost: wife, family, money?"

People loved it, because he was using the same method as Jesus who taught from everyday life: plants, animals, people. Besides, it was clear that these were things that came from Pedro's heart and experience.

But suddenly the messages began to change. They were more stylized, with an introduction, three points and a conclusion. With illustrations and good anecdotes, but they didn't seem like Pedro's, at least not the Pedro we knew. Besides, the themes themselves seemed to have nothing to do with the reality they were living in that place in Argentina, in 1988.

The change had an explanation. At this stage of the F&G consultancy, they recommended working with a series of sermons, with outlines they sent from the headquarters in Houston, along with the illustrations, examples, and workbook, to be implemented in the islands. At first Pedro resisted the idea, because he liked the sermon preparation time, the challenge of choosing the topic—always the most difficult part—the choice of the passage, the meditation, the way of applying the text to the concrete situation of his church. It was a way of keeping the link with his congregation now that he wasn't doing so much overt pastoral work. Because when he struggled with the sermon, he tried to think that he had concrete, flesh and blood people in front of him, an excellent practical advice from the Seminary's Homiletics class. So, during this time, Ariel and his problem with asthma, Grandma Máxima and the rheumatism that kept her from walking, the Pintos' and the discussions with their children, Valerio and his desire to go to the Chaco... Later he would realize that this would be the last stronghold of real contact with real people and their real problems that he had left. Moreover, he always had a very deep time of prayer, asking with holy fear that the Lord would bless his preaching, but also interceding for each of those people who had accompanied him in that time of preparation. When he shared this inner struggle with Tony Vidal with whom he met once a month he got this advice:

"Look, Pedro, I understand you perfectly, and you're not the only one who's been at this crossroads. But you must be a good steward of what God is giving you. He is giving you a thriving church, and neither you nor I know how far it can go. At some point you must take the leap to optimize your sermon time and make your interaction with the islands, youth, and women optimal as well. In addition, the fact of making a sequence allows you to achieve a greater penetration in time. We have studied everything. Trust us. Finally, the possibility of planning the themes and contents of the sermons well in advance coincides with the guidelines and the way of working of the largest corporations in the world.

"And what place is left for the Holy Spirit, for the unexpected, for creativity?" asked Pedro, with the last breath of resistance.

"Precisely, by organizing yourself better and having the basic activities of the church organized, you will have more free time to seek the guidance of the Holy Spirit. Remember that God is a God of order. Look, I'm asking you to try it for a year, and then we'll talk. *A year's trial,* Pedro thought, *the same thing I asked Virginia. Could it be that this Central American guy was using the same trick as me, knowing that once you start something it's very hard to go back?*

Pedro agreed to use the prepared material, and once he got used to this resource, he stopped having his time of challenge and spiritual struggle in the preparation of the sermon, and also stopped thinking about concrete people at least once a week. Simultaneously, his prayer time became shorter and colder. Sometimes he used the Prayer Guide for the Pastor, which came with the material. It was good because it helped him concentrate on the material of the week, or the month: 4 Steps to Being a Faithful Member, The Month of Blessing, Giving to Receive a Hundred Times More, How to Help Your Pastor... It was a great way to get the whole church in line and avoid improvisations. In addition, the material arrived well in advance, about six months before the beginning of the year. "Hats off to Americans in these things," Pedro always said. They were masters at organization, but even better at the 20th-century science: His Majesty, Marketing, and his Prince Consort, Sales.

The debate took place a month later, but not about faith, since Nita feared that no one would come to such an abstract and "religious" topic. With a good eye towards her target audience, she promoted the event as "Manipulation or reality - the rise of cults." The presence of Nicolás Peretti, a researcher of cults, Father Nicanor Tosca, from the Catholic church, and Pedro Terrero, pastor of the New Church of Blessing, was announced. This last contact had been mine, when I was asked if I knew any pastor who could participate in the debate. I proposed several professors and theologians that I knew, because they would have the knowledge and the necessary prestige to face the challenge, but Nita said that it wouldn't have the same appeal as a pastor who was actually leading a church that was considered a cult, by some people and by the Catholic Church. So I asked Pedro if he could participate, and he agreed immediately. What motivated him to make a place in his crowded agenda was that he was very annoyed that people and journalists considered churches like his to be cults and that they were put in the same bag as other groups that barely had anything Christian.

We had asked for a room in the town hall that seated some fifty people. That Wednesday the place was full, to the point that they had to add chairs in the aisles and even so there were people standing in the back.

"Good afternoon. It is a pleasure to welcome you to this talk-debate entitled "Manipulation or reality - the rise of cults." Nita had stood in front of the microphone and the table, where the three panelists were seated. "We all know that there is manipulation in different areas: in politics, in the media, at work, even in marriages. What is manipulation? I propose this definition: Trying to get us to do something we don't want to do, without our realizing it. Perhaps later in the debate we can improve it. But, while we are used to manipulation in the areas I just mentioned, we find it harder to think that it can happen in an environment as... sacred... as religion. To think that religious concepts can be used to force the will of a person, or a group of people, precisely in a field where freedom, the fulfillment of the human being is pursued, is shocking to us, isn't it? Having made this brief presentation, I'm delighted to introduce our panelists for this evening. To my right, Nicolás Peretti, researcher of cults and *chantas*, may I use that word?" —laughs from the audience and Nicolás— a dog of prey for all those who try to deceive people with pseudo-religion or pseudo-science. We had the pleasure of having him here last month, presenting his book "Chantas y encantados." At his side, Father Nicanor Tosca, of the Congregation of St. Paul, a Catholic, a researcher of the phenomenon of cults, Christian and non-Christian. And to my left, Pastor Pedro Terrero, of the New Church of Blessing, one of the fastest growing evangelical churches in... Argentina?" looking at Pedro.

"Yes, that's right, and also in Latin America," he added smugly.

"So, without further ado, let's begin this debate. The mechanics will be as follows. Each participant will have fifteen minutes to give his view on the subject. Then I will make a brief summary of the three positions, and then we will go to the juiciest part, the dialogue with the audience. If you agree, I will moderate the debate. Let's hear from our panelists."

The three spoke in the order in which they were introduced. Fifteen minutes strictly, under the control of Nita, who warned them when two minutes were left and didn't let them go over the stipulated time. Nicolás, serious and with a combative air; Father Nicanor, slow and friendly, as if giving a conference; Pedro, dynamic, with good command of the scene, using examples and with a good order of subjects. Then came Nita's summary.

"Well, do we have any questions? Yes, in the background... the blue shirt."

"For the Father. Don't you think that just when the Christian church stopped being a sect persecuted by power, and became part of power, with Constantine, it lost its essence of a revolutionary body that questioned the system?"

"Yes, looking back, the church in power was more powerful, on the one hand. It had the peace necessary for a lot of things that couldn't be done while underground, but it was no longer so dangerous to be a Christian... The issue with these things is that perhaps the Christians of that time couldn't choose ..."

"What I wonder is if the greater visible power, the greater structure, aren't signs of weakness... For example, how do you know who is in the church by vocation and who because it suits them, gives them security, a job..." insisted the young man.

"Impossible to know. The church is in the world, and the world is in the church. Jesus tells a short and powerful parable. He says that a man found that in his field he had wheat and tares. The workers ask him if he wants them to pull out the tares and he tells them no, because they might pull out the wheat by accident. He tells them to let the wheat and the tares grow together, so that on the day of harvest they can be separated. It's short and simple but the idea is powerful. We can't help it if there are people in the church with the best intentions and others with the worst... But the wheat grows, mind you!" Pedro was delighted with this explanation from the priest, especially because he had used a Bible text that was very appropriate and clear.

"Yes, the lady in grey..."

"For the investigator... What's his name? Yes, Mr. Peretti."

"Nicolás, please."

"Well, Nicolás. Look, I agree with the task that people like you do, trying to warn people, 'unmasking' them, unmasking the *chantas*. But I have the idea that people believe what they want to believe. Astrology, Chinese horoscope, aliens, alternative medicine of any type... Precisely the sort of people who get into those things already have a predisposition to believe in things which may not have any logical basis. And they are willing to pay money without much concern for strict accountability..."

"Specifically, what's your argument?" Nita thought it was a good proposal that could be lost in vagueness.

"Specifically? I fear you'll only convince people who already have a logical or rational predisposition. Other people, deep down, don't want the 'pacifier' taken away from them, which reassures them, gives them a sense of identity... even allows them to feel superior to others in that specific area."

"Maybe, maybe. But perhaps if there were many more people willing to investigate these issues it would be much more productive. Perhaps we need to go deeper into the subject, seeing that we are a society with little sense of prevention of danger, little social sense, little dedication to effort. 'If nothing happens to me, I won't do anything.' 'If a son of mine wasn't caught by a cult, if he wasn't brainwashed, if he wasn't abused, why should I get involved?' But we've suffered enough from this 'don't get involved' attitude in the past decade."

"If you'll allow me, Nicolás... Nita..." Pedro jumped in as he found common ground... "Something similar happens with faith. One could say that only people who are already open to faith will believe, either because of their way of being or because they have had an experience that leads them to faith, but we have the responsibility to preach the message to everyone."

"Maybe..." Nicolás didn't like being associated with a pastor like Pedro, whom he could criticize for so many things that he didn't like. "But what I criticize in many people who talk about faith is that they could actually believe in anything. They need to believe, so the first thing that comes their way is good for them. It could be an evangelical church, a Catholic church, an Eastern religion, a seller of illusions, a cult... anything. What I... what we intend to do is to show people that there are unscrupulous people who trade with this need for faith, and they don't give them what they need but what they think they need. Let's see... it would be something like a doctor giving a placebo to his patient, knowing on the one hand that it won't do him any harm, or good, in his physical condition, but it will help him emotionally, psychically."

"Continuing with that idea," an older man who appeared to be retired and obviously a regular attendee of events like these, by the way he spoke and addressed everyone. "I would make a difference between a doctor giving a placebo to a terminally ill patient and one who gives it to the patient instead of a proven remedy. In the first case, it can be mercy, wisdom, using the transference effect for good. In the second, it would be what you call a *chanta*, a seller of colored mirrors. A con artist."

"The first one isn't so serious, we agree, as long as he doesn't profit from false hope. But the second case makes us feel bad, because they are cheating people who could find the real remedy," said Nicolás.

"I'd like to Pastor Terrero a question," the same man, looking at a notebook he had in his hands. "How do you explain the fact that there are so many evangelical churches with rich pastors, or very rich ones, with poor congregations? How do you justify that difference?"

Pedro tried to take the blow elegantly and sought to gain time by asking the clarifying question, recommended in these cases.

"If I understand you correctly, you are suggesting that wealth is a bad thing, that it is better to be poor?"

"No, what I'm saying is that it seems to me that something is wrong when the pastor is rich among a poor congregation, and he is flaunted as an example of success, when all the pastor's income comes from donations from his congregation, and not from any... productive activity."

Nicolás couldn't avoid a smirk, which he tried to hide. This man was saying things that he thought, and he couldn't help but add fuel to the fire.

"To which must be added the promise that the more the congregation gives, the more God will prosper them... especially the rich pastor who leads them."

"That's another thing entirely. God promises in his word that he will reward those who are generous!" Pedro tried to calm down.

"Then it's not generosity, it's a kind of... long-term investment... with high risk and high return." Nicolás retorted, sure of the effect he would have on the audience, who laughed heartily.

Nita had to intervene to prevent Pedro from raising more pressure.

"I think we all understand that Nicolás only wants to reduce to an absurdity situations that seem one way from inside and another way for the person who is outside the church. I ask for a round of applause for our guests and invite you to continue the talk with them along with the coffee we prepared.

The faces of the three panelists reflected how the short debate had turned out. Nicolás was in his sauce. Pedro, livid and restless, knew that he hadn't been able to stand up well and knew, deep down, that it was his fault. Father Nicanor, in the middle, was the point of balance and had left the debate just as he had entered it.

6

THE PEOPLE WE KNEW

Enriched by each other, sharpened like axes
We all are a part of a whole that enlarges

Juan and Mariela left the Pueblo Santo community in May 1989, along with the presidential elections of that year. The initial ten identical and simple houses around the temple and Bible institute were followed by twenty more, each more luxurious than the other. They had never been part of the inner circle, those who had moved with their families into the community. Maybe that was what kept them from being drawn into the cloud of mysticism and irrationality that grew over time. Living in a normal setting kept them in touch with people in the real world, with its "secular work." Juan found this concept odd, especially when it was contrasted with "work for the Lord," "ministry" or "the work." The impression was that the work of a pastor or a person dedicated "full-time" to the Lord was of a higher quality than that of a laborer, an employee, a businessperson or a housewife. You began in a secular job and as you grew in spirituality you were promoted to pastor, minister of something, or leader of something else.

This concept was transmitted to the young people, encouraging them to study at the Bible Institute and enter directly into the ministry, without having the possibility of having a reference or a contact with the "real reality," as Juan liked to say. The call of these kids was, to say the least, suspicious. The worst thing was that this path of least effort was exhibited as that of the greatest spirituality. Those who studied in the Institute, those who graduated, those who started a pastoral work, all received abundant prayers and recommendations, along with "words" about their future success. On the other hand, students of administration, medicine, teachers and even—perish the thought! —lawyers or scientists were hardly mentioned.

Juan was glad that he hadn't given in to this concept. He also congratulated himself for having that little voice, that inner impression, that appeared at critical moments of his life telling him, so softly, "Don't do it" or "Go ahead." He heard it and paid attention to it when he left the army. The same thing happened when he had the opportunity to study at the Seminary. He wasn't convinced at first, but something told him to enter, and he never regretted it. It reappeared when he met the prayer group at the Varela home, when Pastor Flores spoke to him, and now when they left the Pueblo Santo community. The last time he had heard it was during a series of meetings in April 1989 with the prophet Jerry Solis, a Puerto Rican who had allegedly received direct revelations from God in Miami about our community, and specific people in it, after which he communicated with the four leaders and they prepared the prophetic series. There, in an atmosphere of much excitement for what this man, so far from our country, would bring, he spent much of his time giving specific words for specific people.

One of the prophecies said somebody had a special calling and was called to the nations. The prophet had come down from the platform and rushed to a somewhat timid man who didn't know how to handle such an awesome prophecy.

"Glory to God! Hallelujah!" said Mario Morales, accompanied by the expectant congregation.

In another prophecy to a young man, he was told: "There is a new land of blessing... to the west! Yesssss!"

"God wants you to sell everything and follow him!"

"Don't stop at what you're planning to do! This year you will marry!"

"God is going to change Argentina from here!"

"He's going to change the world! And you will be his soldiers!" That was when Juan heard that silent voice.

The growing sequence of prophecies, from the personal and small to the general and great was stimulated by an increasingly enthusiastic congregation, with the background of music and the praise leader making the people repeat song after song as a background. When there were practically no more prophecies to give, or because he had reached the ceiling of possibilities, the prophet sat down, exhausted.

The prophet Jerry left, leaving behind a trail of illusions and decisions that had to be made if one was to be obedient to the word of God that had come from so far away and with so much effort. Some results of this series of conferences were that Marcos Naranjo, the shy man of the prophecy was sent to Misiones, where he spent a few months in the middle of the jungle until he decided to return, convinced that his calling was not missions, let alone nature, the wild and solitude. Héctor Olmos traveled to San Juan, in the west, and ended up marrying a local woman from the same group, but he had to return a year later because he couldn't get a job. Teodoro sold a house and a car and brought the proceeds of his sale to the community, despite strong opposition from his family. Eduardo Jonte married Miriam Ruiz, his girlfriend of just one month, producing a stunted marriage that lasted barely two years. Needless to say, Argentina didn't change, unless the debacle of Raúl Alfonsín's government in July of that year and the arrival of Carlos Menem could be considered a response to that prophecy. Is it necessary to say that the world didn't change either, at least thanks to the Pueblo Santo community?

Juan remembered one of the many talks they had had at the Seminary, when they really felt that they could change the world by doing well what their predecessors had done wrong.

"There should be something like 'prophetic malpractice,'" Pedro had said, with his usual humor.

"Prophetic malpractice? Like doctors?" Nacho had told him.

"Yes. If a doctor does what he knows, or what he's supposed to know, wrong, he can get a malpractice suit," Pedro argued.

"What are you aiming at?" said Nacho.

"A doctor studied to be a doctor, took the exams, and everyone assumes he knows. There's no doubt about it. This also means that a prophet should take a kind of exam that qualifies him as a prophet. If not, anyone can say he's a prophet..."

"Get to the point." Santiago of all people asking to be precise!

"Well, you know the doctor knows, but if he makes a mistake, for example, by giving the patient the wrong diagnosis, or the wrong medicine, or he doesn't do something that should to be done, and the patient suffers serious harm, or dies, then he can be put on trial."

"So?" asked Santiago.

"Let's consider the prophet. Supposing he is qualified to give prophecies, and he prophesies that you must marry a person, you get married, and the marriage is a disaster... Or he tells you that you have to go as a missionary to another country, and you leave, and when you arrive you realize that being a missionary isn't your thing, that you have no idea what to do, and as a result you go astray and lose your faith. Shouldn't the prophet be judged for malpractice?" Pedro continued.

"What for? What do you want to achieve?" Nacho, again.

"On the one hand, remove him from the circuit, so he stops causing further harm. On the other hand, to make anyone who wants to become a prophet think twice."

"I agree. After all, a striker who misses three easy goals in a row is replaced and leaves the pitch whistled by the crowd. And what about the books that tell you what's going to happen, interpret the apocalyptic passages the way that seems best to them, and then what they say doesn't come true?" Nacho had bought one that was so pro-American that all it needed was a recommendation by the CIA on the back cover.

"I'd make them give back the money they earned from selling those books," said Pedro.

It wasn't that Juan didn't believe in the gift of prophecy. On one occasion, a person who had that gift came to a church he had visited with Mariela and, when he came to the front, said a series of things about his life that astonished him, since the man had no way of knowing them naturally. He remembered that he had correctly said that he had been in the army in the north, what he did for a living, that he was going to sell a property and that his father had died during the last year. One hundred percent effective, just like in the Old Testament. At that time, if they didn't get it a hundred percent right, they risked being stoned. Not everyone wanted to be a prophet then! In fact, what irritated Juan most about this gift and all the other gifts was that, because of people who simulated or misused them, the authentic gifts of the Spirit were not recognized.

The New Church of Blessing had entered a stage of steady growth. In the beginning of 1990 it had over six hundred members and the Sunday morning and evening services filled the eight hundred seat hall that had been built around the corner from the previous rented shed. They now owned this building and had plans to expand, both upwards and sideways. They wanted to have an evangelical school, a Christian radio station, a Christian newspaper. It was a time of great activity, and everyone who came found a place of service. Counseling, music, and worship, teaching children, maintenance, sports, visiting prisons and hospitals. The church's finances were also sound, requiring more time for Pedro from planning and evaluation meetings. Fullness & Growth continued to make their annual visits. Tony Vidal, after being practically a member of the church family because of his frequent visits, had been promoted in the organization, and the new church contact/consultant was Nelson Torres, a 24-year-old high-powered Mexican who made Pedro and Tony look slow and indecisive. Much more ambitious and worldly than his predecessor, he talked about almost nothing but money. The first time he came, and they met, Pedro saw that haunting red light again.

"How are you, *ché*?" Nelson approached Pedro extending his hand and with the typical Central American dig of Argentines, with that tango tone they thought we all used in Buenos Aires.

"Hi, nice to meet you. You must be Nelson Torres…" They met in the pastor's office after the Sunday morning service.

"That's right and forgive my kidding. But we admire the *"chés"* a lot in my country. I am excited to work with you and your spectacular church. We've heard so much about you and your team. Today's service was tremendous, pastor."

"Yes, I think the material on Christian success helps to lift spirits, to have a positive attitude towards life."

"'Christian success and the successful Christian'. It's one of our best materials. We have orders for the next three months and it's already in its third edition. One of the things that your fellow pastors appreciate most is how we have managed to integrate the message with worship, with song, and even with the moment of the offering."

"Well, please sit down. Do you want something to drink? Coffee, a soda?"

"No, thanks. I must watch my health." Did Pedro hear an insinuation or a hint in relation to his excess weight that was becoming more difficult to conceal? "If you have some mineral water, it would be great."

That half-hour conversation after the meeting would be key in the life of Pedro and his church. Because it was there that he was introduced to what he saw as an inexhaustible source of financial resources: the churches of the United States. If he had paid attention to that little red light at this point in his life and ministry, things wouldn't have followed the course they did. Because Nelson wasn't Tony. While on the outside they were similar and belonged to the same organization that had taken them from a mediocre church to a successful, thriving, project-filled one, over time Pedro realized that they were completely different. Perhaps their backgrounds marked their differences. Tony had known the church since he was a child and was a faithful believer. It was this "loser mentality" that he criticized and exasperated him. He thought that the church—and by church, he meant the evangelical church—should take off the mentality of scarcity, shake off the mental barriers, and think big. When he traveled from Puerto Rico to the United States for his studies, he was impressed by the size of the churches and para-church organizations in that country and was amazed at the organizational capacity of the Americans. But, with all the business attitude and efficiency he wanted and managed to convey, his interest was still "winning souls for Christ," evangelizing, teaching the Word, albeit indirectly.

Nelson, on the other hand, had been converted very recently, about three years ago, in one of the megachurches in Houston, Texas, the city where F&G had their operations base. He had been recruited through a formal search, considering background, interests, skills, and profile. He had surpassed all his competitors in what was sought, in part because he was a second-generation Latino who should get along with their Latin American customer base, and because he was a born salesman, especially of himself. He entered with a significant annual salary, even at a secular level, and with a strong system of bonuses and commissions that multiplied his natural commitment. But—and this was a big but —Nelson's main symbol wasn't a cross but the dollar sign. You didn't have to have the gift of discernment to see it. Pedro opened the doors wide for him and lowered his guard because of his profitable relationship with F&G for years.

"Have you ever visited the United States, Pedro?"

"Yes, a couple of times, with Tony. He wanted me to meet other churches that were implementing the method, and for those over there to meet me."

"Sure, perfect. Now, I think we can make much better use of this possibility... Let me explain. The brothers there are very eager to help brothers, pastors, churches in other countries. They have the money and they're very organized. The only thing, as you know, is that they want things to be done right, professionally. And that's where we can help you."

"I don't quite understand what you're talking about," Pedro said.

"I'm proposing that we go on a tour of some churches in the south of the United States, presenting the needs of Argentina, of your ministry, and especially the huge social drama you're suffering because of the economic crisis. I can assure you that you will be surprised, and this will extend the limits of your vision tremendously.

In addition, the idea is to establish links between churches in both countries. They would send people and youth groups here, since they are very interested in the spiritual movement of Argentina, in addition to supporting projects and works of your church.

Another stage had begun for the New Church of Blessing—derived prosperity.

With Mercedes we took charge of the home for street children that the New Church of Blessing started with the money sent by a group of churches in the south of the United States. This was one of the fruits of Pedro's last trip to that country. Another fruit was the Christian school project that was to be built on the 20 x 50 meters lot next to the church, purchased with some of that same money. Mercedes was excited about the project, since she had always been interested in serving the dispossessed, especially the children and women who were increasingly appearing as a result of the economic policies of exclusion implemented by successive Argentine governments. She had graduated as a social worker but hadn't yet managed to practice. When the project was raised in the Pastoral Council, it seemed logical to propose her for this task, and both the Council and she accepted with great joy. In a few months, the church rented an old two-story house five blocks away, which became Casa de Esperanza.[33]

There was some discussion about the legal structure it should have in order to give it more executive agility and not be entangled by the red tape that drowned so many good intentions and promoted corruption in secular media, especially in the government. Finally, we established an Operational Commission—the name was intended to indicate the functional and efficient nature of the structure—in charge of Pastor Pedro, Pastor Virginia, Mercedes, the Ojeda couple and myself. In the emotional presentation to the church on a Sunday morning, Pedro mentioned who would be leading the project and we

---

[33] In Spanish, House of Hope

all went to the front. We saw nothing but good things for the children and women who would benefit from the work, thanks to the financial support of our American brothers and sisters.

In the first meeting of the Commission there were some differences that seemed minor at the time, but that would ultimately be decisive.

"Well, it's an honor to have this group of brothers and sisters for this project so close to God's heart." Pedro's presentation. "Do you all know each other? Let's go around saying briefly who we are and what we expect from our participation in Casa de Esperanza. We'll start... Pedro Terrero, pastor, President of Casa de Esperanza. We hope to be able to take many children and women off the streets, give them a decent home, teach them about the Lord, and bring them back into society completely new."

"Yes, I am Virginia Terrero, pastor, Vice President of Casa de Esperanza. As Pedro said, we want to be the hands, eyes, ears, and mouth of the Lord in this place, to embrace these helpless creatures..." She was moved.

"Well, I'm next. I'm Mercedes Encinas, Director of Casa de Esperanza. It's really a dream come true for me to take on this responsibility and serve among street children and women. It's something we've talked about and dreamed about with Raúl for years, so I hope to live up to the expectations..." I was sure she'd be thinking of the difficult time she had gone through with her mother.

"I'm Raúl, husband of the most beautiful woman in the world"— laughs— "and I'm going to serve as the Administrator of Casa de Esperanza, although it's a topic I'd like to discuss in more detail."

"Ah, yes, of course, after the introductions." Pedro didn't seem to like this interruption of the natural order of a smooth meeting that he had foreseen. "Let's move on. Virgilio?"

"Thank you, pastor." The good-natured man of about sixty-five seemed somewhat out of place in that setting, together with his wife, with the air of a granny more than a committee member. "What can I tell you? For me, and for Rosita, it is a great honor and satisfaction to be in this group of service to the most deprived and needy of our society. We are so happy with this church, with our pastors, with everything they do... And we are here to serve in whatever it takes, from cleaning to prayer support... or getting people to collaborate... Whatever it takes. Rosita and I have no experience, so it seems strange to be on a committee with people as capable as you... but we'll do everything possible..."

"Virgilio, I want to clarify to the whole group why we think that you and our dear Rosita would be useful and of great blessing in this commission. We want to do something different from what is always done in these cases, both in the world and in the churches. We don't want a group of people who know a lot but don't have a heart. We need, and I think we all agree" —looking especially at Mercedes and me— "people with a prayer life, with a spiritual life, and I don't think anyone can say that Virgilio and Rosita aren't that kind of people."

It wasn't clear to me whether efficiency or spirituality was being sought, but it was impossible to object to anything at that time, since one would be questioning the spiritual character of these dear brothers. The presentations followed.

"Rosita?" said Pedro.

"Well... I am Rosita, everybody knows me. I always accompany Virgilio in everything he does, and I will support him and the pastor and the *pastora*, because I think it is a work that needs to be done. As the general said, 'better than saying is doing, and better than promising is delivering." The reference to General Perón, in that context, sounded strange. "So I think we must support those who do and not put stones in the way, which is what the devil does..."

"Well, thank you very much, Virgilio and Rosita." *The less you talk, the better,* Pedro must have thought.

"If you will allow me, I would like to know what's the purpose of this Commission. What are we expected to do?" I asked.

"This commission is a requirement of our brothers in the United States, because they want there to be control of money, of its use. Between you and me, I think they have some prejudice... they think we are all criminals or corrupt, just because we are from a Latin American country," said Pedro.

"I think it's right that they try to make sure that things are handled with transparency. We ourselves should make sure that everything is done correctly," I insisted.

"Yes, but this isn't a business, it is a church, and I think we know each other, and you trust us, don't you?" It was Virginia this time.

"Of course, pastor... and *pastora*. It wouldn't be right for people to think we're controlling them, as if they could do something bad." The Ojeda's, in unison.

"I would say the opposite." I knew my dissenting opinion wouldn't be well received. "We have to do everything to show that there is nothing wrong, to protect the work, the testimony, the pastors, and the Director," looking at Mercedes.

"So you're questioning this Commission, then?" Pedro, obviously upset.

"Well, I don't know if it's right for us to be three married couples since it doesn't give much idea of mutual accountability... on the one hand. On the other hand, is there a formal procedure so that there can be a regular record of meetings... an organization chart, minutes?"

"Minutes... Yes, of course. We'll coordinate it over time, but let's not let the red tape ruin the spiritual aspect and the urgency of this project. I have a brief word that I would like to share from the book of Acts, when the apostles appointed the deacons, and then I propose that we spend some time in prayer."

I was no longer surprised by his repeated use of the technique of spiritualizing everything with a word and prayer, so as not to leave room or time to address the issues that needed to be addressed. Of course, the promised procedures never appeared, and the Commission meetings were held whenever Pedro decided, usually before a visit by the brothers in the United States or a visit by Pedro to that country.

The house was refurbished and inaugurated, with the presence of Mayor Mejías, and began to function under the auspices of the municipality, housing ten street children and four single mothers. Mercedes was happy and excited, seeing changes and advances in the children and mothers of the home every day. They were given food, shelter, and taught a trade, as well as Bible lessons. Casa de Esperanza was featured in the new brochure of the New Church of Blessing, along with the Christian school—in fact, it helped pave the way for this latter project. It didn't take much to raise the funds for the purchase of the land and the design stage of the school, as well as the authorizations and all the support of the municipality, increasingly part of the activity of the church. Pedro visited the municipality and the mayor regularly, and several officials attended the church's non-religious activities. The New Church of Blessing appeared in secular and evangelical media as the model to follow, and Pedro was often invited to recount the process of going from a small church in a shed to this institution that was setting the pace in the spiritual, social and educational care of society. Things couldn't be better.

Nicolás had married and had two beautiful children. His wife, Isolda Neves, was a charming Brazilian he had met on one of his research trips of the neighboring country's Umbanda groups. He met her for the first time in a talk he had given about multilevel marketing (MLM) groups in São Paulo. He remembered perfectly her deep brown eyes and her melodious voice when she asked him a question.

"So you're saying that these groups are like religious cults? Doesn't that seem a bit exaggerated?"

"Look… what's your name?" He wasn't going to miss the opportunity.

"Isolda," with the "o" so characteristic of Portuguese.

"Look, Isolda, I could give you a list of people we've treated at our center who had all the symptoms of brainwashing we saw in religious cults: estrangement from family and friends, domination by the leader, fanaticism about getting new members… increasing occupation of time by the organization. People who knew them said that they had seen them change their personality, and when they told them about this change they answered with ready-made phrases, such as 'you are the one with the stagnant mind,' 'I don't want to be the same as yesterday,' 'I am not going to let happiness escape me'."

"What about the Vonaite company? Do you know it?"

"Yes, I've been told about Vonaite, the ones that sell articles for young people, right? They have a motto in English..."

"Yes, 'Teen to Thirty.'"

"Look, I'm not going to talk about specific companies from this place, but all companies that use MLM, pyramid selling or whatever you want to call it have a psychological control component that affects some more than others."

"And what do you say about the financial aspect? Is it a scam?" This was a man in a neat suit, probably a salesman for one of these companies.

"You have to study each case, but in all these systems the trick is to be at the top of the pyramid. The sooner you get into the structure the quicker you get up there and get others to work for you. If you are late you end up working for those at the top and you never get enough people down there to work for you."

"Would you say that these systems have penetrated the church as well?" This was a young man sitting dangerously close to the brunette.

"For sure. What many religious leaders don't realize is that their churches take everything good and bad from the societies around them, like pyramid systems. I have spoken to many sincere pastors who think their church or community is hermetically protected from society, that when new members enter, they leave their ambitions, their misconceptions, their manipulative habits at the door."

"Sincere pastors... and the others? The ..." The young man used a Brazilian term that caused laughter in everyone. Nicolás supposed it was the equivalent of *chanta*.

"The others find the way open, the ground plowed to implement their methods. How many pyramid schemes use church contacts to start operating? Notice that what a person brings into these schemes is his network of contacts: their uncles, cousins, friends, loose acquaintances. So what better than a church's contacts, which can be at least fifty people?"

After the talk, he made sure to take the data from the Brazilian girl and they arranged to meet in the evening. Isolda was in her third year of psychology at the University of São Paulo and was especially interested in the functioning of social groups in extreme conditions. She had read a lot about World War II from the point of view of the German population, the rise of Hitler, the Third Reich and the "final solution." The more she read and studied the more she became convinced that any person and any group, given the right conditions, could become a monster, a torturer, a murderer, a rapist. Her ambition was to write a book that would be like a practical manual that would alert people to the danger of any such situation. They talked extensively with Nicolás about the Argentine experience with subversion and repression and studied the parallels with the Brazilian and Latin American situation in the same period. They went through the Ku Klux Klan, the Children of God, Nazi propaganda, as well as other attempts at manipulation such as the CIA, the KGB and the press.

But above all, they fell deeply in love. Nicolás's extreme rationalism needed Isolda's exuberant passion. She felt everything he said, from the inside and not from above, in her head. She accompanied her arguments with her whole body, especially her eyes and hands. Nicolás was struck by the level of passion she showed for these subjects so, as they walked along Avenida Paulista, he asked her:

"Can I ask you something?"

"Yes, of course."

"Did you have a bad experience... or someone in your family... with sectarian or religious themes..." He interrupted the phrase, because Isolda's face became serious, like when a cloud passes in front of the sun.

"No, it's okay..." She wiped her face with her sleeve and looked ahead. "My father was in the military, and he was killed with a bomb when I was five... He was such a good man, my mom tells me... I hardly remember him... only from photographs."

"Oh, I didn't know... I'm so sorry." He really didn't expect this. "And who were they? Did you find them?"

"Terrorists, revolutionaries... And to think that my parents always fought for the poor. I don't understand why they killed him. Just because he was in the military."

"What an injustice!"

"Do you understand now why I started studying these subjects? If I could have talked to the ones who put the bomb, if they had known my dad, they might have been friends even. But the manipulation, those who don't want agreement, those who use young people, only ended in death…" She couldn't hold back her tears, and Nicolás hugged her tightly. "I'm tired of so much useless death, of so much hate!"

Nicolás then told her about his sister Susana's case, and how this had prompted him to investigate these matters. The common suffering united them even more, and they continued their walk with the feeling that they had taken a weight off each other. Or perhaps they were now able to share those weights.

Juan and Mariela had been without going to any church for a while after they left the Pueblo Santo community. It had seemed strange at first, because since they had known each other most of their life and their conversations, their projects and even their problems had to do with the church. It was the center of everything, the point of reference. What had to be protected, defended, and made to grow. It was there that the Lord revealed himself, where he indicated what to do. There also were the people closest to them, the examples to follow. It was the place where they wanted their children to be raised, have their friends, and meet their partners.

But this feeling wasn't something Juan had recognized when he was inside. He only became aware of his "church dependence" when he came out, when he took distance and was able to identify how much it dominated him. And he didn't like the feeling. He had left because he didn't want to depend anymore, but he didn't realize how much he already depended. He recalled typical conversations between them over the past few years:

"What did you think of today's message?"

"Very good. Maybe a little long. I didn't really like the music."

"Yes, they could change some lyrics... They don't say much."

.....

"I ran into Gerardo. He wanted us to meet for the construction of the new building. I told him we should try to have fewer meetings."

"What happens is that he doesn't know how to do anything else. I don't see him in a more spiritual job."

.....

"Pastor Flores wants to start an intercession group and wants me to lead it. What do you think?"

"I don't know, you'd have to give up the Bible study."

Just a sample, but enough to realize how many of those conversations revolved around people and church activities and how little was left of those relationships today that they were outside of that group. He had an unpleasant feeling of wasted time. Now, instead, they were talking about each other, they had started going out with the kids, even on Sunday mornings. They had found a beautiful place where people went with their families, with chairs and folding tables, and simply enjoyed the sun and nature. Mariela remembered when she used to do this as a child, with her parents, and it brought her a very pleasant feeling to be able to do it with the people she loved most. And she had them all to herself, without having to share them with the church.

Soon after, almost without realizing it, they began to work in a slum five blocks away from Pueblo Santo. It was strange they only noticed it when they left the community, although they had to pass by each time they went there at least twice a week. They lived about half an hour from there, in Sarandí, and it meant no effort for them. Mariela sang and played the guitar and Juan accompanied her quite well. At least he had a powerful voice that could be heard from a distance. The first time they entered the slum, they walked until they reached a kind of clearing where there was a group of kids playing and they asked an older man who seemed to have certain authority if it was okay for them to play some songs for the children.

"Ah, you're evangelists, aren't you? Good people. It won't be a problem."

No longer had they started playing the guitar than ten, then fifteen kids came running, curious, and sat on the ground. The old songs they had learned and used hundreds of times in the previous church began to flow: "I have a friend who loves me, loves me...," "The Way to Heaven...," "Three Little Words Alone..." At one point Juan and Mariela looked at each other and confirmed what they were feeling: "This is what we want to do. This is the gospel."

Several months passed and they were joined by two more couples they had known from the community and who lived in the area. The singing meetings with Bible stories for children had turned into increasingly numerous gatherings in a room they rented across the street, which had once been a spare parts depot. It was clear that the main need was food, and that if they wanted to talk about God's love to people who lacked the most basic things it would be a futile effort, apart from sounding hypocritical. So they began by offering a snack before the Sunday afternoon meeting. The *mate cocido*,[34] the ham and cheese sandwich, and the *alfajores*[35] donated by a believer's company were very welcome and acted as perfect complements to the message of love that followed. The initial distrust, the product of years of being used by politicians and others, slowly subsided as they saw that they weren't asked for anything in return and these were really "good people."

It was there that they had their first contact with the different people and groups that have other interests in the deprived, and only think about using them for their own benefit. There were the various *punteros*[36] of the political parties, who saw in them simply votes that could be bought in one way or another. They emerged from their burrows a few months before the elections, or when a manifestation was to be held in favor of the politician they supported. There were

---

[34] A drink prepared like tea with *maté* leaves
[35] An *alfajor* is a sandwich cookie popular in Argentina
[36] Point men/women who work to get votes for their political party

the drug traffickers, with their well-defined areas and networks that included local, provincial, and national politicians, police, judges and officials from various government agencies.

Juan and Mariela seriously questioned what kind of message they should give these people, if only one of resignation and contentment, including blind obedience to the authorities, which they had heard so far in all the churches, or a more contextualized and combative message, more incarnated in the very unjust reality they were living. He remembered the controversies about Liberation Theology that they had had so many times in the Seminary, how they distorted the Gospel because Jesus wasn't a socialist or a Marxist. But, of course, it's one thing to say it from the comfort of having all the basic needs covered and within a family that can give you everything you need, and quite another to say it from a place where there is little work, where alcohol has ruined lives, where drugs serve to mask suffering, where those who are paid to protect you—policemen, judges, politicians—look the other way or become part of evil. Where there is no justice and no hope.

As a group they proposed to read the whole Bible again from this context, sharing what appeared and which could be of practical application for these specific people: Don Máximo, the Leiva's, Marquitos, the twins... At first they were frightened, because they began to see things that they hadn't seen before: the emphasis on justice, suffering, terrible stories, messages of condemnation for those who didn't follow God's will... Then they became excited, seeing a God who was much more aware of what was happening and who empathized with his people. A God who bent down to help those in need, who had become incarnate. They also identified with cry after cry of men and women of God asking for help and justice in the midst of oppression, hunger and loneliness. And, of course, the ultimate example was Jesus himself, who had suffered immeasurable injustice, but with a purpose of love. The message changed as they were changed, getting closer to the people and their concrete situation and to God in times of prolonged prayer and fasting, wanting to do His will, fearful of distorting his message.

Already the group, which had given itself the name Pan de Vida,[37] functioned to all effects like a church, although without a formal structure. They had worship services on Sunday afternoons for adults and children, prayer meetings on Wednesdays, cooking and sewing classes, carpentry on different days of the week, soccer and volleyball on Saturdays for the young people. The team, led informally by Juan and Mariela, consisted of about ten people for the different activities, with the support of a nearby Methodist church and the neighborhood Catholic parish, which was delighted to have a place where the youth, especially, could put into practice what was taught in Catechesis. Father Venancio, an engaging and helpful Galician, came from time to time and jokingly asked about the images that were missing in the hall. He had a long history of working in deprived places and at Don Orione's Cottolengo,[38] so there was no situation that was unfamiliar to him, and he was a valuable source of advice for the team. Several times he had engaged in theological discussions with Juan, but always looking for the practical consequences of the different positions. One example was Father Venancio's celibacy, which, regardless of the reasons that had led him to practice it, had undoubtedly allowed him time and dedication to the work among the humble and dispossessed, impossible for a person with a family.

Then the phone call came, a Tuesday at noon.

"Hello? Pastor Juan Cristante?"

"Yes, who is this?"

"We're calling from the municipality. Dr. Salvador Mendiyeta, Secretary of Social Assistance, would like to have an interview with you."

The municipality? Juan thought. *It must be a mistake. How do they know my name... and what am I going to do there?*

---

[37] In Spanish, Bread of Life

[38] A Catholic center dedicated to the disabled

"What's the reason?"

"The Secretary would like to talk about the Pan de Vida project you're leading. Is Thursday at 10 a.m. okay?"

"Yes. Who else could accompany me?" asked Juan, still surprised.

"Actually, the interview is with you only..."

"I'll see who I can go with. We are used to do things as a team."

"I understand. We'll be waiting for you then, Thursday, 10 a.m., at the Social Assistance Secretariat, on the second floor of the municipality."

Juan's heart skipped a beat and he called Mariela immediately to tell her. He had never had contact with government officials, and now suddenly he had a personal interview with the Secretary of Social Assistance of the municipality of Quilmes. Would this be an answer from the Lord to so many prayers for the needs of these people? If only they could ensure a dignified and nutritious meal for all the children and mothers in the village... But they were talking about more than 300 people, every day, including weekends. And work, and school support. Of course, it wasn't just a question of money. People were needed who could be there full-time, apart from the volunteers. The worst thing they could do was to start something that would later fall through the cracks. In that case it would have been better not to start and avoid the false expectations and frustration.

He called Ana, a very active and practical sister, who had worked in the slums with Father Venancio and was saved from being a missing person because someone—she never knew who it was, and for her it was an angel—warned her not to go home that night.

"So Mendiyeta called you? I'd like to accompany you if it's okay with you."

"Of course. I told his secretary I was going with someone else, and you would be my first choice."

"And what did she say when you told him you were going with someone else?"

"She gave me the impression that she preferred I went alone."

"Of course, of course. Well, tell me when and where, and I'll go with you. Mendiyeta..."

When they arrived at the office, the secretary was waiting for them, and sent them in immediately. Dr. Salvador Mendiyeta got up from his chair and received them with that forced friendliness typical of politicians.

"Pastor Cristante, what a pleasure to finally meet you! I have heard so much about your work in the slum. Who is the nice lady who is with you? Your wife?"

Ana's icy gaze stopped him in his tracks. She seemed a familiar face, but his memory wasn't as quick as in other times.

"No, this is Ana Zamorano, one of our most faithful and active sisters, in charge of the lunchroom."

"Zamorano... that name rings a bell..." He also vaguely remembered her face and tried to quickly classify her as good/bad, friend/enemy as he extended his limp hand.

"I'm sure you remember me from Jardín de Sol, 1978, La Plata..." Juan didn't understand what was happening, but obviously Mendiyeta did.

"Ah, yes, you... you were one of the student activists at the university then."

"Yes, one of those who are still alive."

"Of course, I was in the municipality at the time, in charge of security, and we had some unfortunate incidents that were never cleared up. Thank God that's all over now and we're in a democracy," anxious to change the subject quickly.

Ana answered with a blank silence.

"Well, thank you for the invitation," said Juan, sitting with Ana in front of the Secretary, who had turned around the desk and made a gesture inviting them to sit down.

"Yes, well, I want to get to the point. We are aware of everything that you are doing in the slum, and we'd really like to offer you an important financial contribution that comes straight from the government of the Province of Buenos Aires. Are you interested?"

"Of course, you know that the needs are increasing, and we haven't found an echo in the municipality or in any other official body so far, despite the letters we have sent. Sometimes we have the impression that politicians are only interested in the people when there are elections..." Juan began to tell him.

"Ah, politicians. It may seem strange to you, but I don't consider myself a politician, despite being in a political post. I consider myself an executive, a person who does things, a problem solver; someone who manages, who acts as a bridge. For example, in this case we are in a position to offer you a very important donation, so that you can use it as you see fit, without us controlling what you do." Hoping to get the maximum effect, he then said, "What amount would you need for your most immediate plans?"

"Let's see, Ana, you have the data there, don't you?" said Juan, looking at her.

"Yes." Ana opened the folder she had brought with her. "The extension and remodeling of the lunchroom is 200,000 Australes... the first part of the hall, 350,000 Australes. And then the monthly food expenses, 200,000..."

"How about a donation of 200,000 US dollars?" interrupted the Secretary.

If a bomb had fallen, it would have made less effect. Juan managed to ask as he recovered:

"How much did you say?"

"200,000 dollars, that is..." Keying on his desk calculator, "200,000,000 Australes."

"And what do you want in return?" asked Ana, always suspicious of anything that came from the government.

"Nothing. You can do what you want with the money. All you need to do is sign this receipt, which we can do in the name of you, pastor, or the church, or the institution you designate. What's more, next year we could repeat this same donation."

Juan took the receipt and noticed that it was for 300,000 dollars.

"It says here 300,000 dollars..."

"Exactly," Mendiyeta replied without showing any emotion.

"So..." Juan looked at the Secretary's expressionless face and at Ana's withering look. "No ... no way ... this is unbelievable!" He rose so abruptly that he threw down the chair in which he was sitting.

"Please, pastor, think of all those children, those mothers, all that you could do. Remember that the Bible says that you have to be cunning as a snake..."

"Don't you dare quote the Bible for your dirty business!" Ana had never seen Juan so angry.

"Pastor, Ana, think about it... Pray. I'll give you until tomorrow. Just call me and say 'yes'."

"Mendiyeta, always the same corrupt and thieving man!" Ana wasn't one to keep quiet, slamming the door as she left with Juan.

With the change of the F&G representative, the New Church of Blessing embarked decisively on what came to be called the Theology of Prosperity. In essence, it says that God wants you to be rich and healthy, and that one way to achieve wealth and health is to give money to the current organization, church, or leader. If you have faith and give money, you should do well—financially, in health, in work, and in all areas. The wealth and success of the leaders of these movements is exhibited, in turn, as an example that God blesses those who have faith.

The strangest thing about this movement is that it assumes that the majority of the characters in the Bible lacked faith or intelligence, since they were neither rich nor successful in human eyes, ending their careers in prison, murdered or in loneliness and poverty. To this must be added the vast majority of Christians throughout history and in the world today: poor, persecuted, sick, giving their best witness in the midst of hardship and suffering and not from opulence and well-being. How is it that no one told them about the discoveries of the prosperity theologians?

Pedro was converted to this new version of the gospel when he traveled to the United States in 1991, this time to a group of churches in California, with Nelson Torres. He was faced with a new world. While he had seen large churches and knew the numbers they handled, both in people and dollars, and had tuned in from time to time to a television program of some famous televangelists, he had done so out of curiosity, and not as a concrete possibility to use in his own church, as happened on this trip. He had seen big and very big churches; now he saw powerful and rich megachurches. With single service offerings of fifty thousand dollars or more. With thousands of members, with associated businesses. With pastors in expensive cars, private planes, dressed in designer clothes. Ministries with their own buildings and hundreds of employees. Christian TV channels that handled millions of dollars. At one point, alone in his hotel room, after a week's tour with Nelson, he realized he was looking at a gold mine. He also thought he saw that annoying and unwelcome red light.

When he returned from that trip, Pedro's messages changed dramatically, as did his dress, his car, his clothes, and Virginia's. They even moved to a bigger house in one of the best parts of San Isidro.

"God doesn't want us to be poor, that's a lie from the devil. If we think like poor people, we'll be poor. If we think rich, we'll be rich. Let's reject all negative thinking, let's reject the loser mentality. God wants us to be generous so that he can show that he can be ten, a hundred times more generous to us. Are we going to believe God or circumstances? What is the reality, what we see or what we believe?"

The moment of offering in the worship services, until now preceded by a simple presentation and followed by a prayer, came to occupy a central place of five to ten minutes in the meeting, "the most important moment of the worship service," according to Pedro. The preceding harangue included Bible passages that spoke of God's promises, suggestions that God rewards the generous, with occasional testimonies from people who told how God had prospered them after giving much money or effort.

The obsession with numbers appeared. Everyone knew about the attendance at the meetings, the baptisms they performed, the number of pastors they had— two assistant pastors, a youth pastor, a children's pastor— the money they handled, the annexes that were being opened by the central church. Pedro also skillfully handled all these figures in his meetings with other pastors, in radio interviews, in the Christian newspaper, and in his books. Growth statistics, percentages of active, waiting, and potential members, hours of travel, annual mileage, number of messages, square footage covered, everything was quantified. And the numbers shown were always increasing, compared to previous numbers and figures from other churches, evangelical and non-evangelical. The message was clear: God was blessing this place, and if you wanted to participate in the blessing, to be with the winners, this was the place.

Books and tapes began to appear of Pedro (Fear of Failure, Fear of Success, How to Rise Above Failure, Against the Spirit of Miserliness, Always Winners), of Pedro and Virginia (United to Boost our Success, Marriage as the Foundation of Prosperity, How to Avoid Infidelity), and of Virginia (Holding on to Success, Your Perfect Image, Never Again a Doormat), which were sold in the church bookstore and at the end of every service. They were also sold when they went to other churches or gave talks at conferences. It was a condition they always put, with the idea of giving people the opportunity to benefit and counteract so much negative material from the world that was on the loose. There was a New Church of Blessing magazine, a New Church of Blessing radio station, stickers, T-shirts, and even editions of the Bible with notes by Pedro and Virginia (the latter for women). They had hired an important advertising agency to design their penetration campaign for 1991, and they came up with the slogan "Up and Ahead," whose blue and red logo, a veritable explosion of optimism, went on to occupy all the previous material, as well as the walls of the main church and the various annexes, in Greater Buenos Aires and the rest of the country, with contacts established in Paraguay, Chile, Peru, Colombia, Guatemala and even Brazil, where it was called A Nova Igreja da Benção.

Even the hiring—yes, that was the name—of Pedro and Virginia, which had to be booked several months in advance, had a commercial tinge, and went through Pedro's very efficient secretary, Sara Oviedo.

"Good morning, Pastor Terrero's office."

"Yes, we would like to have a visit from the pastor at our church in Concordia, Entre Ríos."

"It will have to be after August. What kind of activity do you have in mind?"

"Well, we'd like him to speak to the men of the church. We listened to one of his tapes and thought it would be very useful."

"How many men would that be, and what kind of meeting?"

"The number? Well, usually there are twenty, twenty-five of us... It's a new group, but it's growing. Surely with the visit of the pastor, who is so well known, and with time, we can reach forty, or fifty."

"Forty... Actually, we are taking reservations starting with a hundred people, especially in the interior. The pastor is a very busy person, and he is receiving requests from all over, even from abroad, and it would be very difficult for him, it wouldn't be very productive, if you understand me, brother, if he were to set aside a whole day for only forty people. Surely the Lord will be able to provide another person who can take care of that ministry in this stage of growth."

"Look, sister..."

"Sara, Pastor Terrero's secretary."

"Sister Sara, I understand you, even though I may not share the... engagement policy of your church, or of the pastor. Surely you weren't always such a big church, you must have started with a small group, like us, and someone must have helped you. But we could make an effort to reach a larger attendance. We can take it as a challenge, talk to other churches in the area, invite businessmen, shopkeepers, professionals."

"Yes, I understand. As the pastor says, we appreciate what costs us something. We always have to set ourselves goals that are much higher than what we are used to achieve, because if not, they aren't goals."

"Of course, in 'Setting unattainable goals.' We loved it!"

"There's one more issue, closely related to goals."

"I'm all ears, Sara."

"What possibilities of offering would you have in mind? We don't charge for presentations, since it is a work for the Lord, of course. But we do have expenses. Keep in mind that in order to take this commitment, we leave another possibility aside, and there have been times we made a very great effort, rejecting more interesting possibilities, and received an offering that isn't in accordance with what the Lord expects."

"Look, our church is very generous, but we don't have resources to spare. We don't believe in forcing people to put up money; we believe that it is the work of the Holy Spirit, an intimate commitment of every believer with the Lord."

"I understand perfectly, but we must be practical. Can't you guarantee a minimum offering? We need a number for our spending plan. In our ministry we believe in order, planning, goals—without, of course, leaving the Spirit out—and then we evaluate each activity in all its aspects: spiritual, relational, and financial. I don't think it would be right to return from a trip to Concordia with an offering of, say, 10,000 Australes, do you?"

Pastor Verón, at the other end of the line, said a polite goodbye and breathed a sigh of relief. His wife was right: to invite these people, however successful they were, wasn't from God and they wouldn't be a blessing. He had many visits to make yet. The *matés* and cookies that the humble people shared with him were a delicacy from heaven, as well as their warmth and sincerity. That was something he could "guarantee."

Mercedes had noticed the changes in Pedro, especially in the way he treated Virginia, much colder and more distant, even in public.

"I ran into Virginia at church today. As always, she was busy, running back and forth, answering the phone. I had to take her by the arm and practically drag her out for coffee."

"Yes, on the one hand, I think they deserve what they have achieved, they are both very hard-working. But I don't envy their lifestyle," I answered, as I fed Melissa, our two-year-old daughter.

"Exactly. As soon as she sat down, I took her arm and asked her what was wrong with them, and she burst out crying inconsolably, in the middle of the bar! Since people began to look our way and many of them know Virginia, I asked them for a place upstairs and we went to have coffee there."

"Virginia, crying... and in public? You're kidding me..." It was hard for me to imagine it. I'd never seen her cry before.

"Yes, and they're getting along very badly... although on the outside they're the best couple in the world."

"If I were in a church meeting, I'd say it was an attack by the devil."

"The devil's attack my foot! The problem is they're never together; he is always travelling, from meeting to meeting, from conference to conference, in the municipality, on the radio, with F&G... And she holds the fort for him when he isn't there, because he doesn't trust anyone else. Apart from the women's ministry, the leaders' wives, the books with the publishers' deadlines, the book presentations..." Mercedes was building pressure with every word.

"It's like a machine that can't be stopped, and it's going faster and faster. I get the image of a whirlpool, which as you get closer to the middle, it spins faster, until there comes a moment where it is impossible to escape. Or a black hole..." My work in advertising had led me to think constantly in images.

"When she calmed down, I asked her if they had outings of their own, if they had any friends, if they could go on vacation."

"And what did she say?"

"She said no, that no one saw her as a person, not even Pedro, that she wished someone had taken her out by force before as I had done. That everyone respected her, treated her well, but no one knew the agony she was going through. And to top it all off, she had to pretend that everything was fine, she had to smile, speak well of her husband... and all that... stuff."

"What stuff?"

"Actually, she used a stronger word, completely unusual in the Virginia I know."

"Poor thing. If she said it, it's because she thinks it... and because she trusts you. Amazing! You see her so sure of herself, so confident, so well groomed. What they call a golden cage."

"She even told me she'd played with the idea of suicide, more than once. 'Don't tell anyone, please,' she asked me! She was a wreck, poor thing. And she told me that the kids ask about their dad, that they miss him, and he's always busy, always with others, always smiling... for others."

"And did she tell Pedro how she felt? Did they look for help?"

"You know what he told her? 'You have to be strong, because there are a lot of women who are looking at you. Reject that inner voice.' And he promised to go on vacation, and to leave Mondays free."

"That's good!"

"No, he's already promised her countless times, and he never delivers. What I proposed to her was to gather a group of her friends, which she would choose... three, four, to talk about anything, to pray, to support each other. You can't imagine the relief I saw in her eyes when I proposed something as simple as that. She immediately said to me, 'You, Camila and Sabri,' with a certainty that impressed me."

"Camila Reyes and Sabrina Maza? If they hardly come to church, they aren't on any commission, they hardly see each other."

"Exactly! She wants people who aren't in that environment, where she can feel comfortable. It's strange she included me, since I'm on the Women's Commission."

"Yes, but you're different. Like me. We don't trade our life for a position, a title. Besides, we've known each other for so long... And how would you feel about that group?"

"Great! I don't know Camila that well, but I've always had good vibes with her. And Sabri, you know how I get along with the little one. When we finished, I told her that I was happy to meet the Virginia I had known years ago and that she could count on me for anything, anytime. The hug she gave me! She almost smothered me."

With this information and concern, I tried to meet with Pedro. I called him several times, and Sara always answered and told me that she would take notes and notify the pastor. Finally, I caught him at the end of a meeting, when he was greeting people, and I practically pushed him aside and told him:

"Pedro, I have to talk to you... urgent!"

"Wait, what's wrong, Raúl? Don't you see I'm busy?"

"That's what I have to talk to you about. You're always busy, always with people. What about your friends, your family, your wife?" I was almost shouting at him.

When he saw my intensity and realized that people around us were watching, he said,

"Well, OK. Tomorrow morning at 7 a.m., in my office. Later, I can't; I'm busy all day." He gave me a forced hug and went back to the people who were waiting for him, with his plastic smile.

The meeting didn't go well. Pedro began by reproaching me for the scene I had made in front of the people at the end of the meeting. He told me that there were many people who were against the church and its ministry, waiting for an opportunity to find fault and thus throw away so much effort. According to him, I had no right to intrude in his private life, his friends, let alone his wife. He was much more upset when I asked him about his physical care, his excess weight, his hypertension, whether he was having medical checkups. I saw him irritated, upset, angry. So far from the image he carefully conveyed in his messages, his videos, his books and even the way he treated people who approached him. *That's why,* I thought, *he was so upset about yesterday. It was a crack in the perfect image that he had built with so much care.*

"Pedro, let me remind you of one thing. Then I'll leave you alone. Year 1980, SeBiPa..."

"Don't give me prehistory, please. We're reaching the year 2000."

"Class of Pastoral Life," I continued, unperturbed, "Professor Vega, 'The Pastor and the Accountability Group.' Do you remember? Just in case, I brought you a copy of the notes. If I'm not mistaken, many of the notes and the underlining are yours, from when we studied it together," and I handed him the twenty-page booklet.

Pedro took it and barely glanced at it, relieved that it was the end of the interview and he could now focus on the important things that lay ahead. We greeted each other and I went out into the street, where the day's activity was beginning. I had taken a load off my mind, but I was leaving with a much worse one, to be confirmed by the facts.

I resigned from the Pastoral Council, convinced that, increasingly, it was superfluous and even counterproductive, because it conveyed a false sense of a collegial body to which Pedro responded and consulted, when he had already ceased to fulfil both functions a long time ago. It met only when Pedro deemed it convenient, without an agenda, without time to deal with the important and necessary subjects. In reality, the time was spent in a report—always positive—of all that was being done, plus some subliminal messages about troublesome members. But Pedro didn't consult anyone or listen to anyone. His only circle of relationships was the group of wealthier families, who invited him to their homes, to their birthdays, their weddings, and whom he invited to his home. I found out that people had given it a name, the "VIP group," and I congratulated myself for never being part of it. They flattered him; he gave them his presence. At the same time, he had lost practically all contact with ordinary people, those who weren't in a position to invite him to their homes or to give him expensive gifts.

The hardest thing for me to accept was the handling of Casa de Esperanza's money. I never had problems accepting corruption or scams in business or government. I considered it a natural product of the inherent evil in certain people. But it was a big blow to me that someone could defraud or deceive using a noble cause, using the needy and the weak for personal gain. When I saw that many people who worked for AIDS, the sick, the homeless, the poor, did so only to benefit themselves, I found it hard to believe initially, and then I was repulsed. To know that there were Christian, evangelical organizations that did the same thing was beyond me. The straw that broke the camel's back was to suspect and then confirm that a work of our church, in which I was part of the commission, along with Mercedes, was doing this. Fortunately, I couldn't be accused of not having given the warning, and I withdrew from the commission and Mercedes from the administration as soon as we heard about the shady mechanism.

It worked like this. Casa de Esperanza was supported by churches in the United States and by the municipality. We found out how much was coming in from the churches and acknowledged the donations promptly. It was never clear how much the municipality was contributing because officials said it was coming from a social support account that didn't require a punctilious accountability. In short, neither source of income had transparent accounting, and all the money passed through Pedro's hands. This arrangement, which was to be transitory until the Casa de Esperanza Foundation was created, continued indefinitely. What both sources of income insistently demanded were photos and testimonies, which appeared in the reports of the municipality and in the missions departments of the churches in the north.

The work was carried out. The children and mothers were fed and attended school support classes and workshops. But there was always the lingering impression that not all the money reached the recipients, that the number of people on the payroll was excessive, including a cousin of Pedro's and a friend of Virginia who, to make matters worse, showed up very little at Casa de Esperanza. The comments of the people of the neighborhood and some of the church mentioned terms like *curro*,[39] *avivada*,[40] *tragada*[41] and *ñoqui*,[42] which I had never heard associated with evangelicals, considered in my time and those of my parents as honest and transparent. It was hard for me to finally accept that the people were right, that the money wasn't only for the needy, and that the municipality was complicit by action, the churches in the United States by omission or ignorance, and I had helped to unwittingly set up a scam that stained the name of the church and its Lord.

---

[39] Rip-off

[40] Con job

[41] Grab

[42] Person who has a job but hardly or never turns up to work

7

THE MISTAKES WE MADE

We took the wrong turns, blundered a little
People were hurt as we went through the thistles

Juan and Mariela felt it was time to look for a church where they could meet and where they could be spiritually nourished, apart from their work at Pan de Vida. Also, the twins, who were already six years old, were going to need a place to grow up in a Christian environment, learn the Bible and have Christian friends. When there were children involved, things were very different. They felt like they were passing the baton in a relay race. They felt it in their work with people, too. They were a link in the long history of people who had kept the flame of faith alive, many at the cost of great suffering, pain, persecution, and death. And they felt they were fulfilling that historic commitment. But what about the children? What about the syndrome of the pastor's son? Why did many pastors fail to keep their children in the faith, and many ended up denying it? How could they avoid that tremendous pain? Their desire for the twins was that they love the Lord, love the church, and love the people. They had the responsibility to teach them many things, but their greatest responsibility was to provide them an example to follow.

They had gone to visit Christ the King Church several times, some ten blocks from Pan de Vida, close to the Quilmes Atlético Club stadium. It was a church of working people, many from the textile factory, many self-employed, construction workers, salesmen, with a couple of doctors who worked in the local hospital. The pastor, Bedros Samarián—whom many called Pedro—was a large, bearded man with a Santa Claus look. He had been a shopkeeper for many years before becoming a pastor, so he knew firsthand many of the problems his faithful brought to him, including suffering for his favorite soccer team, San Lorenzo. While Juan and Mariela wouldn't have chosen the church or the pastor for its theological rigor—Juan had a hard time placing Bedros in a specific position, since what he said one Sunday might logically contradict what he had said the previous Sunday, and no one seemed to care—it was a place where they felt very comfortable, part of a big family. The problem was precisely that they were a big family. Something they learned as time went on. Almost every time they talked with or about someone, they found they were related to someone else in the church.

"You have to be careful when you talk here," Juan found himself saying several times when potentially embarrassing situations arose. "Everyone is related to everyone else." Curiously, people didn't laugh so much, as if implying that it was normal for there to be so many family relationships in a church. The pastor's brother, Samuel, was the Treasurer. The one who replaced the pastor when he wasn't there, and who gave all the impression of being his successor, was his son, Eduardo. The choir director, Manuel, was another son of Bedros, and the choir itself reflected the church's mosaic of relationships: of its thirty members, only three weren't related to any other member of the choir. The Sunday School Director was Elisa, Bedros's wife.

But they had a very good Sunday School. The children were divided by age, from the Cradle Class, through Kindergarten, the three classes in which the primary students were divided, the youth class and the adult class. Everything took place on Sunday morning, leaving Juan and Mariela free in the afternoon to go to Pan de Vida. Pastor Samarián knew the work and had come several times, and the people received him with great joy. He was a typical neighborhood man, and when they called him "Turk" he pretended to be angry with them for giving him the nickname of the people who had decimated his ancestors, the Armenian people, at the beginning of the century.

That church was the place where they saw the most miracles. The whole atmosphere was impregnated with faith. The children, the adults, even the visitors perceived something different that led them to believe. In the services it was common to have prayer for healing, and although not everyone was healed, Juan saw before his own eyes how a paralytic began to walk, a deaf woman began to hear and a medically documented cancer disappeared completely. Pastor Samarián had the gift of healing, but he didn't make too much of it; it was as a natural part of his preaching and his pastoral work. There was also a group of brothers dedicated to the liberation of demons. Many people came with serious problems that were diagnosed as demonic possession. After a time of prayer and asking some questions, if it was considered that they might be facing a case of oppression or demonic possession, the person was taken to a room specially prepared for this purpose, where a group of people prayed for them, sometimes for minutes, sometimes for hours, struggling with the devil and demons. The results, in many cases, were astonishing: people who came in alienated, with hardened faces and defiant look, left exuding peace and joy.

Juan and Mariela went there for a couple of years, creating bonds and friendships, working in different areas of the church. Juan taught in the adult class, and Mariela attended the Cradle Class. But everything changed drastically when Yamila, the pastor's niece and Samuel's daughter, became pregnant. It was a tremendous blow, for several reasons. On the one hand, Pastor Samarián, and the church, had a very firm attitude toward holiness, which they considered essential to the church's power and ability to confront all the spiritual and other pressures of the world. Premarital and extramarital relationships, of course, were condemned. It was an issue that was addressed from the pulpit and in the youth meetings. But the second factor was critical: the way people found out, or rather, the way the pregnancy was concealed. The third, fatal factor was how the problem was dealt with once it was known.

It all started in the strangest way. Mariela was in the neighborhood butcher shop, and there were two women chatting.

"What an outrage, the young people of today! Did you see that the janitor's daughter got pregnant? Fifteen years old! We saw her grow up..."

"Really? And she's going to have it? Because now the girls get pregnant and they take it out, like a pimple. It wasn't like that in our time."

"I don't know if it wasn't like that. Besides, we've heard about these, but how many of them are there that even the parents don't know about..." Here the older one lowered her voice, which made Mariela more interested in what she was going to say and made her prick her ears. She was hoping that the butcher wouldn't call her at that moment. "They told me that Yamila is a bit large too."

"The pastor's niece?" in a whisper that was louder than a scream. "I can't believe it!"

"Chola told me because her daughter is a schoolmate. There you go... with such insistence against sex, look what they get."

"Twenty-two!" The butcher's call put an end to the situation, and Mariela tried to pretend she hadn't heard anything. But inside she was devastated.

She walked home, stunned by the news. Maybe it was old women's gossip, and it wouldn't be true. Although the news of teenage pregnancies kept hitting her and she had seen so many cases at the Pan de Vida center, the thought of sweet Yami, who had received good teaching, who had been surrounded by good influences, pregnant, losing much of her adolescence and youth from a moment of madness... didn't enter her head.

As soon as she got home, she poured out her anxiety on Juan, who had come to lunch that day.

"Yami, pregnant? But was she dating, was she seeing someone?"

"She'd been dating a classmate lately. But how can we know if it's true?"

The confirmation came very soon. Mariela was called to the front to pray for the people who came after the message the next Sunday, and it was her turn to pray for Yamila's friend, Nuria, who wouldn't stop crying. When she asked her what was wrong, she just said, between sobs, "It's because of Yami, Yami... I don't know what can happen to her, what she's going to do. I'm afraid she'll do something crazy... pray for her, Mariela." She tried to find out discreetly what was happening to Yamila but realized she couldn't go any further. She ended up hugging Nuria and giving her strength with a biblical passage that came to her mind at that moment. But she also got confirmation through Sister Azucena, from bigmouth Juan Zóttoli, and especially from the sudden absence of Yamila herself.

Juan decided to find out directly. He arranged to meet Bedros Samarián for coffee at the corner bar the next day. The pastor preferred that place to the church office for almost everything, since he said that Jesus had no office, no secretary, and he talked to people at their place of work.

"Bedros, you know why I came to talk to you, don't you?"

"Yes, you want to ask me about Yami, about everything that's being said."

"You know that I, we, never liked rumors, gossip. We prefer to go up front. Is it true that Yamila is pregnant?" Bedros had given him the cue for the difficult question.

Suddenly the pastor began to shake with silent sobs that came from the depths of his heart. In a few moments, Juan thought he saw years of struggle for a cause destroyed like lightning. He felt an immense sorrow and sympathy for this good man, who suddenly seemed ten years older.

"Forgive me, Juan," he managed to say. "Forgive me, it takes me so by surprise... I never thought anything like this could happen to us. It's a nightmare..."

"Bedros, I can't say I understand you, but all I can say is that you can count on us, Mariela and I, you and Elisa, for this moment."

"The worst thing... what hurts the most..." It was very strange to see this man at loss for words. "Do you know that the other day Yamila came to me and said that people were suggesting that she get rid of it?"

"To abort?"

....

"Well, they convinced her not to, didn't they?"

"Yes, but we took the blow. How could she even think of doing such an outrage? Now comes a very difficult stage... very hard. Can you tell me where we failed? What did we do wrong?" It wasn't just a lament; it was a sincere request.

"Look, no one can assure the future. You can be the best father, the best pastor, the best person, and your children, your grandchildren have the right to make their own mistakes."

They chatted for almost an hour. On any subject. About soccer, the last World Cup and Maradona's disqualification, President Menem, house arrangements, things they'd both like to do when they retired. The only thing they didn't touch on that last part was the church. They said farewell with a long hug and the usual promise of meeting at some indefinite moment.

"We'll keep in touch."

"Sure. I'll take your word for it."

It all started out as an innocent game. A glance, a joke, moved on to phrases, words and gestures that went beyond that. Pedro could never say that he didn't have opportunities to stop it or that he lacked advice or warnings. It was even a subject of constant discussion among pastors since the time of the Seminary, and in these years, he had seen one after another great and not so great men of God fall into the clutches of sex and infidelity. Old Tremonti, a great international preacher, tangled up with his secretary. Norberto Valdés, a famous Christian singer, with a member of his church's worship team. Oscar Queijedo, a prestigious Christian businessman, member of every committee that ever existed and of his church in Polvorines for fifty years, led a double life, with two families. Could anyone today honestly say they were surprised when something like this happened? Could any pastor say, with his hand on his heart, that it was only the devil who led these men to throw overboard a life of testimony, leaving hundreds of members so shaken and disillusioned that many would swear never to set foot in a church again?

"Hey, Pedro, watch out with the secretary. Look, you wouldn't be the first..." Pastor Seveso, of the Association of Evangelical Pastors.

"I don't think that's the way a pastor's secretary should dress..." Overheard.

"What do you mean, he went on a trip with Sara?" Mariela to Raúl.

"A round of applause for the pastor with the best secretary..." A comment out of place, but suggestive in a meeting of pastors.

Sara Oviedo was a more attractive than pretty girl, and much better dressed than charming, who had appeared in the church when they rented the big shed, just as the "1984 x 10" initiative began. She came from the province of Tucumán, with the intention of studying. From the day she arrived she had attracted attention, with her brightly colored dresses, impeccably in style. Virginia had detected her before meeting her, and she had never liked her. With a woman's instinct, she put her thumb down the first time Pedro suggested her for the position of secretary, when he jokingly accused her of being jealous. But when Ana, the secretary they had hired, became ill with cancer and had to cut back on her workload, the position no longer allowed delays, and Sara was the only one who answered the ad placed on the church bulletin board. Virginia budged this time out of need, but also because since she spent much time in church, she thought she would be able to control this mysterious girl.

But it wasn't like that. Pedro spent more and more time at the office, and less and less time at home. Sara also increasingly took over all the administrative aspects of the church, to the point that practically everything had to pass through her hands. She knew where the information was, the contacts, who was who. Although she occupied a secondary position in the structure, she was the unseen hand of the church, monopolizing increasingly institutional power, as well as the heart and will of the pastor.

"Sara, can you call Pastor Ovejero? I want to see if he can come and preach on Sunday the 28th. I asked Virginia, but she's busy that week."

"Ovejero? Don't you remember what he wrote in Profiles magazine? He's very legalistic..."

"Ah, well. See if Fleitas is in Buenos Aires. People like his style... What, you don't like him? Let's see..." with a smile of complicity. "I'm beginning to recognize your faces."

"Fleitas isn't an important pastor, I mean for this church. I'm sure he'd come, but I think we need someone of a higher level." Her soft voice and penetrating gaze worked wonders with Pedro, and he always ended up giving in.

"Careful, this isn't a business, as I am constantly accused. If they heard you, they would misunderstand. Let's see, who does my *tucumanita* recommend?" She smiled back at him seductively.

"Oh, pastor, don't say that... I only want the best for you. I don't want you to be hurt, I don't like to see you suffer. That's why I'm trying to take care of you."

Pedro had opened a door he couldn't close. If there was one weakness in his psychic structure, especially at this time, it was the need for recognition from those who loved him most: his wife, his friends. They were always reproaching him for his excessive activity, his attitude, his way of preaching, his organization, everything. On the other hand, this simple and pretty girl—Sara had lowered her eyes to give him enough time to watch her at ease—understood him more than all of them. She took care of him, helped him in his work in the church, she was capable, silent. And mysterious. Suddenly, he realized that what attracted him most was what he didn't know about her, and the seductive smile of a few moments ago indicated that he had much to discover in this creature.

"So?"

"I would try to get Corredes."

"The evangelist? I'm sure he's busy, or on a trip..."

"I already checked. He's in Buenos Aires, and on the 28th he's free. I just spoke to his wife, Rita."

"Well..." He was amazed, grateful, confused. "Then, yes, call him. It would be tremendous if he came."

"And he owes you a big favor, too, from the Congress."

"Of course, it was nice to help them on their trip..."

And then it happened. Without thinking, without paying attention to the red light that flashed desperately, he said it:

"Do you want to go for a coffee? You're going to be late, and I can take you home after."

Something in Sara's eyes screamed that she wasn't surprised by this invitation. Pedro was already blinded.

"I'd say not around here, so no one can thing badly," he said with a nervous laugh. "We can go further out, maybe at the Cuzco bar, closer to your place. What do you say?"

That night it was no more than an outing, a couple of coffees and a pleasant chat, with much guilt. It wouldn't be the only one, always in Cuzco, where Pedro had made sure no one he knew went. But it wouldn't stop there.

In September 1998, a church group attended a leadership conference in Mar del Plata, and Sara went as secretary to Pastor Pedro Terrero, one of the stars of the event. She was indispensable to help him with all the material, to organize his contacts and his interviews, so that he could concentrate on the messages. Virginia, who couldn't go, didn't object because they were in a group, with several ministry leaders, youth, and several members.

One night they had to stay late working on the notes of the final message of the congress, in the room that the hotel had prepared for the convenience of the speakers. The rest of the group had gone out to dinner with people from the church and others who used to attend this kind of event. Sara had been invited by her childhood friend Teresa, who had come from Tucumán. They hadn't seen each other in five years and had crossed paths several times in the past few days.

"So, are you coming?"

"No, we have to work with the pastor on tomorrow's message, the closing of the conference."

"Come on, let him finish it. That's what he's a pastor for."

"What happens is that it's an important message, and he has to organize the notes and the outlines they ask him for."

"Stop messing around, Sarita. Hey, there isn't something going on between you two, is there?"

Sweet little Sarita glared at her with a look that froze her. She'd never seen her like that before.

"Well, it was just a joke. I wanted to tell you about Aldo and me, about Chelita, like we did in Tucumán."

"Forgive me, Tere, but seriously, we're... I'm very busy and this message is important. It's the closure, they'll all be attending. Besides, it's about the life of the leader, and you know how the enemy wants the message to go wrong, the attacks he makes against the Lord's servants."

"Sure. Well, I'll see you tomorrow." Tere said goodbye with a kiss, and she couldn't help noticing the rich smell of perfume.

That night they worked hard from ten to half past one in the morning. At first there was a group of about fifteen people, who slowly thinned out until only the two of them were left. When the time came to finish, he accompanied her to her room. There was nothing to justify the hurried kiss on her mouth, but it happened.

Someone smiled contentedly. It was the desired point of no return.

Nicolás's last study was on sex in cults, and he was in the midst of researching the material he planned to incorporate into his next, as yet untitled, book. What had prompted him to do this work was that he saw that in practically all cults and closed groups it was an important issue. A subject that was repressed or exacerbated, but hardly occupied a balanced place. Abstinence, sexual abuse, group sex, child and adolescent prostitution, sexual symbols, perversions. He had asked himself why, and hadn't yet found a satisfactory answer, especially considering that many of these groups were radical protests against defects in the "system" or the "world" that restricted freedom and happiness. In these groups one would supposedly have to find the solution to a distorted view of sex, rather than the aberrations he had seen.

"On the one hand, you have the priests, who don't marry. Are you going to tell me that they don't feel the same things that you and I do?" Nicolás had once told me.

"Of course, but there's such a thing as celibacy and the vow of chastity." Although it was hard for me to understand, I knew it existed. The Apostle Paul himself had practiced it and recommended it.

"But how can they give opinions and advice on things they don't experience: marriage, sex life, birth control, parenting. It seems crazy to me. Pastors and rabbis at least get married and speak from experience. Besides, they can't say what they want because there's the wife, the kids, what people see. When you speak from theory it's much easier," Nicolás insisted.

"Yes, I totally agree, and I agree with you that the subject is difficult, within the churches, in the sects, in the relationship of the churches with society. But why does the subject of sex always appear in regard to cults?"

"It seems to me that it is one more form of domination. For example, in cults that say that having relations with the leader purifies them or brings them closer to God, the one in control is the leader. Also, if the leader, or the cult, is the one who sets the sexual rules, which are usually different from those outside, from society, then they also have the control. They are the ones who say what is right and what is wrong."

"In cults, what is forbidden outside is approved and encouraged inside," I thought aloud.

"Or what is approved outside is forbidden inside," added Nicolás.

"But they find another world of rules... and those who impose the rules are the ones with the control, as you said," I said.

"In churches, evangelical or Catholic, there are usually stricter rules than society, so to progress in these groups those who best follow these self-imposed rules are rewarded," said Nicolás, making notes to be used in his book.

"Or imposed by the Bible," I wasn't going to give in on this.

"Every church imposes its own interpretation of the Bible. The others are wrong." Nicolás was partly right, but he also had his particular interpretation of the Bible— which parts he liked and which he didn't.

"Now, tell me one thing." I was interested in his opinion on this. "Nowadays there seems to be a struggle between free sex, at a younger and younger age, and the restrictions which most Christian churches place on it, basically abstinence, chastity until marriage. Would you say that the secular solution is superior to the religious one, when you see pregnant teenagers and abortions?" I wanted to take it to the practical level, to the real consequences of so much free experimentation.

"I believe that you win on the one hand, with greater freedom and sincerity, and you lose on the other, with the practical consequences of greater freedom without responsibility," he answered.

"And always with the weight of the consequences on the woman, on her body or on her life. Don't you think from that side that the argument of free sex doesn't hold water?" It was clear to me that the consequences weren't the same for the man and the woman.

"Maybe... Maybe. If the damage were to be graduated, it would be first the child, who didn't choose to be born as an 'accident'..."

"Or is killed in an abortion..." I added.

"Yes..." Nicolas thought and wrote, meditating on every word, "then the woman, who could lose her adolescence, her possibility of studying or getting a good job... then perhaps the girl's parents would come, who instead of making life as grandparents make life as parents... and then the man, who can continue his life without major modifications... Does the order seem right to you?" looking at me.

"Yes, that's a bit what I think..." I had one more topic. "What about all the cases of sexual abuse by priests that are appearing all over the world?"

"It seems to me to be indicative of a serious problem which can't be solved unless the present restrictions are changed. Incidentally, the cases of pastors who have had similar charges should be reviewed. The problem is that if anyone in a position of authority feels or perceives that they can do whatever they want, there is no limit to the evil they can do. And if when something happens, the institution covers it up instead of bringing the truth to light, worse. The same goes for governments. Democracy is the control of the desire for absolute power that every human being, every system carries." The relationship between politics and religion had always fascinated Nicolás.

"You say that the way to limit sexual and other abuse is to have a system of control, a system that is basically saying, 'We know that we are all fragile, that we can all sin, so we all need a system that controls us, so that we don't do the evil that we can do, or at least to limit it?'"

"That's right. Without control, without limits, there will always be abuse, of one kind or another."

Juan would have liked to be able to say that after his talk with Pastor Samarián things took a positive turn, but they didn't. Despite having opened up with him on that occasion, he perceived that Bedros avoided him or brought up the subject of soccer as soon as they started talking. Juan even thought about calling him by phone, but he realized it would come to nothing.

Mariela couldn't get Elisa, Bedros' wife, to say anything either, even though she gave her several cues.

"Yesterday Juan met Bedros. He loved the talk..."

"Yes, Bedros loves Juan very much. How are your things, Mariela?" *Stay out of it, we're fine.*

On the other hand, the way in which the pregnancy of a person so closely related to the pastor was handled, in a church with a clearly family structure, couldn't have been worse. Initially, the decision was made to say nothing and to take the girl out of the picture. Later, in response to insistent questions, it was said that she was visiting family in Santa Fe, which only underlined what was an open secret. The boy—the alleged father—was never seen again and disappeared forever. The young people also failed to get any information from the other young people who were part of the large extended family. There seemed to be a gigantic and efficient pact of silence.

What made it worse was that there had been a couple of extra-marital pregnancies during the last year that were treated very differently. The first, a nineteen year old girl, a Sunday School teacher for a couple of years, was removed from her position, had to have a meeting with the pastor, the Sunday School director and her parents, and it was publicly announced that she couldn't continue to teach because of ethical problems. The second pregnancy was of a twenty-three-year-old girl who came from a humble home and had come to the church through the Pan de Vida lunchroom and became pregnant a couple of months before her marriage. Although she could have concealed it, she chose to announce it, ashamed and repentant, but was immediately removed from the church choir, the reason being announced in the group. In none of the cases were the girls related to the family that ran the church.

So, when this incident occurred, the jurisprudence indicated that there would be a public announcement and a suspension of the position in the church's musical group, where Yamila played the piano. None of this happened, and when the pastor's niece came back a month later as if nothing had happened and took her place in the group again, many screamed blue murder. Pastor Samarián and everyone in the family denied all the pregnancy rumors, unaware or perhaps not interested that everyone knew what had happened, compounded by the inevitable conclusion that the "solution" had been through something so strongly and repeatedly denounced from the pulpit as murder and the worst of deaths.

Anyone who had followed up on the issues addressed by the pastor would have seen a clear shift toward less controversial issues, avoiding abortion and sexual issues altogether, and a greater emphasis on issues of forgiveness, grace and understanding. The pastor no longer shouted so much and gestured much less. When people began to leave the church, slowly at first and then more quickly, he did little to stop the bleeding, as if he knew it was the price to pay for what he had done, what he had failed to do, or what he had left undone. In his conversations with those closest to him, he wouldn't cease to reproach his niece for the harm she had done to his ministry, his family, and the church, even though in his innermost self he knew that she wasn't the only one to blame. During the long sleepless nights he spent after the incident he was constantly haunted by the image of the baby sacrificed on the altar of appearances.

Yamila wasn't the same since the incident either, and after fulfilling her assigned role in the play she had helped write, she ended up leaving that church and never stepped foot in that or any other church again. They say she married a nice kid, an "unbeliever" and went to live in Germany, but they couldn't have children of their own and adopted two beautiful babies. The family never saw her again, she never answered their calls or letters, and when she visited Buenos Aires, they all stayed with her husband's family in Longchamps.

The chink in Pedro's armor got even bigger when he discovered the world of hotel pornography. Oddly enough, it only happened after he let his guard down with Sara. Until then, watching TV in his hotel room when he traveled abroad was limited to news, sports, and the occasional local show or well-known series, either at the end of the day, before bed, or early in the morning, before he went downstairs for breakfast. But now there were channels with clearly pornographic content that were interrupted after five minutes, with the option of signing up to watch more and the convenience of being able to pay for it on the bill when you left. Travel was becoming more and more frequent now, spending between sixty and ninety days a year away from home, half of which were abroad, in first-class hotels. When he discovered this, he was limited to the five free minutes, because even if he wanted to make use of the rest, the detail would appear on the bill, which was paid by the churches or organizations that invited him. But then he found that he could pay this item separately, and no one would notice the little slip-up. After all, it was a way of looking at what people in the world were doing, and it wasn't doing anyone any harm. And it would be just this once. Well, once again. By the time he realized it, he had become addicted to pornography, consuming it in airports, where no one could see him.

Pedro's messages were also changing, from an emphasis on personal effort and self-responsibility in the face of life's situations of failure and success, to an extreme determinism where everything was preordained by God and salvation was something impossible to lose. The sermons constantly spoke of forgiveness, of grace, of the goodness of God, and he often broke down while preaching. For many, the pastor had become more sensitive, less harsh. But in reality, he was one more example of accommodating doctrine to personal convenience, and also of the silent struggle he was having inside.

Then the accident happened.

Pedro was driving Sara back from church late in the day when it occurred to him to make a detour along the river so they could be alone. He was worried because Virginia was suspicious of their relationship and had demanded that he fire the secretary, and he didn't know how to tell Sara. He didn't really want to. He didn't dare to imagine himself without her and that not so innocent game of seduction and fantasy. He parked the car by the curb. Sara noticed he wasn't well.

"What's wrong with you, Pedro?" Pedro was always worried that this way she addressed him would come out when they were in public.

He put his arm around her shoulder and kissed her lightly on the forehead, in preparation for what would be difficult news to convey. Just then he saw the lights of an electric blue car shining on them from the opposite lane. There was no doubt about it. It was the car of Pastor Jiménez, one of those who had warned him about this relationship and that Pedro had strongly denied. When he saw it slow down in the rearview mirror, he panicked. He started the engine and accelerated abruptly, without seeing the cyclist coming through the blind spot in the side mirror. The simultaneous crash and scream seemed to come from his worst nightmares.

"What's the matter with you! You've gone mad!" Sara's desperate cries seemed unreal.

"Get down!"

"Aren't you going to stop? He's lying on the street!"

"Someone will help him. Now we must get out of here, fast."

"You're crazy! We can't leave him like this! Stop the car, I'm getting out!"

"Don't you realize they saw us?"

"What do you mean, they saw us? Who saw us? If we weren't doing anything..."

"Jiménez! In the blue car. I'm sure he saw us. And now this. I can't stay..." And then in another tone, amidst tears of helplessness, "You've got to help me, Sara! Don't you realize what can happen? Don't you realize?"

The car picked up speed along the promenade and drove into the dark as soon as it could leave the road. In silence, they both knew it was the end. So absorbed were they in what this incident meant to them that they forgot about the cyclist who had been run over. Pedro was thinking about Pastor Jiménez, whether it would be his car, whether he would have seen them, whether it might have been only an impression, who would be in the car, how he would face him the next time he saw him, the consequences for his ministry, what Virginia would think. Sara was certain that she could no longer be the church secretary. In fact, she already suspected what Pedro wanted to tell her before the incident. But she wasn't going to go out and look for work like some random person.

"I'm not leaving, Pedro," she said resolutely.

"What?" He had no idea what she meant, so absorbed was he in his thoughts. Suddenly he looked at her and understood. He chose to play along. "I don't understand. What are you not leaving?"

"You were going to tell me to leave the church. I know your wife doesn't like me. She blames me for everything, but I only tried to help you."

For Pedro, everything was more than he could handle in such a short time. The interrupted talk, the encounter with Jiménez, a man run over, and now this challenge from Sara.

"Look, I have a lot on my plate now, but since you brought it up, you're going to have to leave... You know how much I lo... appreciate you, how much I value your work, your loyalty... but this can't go on. Look what you've achieved!"

"Take me home now. You're ungrateful, worse than any other man! Pastor... you're pitiful! And I warn you... tomorrow I'll be in the office as usual."

"Are you defying me?" It was amazing how quickly a beautiful relationship can deteriorate.

"No, I'm informing you that I won't be used. I know all my rights. I've already spoken to my lawyer and you can't just kick me out. Besides, pastor" —the final blow, with the informal address already put aside, was devastating— "you don't want people to know about tonight, do you?"

The slap he gave her didn't seem to come from his hand, but from some force, someone, who had him under control and wanted to make sure there wasn't a shred left of a relationship that had meant so much to him.

After that 7:00 a.m. talk, I never spoke to Pedro again. Mercedes started meeting with the group of girls and Virginia. They did it on Wednesday afternoons, when the kids were at school. They took turns carrying *facturas*, sandwiches, a cake. They drank *maté*, tea or coffee and talked about their things, ending in a time of prayer. At first, this time was a single, brief prayer when everyone had to leave, but it was extended later to take up almost half of the time, with all of them praying, first in a round and then freely and spontaneously. They also incorporated a Bible reflection at the beginning, and each of them in turn used this to prepare the spirit of the meeting and give some order and purpose to their shared time. The meeting went from an hour every two weeks to two hours a week, such was the need they had and the benefit they derived from it. And this was happening with the four of them. Although they had initially been called to support Virginia, the others began to open up and show the areas of their lives that needed the support of a friend, in word, action and prayer. Camila was suffering a lot because they couldn't have children, and Sabrina was carrying a problem of loneliness from her adolescence that hadn't been solved by her marriage.

Virginia changed dramatically. In fact, for those of us who had known her for a long time, she was back to her old self. She started laughing at simple things, sharing everyday news and gossip, letting herself be seen for who she was. She got off the pedestal on which Pedro had put her for purely selfish reasons. At least for that little group, she stopped being "the pastor" to become "la Virgi" again. But she also changed her role in the church, when she was on the platform or when she led the women's groups. Or when she replaced Pedro on his travels.

"*Pastora*, I see you more...more..." said a woman at the end of a service where Virginia preached.

"Oh, come on, Doña Clara, tell me."

"I see you more... human... more like us..."

Virginia laughed heartily and hugged the lovely old lady.

"And that's good or bad?"

"It's good, it's good! You don't know how I'm praying for you two, and for the kids."

When they had built enough trust, and when Pedro's problem couldn't be avoided in the group and in the church, it came out, first as an undefined prayer topic for her husband, "Girls, I need you to pray for Pedro. He's going through a lot of pressure," then a more specific request for both of them, "We need prayer. We're having a hard time getting along, and we can't stop," ending with a desperate cry for help, in the face of the reality of what everybody knew—the relationship of the pastor with the secretary. That day the four of them were there. They had had a coffee and a piece of cake that Mercedes had brought, and Sabrina had a reading and a reflection on Psalm 23.

"Girls, I'm a shamble. I don't know what to do," in between sobs. They all knew what she meant. But she had to take the initial, courageous step of telling them.

"Tell us, Virgi." Mercedes took her by the hand and squeezed it tightly.

"I never thought this would happen... that I would have to tell you this... It's so difficult... I'm so ashamed..." Suddenly she pulled herself together, took strength from deep inside, with the determination we had always admired, looked at the three of them one by one and said, in a sure and slow voice:

"I think something is going on between Pedro and Sara. Besides, I think everyone suspects it. You are my friends; you are the only people I can share this with."

The three friends kept silent for several minutes. They sensed that the air had been purified, that the burden of one was being shared by all, that they were closer than ever. The silence was healing, the silent tears of each one were cleansing the pain. Any word, the best, the wisest, the most comforting, would have interrupted the process. Suddenly, Sabrina, the toughest, got up from her chair in front of Virginia, hugged her tightly and returned to her seat. Mercedes kept squeezing her hand. Camila didn't say anything but kept on praying silently.

Then, as if someone had given the order, they started talking from another place, one of protection, of her and the kids. Here the "witness" was irrelevant, the ministry, the church, what people would say. These three lionesses were going to fight to protect the wounded lioness, and no one was going to stop them.

"I'm going to tell Raúl to talk to Pedro. He can't do this to you," said Mercedes.

"Did you confront him?" said Camila.

"Yes, but he says that there's nothing in it, that I'm jealous, that I don't understand the pressures, that there are always people who are envious and who talk just for the sake of talking."

"And who else could you talk to? Is there a body that runs the church, a council, anything?" Sabrina asked innocently.

"I wish. There was a time ago, but it never worked. Pedro always said he wouldn't let red tape hold him back, that he wouldn't waste time on reports, on meetings, when there was so much to do. That he didn't want to feel tied down. And I supported him at the time..."

"Yes, Raúl was on that Pastoral Council and realized that it was useless. Well, it was just to say that there was a council," said Mercedes.

"And doesn't Pedro have a reference pastor? Isn't there anyone that he consults, that he asks advice from?" Sabrina, again.

"No, he's been alone for years. He was always self-sufficient, but when he left the Seminary we had learned to work as a team, to have people of reference. But lately he's been getting more and more lonely..." The confession that followed seemed to cost her a lot. "Actually, it was Sara who filled that role, and I feel guilty, because I saw it coming and, in a moment, I let my guard down. And then I let her occupy more and more space..."

"Do you think that...?" Camila was saying what everyone, the whole church, thought.

"I don't know if anything happened, but for me it's over. He's never lied to me before, never looked away from me. And I've never had to feel the shame of people's looks before. I was always proud of what we had built, and, in a way, I wanted us to be a model for others to see. Especially after the disasters we saw in our parents' generation, who kept together out of obligation, because of the testimony, but without love, without passion, without spark."

"Did you consult a lawyer?" Mercedes always saw further than the others.

"What for?" Virginia showed that the idea hadn't even crossed her mind.

"Do you realize that if this doesn't get fixed, you could be out on the street, out of work, and with the kids? Besides, it's the way to show him that you're not stupid and make him think about the consequences of his little game."

"I don't know, it goes against everything we teach, that things have to be fixed inside the church. At least we should try, before going to court, with lawyers and judges."

"Yes, but if it were a church with some kind of structure, one that defended the people, not a painted cardboard shell to support the pastor," Camila said.

"The pastors," said Virginia, "I am also to blame. But it's really a lead lifesaver. Look at this case... We are so protected, so high up, so unreachable, that no one can help us... except you girls," with a faded smile. "What's more, many people must think that we don't have problems, or that when we do, an angel comes from heaven and solves them..."

What she said was true. And the pastors knew it. They believed the fiction the church bought about their life. What's more, they were constantly feeding it, putting themselves on a higher level than mortals, spiritualizing everything, surrounding themselves only with other pastors, always giving advice, never receiving any.

"The kids, how are they?" Sabrina asked.

"Of course, they don't know anything. But the other day Valeria said to me, 'Mommy, why are you fighting so much? Doesn't Daddy love you?' It broke my heart."

"So you're arguing. Is it because of the *tucumana*?" asked Sabrina.

"We never really talk about her, although Pedro knows how I feel about her. I told him the first time he proposed her as a secretary. Actually, I think we talk about anything to avoid touching on the subject, and she's present without being present... I don't know if you understand me."

"Give us an example."

"Yesterday, for example, I was late for the parents' meeting at Roque's school... he's terrible, aggressive, answering back... Pedro never went to a parents' meeting, but here the teacher called us personally, and he had no choice but to go... He's always busy, traveling, in meetings... He's a pastor, so how can he go to a parents' meeting? That's a woman's thing... Well, I was late, and he was there and treated me badly in front of everyone. When we got home, he let it all out, that he had cancelled a pastor's meeting, that this and that. Of course, I knew or suspected that he had in reality taken time away from Sara. Since I didn't tell him, he assumed I assumed, and took a defensive attitude. He told me that he was tired of me questioning him and that I didn't value the effort he was making, that I could accommodate my schedule, but he had many obligations, and that he would never again suspend an activity because of a stupid parents' meeting... You can imagine I went crazy there."

"And with good reason... But I think it's your fault as pastors, and our fault on this side, that we want you to be perfect, we demand that everything is fine and we don't want to know that you have problems. Perhaps because then we would have to do something, and we are comfortable, or we are afraid that you will reject us... That you will say to us: 'How darest thou interfere in this our palace of bliss and superior spirituality, you mere mortals, with all your inadequacies and failings? We have direct contact higher up. Do you not see that we are much closer than you? Go, forsooth, make haste.'"

Camila's exaggerated voice impression and words made everyone laugh, but it also transmitted the message with much more power. It was the real feeling in the church and in the relationship between the pastors and their "sheep," in this and most other churches we knew.

"You have to get a job now," advised Camila.

"Of course. I'll introduce myself and say, 'Good afternoon, I'm here for the job.' 'Yes, what experience do you have?' 'I've been a pastor for fifteen years, no, actually, I'm a pastor's wife.' 'Sure, of course, fill out the form and you have the job. It's yours. Everyone wants to have pastors or pastor's wives in their companies. How much do you want to earn?'" Virginia was also good at saying things with humor. As Pedro had been. As they had been together... "Sorry, girls, but I don't see it."

"Forgive me for meddling... maybe it's not the best time... But, this girl, the secretary..." It was Camila.

"Sara." Virginia forced the name out.

"Yes, Sara, does she belong to any group, any... what do you call it? Cell, boat..."

"Island."

"Island! You've already noticed how little I go to church. Well, who's pastoring her? Does she have any friends? Is there anyone you can talk to?" Camila, always thinking of flesh and blood people, real problems and situations.

They looked at each other, surprised by the obviousness of the questions. Of course, they had thought about Pedro, about Virginia, and no one had considered this girl from the interior. Why was she doing what she did? Was she the culprit or a victim? If she was doing something wrong, did anyone at least tell her? If she wasn't, who would protect her?

"To me she was always a very lonely, quiet, mysterious girl," said Virginia. "I think it's that quality that makes her more... seductive. But the truth is, I never worried that she had no support, that she was on her own... that no one was pastoring her. Oh, God, how much of this is my fault! I'm so stupid!" She held her head with her hands and began to walk around the room with a desperate gesture.

"No, Virgi. In any case, we're all guilty of not taking care of you. Look, I'll do this. I offer to talk to Sara. Once, when I was in church and saw her, I got a mental impression of who she was, what kind of life she'd had. I think it was from the Lord, but I'd like to confirm it with her. Will you let me?"

"Yes, talk to her if you like. But don't ask me to love her, to forgive her... Thank you, Cami. I love you so much. I love you all very much."

After the pregnancy incident, Juan and Mercedes tried to stay at Christ the King Church, but they found it impossible. The climate had changed, and the spiritual power had diminished significantly. The miracles and signs practically disappeared, and it became a more conservative church in all respects. Gone was the open and free attitude that had attracted them so much. Now you had to be careful what you said. Instead of taking advantage of the crisis to renew the leadership, the pastor dug deeper into the family, and the few who remained and didn't belong to the family chose to leave.

Juan and Mariela took an interest in those who had left because of this crisis, calling them and meeting with them.

The talk with Vicente Rauch was characteristic of others he had had when they left Pueblo Santo and many more he would have in the future with people who had to leave the church because of problems or mistakes of the leaders. The pattern repeated itself invariably.

"It's been a few months since we've seen you at church. Is something wrong?" Juan asked.

"There are several things. I'm not going to lie to you. But the last straw was the pastor's niece. You know how much I love Bedros. He seems like a great guy to me. He helped me and Adriana a lot. We had him home tons of times. Our kids were raised with his kids."

"But?"

"Look, the family thing always existed. If you weren't family, you were second rate. All you had left was for one of your kids to marry one of them. Like royalty. But I didn't mind that so much. What drives us crazy is that they say one thing from the pulpit and do another when they get off. There's one law for insiders and one for outsiders. Then we want to teach everybody ethics, and we point out the mistakes..."

"What can I say? You know what I think."

"Yes, that's why I'm opening up to you. Besides, when you're inside and you work, and you put up money for construction, for the pastor's salary, for missionary trips, you're a hero. The day you leave, 'slam, bang, thank you, ma'am'"

"Nobody called you?"

"You're the first."

"None of the leaders?"

"Oh, yes, now I remember. The other day Clara, the secretary, called me to ask if I had the key to the kitchen cabinet. Can you believe it? Three months without showing up, I could have died three times, and all they care about is a stupid key."

"And Clara didn't ask you anything?"

"Nothing, and she's always the first to talk about those who leave. I heard quite a thrashing when the Restrepo's left. She went at them ruthlessly. Yes, the pastor was wrong, the leaders too, but neither did any of who worked with us, those who helped, those who shared prayer meetings, vigils, retreats... It's twenty years, Juan! Twenty years! I feel used..."

"Disposable..." He said it without realizing it, but it was the first image that came to Juan's mind: a used plastic cup, a spare part.

"Precisely, disposable."

"And what are you going to do now? It's hard to imagine you outside a church, staying at home..."

"Yes, it was a very strange feeling to be home on Sundays. But we took the opportunity to talk, to walk around. We realized that we had done many things just for the sake of it, thinking that we were doing it for the Lord."

"Something similar happened to us too when we left the previous church. But then we began to miss it all, and we found this church. We knew it wasn't perfect, that it wasn't exactly what we were looking for. It was hard for us to fit in at first, to know the people, the customs. Now that we've fit in, this happens. To make matters worse, the people we love, the ones who have worked the hardest, the most valuable, like you, leave..." It was Juan's greatest pain when there were ruptures.

"Of course, those who don't think, the lazy ones, the pastor's kiss-ups... the relatives, stay. They cover everything up. To make matters worse, they criticize those who leave. Or they ignore them completely. The other day, I met Sammy Santillán— *Sammy*! —at the supermarket. First he pretended not to see me, and I was going to play along, but I said to myself, 'No, if I didn't do anything, I did nothing wrong to anyone,' and I went to say hi. Three months had passed without seeing us! Before, we used to see each other every week in church, we talked, we played soccer, we organized a thousand youth camps... It was as if I were the plague."

"You tell me this and, on the one hand, I find it hard to believe. On the other hand, I'm not surprised. It's a strange way churches operate..."

"And the pastors, c'mon! People are like that because that's what they put into them. All they care for is there little kingdom, their work." Vicente was obviously very hurt.

"Yes and no. Remember the phrase 'the people get the governments they deserve'? Here I think it's the same thing. The people have the pastors they deserve, or something like that. I mean, for there to be a pastor Bedros, there must be people who like a pastor like that."

"And the one who doesn't like him, should leave, right?"

"That's the worst part, I think. The unwritten message that's all over the walls, is, 'If you don't like it, leave.'"

"And the pastor always gets off well, no matter what he does."

Juan spoke, by phone and in person, to about five people or couples who had left because of the pregnancy incident. The pattern he found was systematic and constant: lack of interest on the part of the pastor and the rest of the church members in those who were leaving, feelings of abandonment and of having been used by them, disillusionment with the relationships of years in the church, lack of protection from injustices or things done incorrectly, and lack of accountability on the part of the pastors.

Having gone through that situation themselves, he wondered how many cases like these would be repeating throughout the evangelical world. Was it just a situation in the churches he had attended, was it a problem of some churches only, or was it a trait, a generalized defect, characteristic of "being evangelical"? If it happened only in some churches, why in those churches and not in others? He also wondered if someone was doing something for these people who were suspended between a church they had just left and a mass of churches from which they would have to find one, praying that the recent experience wouldn't repeat itself. Would it be a concern of the pastors, of some pastors? If not—as seemed to be the case—shouldn't someone do something to put an end to the bleeding and protect those who simply didn't fit into a specific church at some point, but kept alive the desire to serve and the need for Christian fellowship? He made a mental note to look at the issue at some point.

The cyclist had no major injuries, although his bike was wrecked. But for Pedro the uncertainty was much worse than reality. He had nightmares several nights in which the vividly saw the man's bruised and broken body with several witnesses shouting "Murderer, coward!" one of whom wrote down the number of his car's license plate. In an improved version, a woman shouted, "It's Pastor Terrero!"

The worst one included the phrase, "and he's with his lover, the secretary!" The other idea that constantly haunted him was the possibility that someone had seen who had run over the cyclist, and that at any moment they would call him to tell him that they had seen everything. Perhaps they had picked up the man and accompanied him to file the complaint. Or he had become a quadriplegic and the family would be making a multimillion-dollar lawsuit against the church, as happened with that worker who fell while working on the construction of Grace Church last January. Now the congregation had been left on the street because they had to sell the building to pay for the lawsuit. He found himself perspiring thick drops, and panting.

Finally he used his political influence to find out if any cyclist had made a complaint on the night of the incident or the following week, and they replied no, that it had been a quiet night, with no accidents or complaints.

The other nightmare he had, no longer asleep but awake, all day, was what the occupants of Pastor Jiménez's car would have seen and thought. Was it really the pastor's, or was it similar? And why did he slow down when he passed him? Or did he think it was slowing down? Was he going crazy?

It was funny how he found out his fantasies were unfounded. A week later there was a pastors' convention he couldn't miss since he was one of the speakers. He assumed he'd meet Jiménez, and he did.

"Hi, Pedro, what are you going to delight us with today?" Jiménez said with a smile. Then, addressing the man who was with him, he added: "This man is the most motivating pastor I have ever met. You listen to him and you just want to start off and run over anybody who crosses your path..."

A chill ran down his back. Was the figure chosen a hint or a coincidence?

"Yes, of course," grinning nervously. Was another stab on its way?

"Thanks to a message I heard on one of your cassettes a couple of months ago, I think it was called 'If you don't want to change...'"

"If you don't want to change, you won't."

"That one! Well, as I was saying, thanks to that tape I sold the truck and the car, I set up a pizzeria, and now I have the whole family working, plus a couple of brothers from church..."

"What? You sold the electric blue car... you sold it? When? Who did you sell it to?"

"Yes. Why, did you want it?"

"No, no. To whom? When?"

"Actually, I gave it in part payment to the owner of the pizzeria, a couple of months ago."

"A couple of months... How wonderful!"

Pedro felt like shouting 'Hallelujah! Praise the Lord!' but someone would suspect it would be too much of an expression of joy in relation to a simple business transaction.

Two out of three. Two favorable—the cyclist and Jiménez— one to go. But the third would be a headache for a long time. Sweet Sarita, the efficient, silent platonic lover, became a monster, also silent. After all, she felt cheated, scorned. As promised, she showed up at nine o'clock the next day in her office and started to work nonchalantly. Anyone observing the situation from the outside would say "Another day at the New Church of Blessing." When Pedro arrived at ten o'clock, he had a very unpleasant feeling. There was the girl who had always given him one more reason to get out of bed and face the problems and challenges of the pastorate. The one who always understood and listened to him. The one who didn't ask him too many questions. The one who arranged his schedule, always looking after the last detail, so that he could devote himself to what he knew best and wanted to do—preach and teach. It seemed to him that this time she had dressed more attractively than ever, and the familiar perfume could be felt from the entrance. She received him with a cold look and he barely managed to stammer:

"Good... day... Sara."

"Good morning, Pastor." Yes, words could be even colder.

He went quickly to his office and closed the door, as if he were being chased. He didn't even ask for his usual morning coffee, an excellent excuse to exchange the first words with Sara. He laid the unopened briefcase on the floor and collapsed on the leather chair.

As he dozed off, he relived nightmares and feelings, doubts, and fears, in a chaotic way.

"What were you doing with that girl in the car, alone? How many times did you go out together? Did you sleep with her? I want a divorce! Everybody's going to know! I'm going to get you, you scoundrel!" Virginia's fuzzy image screamed at him what his conscience had tried to tell him repeatedly.

"So, pastor, huh? How nice! They're just like us, only more hypocritical, and more repressed. The worst thing is that they stay halfway there, they don't even dare to do it." In his nightmare, a classmate from high school had mysteriously appeared, Skinny Miguens, who had a negative concept of all religious people, but especially of the "evangelists." These were the exact words he had said to him years before.

"What a disappointment for the family! What are our friends, the pastors, the people we know going to think? Don't just stand there! Try to reduce the damage, try to talk to Virginia, before she makes a scandal. Don't let that country girl ruin you. All they care about is money, and she took advantage of you." His parents, with their fixation with image, their practical approach to problems, their poorly disguised discrimination.

"It's not that bad. It happens every day. Too bad you lost Sara. But did you see how nice it is to have a little friend? Find another one, you can't say you're innocent anymore. You've already crossed the line. Have fun. Don't let them run your life. You have the right to enjoy..." He was the most talkative, the one who seemed most pleased. He seemed to come from far and near. From outside and from inside. Sometimes he didn't seem so bad to him. He understood him very well.

The buzzing of the intercom woke him up. He pulled himself together and said, in a serious voice:

"Yes, go ahead."

"Pastor, Dr. Zavalía is on line two. He wants to talk to you." Sara said.

"Who's Dr. Zavalía? Does he have an appointment?"

"He's my lawyer. Shall I put him through?"

His voice was shaking so much when he started talking to the man, that he asked him:

"Do you feel all right, Pastor?"

They arranged a meeting outside the church, between Pedro and Sara's lawyer, that same afternoon. Pedro attended, expecting the worst, some legal gimmick that would demand an exorbitant amount of money or blackmail. But the meeting was peaceful. Dr. José María Zavalía, who was a practicing Catholic, told him about the things they were doing in his parish, a visit he had made to Rome, to Saint Peter's Square, the importance of Christian ethics, how we should stand out from the prevailing corruption. On the one hand, as time passed Pedro relaxed, as he had expected a much tougher meeting. He assumed that the best part, the reason for the meeting, would be at the end of it all, when they said goodbye, like Columbo. And it was a bit like that.

"Well, pastor, it was a great pleasure to meet you and see how many things we share as Christians. Miss Oviedo has told me a lot about you and your work, and how she would like to continue working with you for many more years. Between you and me"—with a very studied accomplice attitude, after all he was a labor lawyer— "she could do with a raise, let's say, twenty percent, don't you think? Especially after the little... incident... last night. I understand there won't be any problem. It was so fortunate that no one else got hurt. I also checked on the cyclist, a man named Gervasio Solanas. He only had a couple of scratches, and he was riding without lights. There were no witnesses, so rest assured. Oh... and the blue car stopped because they were going to a house on that block.

"That's OK, Doctor. There won't be any problem and thank you for your interest."

On the way back to the office, he felt relieved, manipulated, violated, thrashed, like he'd never felt before in his life. It was a perfect lesson in how to destroy somebody with elegance, and he knew he deserved every bit of it.

Camila went to greet Sara at the end of the next Sunday service. She noticed that she no longer sat in one of the first rows and found it difficult to spot her among the attendance of five hundred people. But there she was, with her red dress and her raven black hair tied back. She also had dark glasses, like those people wear so they can't see their face, or to hide the fact that she had been crying. She never stayed to chat with the people in the next room, where coffee and soft drinks and cookies were served, but waited a few minutes to see if the pastor had any urgent needs, and then she would head for the door and disappear into the city. It was as if in the service she wasn't just another member of the community, but was still the pastor's secretary, fulfilling her duties.

"Sara? Hi. My name is Camila Reyes. We've never greeted each other... It's always so crowded."

"Ah, hi, Camila. I was just leaving." She still had that beautiful Tucumán accent.

She had never seen her so close up, as a simple person. She was always the secretary, the one who took the calls, who got stuff. And now she was the baddie in the movie, the "home wrecker," the social climber. But standing there, a meter away, Camila's sensitive heart and the Spirit within her perceived a tremendous loneliness and sadness, which clearly came from her childhood. It was similar to what she had felt the first time she saw her. The impact was so strong that Camila had to make a superhuman effort not to cry and embrace her.

"I was leaving too. If you want, I'll go with you. I have my car outside, and I don't have a boyfriend waiting for me," with a smile, which immediately brought another smile in Sara. The ice was broken. She could see how someone like Pedro could be attracted to and reassured by such a... profound person.

"Well, I'm going to Lugano."

"That's fine for me. Let's go. My car is the black Taunus. A bit old, but it takes me and brings me back."

They became friends. In reality, Camila became the first and only friend Sara had had since she arrived in Buenos Aires six years ago. Sara's house was very roughly on her way home—she actually had to make a detour of about fifteen minutes, but it was worth it—so they went back and forth from church together. As they got to know each other, she met a very smart and capable girl. Her dream was to be a biochemist, but she had had a hard time adjusting the first few years, and now she lacked someone to push her, to stimulate her. Although she had a tendency to shut herself off and didn't dislike loneliness, she had made efforts to integrate into the church, but she had always been seen more as a secretary than as a regular young girl who needed to have a group of friends, have a good time and fall in love.

One day, as they were returning from an evening service at the church where a Uruguayan missionary had spoken and motivated them a lot, talking about life's wounds and the possibility of healing them in the Lord, she felt encouraged to ask her:

"Sara, can I ask you a question?"

"Certainly, Cami. What are you going to ask me? If I like Adrián?" She already had issues of her age.

"No. But, by the way, do you like him?"

"A little, he reminds me of a friend from Tucumán. The jokes he makes."

"Look, you know I have a special sensitivity that the Lord gave me for people. It's a gift I know I have to use more to help people."

"How I envy you! I have a hard time understanding people..."

"Don't envy me. Sometimes it becomes almost a burden, because it is as if I feel the pain of the other person... It happened to me, the first time I greeted you, on the way out of the church."

"With me? And what did you feel? Something bad?"

"Maybe I'm wrong, but I don't think so. The Lord showed me that you were carrying a pain, an ugly experience from childhood, when you were five, four years old, no more."

Sara looked at her with eyes wide open. It seemed to Camila that a cloud began to rise from her face.

"Let's talk about it at home. We'll order a pizza and I'll tell you about it."

They continued the trip talking about the meeting, arrived, ordered the pizza and a couple of beers, and when they were finishing eating Sara shared a heartbreaking story of rejection in pregnancy, abuse and rape by her stepfather and how she was rescued by her uncles. She didn't shed a single tear, but every word she said, every word Camila heard, was bringing her out of the torment of silence into a shared pain.

From then on, she added other friendships and activities. She joined the church's youth group and signed up to start studying biochemistry. She began dating Adrián and started working in a pharmaceutical company. Over time, she left for another church.

8

THE PAIN WE SUFFERED

The bruises we carry hurt more every day
And the stabs in the back refuse to go away

Wednesday, March 15, 2000. The rally, which had been growing steadily during the afternoon, was already massive at 7 p.m., a hot and humid afternoon. Thousands upon thousands of people, young and old, families, with their flags, banners, and songs, filled the River Plate stadium and its surroundings. Evangelical Convocation had gathered half a million people, according to the organizers, one hundred thousand according to the police, fifty thousand according to one of the newspapers. For many, quantity seemed to be the most important thing.

"Evangelical Convocation, representing five million evangelicals, as we start this new millennium, is seriously concerned about the events in the country, the corruption in the government, the family crisis, the problem of youth and the lack of values," the voice of Pastor Bernardo Quijada, President of the United Argentine Evangelical Association and one of the main leaders of EC, sounded from the microphone of the platform that had been erected in the center of the stadium. "This massive gathering is a response to the lack of hope of a society that has turned its back on God!"

To the right of Pastor Quijada was Pastor Pedro Terrero, who would have the closing words of the rally. It would be one of the key moments of his life, when he would be heard by hundreds of thousands of evangelicals, would appear in the main media of the country, and his words would be transcribed in many national and international evangelical media, and also in several secular media. He certainly fit the profile for such an important event. A skillful speaker, he knew how to capture the interest of audiences of all kinds with a well-structured speech sprinkled with anecdotes and examples. He had also learned all the tricks to keep the audience's attention. He would raise and lower his voice, in intensity and tone. He made dramatic silences. He used rhetorical questions frequently. He liked to take the microphone off the stand and walk around. In addition, he had been taught, and he had incorporated into his way of being, that when it was a public event, when there were cameras present, to do everything thinking about how he would appear on television, the most important and cruelest medium.

"I have the great pleasure of introducing our main speaker on this glorious afternoon, Pastor Pedro Terrero, whom you all know. Pedro is a personal friend and he is the pastor of one of the fastest growing churches not only in Buenos Aires, not only in Argentina, not only in Latin America, but I would dare to say in the whole world!" A round of applause crowned Quijada's enthusiastic and exaggerated phrase.

"Thank you very much, Bernardo, all the glory be to God!" Pedro got into the role immediately. "Today is a historic day for Argentina. Half a million of us evangelicals have decided to take to the streets to say 'Enough!' No more corruption, no more lies, no more using people only for the votes! We are an army ready to put an end to years of economic stagnation, a product of the moral deterioration of the leaders, who should set an example!"

He had already warmed up, and with the microphone in hand he was heading to the right side of the stage, when the crowd froze. The speaker stumbled and lay inelegantly on the floor, while a couple of youths from the brass band came running up. Barely seconds passed before he stood up again, trying to resume his speech, like a knocked-out boxer who wants to continue fighting. But Pastor Quijada had already taken the microphone and, with great professionalism, addressed the audience, while looking at the corner where Pedro had been deposited on his seat.

"We see that Pastor Terrero has had a problem, probably due to the heat. I suggest that we pray for him... There, I am told that he is better, he is recovering well, thank God."

Quijada led a brief prayer for the health of Pastor Pedro. Suddenly, without anyone telling him, don Ramiro Huarte, an old and admired evangelist who was seated on the platform with ten other pastors, went up to the microphone decidedly and improvised a powerful message, quite different from the one that Pedro had begun to outline. He began by opening his old worn-out leather Bible in a passage that was marked with a bookmark, and read, in a slow and heartfelt voice, marking each phrase, repeating the words to give greater emphasis:

"If my people... my people... upon whom my name is invoked, shall humble themselves, and pray, and seek my face, and turn from their wicked ways... from their evil ways..."; *then*"—he shouted the word and left a dramatic silence, repeating it again in a much lower pitch—- "then... I will hear from heaven, and will forgive their sins, and will heal their land."[43]

What happened next has no logical explanation. First, the silence left by the evangelist from the pulpit was followed by another awesome, stunned silence from the whole crowd. It was as if there was a wordless message that everyone wanted to hear, and no one should interrupt with a single sound. Then, there rose a spontaneous applause, first timid and then increasingly loud. If ever there was a beautiful applause, it was on this occasion. It wasn't to celebrate some artist, nor was it the domino effect that usually occurs in large groups. It was something that emerged from the bowels of that group, functioning as one body and that had recognized in those words something superior, something powerful. Something authentic. Something they needed.

The applause faded to make way for another silence. This time it was the expectation of what the evangelist would continue to say. Even Pedro, sitting now on a chair below the stage, partially recovered physically but beaten up mentally and in his pride, was looking mesmerized at the place he had just left not by his own will.

---

[43] 2Ch 7:14

"We are the Lord's people. But we are not *all* the Lord's people. There are many who couldn't come. There are many who didn't want to come. But they are just as much a people as we are here." The short phrases, clearly pronounced, separated by silences, had an impressive effect. "There are brothers and sisters in other Christian groups. We believe in the same God. The same Jesus. The same hope. The same struggles. The same mistakes. Same persecution. So let us think of all the true Christians in Argentina, who believe in the Lord and follow His Word."

The applause wasn't as loud as before. An observer might interpret it as they were digesting what the speaker was saying. Was he talking about the Catholics? The man didn't seem to care much.

"We're part of another people, too. The Argentinean people. And we participate in everything. Its successes and mistakes. Its cowardice. Its comforts. Its 'Stay out of it'. Its pride. We are no better. We are not apart." Many already realized that what he was saying wasn't a continuation of the initial aborted message, but quite the opposite. A couple of people sitting on the stage began to look at each other nervously. One could read what they were thinking, *Where was Huarte heading?* "We are not better because we are evangelicals. Because we go to an evangelical church. Or because we are evangelical pastors. We will be closer to God's will, and we will be salt and light of this dear land, only... only... *only* if we fulfill the passage I just read. Let's read it again. First Chronicles, chapter 7, verse 14." He finished reading, closed the Bible, and sat down again. A couple of songs and announcements later, the rally ended, but few would forget for some time the last ten dramatic minutes they had witnessed and shared.

Juan and Mariela received an invitation to pastor the Church of the Open Word in the Núñez neighborhood, so they left Christ the King Church for good and moved into a house near the new church, only five blocks from where Juan lived before he got married. It was a relief to have an assigned destination, because even though they had already made the decision to leave, they didn't want to be adrift again or to be wandering through different churches in search of the best option.

The contact was through the SeBiPa, and when the invitation came, they realized that it would be the first opportunity for Juan to carry out the function of pastor, with a salary and a house. None of the benefits were substantial, and it didn't allow them to think of going full time. Perhaps, if the church grew and had a higher income, it would be possible.

Juan kept his main clients from his work as a mechanic, although he tried to organize himself to have his afternoons free, starting at four o'clock, for the work of the church. When the opportunity appeared, they were both excited, and when Juan was shown his office, with its library of Bible commentaries and reference books, many postponed dreams came to mind. He hadn't looked for it, but he knew it was what he wanted.

In the room next door, two men and a woman were waiting for him. Brother Francisco Gómez was the oldest and most senior member of the church. He had been there for forty years and had known all the pastors who had come to the church. Brother Antonio Cervantes, a Spaniard who still had a Spanish accent, was the one with the most theological knowledge. They said he was a good preacher, with a strong emphasis on doctrine; on maintaining it, rather than developing it. Sister Ángela Otranto, a widow, was Antonio's sister. A woman of strong character and straightforward. She said what had to be said, did what had to be done.

"We are very pleased to have you with us, Pastor Juan," said Antonio.

"Yes, it's a pleasure for me too, a challenge, to be able to work in this church of so many years. Fifty already?"

"Fifty-six, in October," said Francisco.

"You have a wife and three children, Pastor, don't you?" said Ángela.

"That's right. My wife's name is Mariela. And we have two twins, Mateo and Marcos. Like the gospels. And the little girl we adopted, Celeste." *Somewhat stiff*, thought Juan. *We'll have to work on this.*

197

"Well, they must have explained to you how this church works. We have the annual assembly, the Council, which is the three of us, and Brother Armando Vanone, who couldn't come today."

"Do you have anything in writing?" Juan asked.

"What should be in writing?" replied Francisco.

"The way the church works. The declaration of faith."

"We aren't one of those formal, bureaucratic churches. Here we are guided by what the Bible says. It's that simple."

"Of course, but it usually helps to have things in writing... so there's no confusion or misunderstanding..." *Change the subject right away,* he thought. "Well, it's not critical, it's just ways to work."

Despite the cold reception, Juan was excited. Even knowing that it was a church considered "difficult" or a "pastor-eater" in the scene and that its structure, history, and way of being were very different from all the church experiences they had had until then, he took it as a challenge. A challenge sent by the Lord. He thought that in church, just as in the secular world, you didn't do only what you liked. You only grew when you overcame barriers and went into new territory. Comfort never taught anything and only led to accumulating fat. Furthermore, he was convinced that the search for a deeper spiritual life didn't necessarily have to occur in churches that were open to the work of the Spirit. Why not think that God could use them to infuse life into a rigid and closed church? This seemed to be the case. Not because it had no activity. Quite the contrary. Juan found himself with an impeccable schedule, organization, program, church bulletin, hymnal and songbook, punctuality, and strict financial accountability. The ideal of foresight and order, except for the organization of the church and the creed, curiously enough. He had already been warned to forget about trying to change anything there.

"The Open Word Church? Don't even think about it!" Mariela had said when Juan mentioned the possibility. It was the last place she wanted to go. "A pastor there lasts no more than a year. And they are so rigid and cold."

"I know," he said. He didn't like to argue with Mariela, especially when he knew she was right. "But I don't think we have to be guided by the past or by what people say. Why not think that we can change things? Why not think that the Spirit can renew dead structures? Remember Ezekiel's valley of dry bones."

"I don't know, you know I'm not going to be intimidated if that's where the Lord wants us to be. But is it so? Couldn't it be your desire to be a pastor?" with her usual insight.

"Maybe, I don't deny it. But I also think that by now we have enough experience and maturity to face difficult people. In fact, I believe that you can melt the hardest hearts with love, giving them time and affection. Showing that you love them, that not everything has to be in one way."

When he came home from the initial presentation, he didn't hide anything from Mariela. He told her the details and his impression, which could only be negative, from a human point of view. But he also shared with her the fire he felt at the possibility of working as a pastor and being able to touch lives, inside and outside the church, from that position. After all, that was what he had studied for, even though he still lacked the practical knowledge of pastoral work. It would also be an opportunity to avoid many mistakes he had seen in pastors and leaders they had had, especially the desire or need to manipulate people in one way or another. Or to perpetuate himself forever. Or to make distinctions. He was going to show them that with respect and dialogue everyone could win. He had no desire to change or destroy all the good they had as their best asset. What he was going to propose to them, explicitly or implicitly, was that on a foundation of order a structure of spontaneity and dynamism could be built that would be unbeatable in the fight against darkness.

Mariela couldn't help but be infected by Juan's enthusiasm. This is how they both worked. One encouraged the other, and both bore the consequences of their joint decisions. So after a week of prayer and talks they decided to accept the post and Juan became the new pastor of the Church of the Open Word on his birthday, September 17, 1995.

Mariela tried to work among the women, at their weekly Wednesday afternoon meeting. But it was a very independent women's group in a denomination that gave women full participation, so she found herself in the uncomfortable situation that no one expected her to do anything. Unlike other denominations, the pastor's wife had no special status; she was just one of the crowd. But she didn't mind much, because she thought she could lend a hand with the young people. The group was led by a forty-five-year-old "young man," a bachelor who had held that position since time immemorial, when he was really young. There, too, she didn't feel needed or welcome. She thought of helping at the Sunday School, where she had quite a lot of experience, but found that the director, Sister Hortensia Vélez, wasn't going to let anyone come up with new ideas, after twenty-two years of seeing how "one hundred and forty-two boys and girls had passed through the School and had learned to know and study the Bible."

Juan, even though he was the pastor, found himself in a similar situation. It was as if he were simply filling a vacancy, a position that had its job definition stipulated by years of use. He remembered that tragicomic phrase he had heard in the Seminary: "There are churches that, if one day the Spirit decided to withdraw, no one would notice, and everything would work exactly the same." Here it seemed that not only would they not miss the Spirit, but also the pastor. But Juan was a man of faith, a man of prayer, a man of action. And, if others had failed, he would look for ways to avoid the curse that that church seemed to have, not because he was better, but because he would learn from the mistakes of the past.

"So there have been several changes of pastors in recent years, I see." In their effort to get to know the members, they had made it a point to invite several key couples to dinner and chat informally at their home one day a week. Mariela loved preparing special meals and hosting people, so that part was covered and helped Juan a lot to break the ice.

"Yes, unfortunately the pastors who came couldn't adapt to our church, to our way of being. I admit we are something special, but it is not for nothing that we have remained more than fifty years without losing people, even with some increase in membership." Don

Francisco shared this unlikely statistic while enjoying his cannelloni, as was his wife, Doña Clara.

"But, if I am not mistaken, don Francisco, there were six pastors in ten years?"

"Seven, if we count the American... Johnson."

"And where was the mistake, in the selection, in the adaptation... the theology?"

"It's very simple. I could say, if I wasn't a believer, that we were unlucky. Carreras, who spent almost a year, didn't know how to preach, and didn't visit people. López..."

"No, then came Jiménez, the young man..." corrected his wife.

"Yes, Jiménez. Well, he wanted to run us over, with all his ideas from the seminary. He lasted four months. Then came, yes, López. A seminary professor. An eminence. He knew Greek, Latin, Hebrew... church history... everything. The church was filled with intellectuals, but he didn't go out to evangelize. He didn't want to change and left after a year and a half.

"Remember Valenti, Pancho," said Clara, without taking her gaze and the fork off the food.

"Valenti had problems with everyone in the Council. He wanted to write a rule and a declaration of faith, and we didn't agree. One day he decided to leave without warning."

"Just like that?"

"Yes, we heard about it from the neighbors. You realize that we have had to deal with difficult people..."

"It seems so. Let's hope we're not difficult too," half joking, half as a wish.

"Sure. Well, we were with Valenti. Then Rosas, a very messy guy. Very nice people with his wife Viviana. They were the best. But he was into the renovation, he spoke in tongues, he brought a lot of new songs, and we didn't want to have anything to do with that weird stuff." Juan felt that the last phrase was meant for him. *Don't you dare bring any weird stuff in here.*

"Then Johnson came."

"The American."

"Yes, the American. He didn't speak Spanish well, he dressed funny. He was here one year, I think. And then we went a couple of years without a pastor, until now, when you came."

Pedro's incident in front of the evangelical crowd marked a turning point in his public life, just as the incident with Sara marked his private life. They both pursued him for years and appeared often in his nightmares. Looking back, he realized that it had been a mistake to agree giving that speech under those conditions, just a month after the other episode. Raúl had been dead right, after all. That month had been a nightmare for him. How would he tell Virginia what had happened? Should he tell her? What if she found out some other way? What if Sara took it upon herself to let her know? He tried countless times to imagine how he would tell his wife—knowing that it was the right thing to do—and he came out in a bad way. What would he say, that he had gone out to make things right with Sara? "What things?" she would say. And if he said he was going to fire her, she would say, "Why didn't you tell me? Did you have to do it at night in your car? Couldn't you do it in the office, in the daytime?" There was no way out. It was like choosing to die by hanging, the electric chair or with a firing squad.

Suddenly he had felt the overwhelming need to talk to someone other than Virginia. A friend, someone who would listen to him and not give him professional advice, but an opinion, something. To tell him at least, "What an idiot you were! Do you realize you could lose a lot more than you've lost so far? Don't be stupid, talk to Virginia! Now!" But he realized he had no one. Ah, of course he always boasted about his great "friends," the important characters he showed as the figurines he collected when he was a child, especially the hardest to get. "Johnny Sookes? A great friend... Tell him I send you. We spent some great days with the *yankee* the last time I traveled to Miami" or "Zacarías is a great guy! Ask him if he remembers what we ate at the convention in Rosario" or "Mejías—the mayor— owes me several favors, so tell him from me, from Pastor Pedro, to ease the pressure." And he knew that he too would be a "figurine" in these men's pockets. "Pedro Terrero? We're close. Tell him I send you. Call here and Sarita, the secretary, will attend you. Let me know anything you need, but he'll give you a hand."

But none of these "friends" would serve him now... because, in fact, they weren't friends. He didn't have a single friend! And, the only friend who really knew him and loved him for who he was, Virginia, he had cheated. He thought of the church's VIP group, with whom he had shared barbecues, birthdays, and year-ends, and realized that none of them, not one of them, could help him in this, the worst time of her life. Osvaldo was very good, very generous, but also very superficial spiritually. He always congratulated him on his messages, always agreed with everything he said and did, but he had no spiritual life of his own. Sergio and Sonia lived for money and prestige. Mariano was a worldly guy, who had simply found in the church, and in this group specifically, his social nucleus. He had felt no need to sever his ties with dubious acquaintances. He played both sides. And then there was Héctor and Nadia, and the Suárez Rosas'... They were just an interest group, a band of people interested in supporting each other to achieve their goals, but without any real friendship.

He remembered how Raúl had come up in his mind after the accident with Sara and how he had relived in ten seconds every detail of their last talk, at seven o'clock in the morning, how he had gotten rid of him, and how he had congratulated himself on his handling of the situation, his determination and his efficiency! Suddenly, he had remembered that the Bible had some phrases about friendship... yes, in Proverbs. He searched in the Concordance, under "friend," ran through several quotations and stopped at one: Proverbs 27:6. He desperately opened the Bible on his desk and read: "Faithful are the wounds from a friend, but the kisses of an enemy are deceitful."[44] He ran to the library, looked up another version, and read: "Wounds from a friend can be trusted, but an enemy multiplies kisses."[45] He

---

[44] KJV
[45] NIV

took the Jerusalem Bible, a Catholic version, and looked up the same passage: "Trustworthy are blows from a friend, deceitful are kisses from a foe." Of course! It was all the other way round! The people who told him everything was fine, the people who rubbed his back, were not his friends. And the only one who had taken a risk for him and had endured his mistreatment, that was his friend! He was his only friend! Or maybe he had already lost him... Maybe the difference between Raúl and Mercedes and the others was that they didn't expect anything in return. They were simply interested in him and Virginia being well.

He remembered that phone call at 9 p.m.

"¿Hello? With Raúl, please."

"¿Pedro?"

"Mercedes?" He had recognized her when she answered from the other end of the line, but he hadn't dared to identify himself. "How are you? You still have a good ear."

"How can I not recognize you, Pedro? Do you want to talk to Raúl?"

"Yes, is he in?"

"I'll put him on... Raúl! It's Pedro!" He could hear Mercedes looking for her husband.

"Pedro! I'm so happy to hear you!" Raúl's sincere voice was already reassuring him.

"Hi, Raúl. Sorry to call you at this hour... I don't know if you're busy..."

"Is something wrong with you? You're voice doesn't sound good... Ah, well, yes... Of course... But are you okay? Are you sure?... Of course... At the church? I'm coming... No, I was just finishing... Please! What are friends for, if not?"

When Raul said the word "friends," Pedro felt a tremendous relief. So he still considered him a friend, despite the way he had treated him. And he was willing to come and see him, without warning, at this hour of the night... Precisely, something that a pastor was expected to do. Something he hadn't done for so long.

As he drove the thirty blocks from his house to the church, Raúl had begun to think about that interview. They hadn't had any contact since then, but he knew from Mercedes that things with Virginia were going from bad to worse. What could have happened to make him call and arrange to see him at this hour? *Or too early or too late. Never a normal hour* he thought, smiling to himself.

Pedro opened the door as soon as he heard the car arrive and greeted him with a half hug that Raúl completed with all the strength he had. He felt that the barriers that had been erected between them lately were no longer there, that he was meeting again with Pedro, not the pastor.

"Come on, give me a good hug! Did you eat something? Shall we order something?" Food was essential for any chat between friends.

They ordered a dozen of *empanadas*[46] and beer, and right there Pedro told him his situation. He thought it would be hard to recount the incident with Sara, but the words came pouring out, along with the feelings, doubts, and fears. And he didn't stop at the incident alone, but went through his whole platonic and not so platonic relationship with Sara, how he had cheated on himself and had wanted to cheat on his wife—how much he loved her!—and how he saw everything black ahead.

"Mind you, if I didn't have to give the final speech at Evangelical Convocation next week, I'd be thinking of something more drastic…"

"Stop, stop! On the one hand, get that idea out of your head… Actually, get both ideas out. What drastic thing are you talking about? Are you going to jump in front of train, shoot yourself?"

"I didn't tell you I would, but I can't say it hasn't entered my head."

"Well, let's pray about that later. But, the other thing. You'll call to cancel the speech right now! You're in no condition to take on that responsibility."

"Don't ask me to miss this opportunity. It's a recognition of all we've done over the years. To our church. Besides, it's a message I've been preparing for months. They say there's going to be a lot of people… half a million, maybe!"

"Do you want my opinion? Settle things with Virginia, right now. Take a few days both of you alone. We can take care of the kids. I'll talk to the people in the Council. They'll find someone to replace you. But don't take on such a big responsibility like this."

---

[46] Typical hand-held pies filled with meat.

"But Quijada asked me especially. He says everyone wants to listen to me, that they need a motivational message. That I'm the best person for the media. It's not for me, it's for the evangelical church, for the Lord's work. We finally have a unique opportunity, and if I have this responsibility, I don't want to fail them..."

"Who are you going to fail? Quijada, the church, society... the world? Think of yourself, the Lord, Virginia, the kids!"

Sometimes, like the Israelites in the desert, we are the ones who prolong the recovery treatment the Lord has prepared for us.

Yes, he should have listened to Raúl.

Nicolás had partnered with Javier Urzaga, a sociologist who advised political parties, to form the consulting firm RePol (Religion and Politics). Javier's idea was that Nicolás's experience in the behavior of religious and pseudo-religious groups could be useful in understanding certain aspects of the functioning of individuals and groups in society, and this input could be useful to politicians. It was good for Nicolás, because he now had two children and a wife, and they couldn't eat out of the air. Javier was in his fifties, about ten years older than him, and taught him many tricks to achieve a better effect in his presentations. And Nicolás brought to the society a passion for defending freedom that was missing in his partner's more academic and polished style.

They had met at a Latin American meeting on cults in Quito, Ecuador. When they recognized each other as Argentines from their accent, they first had a coffee and then shared their free time. However, the idea of doing something together came up only when they returned to Buenos Aires. Javier came from a wealthy family and was well connected. He had no financial problems, and he liked to try new things, without the pressure of having to keep to strict schedules or commitments. So, when he met Nicolás, he felt he could venture into a new area of obvious sociological interest.

"Shall we go over some of the characteristics of cults?" They were going to give a joint talk in the hall of a consulting firm, a kind of presentation in society. Nicolás had prepared the slides and, as Javier had taught him, the best thing was to do a full rehearsal, including position, tone, timing, when they would take turns, and when it was convenient to stop. The more they planned, the fewer surprises they would have, and the more solid the presentation would be.

"Okay. I'll make the presentation of the consulting firm, I'll introduce you, and I'll start with the first five," said Javier.

"Yes, and we'll alternate five and five."

"The first one: Control. I like the drawing." It was a cartoon with a character driving a joystick that managed a lot of people moving to the beat of music with empty and happy faces. "Here I talk about leaders, with their strong, controlling, manipulative personalities..." Javier began.

"Who do not accept conflict," added Nicolás.

"Yes, that's important. Total obedience, the use of fear..."

"...of the leader, of God, of hell... anything goes." This was a theme that Nicolás mastered.

"Added to intimidation and accusation. To question authority is rebellion, distrust. Suppressing questions, discouraging critical, independent thinking. Over-simplifying the deep questions of life. Everything is black and white."

"All that under the theme of Control only?" Nicolás said.

"Yes, there is a lot to be said. Let's go to the second point: Interference in intimate matters. Telling them when and who to marry. Here comes the sexual issue: chastity or promiscuity. This is a topic you've been looking at, right?" asked Javier.

"Yes, it's mixed with the theme that leaders think they have their own laws, that they are above the laws of others. Or they write the laws themselves," added Nicolás.

"Let's go to the third slide: Trust in the group. Group confession sessions that can then be used to manipulate, blackmail those who want out. The fourth one talks about what you just mentioned: Duplicity. One standard for followers and another for leaders. The fifth concerns the free use of the Bible. Here it could be any holy book, I understand..." asked Javier.

"Yes, but it is interesting because the same book has such different uses and interpretations. In my experience I have seen how the same book can be extremely liberating and also extremely enslaving." This aspect of the Bible had always caught his attention, and a subject that he had discussed at length with Raúl.

"Private revelations and interpretations are added. Passages are taken out of context, certain passages are emphasized over others, or over the entire book. Inconvenient text is ignored or discredited. Opinions contrary to the leaders' interpretations are not considered, or are ridiculed," Javier ended his part.

"Well, now it's my turn." Nicolás came forward as Javier sat down. "The sixth, Loyalty Changed. Loyalty to God, to Jesus, is replaced by loyalty to the organization, the church, the leader. The follower is confused, identifying one loyalty with the other."

"Try never to turn your back on the public and remember to make frequent eye contact. But you're doing well," Javier, encouragingly.

"The seventh... Oh, yes, Isolation. Very important. It always comes up one way or another. Members are not allowed, or are discouraged, from having contact with family members outside the group, or with other organizations that might influence them. To prevent information from coming out of the group and to keep it from coming in from outside, especially if it includes criticism of the group. They try to get you to read only the "approved" books, listen to the "approved" people. In particular, you are completely discouraged and virtually forbidden to have contact with those who have left. If someone presents evidence against what is said in the group, that person is attacked, rather than dealing with the evidence. The eighth. An attitude of 'us against them.' Everyone who is against them is an enemy. They feel persecuted. They are warned that they are going to hear negative things about the group or the leaders, but they must ignore them, they have to trust their leaders. Then, it becomes a self-fulfilling prophecy: they receive criticism, and this reinforces the authority of the leaders. Here I see that the ninth says 'Focus on an imaginary enemy.' Maybe we can put it together with the previous one. What do you think?" said Nicolás.

"I think this one is more specific: The government, Freemasons, Jews, even the devil, who comes in handy for a lot of things," Javier said.

"Yes, you're right. Having an enemy outside keeps them from looking in and keeps them busy and distracted. Like blaming all the country's ills on the IMF, the United States. Now would come the tenth: 'Motivational teaching.' Lots of stimulation of emotions, with loud music, group participation, smiling faces, hugs. It is also called 'love bath.' A place where everything is fine," concluded Nicolás.

"My turn. Eleven: 'Rules of silence.' Rules that are not usually said, let alone written. Much more dangerous and rigid than groups that have their principles in writing. Because they can't be discussed and are usually handled by the leaders."

"You should give some examples here," suggested Nicolás.

"Let's see. A usual unwritten rule is 'Do not disagree with the group's authorities.' Silence allows you to protect your positions of power from scrutiny or questioning. Another example: 'Do not talk to others about a problem.' If you do, you become the problem. Talking to those who have left is considered treason."

"Talking inside is considered murmuring in evangelical churches," said Nicolás, surprised by how often pastors and leaders talked from the pulpits against murmuring, when there were generally no established channels for objections and complaints in one direction, or for systematic information in the other.

"The twelfth: 'Knowledge by revelation.' Emotions, intuitions, revelations, and mystical perspectives are promoted over objective knowledge. Thirteen: 'Altered mystical states.' It seeks to 'annul the flesh and stimulate the spirit' with word repetition, relaxation techniques, chanting, hypnosis, meditation, trance states, guided imagination or visualization, deep breathing exercises. The aim is to bring the person to an altered state, with a psychological imbalance," explained Javier.

"Everything makes it possible to handle people better," Nicolás said.

"Of course, deep down it's what you want. Fourteen: 'Group pride.' We are the only ones who are right. If you're not with us, you're going to hell. We are the only ones who have the right doctrine."

"In this sense, what they do is also give new meanings to common words, which only those on the inside understand. It is like a hidden jargon." Nicolás always knew the terminology of a sect when he heard it. "I would add here the concept of unity that these groups handle. Since they have arrived at the truth, others can join them, but never the other way round."

"Okay. Fifteen: 'Brainwashing.' A gradual and constant process to indoctrinate new members. Your turn." Javier took his seat.

"Well, the sixteenth," Nicolás continued, 'Distorted tithes or excessive donations.' More and more money is demanded to achieve or demonstrate a higher level of spirituality. Or handing over property. Giving so that God will give. The more you give, the more God will give you. The counterpart is even stronger: if you do not give, God will not give, or even take away what you have. Seventeen: 'Promote the kingdom now to change society and the government, even using force.' For example, by Christianizing the government and the people to bring about the coming of Christ. Eighteen: 'Total commitment.' Everyone is expected to commit to the leaders. This includes time, talent, and money. Nineteen: 'Individuality is sacrificed to the goals, needs, and aspirations of the group.' The end justifies the means. Everything is justified to promote the goals of the group, even lying. I've seen it a lot. Twenty: 'Inconsistent disciplined life.' Very strict rules in some things, very free in others. Lack of balance. Twenty-one: 'Martyr complex.' They consider themselves misunderstood and persecuted and are willing to die for what they believe to be true. Twenty-two: 'Curses and threats.' Sent on those who leave the group or oppose them later. They are told they have nowhere else to go. It is very difficult to leave these groups, and those who do so lose friends and family relationships. Sometimes you must choose between one or the other.

"Twenty-two characteristics. I think that's enough, although there are more," Javier said. Now the interesting thing would be to see how we can find common points between sectarian behavior in religious groups and the political behavior of society. That is the part I would like to work on more and leave as a message."

"Let's see quickly," said Nicolás, "which ones could be applied readily. Control, yes; Duplicity, yes; Free use of the holy book... could be applied to the Constitution; Changed Loyalty, if we replace God with the country, or the political party, or the government in power. Us against them, no doubt; Focusing on an imaginary enemy, we already talked about it; Motivational teaching could associate it with the official propaganda; Rules of silence, not to criticize the government... could be; thirteen, leaders cannot be judged, makes me think about when they say history will judge them."

"I think we have plenty of material, without forcing ideas. Maybe it would be interesting in this talk or in another one to go the opposite way," suggested Javier.

"Things about politics that can be applied to religion or sects?" It was something Nicolás had already thought about.

"Yes, I am convinced that there is something deep in man, in society, that leads us to be willing to give up our freedom in exchange for security," said Javier. "As if we were teenagers who preferred to stay in the comfort of home, under the care of our parents, criticizing them and lamenting what they don't let us do, but never taking the logical step of maturity to become independent, to become emancipated."

"A step that is necessary but painful," said Nicolás, recalling his own experience.

"Mind you. For both, for parents and teenagers," a topic Javier had seen repeatedly in the different societies he had studied.

"And there are people who know about this fault of ours and take advantage of it in both areas: religion and politics," added Nicolás.

"Or, looking at it from this analogy, leaders who aren't willing to let go of people, out of selfishness or mistrust."

"It could be that our next talk will have to focus on these people, the manipulators," suggested Javier, "or maybe it will come up in the debate after this presentation, naturally."

Juan lasted two years and two months in the Church of the Open Word, a church record in the last fifteen years, and like all previous separations between pastor and congregation, it wasn't on good terms. The first contacts with the Council showed him the need to make an extreme effort so that his pastorate wouldn't end in frustration for him and Mariela, and one more failure for the congregation. Juan thought they would need a five-year period where they would have to use all their wisdom and patience without letting anything divide them both.

He also realized that he would have to intensify his spiritual disciplines to have the strength to resist what was evidently a mission fraught with danger. More like a minefield. He had always got up early, when it was quieter, and the air was fresher. The first half hour was spent reading and meditating on the Bible, *maté* in hand. Then followed another half hour of free prayer, where he passed from his own needs to those of his wife, his family, his friends, and all that he understood the Spirit indicated. He had always included in the time of prayer the church or congregation where they were, but now he realized that this part must have a much greater importance.

So he kept the devotional hour as usual, but he opened another specific time to pray for the church in general and the members in particular. It was a way of inserting himself into a community that had many years, much history and—as he would realize—many problems in interpersonal relationships. Moreover, once he began to do so he realized that themes and ideas were emerging for the Sunday sermon, which he didn't want to be something cold and theoretical, but clearly related, in a practical way, to the life and needs of the individuals and families of the community he was pastoring.

The second part of his daily time of prayer for the church grew from about ten minutes to almost an hour as he got to know the people better.

"Lord, I thank you for this church, for each one of its members... I ask you to give me your word for Sunday's message... I don't want to give them a sermon, I want to share your heart... Give me strength to resist the enemy, inside and outside... Show me if there is something that is preventing your work from growing here, that no pastor can last... I pray for the members of the Council, for Francisco, Antonio,

Ángela, Armando... Bless them... But also show me why they have that hardness... that pride, that mistrust... I also ask you to help Mariela to be able to fit in... You know how she has felt rejected, superfluous, not welcome... Help me to change what is necessary to be able to help these people... I am thinking of Don Rafael and the debt he has with the bank... Provide for his needs... I ask you for what Serafín told me about the crooked deal in the municipality... May we be light and salt at this moment... I ask you for the relationship with the other churches of the denomination... You know I don't like it that we are isolated... You always talked about unity, so that the world will believe... I also ask you for the relationship with churches of other denominations..."

Mariela often accompanied him in the last part of the prayer, either silently or incorporating her own prayers and thanks. Sometimes Juan was so absorbed that he didn't notice when she came in, and sometimes she would leave while he continued to pray, to take the children to school. Then, when she returned, they would share their concerns and she would make some calls or make some appointments for the afternoon, and he would go to work.

Having kept "secular" job gave him several advantages over the possibility of being a full-time pastor, which had been the Council's initial proposal. On the one hand, it gave him financial independence if he ever had to leave. On the other hand, it allowed him to maintain contact with the real life of the people. Since it was an independent job that gave him the freedom to move around, he took advantage of this freedom and mobility to visit the workplaces of some members or people with whom the church kept contact. For example, he liked to stop by Sergi, a hearty son of Catalans who would leave everything when he saw it coming to his carpentry shop.

"Hi, pastor. Nice to see you here!"

"How's it going, Sergi? I have ten minutes..."

"Sit here," clearing a chair full of tools. "José! Take over while I take care of the pastor."

"I see you have plenty of work. How's that kid José doing?"

"Yes, work is going very well... It allows me to pay some debts.

The kid's doing well, too. Too bad he's a believer!" They both laughed heartily. Sergi was referring to a talk they'd had the week before about the bad experience many believers had when they had believing employees or subordinates. In many—too many—cases, instead of giving an example of dedication, effort, and punctuality, they mixed the church with the work, with disastrous results. "I was late because yesterday we had a campaign and we stayed until two in the morning, a real blessing." "I'll have to leave early because we have a leaders' meeting and I don't want to be late." "The Lord showed me that he has a position for me in the Rosario branch."

"Well, as soon as he does one of these things, out he goes... with a prayer, perhaps... Changing the subject, today I was praying in the morning and an idea came to my mind about you. I don't know if it's from the Lord, but I'll share it with just the same," Juan said.

"Yes, of course."

"Today I read that passage where Jesus says that where our treasure is, our heart will be there, remember?"

"Isn't it the other way around... where our heart is, there will be our treasure?"

"No. Notice that this is exactly what makes Jesus original. It is the opposite of what we are told every day: set your goal and you will have your reward. Come, I'll read it to you from the Bible. I have the Phillips version, which is easier to understand... It's in the Sermon on the Mount... Here: Matthew 6: 19 to 21: 'Don't pile up treasures on earth, where moth and rust can spoil them and thieves can break in and steal. But keep your treasure in Heaven where there is neither moth nor rust to spoil it and nobody can break in and steal.' Now look: 'For wherever your treasure is, you may be certain that your heart will be there too!'"

"You were right."

"Of course, that's why I'm the pastor"—a joke he wouldn't make with others, who might misunderstand. "Well, what I wanted to say was that I saw you and Viviana too worried about money, bills, debts. It's good that you want to make progress, and I know it's not to hoard for yourselves but to help others, but I think the Lord was telling me first, and I think it's to share with you too, that we shouldn't let money manage us. Take it or leave it. I was planning to talk about this on Sunday, so try to come."

He finished the last *maté* and left. He felt up to date with this man, and he felt appreciated. In the afternoon, as he began his day of pastoral work, he had set out to make at least one visit a day to the homes of different people in the church. It allowed him to get to know them in their natural environment, and although many times the homes didn't lend themselves to a quiet chat, it was in settings like these that he learned things that were impossible in church.

A case in point was the first visit to the small department of the Herczuk family. It was tough, but very productive. When Hilario opened the door, the image he found gave him an explanation of the taciturn face he always had. In the main room, the living room, there was an orthopedic bed installed, with a child of about ten years old paralyzed and with a lost look. A woman he hadn't seen before in the church—his wife? —came out of the kitchen drying her hands, with an even more languid face than her husband. He noticed that she was pregnant, perhaps four or five months. Juan took the initiative.

"Thank you very much for receiving me, Hilario. I hope I'm not interrupting."

"No, please, pastor. Come in. Sit down. My wife, Susana."

"Hi, Susana." He shook her hand and smiled warmly at her. "May I ask for when?"

Their faces lit up.

"By the end of March, or the beginning of April." The boy watched him closely from his bed. Juan came over to greet him. "And what is this boy's name?" When he saw that he was trying to answer his question, without being able to, he resorted to a little game that always worked for him with kids.

"Let me guess... Carlos... Miguel... right? Luis..." Susana understood the game and whispered his name. "Ramiro... yes? I guessed it!" The boy was amazed and looked at his parents with a smile.

He stayed only half an hour, but it was enough for him to establish a love bond with that family and to know how to pray wisely for their needs. Hilario's wife had left him shortly after Ramiro was born, with a serious genetic defect. Susana, Hilario's partner of three years, was a nurse at the Central Hospital, where they had met when he took the boy for his consultations. The son they were expecting now had been sought after and they had high expectations. Juan knew that Hilario was a history professor but was surprised by the books of Bible study and deep religious themes he found in his library. When they began to talk about the history of the Church, the predominant theme among the books, it was the second time that Hilario's face lit up. He knew Greek and Latin, as well as English and Russian.

"See you on Sunday, Hilario. Maybe we can see you in church one day"—as he greeted Susana— "before your child is born. Bye, Ramiro!" The boy greeted him with his eyes, as best he could, from his bed.

"Thank you very much for your visit, pastor. You have changed our day," said Hilario.

Then he learned that it was the first visit from someone from the church to that house in more than three years. The second would be Mariela, who made it her task to visit them regularly and call Susana by phone every week.

But not everyone agreed with this style, even though attendance began to grow slowly. Some made excuses or set up barriers when he asked if he could see them, others received him once, but Juan realized that they weren't comfortable with his visit. Others slipped the idea that none of the other pastors had done anything like that, and that it was best to use the pastoral office for contacts, which was its purpose after all. He ended up doing both, attending in church and outside, knowing who preferred each place.

"The humiliation of the year" in the Evangelical Convocation had many repercussions. Some said that Pedro was too stressed, that he was tired and that the day was too hot, while others questioned the decision to invite him, since he didn't represent the majority evangelical thought, and only political interest had prevailed. Under their breath, some said that God had surely punished him, and that no doubt "he must have done something" to have this happen to him.

What is certain is that he disappeared from the star circuits that he had worked so hard to reach and that he enjoyed so much. To top it all off, the picture with his ungainly image on the floor appeared in almost every newspaper in Buenos Aires, with titles like "Pastor on the floor!," "God's judgement," "A stumble *is* a fall." And that image remained etched in the minds of believers and unbelievers alike. Although all his colleagues and personalities that day appeared to take an interest in his health, the fingers of one hand were enough to count those who called him after the "Pedrogate."

But Pedro, instead of coming to his senses, instead of remembering the talk he had had with Raúl and his warning became even more blinded. He took refuge in what he called his "loyal" or "stalwart" followers and the others called the pastor's "obsequious" or "bootlickers." His messages continued to emphasize success, prosperity, blessing, and God's promises. The annual church assemblies, which had already become nothing but symbols of a dying system, disappeared altogether, unannounced. Simultaneously, he began to denounce from the platform those who didn't agree and even those who had already left.

"God does not tolerate murmuring! Look what happened to those who murmured against Moses... God does not tolerate disobedience! God wants us to submit to the authorities, to the pastors, to the leaders! In submission there is blessing... Some say that we don't read the Bible, that we don't study it, that we add other things. I would like you to look at how many people these churches have! Fifty, eighty... a hundred? Here we have made a great effort so that the eternal message of the Bible can be understood by the people of the 20th century... Enough guilt! Enough of a gospel of sin, hell, punishment! God wants you to do well, he wants you to have money, to have health! It's a lie that God wants you to suffer, it's a lie of the devil! No more legalism! No more trying to be good! Let God do the work! And if he doesn't want to do it, don't do it!"

The desperate combination of threats and blessings won the unconditional applause of an equally unconditional audience. How could they object to a message that demanded nothing from them and, to top it off, made those who tried to do what God said look bad? Those who objected to his Manichean, schematic, distorted view of a book that few had read had left or were seriously considering doing so.

Pedro never got to talk to Virginia about the accident and the whole situation with Sara, though for all intents and purposes it was as if he had, but much worse. Virginia knew everything that had happened, especially from the group of three staunch friends who met with her weekly. Pedro assumed that Virginia would know, either from her group or from some casual or Sara-induced disclosure. All the courage he showed from the platform with the microphone in hand disappeared when he had to assume the role of a man to acknowledge his mistake and ask for forgiveness. The distance between them was increasing, although each one fulfilled their duties in the church religiously. That was the word: religiously. They earned their pay, and no one could question it. But these weren't pastors' salaries, but more the salaries of company managers.

Then the bizarre incident happened. On April 16, Easter Sunday, Pedro was preaching on that special night on the power of resurrection. Suddenly, halfway through the sermon, a man stood up in the third row on the right, and simultaneously the microphone stopped working. Addressing the platform in a loud and clear voice, he uttered some words that everyone heard but no one understood:

"*Gorbala masala, sinise tomei!*" At least, this is the version with the most support. Others say he said, "*Gomala masala tomei*" and others "*Gorba mala sini tomé.*" When he got everybody's attention, while Pedro clung to the useless microphone, petrified, he repeated in the same tone and with the same intensity the cryptic phrase, *Gorba masala, sinise tomei!*

Then he turned on his heels and walked slowly down the central corridor without looking at anyone and disappeared into the night. No one else saw him again, and upon further investigation, no one had ever seen him before. The tall, thin, gray-haired man in the elegant blue suit could have been a bank manager, or a doctor. His eyes were the most striking thing on his face, a very deep, piercing, warm blue. The voice was like that of an announcer, loud and with a beautiful reverberation.

The audience was stunned, and after following the character to the exit as if transfigured, they slowly turned their eyes to the platform. Pedro was perspiring profusely. It appeared as if he had understood the man's message, and that that message wasn't good for him. People wondered, "What now?"

But Pedro was a tough person who was getting tougher and harder, like Pharaoh of Egypt. So he reacted by countering, when it was clear that all he wanted was to get off the platform as soon as possible.

"Well, the church has always welcomed special people." The microphone had come on again, miraculously. "But let's not make a big deal out of it. Does anyone know this man?" He made a pompous gesture of looking around the audience, down and up, to see if anyone would raise their hand. "Did anyone understand what he was saying... or what language it was?" No answer. Pedro finished the sermon that no one was interested in hearing in less than five minutes as best as he could.

The meeting ended strangely, so much so that they forgot to pass the offering and make the announcements. Everyone seemed to want to finish as soon as possible to comment on what had happened and go home to tell about it. They also wanted to know if anyone knew this strange but captivating man. Would he come to the next meeting? Would he go to another church next week?

The next week the church was packed to the rafters. Word of the incident with the strange visitor had spread and everyone was looking to see if he would show up. Or maybe he'd fly down. Or he'd materialize out of nowhere. The versions were as varied as the interpretations of what he had said, and what Pastor Pedro had heard or understood. The truth is that no one bought the official version that he was a weirdo, a madman, a deranged person. If anybody had seen and heard him, they would realize that he had said something important, something substantial, addressed to Pedro but with the intention that everyone should hear it.

Pedro never preached in his church again after that third fateful night of his life in only two months. One week it was because he was sick; the next, because the Council had invited an international evangelist; the next, because he had an accident with his car and arrived late; and the fourth, because there was a convention of pastors where he had to go. The last straw was the night of the following week, on May 15, when he had prepared one of the best messages of his life, full of examples, anecdotes, humor, and forgot all his notes at home. While he was speeding to look for them in his car, he was stopped by the police and lost another half hour.

When he arrived at the church, Osvaldo Corridori, the youth leader who had once replaced him when he became ill, was speaking. He had already been told how well he had spoken that time, and he had congratulated him, thinking *Of course, it's the first time. Besides, he's young.* This time he stayed at the entrance, listening to him, sitting anonymously in the last row. Osvaldo was already finishing his message—he had been told that he spoke half the time that he did, and he remembered thinking *Of course, because of his lack of experience, because it's difficult to put together a message*—and the audience was taking in every word he said. Osvaldo spoke without shouting, as if he were chatting with you. In his desperation, Pedro had lately incorporated vices that he had always criticized in Central American preachers, causing people to repeat or nod in agreement one way or another that he said from the pulpit. "Tell the person next to you, 'I'm not trash. I'm valuable,'" "Repeat after me 'God loves a cheerful giver,'" or make them stand up and sit down, like puppets: "Let see, all those who want to give their life for the Lord stand up," "Now sit down all those who didn't mean it," or even with physical contact: "Push the brother next to you, so that he doesn't fall asleep." It was a way to keep people interested and not to be distracted during his messages of nearly an hour.

But that wasn't the case here. And people weren't falling asleep, nor were they distracted. Quite the contrary. It seemed that every word, every concept that came out of the front reached them. He saw three or four people with tears in their eyes. A group of teenagers were furiously taking notes. He was talking about the cross, about

Jesus' interview with Pilate. How many times had he preached on this...

"Jesus didn't say anything, he didn't defend himself. And Pilate didn't understand anything. Because, as a good politician, he expected Jesus to use the opportunity before the authority to reject these unjust accusations. If he was truly a leader, as they said, he would negotiate. 'Today for you, tomorrow for me.' And who knows, this man might return the favor someday. You never know..."

Interesting, Pedro thought, *where's he heading?*

"But Jesus wasn't a politician, he wasn't a leader like everyone else there was... and there is today. He wasn't looking to accumulate, to add power, to make an upward career. Jesus' leadership was a leadership of renunciation, of giving up, of being willing in a moment to throw overboard everything he had achieved in order to have the freedom to pursue his goal, even though no one understood it other than he and his Father. If you want, write down this phrase: 'Leadership of renunciation.'"

Leadership of renunciation? This guy doesn't have the vocation of a leader..., thought Pedro.

"Here are two passages of the Bible to read later: John 6:60 to 66 and Luke 9:51... and you can follow up to verse 62. In the first passage Jesus says extremely hard things that lead many to leave him, but that's not a problem for him, and he asks the disciples if they want to leave him too. In the second, Luke 9:51, it says that Jesus, 'When the days drew near for him to be taken up, he set his face to go to Jerusalem.' At the height of his popularity, when he had accumulated followers, prestige, popularity, Jesus 'set his face to go to Jerusalem,' where he was going to lose everything: followers, prestige, dignity... and his life. Was he crazy? What leader does this, at least voluntarily? How many of us are willing to give up everything we have achieved, what we think we have achieved, what we think we deserve, what is rightfully ours, to fulfill the true mission God has entrusted to us? Well, I leave you with that thought and both passages. I see that our pastor has arrived, so I'll let him close the meeting."

Pedro came forward, deeply moved, thinking to cover it up with

221

some light comment or a joke about the police. But when he got on the platform and looked out at the congregation, he realized that there was a spirit, an atmosphere that shouldn't be broken. God was at work. So he asked them to bow their heads and pray in silence. He felt something, Someone, take hold of him and embrace him very tightly. He began to cry very quietly with his head bowed, as if he were praying. Little did he care if they saw him, nor was he interested in the image he had learned to care about so much. At one point he opened his tear-filled eyes and saw Virginia, deeply touched, sitting as always in the front row, and their glances crossed. Then and there he knew he would never be in that pulpit again. That this congregation was no longer his. In fact, it had never been his. He was unnecessary, and he didn't want to keep fighting with the only true Owner.

Juan's work had two clearly defined directions. With the people who ran the church, formally or informally, he made no progress, and there were constant clashes, questionings. In the weekly meetings with the Council, he was systematically challenged on everything new, everything that hadn't been done before. In the monthly meetings with the larger leadership group, much of the time was spent in inconsequential discussions about schedules, problems, denominational meetings, and finances. At the annual meeting, in which all members participated, he found that he could present new projects that would be open to treatment by all. This was where he found support among people who didn't hold office and among newcomers. But it was also where the biggest conflicts and discussions took place.

For the annual assemblies they used the parliamentary system, with agenda, motions, endorsements, votes, and minutes. It had the advantage that everything was transparent, and the information and participation of all members was guaranteed. The obvious disadvantage was that time could be lost in endless discussions and there was a tendency to produce sides for and against different positions, with their inevitable political action before, during and after the sessions. In the first assembly, three months after his arrival, he saw how all the time was used in useless and even dangerous discussions. The church was divided into two active sectors, which could be called "traditionalists" and "reformists," to which should be added the ubiquitous third majority sector in any group, the "indifferent" or "accommodating" ones. This was the most dangerous, because they didn't express themselves publicly, always seeking the position of least conflict, voting with the perceived majority, leaving in the hands of others the discussions and decisions that would end up affecting them.

The second assembly he attended and presided over was difficult and left a bitter taste that made him seriously consider resigning. He could now understand his predecessors. He felt inside a machine that crushed one by one all the ideas, the projects that tried to change what had been done for years or that somehow dared to reduce the power of the group that ran the church.

The main discussion was the music and songs used in the services. Accustomed to using only bound hymnals that included hymns from a hundred to three hundred years ago, accompanied by organ or sung a cappella, the introduction of printed songbooks with more current songs was considered by some to be a bold innovation at best, a heresy at worst. Juan's position was to use both types of songs, both out of respect for the different ages of the members of the congregation and for the different types of musical expression. Personally, Juan loved old hymns like "A Mighty Fortress is Our God," composed by Martin Luther, or "Nearer My God, to Thee," famously sung by the Titanic castaways as it sank into the sea. He also loved the more modern, or simpler, songs. Sometimes they managed to convey very deep things in a few lines. Of course, he recognized that there were both old hymns and modern songs that weren't useful. But here things had become polarized. Those who wanted the hymns didn't want to know anything about the new songs, and vice versa. The problem was that the discussion drifted to other topics and brought to the surface other more serious latent problems.

"Let's deal now with item 4 on the agenda: Music and songs." Brother Francisco, very efficient and practical, and with a lot of experience in these matters, was presiding.

"I don't agree with the new songs. They don't have the quality of lyrics and music that the hymns have, which have lasted so long." It was Brother Omar, a man whose greatest self-proclaimed virtue was punctuality and perfect attendance at all meetings.

"In relation to this topic, and without wanting to ignore that there are more important topics, or at least of more… theological transcendence, and thinking that the principal mission of the church is to evangelize, although music is very important, and was important in Luther's time, and now"—Miguel had this annoying tendency to beat around the bush and the people were patient with him, but here it was necessary to be more concrete. He realized that he was rambling, so he tried to be more concrete. "Well, returning to the subject, I think we have to let everyone express themselves, use the music they like best, as long as it is for the Lord…"

"Thank you very much, Brother Miguel," Francisco interrupted. "Does anyone have another opinion on this subject?"

"Yes, I think completely different," María was emphatic in what she believed. "I think that hymns must have been excellent in their time, for the people of their time, but now, dear brothers, we are in the twentieth century, almost finishing it. If we don't renew the songs, we're going to miss the train."

"What's happening here, sister and brothers, is that there's something behind this." It was Brother Omar, again. "What's happening here, and I and many of us realize, is that they want to change the church, first with the music, then with the messages, then with a pastor who not only isn't dedicated full time to the church but who goes around visiting people outside the church…"

Several exchanged glances as the level of discomfort rose by several degrees. The attempt to get the meeting back on track by the moderator wasn't successful.

"It seems to me that we are getting off track. I remind you, Brother Omar, that we are talking about music and songs," said Francisco.

"I'm also talking about music and songs, because if we give in here, we're going to allow a lot of influences to come in that we're seeing in other churches of the denomination and in other denominations. Now the fashion is to be Pentecostal, to sing with the guitar... everything has to be new. And if we keep this up, where are we going to end up?"

"This... if you'll allow me..." It was Hilario, who Juan had visited. "For me this is the first time I've participated in a church assembly, although I've been attending for almost ten years. I would like to clarify that I also prefer hymns, but I think it is good that the younger ones have a preference for songs with more modern music. Remember that many of the melodies of the sacred hymns we sing now were taken from popular songs, even from taverns..."

"Impossible! Give me just one example," said Brother Omar indignantly.

"Several of John Wesley's hymns, for example. But I want to go on with what I've been saying. In the ten years I've been coming here, no one has taken any interest in me beyond a greeting, and maybe it's not the fault of many, when all the activity was centered on the building. But, shortly after arriving, Pastor Juan came to visit us at home, and met my wife and son. Who among you knew that I had a disabled son? My wife, Susana, had sworn not to set foot in a church in her life, because she said that they were all hypocrites, that they were only interested in money. But after the pastor's visit, and the calls from his wife, she started coming."

Hilario's participation, although favorable to the pastor and representing the feelings of many, only polarized the positions further, and the assembly ended up stagnant and divided. The cards had been dealt. The next day, Antonio, in the name of the Council, pronounced the fateful words:

"Pastor, we want you to take a break. You are exhausted..."

With Mercedes we decided to leave the New Church of Blessing, after more than ten years. All the enthusiasm that we had shared during the initial growth, from the small group to being one of the largest churches in the country, had been fading with Pedro's self-centeredness and isolation. The decision to leave Casa de Esperanza because of the unclear management of money and then my resignation from the Council seemed to have been interpreted by Pedro as permission to extend his power. From the outside, for those who evaluate a church by the size of the building, the congregation, or the offerings, all was going well. But on the inside, the cracks were showing.

I had done my part by talking to Pedro the first time and listening to him the second time. When Mercedes decided to support Virginia with the group of friends, we found a quiet and helpful service area. After all, it wasn't just a friend who was at stake, but their children.

One thing that was quite discouraging was most people's attitude toward the things they all saw. They chose to turn a blind eye, to look the other way. They thought that accepting what was clearly wrong was better, more spiritual, than confronting it head on or withdrawing for disagreeing and not appearing as accomplices. This was something that was encouraged from the leaders and from the pulpit.

In short, it was a comfortable and utilitarian attitude. For these people, the church and the pastor had to provide them with a series of services—inspirational preaching, counseling, a menu of activities for the whole family, saving them the dilemma of having to decide for themselves what was right and what was wrong—which they paid for through their tithes and offerings. As long as the pastor and leaders provided these services and they contributed the money and silence, all went well. In this context, the questioners, always asking "why" or wanting to know if things were done correctly, always distrustful, always splitting hairs, were a nuisance. In the end, it would be best if they went elsewhere and left them alone.

We saw how within a few years there was a considerable turnover of the members of the congregation, with many of the hard-working and spiritually deep people of the early days being replaced by others who were just looking for numbers, noise and comfort. Ah, comfort...

I could see before my eyes how it ruined the life and ministry of a man with tremendous potential, like Pedro. If I were to sum it up, at least in the last stage, he was a pastor who sought the most comfortable theology, the most comfortable structure, the most comfortable relationships. And this comfort took him so far from the revolutionary essence of the gospel that he didn't realize it and he was unable to recognize those who warned him—those who had not compromised the true Christian life.

We were there on the day of the mysterious visit, and we both tried to figure out who the man was and what his message was, but especially the meaning of the episode itself.

"For you, who was the man?" I said, as we returned home from the service.

"I don't know. I've never seen him before," said Mercedes.

"What I do know is that I don't think he's a madman, as Pedro said."

"Sure. For me, Pedro understood somehow what he said."

"It seems a little crazy, but could he be an angel?" I asked.

"I don't know. I never saw an angel. You?"

"No, it seems to me that what he said came from the Lord. And I don't know if Pedro actually understood what he said, but I'm sure he was touched by it."

"You should ask him," concluded Mercedes.

I didn't feel it would achieve anything, but I decided to give my cousin Juan a call.

FROM HERE
TO THERE

(2000-2003)

9

PEDRO: INSISTENCE AND ACCEPTANCE

Going more and more in the same direction
With the only limit of our imperfection

Pedro managed to meet Nacho the fourth time he went to his church. That day, from his usual place at the back of the room, he saw him sitting on the platform. It was remarkable how different the atmosphere was. All the details he had seen and criticized were the same: the music, the repetition game, the tithe and offering harangue. But they didn't bother him so much in the hands of a man like Nacho Leiva, "a spectacular guy," in the opinion of everyone who knew him.

Nacho had a sad history. When he was just five years old his mother had committed suicide, a victim of deep post-partum depression, after his sister, Cloe, was born. Even today, more than forty years later, he had flashes of the scene when they heard the news: screams, running, an ambulance, the wake, the funeral, his father holding the baby, crying inconsolably. His father never recovered and went from one job and gig to another. He didn't know if it was because he already had a strong personality or because necessity led him to have one, but by the age of ten Nacho was the man of the house. He took his little sister to kindergarten, cleaned the house, cooked, and gave his father emotional support. Nor does he know if by birth or by necessity he had acquired an optimistic and jovial character, always looking for the good side of things. "Life will always give you surprises, so accept the good ones and wait for the bad ones to pass" was a typical phrase of his.

Nacho's message that day was amazingly simple. He walked through Jesus' life, from his birth to his ascension, noting the reactions he caused in people. Those who loved him, and those who wanted to kill him. From the reaction of John the Baptist in his mother's womb when Mary, pregnant with Jesus, visited her, the Magi, the pastors, Simeon, Anna... the Samaritan woman, Nicodemus, the demonized Gadarene..., the Pharisees, the scribes, Herod, Pilate... the centurion and the thief on the cross... Mary Magdalene, the couple on the way to Emmaus, Thomas... It was a message of more than an hour in which Nacho's serene voice led Pedro in such a vivid way that it was as if he were literally next to Jesus, almost as if he were the disciple of the same name and with whom he felt so identified. The people were also engrossed. The silence was as real at that moment as the bustle of a few minutes before. Suddenly, Pedro felt tears well up in his eyes. It seemed incredible, but here a pastor of years, an international preacher, a preacher of multitudes, had met Jesus again!

"...as you can see, Jesus's presence wasn't neutral. It changed everything: the atmosphere, the people, the power relations. Not so much because he set out to do it, but because he had something different, an authority, that went beyond titles, the way he dressed, the money or the amount of people who followed him." He was already finishing. Normally, preachers used this moment to achieve their greatest impact, sometimes dedicating about ten minutes to the final appeal. It was also usual to accompany this moment with soft music, for greater impact. Nacho only needed one sentence.

"Do we have enough of Jesus to affect the places where we are and the people we treat as he did?"

With that simple phrase he ended the message and the meeting. Then he made a very simple invitation, without shouting or screaming:

"We're going to be praying for people who have needs now. I am going to ask those who need prayer to come forward and those who want to leave to do so in silence. Thank you. God bless you."

Pedro didn't hesitate. Without caring if anybody recognized him, he walked down the stairs, making his way among the crowd and advanced resolutely along the central corridor, facing those who were coming out. Four lines had formed in front of the two men and two women who prayed for those coming forward. Nacho's was the longest, and some ushers were trying to even out the rows, with little success. While he waited, Pedro felt as in a cloud, oblivious to the rest of the world. At one point, one of the ushers approached him and took him by the arm.

"Pastor Terrero? This way, please..." gesturing as if to take him forward.

"No, thank you. I'd rather wait here."

"As you wish, pastor."

Incredibly, he felt good here, one in the crowd, without the privileges he'd always had. The woman in front of him recognized him and said something to the man who was with her. Pedro smiled and continued tucked into his own world. He had used and heard so many times the phrase "God is working" and now he was experiencing it firsthand.

When he got to the first place in line, Nacho started with the question he had been repeating for the last half hour:

"What do you need God to do..." and then he recognized him. "Pedro!"

The people who saw Nacho hugging him, with a face of indescribable joy and emotion, thought it was some relative he hadn't seen in a long time.

"Pedro! How nice to see you! Do you know that the Lord told me during the service that I was going to have a surprise, somebody special? I even told Jimena, my wife. But I never imagined it would be you. Man, how we've prayed for you!"

"Yes, Nacho, I know. Look, I don't want to take up any more of your time here. You've got too many people. But I need to talk to you."

"Of course. Take my card and call me at home, at the office, whenever you want, any time. It's wonderful to see you again."

Nacho made a brief but heartfelt prayer, they embraced again, and Pedro left the temple. Many already knew who he was, especially what had happened to him in public. But that was the least of his worries at that moment.

He crossed over again to the bar La Encrucijada, with less of the people he had found the last time because the meeting had finished over an hour ago. This time he found an empty table by the window, facing the street, and asked for a double latte. He needed time to digest what had happened, for himself and to explain it to Virginia. After all, it was she who had suggested that he go to see Nacho, and he had resisted. She had also insisted after the three times he went to church and didn't find him. Suddenly, he realized how lonely he had been this last time and how many people loved him, even if he didn't make time for them. Virginia, Nacho... Raúl. And his children. His oldest son, Roque, was the one who criticized him the most, the one who wouldn't let him off the hook ever. But sometimes he was afraid that all the bad things he saw would take him away from the good things. "Who does he take after?" he thought and smiled. Luciana, the middle one, was his weak point, and everyone told him so. She could get anything out of him. She was the one who understood him best, who always defended him. For her, everything Daddy did was right. "The time will come when she will question everything," he thought. But while it lasted, he would enjoy it. Valeria was a real doll, just like her mom had been as a teenager. Lively and somewhat spoilt, perhaps because she was the youngest, she had the virtue of achieving everything she set out to do. "She has the disadvantage of being too pretty," Pedro had often thought, knowing that she would accomplish many things simply by her beauty.

After all, things weren't that bad, and if others had gotten out of worse situations than this, why couldn't he? Clearly, God hadn't abandoned him, because he had spoken powerfully to him that night. Or was it just emotion? Suddenly, he had doubts. What if it was too late? Would he have the strength to change the things that had brought him to this point?

They met the next day, Monday, in Nacho's church, at 10 a.m. Pedro was well aware that Monday was the day pastors took as their day off after the busy activity of the weekend and Sunday, so he valued Nacho's readiness all the more. He had told Virginia enthusiastically about the experience, as soon as he arrived at the house. For her it was a great relief, because the last time hadn't been easy, and she didn't know what she would have done without the help of the support group that Mercedes had arranged. She had insisted that he see Nacho, because she remembered him from the time of the Seminary as someone Pedro admired. At some point, they had even thought of working together before the church entered the furor of the F&G program. He had always been a very upright, incorruptible guy with strong principles. He remembered that Jimena, his girlfriend at the time, had initially been resisted by the group of friends because of her bohemian, artist-like nature. She was an excellent painter, always in an avant-garde and irreverent style. The house they rented was a real spectacle, with bright and contrasting colors, birdlike doorknobs, colorful armchairs; nothing was conventional. Their discussions about how little importance evangelicals gave to art were proverbial. She associated it with a distorted view of the created world and all the good it had to offer, along with a systematic nullification of creativity by the church system.

"Pedro... You don't know how good it made me see you. You changed my day, yesterday, and we started to remember beautiful times with Jimena." It was typical of Nacho to make the other person feel good, without putting himself in a position of superiority.

"Yes, those were spectacular times. It's a pity... Well, we were very idealistic then, at least I was."

"Everyone. But I don't know if those ideals were bad. They drove us to do many things. Maybe it's a matter of replacing those ideals with others, updating them, without making too much of a fuss."

"I'm a fool... You don't know how many times I thought of calling you, Julio, Marcelo...

"And Juan? I remember you were such friends... And the discussions you had! It was like a River and Boca match."

"Of course, Juan... I haven't seen him in a long time... It would have done me good to see you guys because they were beautiful years. But no, I was always in a hurry, locking myself up more and more."

"You know, that happens to a lot of pastors, I'd say most of them. And many still don't change. You, at least, have the opportunity to react. It's really a problem of leaders."

"And people think you're great... Look, I don't know how much you know about what happened to me, I don't know how things got to you. I was probably the talk of the pastors' meetings."

"Regarding pastors, don't ask me. You know how I escape from that type of meetings: "I have a thousand members," "now we have to do three services a day," "our budget is five hundred thousand dollars a year," "we have a radio..." What do we have to envy the world in jealousy and competitiveness? Now, if it's from what I know, or rather from my experience with pastors who had problems, I'll tell you in three words: power, money, and sex, usually in that order." He saw that Pedro was running a quick check in his mind. "Am I wrong?"

"Maybe, maybe. So is my thing textbook?"

"I'll throw in another prediction; I don't know if it's textbook or mine. I'm sure you had warnings, from people and from the Lord, and you didn't take them into account."

"Yes. Virginia, Raúl tried to talk to me." He also remembered that persistent red light that appeared at key moments. Could it have something to do with that? He didn't dare tell Nacho.

Pedro gave a deep sigh.

"Lately I'm seeing everything through images, so the easiest thing to say is that I feel like I've been on a high-speed train that I couldn't get off. Rather, I thought the train was the destination, that the important thing was to be on the train, and well ahead... going faster and faster. A train with lots of passengers who didn't ask themselves where they were going, but liked to go fast and with lots of people..." Here Pedro got stuck in the description. Nacho noticed and encouraged him.

"Come on, you're doing fine."

"Now that I'm telling you, I realize that the people I love most weren't on that train... they were on the ground, waiting for me to get off... and I was going so fast I couldn't even see them."

"And you didn't get off the train, nor did you try to stop it."

"No, the Lord kicked me off. I didn't. He actually tried twice, and I was hanging on so hard that he couldn't throw me off," he laughed. "The third time was the charm."

"What was the third? Tell me at least that one."

"I had come back to preach after the spectacle at the Evangelical Convocation and I was preaching on Sunday evening. I'm in the middle of the message, when a guy stands in the third row and shouts at me, *"Gorbala masala, sinise tomei!"*

"What did he say?"

"Gorbala masala, sinise tomei." I remember it like it was five minutes ago. He said it twice, to top it off. And I remember that my microphone went off right then..."

"And you know what that means? What language is it?"

"I haven't the slightest idea what language it is, but as soon as he said it the first time, I was very clear about what the message was. The second time was so that I didn't have any doubts. Nothing like this has ever happened to me before. You know I was always very suspicious of the subject of prophecy, tongues and all things of the Spirit, and I still am."

"Haven't you changed yet?"

"No, and I don't regret it after some things you hear... Well, going back to what that man said, it was as if he told me in English."

"And what was that?"

"The time is over. Stop fighting."

"And what did you do?"

"I mean, imagine, I'm on the platform, the guy leaves and everyone's staring at me. I tried to get out of it by making him look like a madman, a weirdo. Then, when I realized that nobody had understood the message, I just kept on going, but you know what?"

"What?"

"After that day I couldn't preach anymore, and I ended up giving up. To top it off, so that I wouldn't have any doubt, it turned out that the youth leader had a great gift for preaching. At first, I was jealous, but then I calmed down and realized that this was the Lord's way of replacing me and that I would be a fool if I continued to 'kick against the goads...'"

"Like Paul."

"Exactly. So I asked for a meeting with the Council and requested a three-month leave of absence, but they gave me a year."

"How long ago was this?"

"Two months. And I'm hanging around, not knowing what to do."

"How's your devotional life?" Right to the point. That's what he expected from Nacho. What he needed.

"Lately, quite sluggish."

"Let's see, can I ask you to be a little more precise? When you say 'lately,' when would that be?"

"Some time ago...months, a year..."

"I'm going to take a chance. I'd say it's been sluggish since before your first PMS incident. Power, money, and sex," seeing he hadn't registered the acronym.

"Mmmm... It's just that the power thing wasn't so definite, it's like it's been building up bit by bit. I needed to have more and more, as if it were a drug. The issue of money... yes, it's more concrete, at Casa de Esperanza, the mayor... I got used to the ethical grey, I lost the initiative. Sex? Yes, definitely, and I'll tell you about it next time. I was doing a lot of Bible studies because of the messages and conferences I had to give. I couldn't find time for prayer."

"It's also very common in pastors that fall. And the strange thing is that they don't realize it. It's a mixture of self-sufficiency with unconsciousness. Why don't you spend an hour a day praying and meditating? With a watch, forcing you to concentrate, without interruptions. Like at the Seminary, but with more need, more desperation. Also, I can recommend something that I think is fundamental for every Christian, but especially for those who are in leadership, or exposed to popularity."

"What's that?"

"Something that is practically infallible, although it's difficult at the beginning—an accountability group, or control group.

238

"The Seminary booklet?"

"Yes, that one."

"Raúl recommended it to me too."

"Raúl Encinas? It's been so long since I saw him and… Mercedes, yes. How are they?"

"Fine, they have a girl. He left me a copy, but I didn't even read it. I don't really remember what it's about. What was it, some kind of cell?"

"Something like that, but it's not the same. Do this. Find what Raúl gave you, read it and we'll look at it together. Okay?

"Yes, by all means."

When he got home, Pedro looked for the booklet and started to leaf through it. He immediately remembered the concepts: a group of people who meet regularly to make an ordered summary of the different aspects of their life: spiritual, marital, social, financial, and work. In that group everyone had the same value, it didn't matter if one was important and the other was not. Total confidentiality. Total trust. The idea of submitting to each other voluntarily. The idea also that we all need to be systematically and periodically accountable to each other to counteract the tendency to go our own way.

He was about to call Nacho and talk about it when the phone rang. They had agreed with Virginia that during this period only she would answer the phone, to protect him from anyone who might harm him because of the situation he was in, but also so that he didn't get involved in anything that would take him away from the recovery process he was going through. But apparently, she wasn't there because the phone kept ringing, so he took the call. The voice was strange, like distant, but very convincing.

"Hello? Yes, speaking... No, I'm actually on leave... Yes, of course I'm interested in working... Can't it be a month from now?... Ah, well, then make it this week... Thursday? Well, yes, at nine... At the Domino... See you later."

When he hung up, he wasn't the same man. His indecision would cost him dearly. If he'd only done the devotional time once in the next three days, he'd probably come to his senses in time. Hiding it from the only person who could rescue him at that moment made it almost fatal. Interestingly, he had stopped seeing that annoying red light.

Thursday came, and Virginia saw him going out.

"Where are you going?"

"To take a walk. I'll be back in a couple of hours." Virginia wouldn't be suspicious, because he had made a habit of going out for a walk almost every day. The doctor had recommended it, and it did him a lot of good.

"Think about me."

"Of course, darling."

When he arrived at the bar, a modern place decorated in black and white, with dots like dominoes, located on the corner of two streets that opened in a "v", he immediately identified the person who had called him. He hadn't given him the name or any particular sign. But he knew that the blond guy in a black suit and white shirt with a black briefcase and black folder was the one who had called him.

"Good morning, pastor."

"Good morning. You called me the other day, didn't you?"

"That's right. Please sit down. I ordered a double coffee, with sweetener for you. And a lard croissant."

"Ah, yes. Thank you very much." *How did he know what he liked?*

"I'll get right to the point. In this folder I have a detailed proposal for the Faith and Progress project. Have you heard of our institution?"

"Not really."

"We have grown enormously in recent years in Colombia, Peru and Bolivia. We are interested in entering Argentina, Chile, Brazil, and Uruguay. We are keeping a low profile for now, but we will soon be out in the open."

"But what is it about? Mind you, I'm on leave. You must be aware that I had a bad experience and I'm recovering."

"Yes, we know about all your stumbles."

"So, what do you expect me to do?"

"Look, pastor, you don't have to worry about the details. Everything is already organized. Just look at pages ten to twelve," handing him the folder open on the page with a bookmark. "We believe that, despite the setback you suffered, you are still a very useful and valuable person. And I suppose you're not too happy with the inactivity, living like a pensioner, are you?" He hit him right on the weakest point.

"No, the truth is I'm quite tired of this."

"Then you won't be able to resist." He got up, left a bill to pay for the consumption, went to the door as he said,

"We'll call you."

Pedro was stunned. The mysterious guy was gone, and he didn't even know his name. And here he was, practically committed to a project he hardly knew, without having the strength to resist.

He opened the folder, which was impeccably assembled, with a shiny paper that practically jumped out at him. The graphics were more than attractive: they were alluring. The tables with estimates of captivating figures and annual projections. Without even reading the introduction he went to page ten. There was a picture of him that he didn't remember having been taken. He looked ten years younger and much thinner, brimming with health. Under the photo, in letters of very intense gold, it read: "Pastor Pedro Terrero - General Manager, Argentina." He then read a brief description of his background, brilliantly written to avoid or disguise all the setbacks he had had recently and to highlight his achievements: "Pastor of the largest and fastest growing church in Latin America, international speaker, author of numerous successful books on Christian life, father of three, president of Casa de Esperanza, with excellent political ties…"

He kept reading. The first section, entitled Exhaustion of the Religious Experience in Latin America, was a brief analysis sprinkled with secular quotes about the problems that all Christian denominations, Catholic and Protestant, had in continuing to advance in the continent. It attacked Catholicism for its formal rigidity and Protestants for their theological superficiality. It attributed this situation to the lack of preparation of leaders in current issues such as mass sociology, political psychology, communication and media theories, and investment projects. The latter attracted his attention powerfully.

The second section, entitled A Solution for the Twenty-First Century, referred to a series of "historical meetings" that had taken place in Cartagena, Colombia, in 1997, called Faith and Progress for Latin America. It spoke of a strategic alliance between three worlds: the world of religion, the world of politics and the world of finance. Recognizing that they had always been linked, it proposed a much more dynamic and open relationship, not so hidden and mysterious.

The third section, Promising Advances, recounted what the movement had achieved since its founding in March 1998 in Colombia, Peru, and Bolivia, with a long list of names taken from the three previous areas of influence. He was impressed to see a dozen pastors he knew by name: Ruiz Oliva, Barrientos, Ojeda Saldívar... Morrison! The names of five national deputies from the three countries and a couple of businessmen from well-known companies and several second-level journalists from well-known media also appeared.

The last part, a series of graphs and tables of a clarity and technical perfection he had never seen before, was called Ten Year Projections: 1999-2008. Starting with the three previous countries in 1999, it ended with all the countries of Latin America. What caught his attention was the level of detail and growth of each of the items: members, media, and finance. He looked for the Argentina section, and he was astonished. The annual columns had very precise figures. Members: 0, 550, 6,700, 18,200... 580,000. Media (audience): 0, 20,000, 350,000, 1,200,000, ... 3,000,000. Finance (millions of dollars): 0; 0.5; 1.1; 4.8; ... 28. How could they have this level of detail? How could they have this level of certainty? The most obvious question—where would the money come from? —didn't seem to trouble him at this point. He supposed that some benefactor or some group of people with money would be behind this gigantic effort. Finding out the origin of that money wasn't his job.

His mind was full of questions. Why had they chosen him? Wouldn't it be an opportunity to evangelize in a massive way and with resources, on another level, and using the latest techniques and technology of this time? What did it matter if those behind it weren't believers or even if they had other intentions? He remembered what the Apostle Paul had said: "But what does it matter? The important thing is that in every way, whether from false motives or true, Christ is preached."[47] After all, he was a pastor and they knew he would speak about the gospel. The idea of power subjugated him, seduced him. It would also be a revenge for all those who abandoned him in his worst moment and hadn't even given him a call. Yes, Pedro Terrero wasn't finished! These people valued him. They were right. You had to modernize, use the media, politics, and money. What was wrong with that? His mind went back to Nacho's Faith and Love Church and saw again all their defects. Where did they expect to go with such primitive means, with people without training? Sure, they would reach the simplest people, but who would take care of the rich, the powerful, those who had influence? Didn't Jesus also speak to the powerful and the wealthy? Wouldn't we be discriminating by taking care only of the poor and the weak? These people need to be reached according to their level, with a proper message, a dinner in a high-class restaurant, talks in five-star hotels. The only thing left was to convince Virginia...

"Who is this person, and why didn't you tell me he called you and that you were meeting this man? You lied to me!" Virginia was angry and felt cheated.

"I didn't lie to you then because I was going to tell you everything eventually. I knew you were going to say no before you knew what it was about. And this man, I forgot to ask his name, but I can find out. The important thing is that it's a chance to go back to work for the Lord, and in a different way, full of possibilities."

"What did Nacho tell you? Didn't he tell you to go back to rebuilding your devotional life first, to join a control group?"

"And I'm going to do that, but this is something that came up now, and I can't let the opportunity pass."

---

[47] Php 1:18

"Check with Nacho... with Raúl. It sounds crazy to me, a trap of the enemy."

The next day, while on his daily walk, a man dressed in black sportswear approached him.

"Nice day!"

"Yes, beautiful."

"How are you, pastor? My name is Ramiro Zuleta, from the Faith and Progress Project," holding out his hand. "Let me invite you to coffee."

Amazed, Pedro shook his hand and accompanied him to a bar on Libertador Avenue. He had never noticed the name before. It was called El Progreso.[48]

It was a very elegant bar, with a place upstairs. Ramiro climbed the stairs nimbly and chose a chair by the railing, from where he could see the entrance, as if he were on a lookout. He ordered, without asking Pedro, two coffees with milk and *facturas*.

"Let's get down to business, pastor. What did you think of the project?"

"Well, interesting. Ambitious. I'm analyzing it."

"We need your answer today."

"Today?"

"Yes. It's a major project and every day counts on the schedule. We think you're the right person, but if you don't accept it or have doubts, we already have another candidate."

The vertigo and determination of these people generated admiration and fear in him at the same time. It was a feeling similar to that which had caused him his first encounter with Mayor Mejia. They were people who knew where they were going, and got things done. On the one hand, Pedro had always said that evangelicals were very disorderly, very lazy, slow to take advantage of the latest technological advances and sociological research. He was comfortable with people who were action-oriented, efficient, and determined. It was a bit the secret of the church he had managed to raise in such

---

[48] In Spanish, The Progress

a short time. But he didn't welcome this pressure in a moment of weakness, where he was rethinking his whole life. The threat of losing a great opportunity if he didn't make up his mind right there, a typical sales technique, shook him. He remembered his first meeting with Tony Vidal of Fulness and Growth, another salesman. In the end the proposal had been good, right? He couldn't bear the thought of seeing another person benefitting from this project tomorrow, another picture in the brochure, with all that it meant in terms of money and security, and he idle at home, waiting for something to turn up, or ending up in a second-rate church, facing retirement and old age like so many pastors he knew. "Besides," he thought, "they chose me. Surely, they saw the conditions I have, and I am the person who can best implement the project."

"I understand. What would be the working conditions?" Pedro replied, assuming an executive attitude.

It was already late. The man took out a folder detailing salary, benefits—a late model car, thirty days annual vacation, office in one of the most modern buildings in Belgrano, surrounded by gardens and amenities, medical insurance—along with a contract and the pen, which he put up in front of Pedro, after removing the cutlery and cleaning the table in a swift movement.

When Pedro told her that he had accepted the proposal, for Virginia it was the last straw. She wasn't interested in knowing the type of work, the conditions, nothing. She knew there could be nothing good in it, and that Pedro, once again, had missed an opportunity to change, to get out of that vertigo that was dragging them towards destruction. She told him decidedly,

"Go away then. I'll stay with the children."

Pedro tried to convince her, but he knew it was a losing battle. If he considered himself a determined person, Virginia was no less than him. In fact, it was one of the virtues that had attracted him to her, and one of the things he always admired her for.

She had lived these last ten years with growing anxiety, seeing the changes in Pedro, gradual at first, and increasingly abrupt in the last few years. It was as if there were nothing left but memories and vestiges of the pure, idealistic boy she had known and who had captivated her when they were eighteen. Pedro had been a funny guy, full of friends, sporty, with a frank and sincere look. Now he had become a person whose only topic was the church and its projects, isolated, overweight, who trusted nobody.

At first, she had liked the push he had given to the small initial congregation and had accompanied it with all the enthusiasm he had, facing each of the obstacles together. She remembered that they started the day by praying and reading the Bible, once the children were in kindergarten or school. Then at night, when the children were in bed, they spent some time talking about what each one had done during the day. There was a unity among them of all kinds that made them a solid block. But the basic, deep things that sustained them were gradually, imperceptibly, replaced by the external things that divided them. The time for prayer and reading became the team planning meeting when she joined in as a virtual and then effective sub-pastor. Talks about what each had experienced individually led to talks about the church, the ministry, and other people.

Sara's appearance was like a wedge that divided them even more and the final incident left open wounds, which she was only able to begin to heal with the group of girls. He didn't even have the courage to acknowledge his participation, and this only tarnished his image further. The Pedro with whom she had fallen in love would have recognized his mistake. When the Council gave Pedro his year's leave, she knew she would have to make a special effort to continue in the church without him, but this would be more like a job than the initial calling they had felt together. She knew this was a transitory arrangement and didn't see herself doing this for long.

In the first meetings with the girls they had shown her how weak her position as a pastor's wife would be if something were to happen to Pedro, and they encouraged her to find a job of her own, one that had nothing to do with the church and wasn't dependent on her husband. When she didn't seem to react, they showed her several real-life examples that ended up convincing her.

"Do you remember Pastor Ruiz?" said Camila in one of their meetings.

"The one who died in an attack?" replied Virginia.

"Exactly. Well, the other day I ran into his wife, Rosalía. She looked so bad... She had an old dress, a sad face... When I asked her what she was doing, she said she was sewing for a living. I gave her what I had. Four kids..."

"And Sarah Miles, the American missionary's wife?" said Mariela, joining in.

"Don't tell me she's on the street. They're well taken care of from there." It was Virginia.

"Yes, in that sense, yes, but nobody invites her to give a talk anymore, or to write an article, and she was as good or better than her husband."

"Better!" Sabrina always stood for her own sex. And while we're on the subject, I'd like to mention Marcela Arroyo, wife of Tomás Arroyo, from Cristovisión Ministry, that went bankrupt."

"I know. She was left on the street," said Camila.

"Not on the street, but she lost the nice apartment they had and had to rent, and now she's looking for any kind of job. The money they gave her will last a couple of months only."

Virginia had understood the message. But what could she do? The idea came from Mercedes, who remembered that Virginia had started studying journalism.

"What if you try doing a radio show?" The church had an FM radio station that broadcast a program all day that, like most evangelical radio stations, was only listened to by the church's own faithful. They sent themselves greetings, music requests, and congratulations. The bulk of the programming was recorded worship or canned programs sent to them from various foreign ministries.

"Do you know that I once thought about doing this, when the radio station was launched?" said Virginia.

"And?" Camila asked.

"But I'd like to do a serious program for people who aren't from the church. That can compete with other radios." The tone of voice and the face showed that it was a project that excited her. "But maybe we can start on the church radio station and then, when we have practice, go to a secular radio station." That was precisely what Sabrina was about to suggest.

"I'm interested too," added Mercedes.

"And I'm sure there are many from the church, or from other churches, who would like to help," said Virginia, as in her best moments of initiative.

They got to work on the project. Virginia led it naturally, and only then did she realize how much she had lost by being in her husband's shadow. Since they started the work, she was always the pastor's wife, the *pastora*, the sub-pastor, never on her own merits. After all, what was the requirement for this position? To be the pastor's wife. What was expected of her? Loyalty. Not to think too much. Had she ever competed with anyone for the position? No. Would anyone tell her if she wasn't good for the job, if she wasn't good at preaching, for example? No. Too easy, and too unfair to others.

She remembered that when they were dating, it wasn't like that. They were Pedro and Virginia, each with their own virtues, the perfect team. Did she have to go through this crisis to get her thinking again on her own? It wasn't costing her that much. She had only one doubt: could she generate a project that was not only interesting to her, that was useful, but also self-sustaining financially? She posed this as a personal challenge, but also in the group. After all, it was one of the pieces of advice for those who set goals for themselves: propose them to people you trust, so that they can function as stimulators for the project.

The program on the Christian radio, which ran on Saturdays from 9 to 11 a.m., was a good starting point, although Virginia realized right away that it would be no more than a rehearsal. It was called "Questions" and the general and vague objective was that people would send in their questions on religious topics and they would answer on the air. But when Virginia asked what the radio audience was, who was listening and how many, no one could tell her. Surely there were many from the church, and perhaps other believers in the area, but no one seemed to care about capturing listeners and keeping them. A little informal market research done in the neighborhood businesses by people on the team yielded a unanimous concept that this was the "evangelists' radio," and no one listened to it. Even worse, they assumed that it wasn't aimed at them, but only at church members, something like a community radio.

So, after a couple of months in Radio Bendiciones, and confident that they could meet the challenge, they decided to hire a space in Radio Nuevos Aires, the FM radio with the largest audience and reach in the area. The initial slot they received was Fridays at 10 p.m. It wasn't the most convenient, but they decided to start and wait for an opening in a better slot. The team consisted of Virginia, Héctor Zapata, a young communications student, Moira Soto, a voiceover student, and Walter Grossheim, a lawyer who was interested in apologetics. They were all believers from the New Church of Blessing. This generated a discussion at the weekly team meeting, which they held on Monday afternoons.

"It seems to me that we need more diversity in the team. We are all from the same church and we are going to say more or less the same thing. Too monotonous." It was Walter's vision, thinking of his colleagues, and the remote possibility that they would listen to such a program.

"Maybe, but do you have any suggestions?" asked Virginia.

"Yes, incorporate people who bring fresh ideas, even contrary to ours."

"You mean from other churches?" asked Héctor.

"Mmmm, maybe, but I'm also thinking of people who aren't believers, who represent the general public," said Walter.

"And forcing us to think in what people think ... I like it." Virginia felt her blood boil. She felt alive. It was a risk she was willing to take. Maybe because she was tired of doing the predictable, what was safe, protected by an institution or by her husband. She would rather take the risk and make mistakes than not risk it and have everything remain the same. She remembered a criticism she had heard on television about evangelicals: that they were only good at talking to each other and when they talked to others all they could do was try to impose their ideas by saying "the Bible says this or that." What about those who don't believe in the Bible? What about issues that are complex, debatable, open-ended questions?

She bought the idea.

"Can you think of anyone?"

"You're going to tell me I'm crazy," Walter challenged her.

"Try me."

"Nicolás Peretti," said Walter, decidedly.

"The cult investigator?"

"Exactly. Don't you like him?"

Virginia was thinking.

"I like the idea," said Héctor.

"Me too," added Moira.

"Let's do it, then!" said Virginia, banging the table.

Nicolás was surprised by the call in the middle of the investigation of one of the last groups that had disembarked in Argentina. Accused of both being an arm of the CIA and of laundering drug money, they clearly handled a lot of money and were trying to buy everything that could be bought—media, buildings and, apparently, political offices. He was particularly struck by the name of the show's host, Virginia Terrero. *This is going to be interesting,* he thought, and accepted the proposal.

It didn't take Pedro long to realize why they had sought him out. It wasn't so much because of his prestige in the evangelical community, since his name was quite tarnished already, and even more so now that he was no longer the pastor of the New Church of Blessing. Nor had they sought him out for his organizational skills and administrative management. Although he was useful to them, he wasn't that important, because all the hierarchical staff, the decision-makers, came from outside. Mostly from Colombia, where the headquarters was, but there were also some Peruvians and Bolivians, along with a mysterious American, Frank Trench, who was at almost every meeting but never said a word. To this day, Pedro doesn't know if he speaks any Spanish beyond "Buenos días," "gracias" or "hasta luego." The few times he heard him speak, it was in English, and with only one person, Wilson Narvajo. For some reason he assumed he was some kind of financial manager, or a representative of someone who put money into the organization. In spite of having the title of General Manager of Argentina, Pedro didn't participate in all the meetings that were held, but only in the one on Mondays, where the week was planned. And even then, he realized that the really important issues weren't discussed there. Maybe later, once they got to know each other more.

Pedro Terrero served them by his contacts. Because he knew all the ins and outs of evangelical politics, and also because of the contacts with the world of secular politics that he had established in recent years. They wanted to know how the evangelical world worked, what things they liked and disliked. Who were the key contacts, who were the most respected figures. What were the most prestigious media, which ones sold the most, which ones were read the most and by what social level. They needed him to tell them which were the most influential Christian books, the most read authors. They were even interested in more subtle information, such as what was the "fashionable message" (literally). Pedro thought he understood what they wanted but preferred to ask.

"What do they mean by the 'fashionable message'? This isn't a shopping center, a 'mall' as you call it, with its fashion items."

"I'm sorry if I didn't make myself clear, or if I hurt your feelings, Pedro." Manuel Cortiloza was the one who called the shots. A Harvard-educated Colombian, he was polite but went straight to the point and never lost sight of his goal. In this case, the apology was only to get his information more quickly. "I don't know if it's the same here, but in my country, and in other Latin American countries, we have observed that in most churches and in the media there is a predominant message that changes in cycles of five to six years.

"I think I understand, Manuel, but could you give me an example?" *These guys are no fools*, thought Pedro.

"Of course. A few years ago, everyone was talking about the anointing. The leading preachers, books, and magazines. Preachers who spoke about the anointing came from the United States and Colombians traveled there for conferences, workshops, seminars on the anointing. After five years, everyone was talking about prosperity, the seed of faith, the abundant harvest. And no one was talking about the anointing anymore. Five more years went by, maybe six, and the fashionable message—now you will understand—was prophecy. Prophets, prophecies, conferences on prophecy, schools of prophets... we even had PropheZion, a concentration of prophets, in our country. About 7,000 prophets were gathered in a kind of 'prophetic think tank,' to generate thousands of prophecies that were fed into a computer with the idea of detecting patterns and generating 'consensual prophecies.'"

"You don't say! And what prophecies came out of the congress?" *Is he kidding me?* Pedro wasn't too sure.

"Nothing specific, other than vague, assorted announcements of destruction and blessing. As it always happens, those who participated and didn't obtain anything don't dare say it was a fiasco, so they return to their churches and say that it was a great blessing. In this way no one asks them to return the costs of transportation, lodging and registration, and they are already in line for the next event. We know that evangelicals never say that an event went wrong; they are always 'wonderful,' 'a blessing,' 'a success.' On the other hand, those who filled their pockets with the event also say it was a success, and they will already be planning another mega event, based on the alleged success of the previous one, aligned with the next 'fashionable message.' Do you realize the importance of this term?"

"But do you also want to take advantage of this trend?" asked Pedro.

"No way! But, like anyone who operates in a market, and I hope you aren't offended by this term, you have to know how it works, and what you expect on the demand side."

"Market, supply and demand. And what do we offer?"

"I am assuming that you have read our material carefully"—making him feel like a student who hadn't studied the lesson—"so I am going to summarize the objectives of Faith and Progress Argentina, adding some information that you may not know about the origins of this project. It all started a few years ago, when a group of Latin American pastors who were studying in the United States saw the power of marketing in that country, and how even children are trained to sell products and services. Something like you with soccer, or the Chinese with table tennis. It's something natural, not to be discussed. Everything can be sold and, using the right techniques, added to any political or military pressure that might be necessary, it is sold. I would almost say that marketing, for the Americans, is as powerful an element as military weapons."

"Well, military occupation in world history has always gone hand in hand with commercial domination," Pedro added.

"Right, with the difference that marketing today is studied practically as if it were a science, and can do a lot of good, or a lot of harm. So we began to unite our two passions, the pastoral, which we brought, and the commercial, which we were learning. That's when the brilliant idea came up: Why not combine both fields? Why not harness the power of marketing for the benefit of the gospel?"

"Interesting..."

"More than interesting! And now I'm going to show you why. We teamed up with several pastors in that country who had financial resources, and we commissioned a consulting firm to do a study of the 'Latin American religious market' and to give us recommendations that would help us sell our 'product,' the gospel."

"Ah, but the gospel isn't a product, it's a way of life..." Pedro began to object. *These people have gone too far,* he thought.

"Of course! We simply put it forward as a mental exercise, just assuming that the gospel could be treated as a product and the Latin American people as a market."

"An 'as if' exercise..."

"Exactly. Now, the interesting thing was that what came out of the study by that consulting firm, Blackman & Blackman, was surprising, something we hadn't expected. When we saw it, we were stunned."

"Why? What did it say?"

"It said that the church's mistake was not to take into account the needs or preferences of the people to whom the gospel was directed. Both in its content and in its presentation."

"But the gospel is only one. At most, it has different nuances, but it has been the same for twenty centuries..."

"Of course, but the genius of these people was that, instead of starting from the message and ending up with the receiver, they suggest starting from the receiver, the 'ultimate beneficiary'"—air quotes— "in what they need, what they look for, what they lack, make them come to the church, and *then* preach the message to them starting from what can attract them the most."

"And the rest of the message?"

"You're talking about the negatives, the demands, the warnings..."

"Sure. Sin, suffering, persecution, for example."

"That can be added as the 'client'"—repeating the gesture with the hands— "becomes part of the group, the organization, the church. In fact, we find that the term 'church' itself isn't convenient, so you will have seen that what we promote are Centers of Faith and Progress."

"And what are the things that people are looking for?"

"Good news, optimism, inspiring songs, lots of music, large groups, action, lights, programs, raising self-esteem, telling them they're important, that they can achieve anything just by putting their mind to it... A leader who thinks for them."

"And what things wouldn't belong in this scheme?"

"Sin, guilt, hell, punishment, poverty, scarcity... persecution, loneliness... silence... small groups... thinking, discipline, effort. In this, we make a lot of use of psychology, and we have several professionals on the team. The idea is to use the latest advances in psychology to motivate people. And we can always find Bible passages that support these principles."

Pedro remembered that many of these things had been suggested to him in F&P and he had successfully implemented them. Successfully?

How could he know he was successful? By the numbers? If he was sincere, he couldn't say that it had been successful for him. Separated from his wife and children, with this group of people he didn't know. What about the people? How could he know if he had been successful for the people? And which people should he consider, the ones who stayed or the ones that left? And those who left, did they leave worse than they came? Actually, he didn't even know their condition.

"So you're basically giving people what they want."

"Yes. One characteristic we notice about Latin Americans is that they find it hard to take responsibility for their decisions. It's always the other person's fault, and he or she is a victim. In politics, they choose caudillos to love or hate. Among countries, there are countries that want to dominate them. And in religion, they have the devil and the demons at their command. So we decided to include these concepts, which are biblical, in our material and our activities."

"And what place would the Bible have in this project?"

"Very important, but of course we consider that there are much more... current... agreeable parts... I don't know what the term would be..."

"Motivators?" said Pedro, who had already found a way around the euphemisms in this project.

"Exactly! Motivators." Pedro knew that probably that wasn't the word he was looking for, but the salesman just wanted to get him on his side. "We use passages that talk about success, blessing, people who succeeded, promises. Of course, we have no problem with people studying the whole Bible or going to a seminary or Bible institute, but we think that the average person doesn't have the time or the possibility to study or read the Bible on their own in this fast-paced world in which we live. So we give them plans for reading key passages, booklets, on positive topics, and the person then comes eagerly to church and leaves motivated.

One of the contacts that interested Manuel the most was Bernardo Quijada, the President of the United Argentine Evangelical Association. Pedro hadn't seen him since the rally, and it had upset him quite a bit that he hadn't even called to see how he was doing. He had felt used. He remembered that a dinner was planned for all the evangelical personalities, local and invited, after the event. He had been invited, but after the incident no one asked him if he wanted to attend. They simply ignored him. Perhaps, knowing Bernardo, he would even have been angry with him for ruining the party, which was so important to him. But Pedro understood that he had to respond to his new organization, and he arranged the interview and sent him some information on Faith and Progress.

When they arrived at the office, Bernardo Quijada received them and hugged Pedro too warmly.

"Pedro! It's been so long! How are you doing? You look great!"

Pedro followed along the best he could, given the circumstances, and introduced him to his boss.

"Manuel Cortiloza, of Faith and Progress. Pastor Bernardo Quijada, president of the United Argentine Evangelical Association."

"It is a great pleasure to meet you, pastor. You will be aware of who we are and our projects, because of the material that Pastor Terrero sent you."

"Yes, and I was wondering how I could help you," said Bernardo, solicitously.

"Well, we would like to integrate fully into the evangelical community that you lead."

"That is something I would have to consult with the Board, but what do you think you could contribute?"

"Dynamism, growth, resources, media penetration..."

The interview followed with a repetition of the origins and principles of the movement. From Bernardo's face, Pedro realized that he was very interested in what these people could offer him in exchange for the contacts and stamp of approval. It was a win-win situation, and it would be one more advance in the process of growth in the last twenty years of Pedro's life.

From then on, the pace became frantic. F&P started opening venues all over the country, at a rate of one venue per week. First in Buenos Aires: Downtown, Flores, Palermo; the suburbs: San Isidro, Lanús, San Justo, Morón; cities in the interior: Córdoba, Rosario,

Mendoza, Salta, Misiones, Río Gallegos. By the end of the year there were more than forty venues. All of them were fully equipped, with rents paid for two years, newly painted, chairs and sound system. Pedro signed all the expense checks and was in charge of approving the premises and signing the rental contracts, but F&P had brought in a team of people from abroad who were in charge of doing the searches and preparing the contracts. He was in charge of the first premises and initial arrangements, but then he was told that there was no need for him to waste time travelling, and that they would simply repeat the basic scheme in the other places, which was the same one they had been implementing in the countries where they were already working.

Once the premises were set up, they started to have weekly meetings, on Tuesdays, Thursdays and Sundays. They all had the same exterior image: a sign that read "Center of Faith and Progress, Free Entry." The messages were the same in all the premises and were distributed the previous week by e-mail. Each week, the people in charge, called Guides, sent detailed reports to the central office— "Center Zero" in the group's jargon— indicating the number of attendees and the amount of the offering. With all that information, Pedro had to collate it and prepare charts and comparative graphs and analyses using a computer program provided by the organization. He would then print them out and display them on the office bulletin board, sending the data to the Cartagena office.

"Good morning, this is Virginia Terrero. This is "Thoughts" the program that makes you think. Hi, Nicolás."

"Hi, Virginia. It's a pleasure to share this space with you. Let's hope that this experience will be positive for our listeners. I can tell you that for me it has been very interesting from the team meetings we have had," said Nicolás.

"That's right. Why don't we explain what this... experiment is all about?" said Virginia.

"Of course. Do it yourself, after all you were the one with the idea," said Nicolás.

"Not exactly. The credit goes to Dr. Walter Grossheim, who is with us today. Hi, Walter."

"Hi, Virginia, Nicolás. Nice to be here today. Let's hope the reality is at least as good as the idea... or better."

Virginia gave a brief account of how the idea came about and introduced Nicolás.

"We're going to share this space with Nicolás Peretti, a cult researcher, international speaker and writer of several books, including "Chantas y encantados" and "Controllers and Controlled — An Unhealthy Relationship." He is also a partner in the consultancy RePol (Religion and Politics), dedicated to researching group behavior in the religious and political world. How would you define yourself: atheist, agnostic?"

"Agnostic. Or maybe a skeptical believer. I mean, I have no problem believing, but you have to show me that it isn't a hoax or a scam."

"Perfectly. A sort of Thomas, who said, 'Unless I see the nail marks in his hands and put my finger where the nails were, and put my hand into his side, I will not believe.'"[49]

"Exactly. And if I am not mistaken, Jesus didn't punish him or reproach him for asking for proof," said Nicolás.

"Precisely. Well, today we plan to deal with two subjects: miracles and control in cults. Let's go to the first one. Do miracles exist? If they exist, how do we know when a miracle has occurred?" Virginia continued.

It was one of the topics they had discussed at the team meeting that week. They had agreed that these meetings would only determine the general issues and formal details of the transmission, but then leave the treatment of the issues themselves to the moment. In this way the debate they were seeking to achieve between a skeptic, Nicolás, and the two Christians, Virginia and Walter, would be much

---

[49] Jn 20:25

more spontaneous and realistic. It was a big risk, especially knowing Nicolás's frontal style, but Virginia was willing to take it, preferring not to come off well in an argument, or even lose it, in exchange for authenticity. It was the only way to achieve credibility, with a genuine audience. In the worst case, it would give them material to study and discuss in a later program.

"If you'll allow me, Virginia, without going into whether miracles exist or not, I'd like to start by clarifying what are *not* miracles. In other words, what evidence of miracles is useless or fake. And they are used also by all the crooks and swindlers who are on the loose, sometimes without knowing it. Let's give them the benefit of the doubt."

"You woke up good today," said Virginia, comfortable in this game of gentle stabbing.

"I *am* good." She laughed. "I'd like us to look at a fallacy that has been well studied and is called 'selective evidence.'"

"Define it, please," said Virginia.

"Yes, this fallacy occurs when we only choose the evidence that supports what we say and discard the evidence that disproves it."

"And how would that apply in the case of miracles, or false miracles?" Virginia asked.

"The best thing is to see a concrete case that I witnessed. I'm in a meeting of about three hundred people, and one person stands up front and starts saying that there are heart, kidney, eye, and spinal diseases, and starts praying for all those problems. Then a person or two come to the front saying that yes, they had some of those problems and they think they were healed. Immediately, that is taken as proof that there was one or several miracles of healing. What would be the fallacies here?" asked Nicolás.

"On the one hand, the supposed knowledge of the diseases among the public is so general and vague that it doesn't prove anything," suggested Walter.

"The sample size, we would say, is large enough and the events are ample enough to guarantee success," said Virginia.

"Right!", said Nicolás, as if they had hit on the right answer in a quiz. "It's something any of us could do. On the other hand, suppose there was a person with kidney trouble, or several, and the person prayed for this problem, and none of them were healed. That isn't a statistic. In everyone's eyes the supposed healer is one hundred percent correct. Of course, the alleged healings aren't followed up either, to rule out subjectivities."

"Okay, Nicolás, I accept that there is no... scientific verification of the healings, but that doesn't mean they don't occur, does it?" It was Walter.

"No, Walter, I'm not ruling out that they happen, even though I didn't witness any of them firsthand. But I have seen countless alleged miracles that can easily be explained as selective evidence, or false evidence. Or suggestion. Remember that people want to be healed, and many like to have their fifteen minutes of fame too."

"The same goes for alternative medicines," added Virginia. "You can always find people who say they've been cured by taking anything or following any treatment, and we don't have the full statistics..."

"Nor the follow-up," Nicolás completed. "Nor do we have a comparison with the placebo effect, or with the recovery statistics without any treatment."

"Like the weather forecast. It seems to me sometimes that the rate of hits doesn't exceed what I might have, for example," said Walter, "but people only register hits and not misses. It's like wanting to believe that the weather service is right, isn't it?"

"Or astrology," added Virginia. "Predictions for the year are sold, but few people check the level of hits after the year is over by comparing it with a normal, random hit ratio. I think there is a very interesting issue that we can follow up another time, something like: Deception or self-deception? But I insist, once we have removed the cases of deception or self-deception in the alleged miracles, can we accept that there are real miracles?"

"At least, I don't rule them out on principle, just as I don't rule out the existence of God, but first we have to remove everything that is not to see if there is something. That's my task, Virginia and Walter, and it's often quite unpleasant."

"If you'll allow me," it was Walter, "one very interesting thing is the concept of faith in the Bible. In both Hebrew and Greek, the two main languages in which it was written, it means something quite different from what is popularly understood as faith today. The word in Hebrew, *emuna*, means a strong conviction that a person has that something or someone exists, is firmly established, is constant, and is trustworthy. The word in Greek, *pistis*, means a strong conviction of the truth of something or someone —and please listen to this—to the extent that you put your total trust in that thing or person. It is not at all the idea of having faith in anything, of having faith for the sake of faith."

"Okay, and thank you, Walter. I think we can close the first subject, miracles, although it goes a long way. The pending issue would be real miracles. Now for the second topic of the evening: Control in cults..."

"Yes, Virginia, I want to say that this is the subject that concerns me the most of all the groups that are out there and that I call cults. The issue of the money they handle and the business, the money laundering and the corruption is unfortunate, and I denounce it when I hear about it, but it is, more than anything, a legal, police issue. What makes me very sad and very angry is that today, in the twentieth century, there are people who enslave others through the mind, using religion, and others who allow themselves to be enslaved, or don't even realize that they are being enslaved." Nicolás put aside the academic style that he had incorporated from the consultancy when he was dealing with this subject; he was very passionate about it.

"I understand that you had very close personal experiences of this... scourge," said Virginia.

"That's right, both me and my wife, Isolda, who is with me today. And I think it's a much more widespread problem than you think, and much more dangerous. Because people are unaware of it."

"You say there are many more cults than we think?"

"No, that's just it, Virginia. It's not so much the cults. What I'm saying is that sectarian behavior, sectarianism, is growing throughout society and in the churches as well."

"There have always been marginal churches, unrecognized, with strange ideas..."

"What I am telling you is that there are sectarian manipulations within long-standing, large, recognized churches." Virginia didn't know what Nicolás was trying to get at, and he realized it. "But I don't know why you are surprised, after all, we are all immersed in a social and political reality that constantly tries to control us, to take away our freedom. Why shouldn't this happen in a Christian church? Do they have a special armor?"

"No, not at all. But the Christian message is liberating, it goes against everything that involves manipulating people, using them... which is what happens in cults, and in politics," answered Virginia.

"Look, without going any further, the last evangelical group we are investigating is buying up, among other things, media outlets all over the country. At any moment they could even buy this radio. Here I have the information." He handed Virginia a folder, with the name Faith and Progress clearly standing out on the cover. He was amazed that she didn't react.

"First, I'm not aware that this is an evangelical group. Lately, every dubious pastor or church that goes around is foisted on evangelicals. On the other hand, there is nothing wrong with wanting to buy media to spread the gospel."

"Sure, but what is not at all clear is the origin of the funds. In fact, they are being investigated in several countries, and I don't know why it's not happening here yet..."

Suddenly, Virginia paled. She had been turning the pages absent-mindedly as she followed the conversation when she came across Pedro's photo, under the title "General Manager, Argentina." She looked at Nicolás and then at Walter, not knowing what to do. Nicolás signaled Walter to say something.

"Yes, of course... The issue of money is critical because we evangelicals in Argentina have never handled much money. In general, they are small to medium sized churches that are self-supporting and dedicate a large part of their resources to helping others, both inside and outside the church. The larger churches came after many years of effort, but none grew overnight." His training as a lawyer had given Walter a great ability to squirm out of difficult situations.

"That's exactly what I, at least, recognize from the evangelicals. Hard-working, austere, generous. But I think that in recent years these ideas and these new influences have been getting more and more..." Now both of them were looking at Virginia, who continued to stare at the page with the photo, completely oblivious to the program.

"Maybe this is a topic to be discussed on another occasion now that it has been raised. What do you think, Virginia?" Walter nudged Virginia.

"Ah, yes, of course... Walter, would you close, please?" She seemed distracted, confused. Completely contrary to the image she always conveyed.

"We left two issues raised for you, the listeners, to think about. You can get in touch by phone or by mail. Until next week, at the same time, on 'Thoughts,' the program that makes you think."

"See you later," said Nicolás, followed by the musical curtain.

As soon as they went off the air, Virginia glared at Nicolás, furious, with the folder in her hand. She wanted to eat him alive.

"How can you do this to me? You made me look ridiculous on the first show! You tricked me!"

Nicolás was perplexed. He didn't look like a person who was satisfied that he had achieved something. On the contrary, he seemed distressed, confused.

"But, Virginia, I told you at Monday's meeting that I was going to bring up the issue of Faith and Progress, and you said nothing. Tell me if this was so, Walter," looking to the lawyer for help.

"Sure, but I didn't know my husband was in this organization. I thought it was one of your cults..." The moment she said the phrase she realized how ridiculous it sounded.

"And how could I suppose you didn't know your husband was in this organization? I assumed that you knew, and that you had arguments to defend it, or some ace up your sleeve. That was the arrangement we had, wasn't it? Not to prepare anything, to leave it to spontaneity, even if it doesn't come out so neatly..." He didn't go on, because he saw that Virginia was in a bad condition, holding back her tears. She seemed so helpless. Nicolás signaled Isolda to go over to her. As soon as she touched her, Virginia embraced her with all her strength, and they remained in silence for a while. Walter knew this was the best thing that could happen to Virginia, even in the midst of the humiliation and shame of having to admit that she didn't know where her husband worked and finding out on a live show that he was the national manager of a highly suspicious entity.

"Look, here's the audience report. Fifteen percent. Is it good?" Walter held on to the paper as a lifeline to get through the bad moment.

"Good? Excellent! It took me a year to reach ten percent..." Nicolás took Virginia by the arm. "Virginia, the idea worked! Don't be discouraged."

Suddenly, Virginia composed herself, wiped her eyes with her arm, and her face took on a fresh glow. She arranged her hair with an assured nod of her head, and said:

"Of course! Let's go on! I am sure that this was not by chance, that it was the way the Lord brought everything to light. Forgive me, Nicolás, for being suspicious of you, but if we take risks we don't have to complain about the consequences of the risks."

"That's the way I like it! And I'm sure that in other programs I'm going to come out badly, because we're not trying to win an argument but to make people think, to analyze options. Remember that." Nicolás seemed completely sincere.

On her way back from the studio, Virginia thought it could easily be the worst day of her life. Much of it was her fault, for not even wanting to know what Pedro was up to. *Would they have realized they were separated? I'm sure Walter knew, but Nicolás... What a humiliation! What must he think of me, of us?* she thought.

Pedro and Virginia had been living apart for a month. The official explanation, which nobody believed, was that he had to be near the new office to organize the work. The whole scheme of concealment was bound to fail, as in fact it did. Not just because of the incident on the radio show. They were both so tired of the situation and having to pretend to be the happy family that they unconsciously thought, *Let them think what they want*. The most affected were the children, who had experienced the strange climate of the house since the church had given Pedro leave. He found himself strange in the routine of the house, used to being always outside. The girls were delighted to have him all day, and he accompanied them to school, cared about them and knew more about their lives. But the quiet atmosphere was short-lived, because arguments began to arise between the parents, often over minor issues. When Virginia told him to leave, they gathered the three kids together and told them the truth, or at least as close to the truth as they could handle.

"Guys, as you may know, this has been a very difficult time for all of us, and with Daddy we decided that it was better to take a little distance for a while…"

"Are you going to separate?" Valeria, the youngest, shouted, incredulous, trying to embrace them both, as if trying to bring them together.

"No, Vale, we hope it's just for a while," said Pedro. It seemed like one more nightmare of the many he had been living lately. "I'm going to be around, I'm going to see you often…"

"What do I care what you do?" Roque, the eldest, didn't mince words. "I'll give you a month to fix your things. If not, you won't see me again."

Pedro and Virginia looked at each other. They didn't expect this answer or this ultimatum.

"Roque, it's not that easy…" Virginia tried weakly.

"And everything you say from the pulpit? So it's all a lie, then?"

This was to be expected, though it was hard blow. Virginia had tried to hide her tears. Luciana, the middle one, had hugged her, afraid of taking sides with that gesture.

"It's not a lie, and I assure you… we are doing everything we can to put into practice what we believe, what we preach… but it's not easy." Pedro was defending himself with what he could in a lost cause.

"And why don't you ask for help?" Luciana's practical advice.

"Yes, we will, if we can't work it out together," said Pedro.

The scene came back to her in detail as she thought about what to do. Virginia turned the corner into Rivarola Street. She stopped at 2245 and rang the bell for apartment 4A.

"Hello?"

"It's me."

"Virgi? I'll be right down."

Pedro ran down the stairs and saw her standing there in the night, helpless and beautiful, crushed by the events. He wanted to shout at her, "Let's leave all this and go somewhere alone, where we can be Pedro and Virginia again!" He opened the door and kissed her on the cheek.

"I'm not going to ask you how you are. But come in. You're freezing to death."

They went up the little elevator quietly and into the tiny apartment. Virginia had never been there before, and the first glimpse gave her a quite different image than she had imagined. Quite simple, austere, with the basic comforts, a bit messy. He made her a coffee in silence and sat down in front of her.

"I listened to the show," Pedro broke the ice, "so I think I know why you're here… and why you're like this."

Virginia looked at him with her beautiful brown eyes and said the last thing he would have expected.

"Now what are you going to do?" said Virginia.

What do you mean, what am I going to do? Pedro thought. She was the one who had suffered the unimaginable humiliation.

"I'll manage. I'm worried about you," he said.

That show of interest in her, so rare in the last Pedro but frequent in the Pedro she had met twenty years before, touched her. She smiled. How Pedro missed that smile!

"Your wife has just told thousands of people on the radio that her husband leads a cult, a money laundering group, a bunch of swindlers, and you're worried about how I'm doing? Look, Pedro…" without realizing it she had rested her hand on his, "on the one hand

I'm angry, but on the other I think we're involved in something... something we don't handle... something that others... are handling."

"You don't know how many times I thought that..." he said.

"And if we don't do something, we're going to destroy ourselves, the kids... And I don't want it, I don't want it. You don't know how often I relive the moment we told the kids we were separating," said Virginia.

"Me too. There too, it was like someone was trying to get us to make the worst decision."

"Why don't we stop this madness? Come home... The kids miss you... I miss you..."

"If you say so... But mind you, you're going to meet another man." They laughed and kissed tenderly, a kiss of a couple that had started their way back.

Pedro didn't wait to be called and sent them the telegram of resignation.

10

JUAN: TEAMWORK AND RESISTANCE

We knew there were others we needed to call
And they were always there heart and soul

It hadn't been easy for Juan to separate from Mariela. In fact, it was the first time this had happened in their sixteen years of marriage. She had stayed with the twins and the little girl. Mateo and Marcos were similar in many ways, but quite different in others. *Like the Gospels,* Juan had often thought. Mateo was more thoughtful, calmer, always wanting to know the reason for things and the instructions he received. Marcos was easier because everything suited him, but he also made mistakes more often, in his choices and in his relationships. But what mattered most to Juan and Mariela was that they complemented each other well. They argued, they had their fights, but they always ended up making up. And woe betide anyone who tried to get between them! Celeste, the little girl they had adopted when she was three years old, was the toy of the house. She had come at a special time when Mariela had just lost a pregnancy. Her mother had died of AIDS and she came to the Pan de Vida lunchroom with her aunt. The attachment was mutual and instantaneous, both with Mariela and the children. Adopting her seemed the most natural thing in the world.

The financial blow had also been great. At the church in Buenos Aires, with the two part-time salaries, mechanic and pastor, they made ends meet. But when Juan became increasingly involved in the church, he gradually gave up his job as a mechanic. If everything had gone well, he could have taken on the job of full-time pastor and used his job as a mechanic to supplement it. But it wasn't so, and the exit he had been offered meant practically a fresh start. He knew that if he dedicated himself fully to his job as a mechanic, in a short time they would be well off financially, but it would have meant closing the door on his vocation as a pastor, which he was only now being able to fulfill.

Mariela had given up trying to get more involved in the church in Buenos Aires beyond what was strictly necessary, while continuing to support Juan in everything. It hurt her to see the effort he made and how he endured so much mistreatment. She had often heard disqualifying comments about her husband that should have been confronted for the sake of the church.

"What does this pastor think, that he's going to change us? If the others couldn't, why should he?" overheard as she passed through the kitchen.

"Today we use a guitar, tomorrow it's going to be the drums. The problem is that the young people do what they want with him," a group of three of the toughest women, unaware that she could hear them.

"Of course, it's the first time he's worked as a pastor. He doesn't know that he can't treat everyone the same," a comment that reached her from a good source.

And even she was the target of several comments.

"She thinks it's like in other churches, that the pastor's wife is the *pastora*. *Pastora*... Here she's just like everybody else," from another good source. It coincided with the feeling she had had since they arrived.

She had concentrated on raising the three kids and was active in the school and kindergarten parent committee. She found it odd that she felt more comfortable and valued in those settings than in church. She saw how meetings were held where issues were decided, allowing dissent, sometimes quite strong, but reaching satisfactory solutions. She remembered the first meeting of the parents' committee in Celeste's kindergarten. They had to decide on the details of the annual welcome meeting that was held every year, around May. As the meeting unfolded, Mariela was able to identify almost all the typical elements of these groups. The oldest parents, who were already in their third year and, within these, the most senior were the two parents who had had more than one child in the garden. The one chairing the meeting, a lawyer, did so in a very professional manner, supported by the most active and talkative of the mothers. A couple of Green Ward parents (4-year-old's) were seen to be making a career of replacing the outgoing Yellow Ward parents (5-year-old's) at the end of the year. They were bringing proposals and trying to get the support of the parents in their ward and the newcomers, the Pink Ward. The person who likes to talk, the one who complicates the proposals, the one who clarifies the complicated one, the opposer, those who agree with everything, those who are present but don't participate, etc., were all there. There were discussions, negotiations, appeals to participation and collaboration, the occasional clarification of misunderstandings... but it was possible to start relatively on time and finish on time having achieved the goal, which was to organize the welcome meeting. There were no divisions, resentment or anyone leaving the kindergarten because they didn't agree with what had been decided. On the contrary, the knowledge of the positions and the ways to express themselves would help the group to face the next decision with greater agility and efficiency.

She couldn't help but let her imagination run wild and think about what would have happened with a similar discussion in one of the churches she had known. For starters, there would be a pastor or leader dominating the discussion, unquestionable, on a higher level. Those who dared to disagree with him would be labeled as rebels, unspiritual, people who caused division. If the meeting took place without differences of opinion, it would be a good meeting; on the other hand, if there was discussion, confrontations, conflicting positions, surely the devil would be doing his job. Then, those who had disagreed during the meeting would continue to clash for a long time.

Shouldn't it be the other way around? Shouldn't the church be an example in handling differences constructively? Why was it not so?

When Saverio left him in the parsonage and after taking a bath, Juan went for a walk through Pueblo Manso, even before putting his things away. He wanted to have a first impression of the place that would be his pastoral field for the next few years. At least, it was what he expected. The stunted period in his first church as pastor had left him with a sense of great frustration. He had a lot of questions that ran through his mind. What had he done wrong? Had he sinned by trying to do things his own way? Did he do things too fast? Had he been wrong in accepting the position, knowing the background? Should he have prayed more, given another direction to his messages? Was it out of pride that he didn't ask for help? Was he good at being a pastor? Apart from a vocation, did he have the required conditions?

Suddenly, he heard a group of people singing a simple, catchy song in the distance, which he recognized immediately from the youth meetings at Raúl's church. It had been years since he had heard it, and he started singing it softly. He realized it came from the Catholic church, opposite the plaza. He felt as if something was drawing him to this unknown place. He entered the old stone church and found a group of standing people, clapping and moving to the beat of the music, led by a group of young people with guitars and tambourines. As he entered, he was handed some printed sheets with the lyrics of the songs. He walked to the last empty bench and tried to join in the songs. When the singing time was over, a priest in his forties came forward and made several announcements. After a Bible reading by a young girl from the audience, he went to the microphone and said:

"Our sister has just read us one of the most comforting passages in the Word of God. Let me repeat the last part."

Even youths grow tired and weary,
and young men stumble and fall;
but those who hope in the Lord
will renew their strength.
They will soar on wings like eagles;
they will run and not grow weary,
they will walk and not be faint.
they will walk and not get tired.[50]

It was a passage Juan knew well, taken from the end of Isaiah 40. He didn't know if it was the priest's voice or the way he read it, or the special time he was going through, but it had taken on a special life for him. The effect was even greater with the words that followed. The priest, as if listening to an inner voice, continued:

"The Spirit tells me that on this night there is a person here... a man... who is very tired, very weary. He has finished a difficult stage, which has left him with questions. Questions that still have no answers... This man loves God with all his heart, and he doesn't want to defile himself. But he feels very lonely and needs the embrace of another brother... This passage is for you, brother, even without knowing you" —looking out at the general public— "and this embrace that we are going to give each other now is for you too. God knows you and hasn't taken his eyes off you at any time" —Juan felt vulnerable already, but the last words pierced him like a sword: "And he is going to take care of your dear wife and your... three children. Let us embrace each other with the love of the Father."

At that moment, the woman in front of him turned around and gave him a motherly hug. He thanked her and went to hug a man who was sitting all alone. He had begun his healing, in the most unexpected place. God never ceased to amaze him. It was better that way. Of course, if it wasn't, he wouldn't be God.

He didn't stay to greet the priest, because he was eager to call Mariela and tell her about the experience. There was a telephone

---

[50] Isa 40:30-31

273

booth as soon as he left the church. He used the few coins he had on the call to tell her how much he missed her, ask about the kids and briefly shared what had just happened.

"It was as if God was waiting for me... you can't imagine what good it did to me."

"Juan, do you know I was praying for you to meet someone who would give you a message from the Lord? Not in my wildest dreams did I think it would be a priest, in a Catholic church. But, after all, why not?"

"I was thinking of talking with him, maybe this week."

"Of course, but go tomorrow," said Mariela, convinced.

"I don't know what they'll think in this town, a pastor going to see a priest. You know that every place has its prejudices, its customs..." In reality, Juan needed Mariela to tell him what he himself thought.

"Juan, we've talked about it a thousand times. We owe ourselves to God above everything." It did him good to hear her say things that they both believed. He felt closer to her than ever. And she knew that he wouldn't renounce his principles for fear of what people could say.

⚮

When he called Father Tomás on the phone, it was as if he was waiting for him. He didn't identify himself as a pastor, but simply as Juan. They arranged to meet at 5 p.m.

He was surprised to find him waiting for him at the entrance of the church. The slightly dark skinned and bearded man with an athletic build was the opposite of the image Juan had in his mind of a Catholic priest, especially since he was wearing "civilian" clothes and a sports hat. The warm handshake confirmed that it would be a productive meeting. He accompanied him to the small office at the end of the corridor. As soon as they sat down, the priest took the initiative.

"Juan, my name is Tomás Valencia, forty years old, seminarian since the age of eighteen, parish priest of The Sacred Heart de Jesús for three years. I love soccer—a fan of Independiente—, chess and people... including their problems," with a wide smile.

He was surprised by this presentation. Usually, the person requesting the meeting is supposed to make the introduction first. He made a mental note to try it out in his own encounters in the future.

"It's a great pleasure to meet you..."

"Please, no *usted* here, only *tú*."[51]

"Better for me, too. Thank you for this meeting. Excuse me for not telling you sooner, but my full name is Juan Cristante, and I'm the new pastor of the Church of the Open Word. I came to see you because yesterday I attended part of the meeting, or mass, I don't know what you call it."

"Meeting is fine. The masses are more formal, more structured."

Juan told him how he was struck by the word Tomás had had, which he understood was directly for him.

"The Lord never ceases to amaze us. How did you feel afterwards, Juan?"

"Good, very good. I felt as if a great weight had been lifted off my shoulders. Besides, it was having that feeling that God hadn't forgotten about me, about us."

"The concept appears in many psalms..."

"Yes. And this morning's devotional time was special. The word *kairos* kept coming to me."

"God's time," Tomás added.

"That's right. God's special time," Juan expanded.

"To your surprise, it was the theme of the sermon at the last two Masses. And I am convinced, at this point in life, that God has his times, and to try to ignore them is to plow in the desert. I'd tell you it's even dangerous."

"It's kind of what I'm feeling lately. What about you?" asked Juan.

Tomás told him his story. He had been born into a wealthy family in Córdoba that had always been close to the Catholic church. He had spent his childhood and youth in his neighborhood parish. With the youth group they had participated in missionary trips to the interior of the Chaco and Formosa, where he had come into contact with a

---

[51] In Spanish, *usted* is the formal address and *tú* is the informal address.

reality that he hadn't even read about in his glass box life. What had always stuck with him from all his Bible readings and theological reflections was that Christianity meant change. An inner change, yes, but one that had to be reflected in the behavior of the individual and in society in general. Without change, it was no more than Marx's "opium of the people."

The life of John the Baptist had always caught his attention in many ways: his calling, his dedication to the mission, his denunciation of hypocrisy, whether soldiers, tax collectors or religious authorities. There was a phrase about John that described him clearly: "He must become greater; I must become less."[52] To live so that Christ will grow, even at the cost of oneself. Finally, the denunciation that had cost him his head and his life, and which he didn't hesitate to make: "It is not lawful for you to have your brother's wife,"[53] to Herod himself. How much this kind of man was needed in today's world!

He had discarded the option of violent, armed revolution, since he understood that it only succeeded in favoring an even more violent reaction of those who would always have the advantage of power and resources. But he hadn't ruled out the idea of risking all for his ideals, even if it cost him his life. What he had seen in the world he knew, the families with power and wealth of Cordoban society, had pushed him more towards a radical solution. Women who met to do acts of charity, undoubtedly useful and necessary, but which didn't alter their well-off lives one bit and did not make them rethink the reason for the tremendous inequality of opportunities between their children and those of the people they helped. Men who gave donations from the companies they ran, also valuable but hardly meritorious, when they were used for publicity purposes and to obtain more benefits than those they gave. It wasn't so much that he criticized them because he knew that, in their own way, they thought they were doing their best. But he knew that they weren't. That their best was their life, their comfort, their safety.

---

[52] Jn 3:30
[53] Mk 6:18

He had enrolled in the seminary and had been caught up in the possibilities of inner change that the Bible and theology study gave him. The more he got involved, the more passionate he became, and the less he was interested in the things of the world, the transient and ephemeral things, that had always accompanied him.

"Did you ever think about starting a family? Did you ever fall in love? That's what I find most difficult to accept about being a priest," Juan interrupted.

"I knew you were going to ask me that, and it's not because of any word of wisdom," he laughed. "It's what everyone thinks, and everyone asks me, or asks us priests. Yes, I fell in love many times, like any high school kid. I went to a co-ed school and I especially liked one girl, Mónica, and we had started dating."

"So? What happened?"

"At one point, I told her everything I was thinking. That although I didn't deny my origins and was grateful for everything I had received, including an education in one of the best schools in Córdoba, I didn't feel comfortable, this wasn't my place."

"Like the Ché Guevara."

"Exactly, but with another proposal. In fact, I think that the Ché's life is a demonstration of what I thought. With all his idealism and dedication, he ended up fueling the most violent response that Latin America has ever known from the military, leaving the revolution limited to a questionable dictatorial and personalistic experience in one country."

"I haven't told you this yet, but I was in the Tucumán jungle, with the army, so I understand you perfectly. Young idealists with wrecked lives and families, while the ideologues stay away, make deals or end up being pardoned."

"And without repentance," added Tomás.

"That's exactly the point!" This village priest he had just met had hit the nail on the head of what Juan had always thought and said. "We agree on that. I think what was missing here was sincere repentance on the part of those who led both sides, starting from the top. I have never heard a single one of those who led the killings say,

277

'I repent. I'm sorry. I regret the death and destruction I caused. I was wrong. I was responsible for bloodshed among Argentines.'"

"I agree with you completely. Especially when you put it in the first person: 'I was wrong, I killed or caused others to die, I ruined lives and families.' It's no use repenting for an institution or a movement." It was obviously a subject that the priest was passionate about too.

"Doing it globally is another variant of the famous 'due obedience.'"

"Yes. And it doesn't help to repent for the military now on behalf of the military twenty years ago. And to think that many of the military were practicing Catholics, and many priests blessed places and weapons..."

"Action or omission," added Juan. "On our side, we evangelicals tended to turn a blind eye or didn't want to believe what we were told. This is a topic I have spoken a lot about with friends and pastors."

The subject begged for greater discussion, and there would surely be opportunities to follow it. Juan was interested to know how a person so like him had ended up in a place quite different from his.

"But you didn't finish telling your story," Juan said.

"I'll keep it short. When Mónica heard me, I think she panicked. I don't know if she thought I would become a terrorist and drag her down with me. Ah, I didn't tell you, but her father was a military intelligence colonel. Later I found out that they had tapped my phones, followed me, and had all my movements recorded in detail. So she started avoiding me, we drifted apart and I went into the seminary. The next thing I knew I was twenty-eight years old and no longer had any dealings with girls. I thought at that moment that I had missed the train. Now I realize that it's not like that, but I don't think anyone will show up at this point in life."

"So, if someone shows up, you'd drop the habit?"

"I'm not ruling it out, but the vow is a serious matter, and it would have to be someone very, very special. A miracle. And I'm not desperate, nor am I thinking about it all day. Especially when I have to counsel some married couples!"

"Yes, I understand you perfectly. Sometimes my wife tells me, when we have arguments, or problems with the kids, 'You should have been a priest.' You'll meet Mariela soon. And the three children... How did you know I had three kids?"

"Ah, about yesterday? I can't explain. It's like an impression in my mind, like an image, but different."

"The gift of wisdom," said Juan.

"Yes, and the more I use it, the less I understand how it works."

Tomás then told him how he had come into contact with the charismatic renewal, a movement born in the 1960's that had its counterpart in the evangelical world, which emphasizes the gifts of the Spirit, such as speaking in tongues, prophecy and words of wisdom, with a simpler and more spontaneous worship. Juan knew about this Catholic movement and shared with Tomás the experiences he had had many years ago in the Varela's home. They were remarkably similar, seeking the same ideals of fellowship and worship centered on the Word and the Spirit.

The themes were far from exhausted, but the most important thing was the bond of friendship and affection that was created in such a short time. Here were two people so similar in their ideals that Juan could have perfectly been a priest and Tomás a pastor. As physicists would say, the only thing that had determined the current situation of both were the initial conditions and the boundary conditions.

Juan left the meeting comforted and strengthened. Mariela was right. It wouldn't have been the same to have the talk another day, without the freshness of spontaneity. He walked back to the parsonage as the sun was setting behind him. He needed time to think and pray.

At the end of the month, Mariela and the kids arrived. Juan had made use of the time to prepare the parsonage. It was an old but spacious house, with high-ceilinged rooms, a large dining room and a garden that communicated with an abandoned lot next door. When the family arrived, he was able to welcome them with a well-conditioned home. The children loved the feeling of space inside and outside the house, especially the back yard.

Mariela was won over by the friendliness of the people. They had managed to rent their house in Buenos Aires, and this gave them some peace of mind. It would be looked after and would mean a much-needed extra income in the first stage. Juan already knew Saverio and his wife, Teresa, quite well. He had had countless *matés* and coffees with him, chatting about the church and the town, and had ended up eating almost every night at their house, despite his insistence that he didn't mind dining alone.

From all these conversations, along with his long walks through the town to learn every detail while praying for it, a fairly complete picture emerged, which Juan shared with Mariela.

"Apart from the Catholic church, there are three small Pentecostal churches, a couple of evangelical churches from other denominations, and us, the Church of the Open Word. Pueblo Manso is a beautiful place to live, especially if you are retired," Juan explained. "It's made for peaceful people, and that's why young people go away, or end up drinking beer on street corners. From there, the jump to drugs is just one step away, although they say it hasn't reached the town yet.

"So you're telling me we're not going to be able to fit into this small town rhythm?" asked Mariela, thinking about the fast pace of Buenos Aires.

"Not necessarily. What I've been thinking and praying about a lot is what we *don't* have to do."

"What we *don't* have to do?"

"Yes, there are plenty of churches in this town, so what we have to avoid is being just another church, just another option on the menu that people can choose from within Christian churches."

"Let's see... I think I understand something, but go ahead..."

"I was thinking about what went wrong in the church in Buenos Aires, and it was clear to me that what I did was to work from within, from what existed, trying to change it so that we could go out, grow and change the outside. We weren't able do one thing or the other, and we only created more resistance. A lot of time and effort wasted."

"So here you propose, what?"

"Work from the outside in. Participate in the activities of the people, help them, stimulate them, and transmit the Christian life in the midst of these activities. Specifically, I am thinking of those activities that require creativity, where there is room for change, improvisation, and fun."

"Art..."

"Yes, but also sports."

"As opposed to teaching them something already established, lessons they have to learn." Mariela was getting hooked on the idea, trying to visualize it.

"After all, Jesus taught as he went along, with examples from life, sharing moments with people... Well, we've talked it over many times, no need to explain it to you..."

"Seeking to teach, but not with formal lessons, right?"

"Exactly."

"I like it. And what will Saverio and Teresa, the Amigó's, Horacio say... Is there anyone else?" Mariela had heard from Juan about the "faithful remnant" that maintained the church which had once had one hundred and fifty people. It was clear that Juan was the last effort they were in a position to make before closing the place and selling the property, a prospect that had filled them with sadness every time it was considered. Juan later learned that his salary came exclusively from the savings of Horacio Sosa, a retired banker who was willing to "invest in heaven," as he used to say. He had made a lot of money as manager of Banco Nación in several towns in the interior, but he had never flaunted his position, and the large number of people who attended his wake were a witness to all the good he had done silently over the years. The central church in Buenos Aires had only paid for his transportation and the maintenance of the hall and the house. This was more in line with their hostile attitude, but in the eyes of Juan and Mariela it spoke more strongly of the Lord's provision despite the manipulations of man.

"I'm sure they'll agree. I've been sounding them out, and none of them want us to have a traditional church, and they have a big heart for the people. I think they're ready for anything, and they have full confidence in me, in us."

As expected, Juan had the full support of Saverio and Teresa, Jorge and Zulma Amigó and Horacio Sosa. The meeting they had to discuss these issues was beautiful, and there and then each one of them began to suggest names of people who were still in the town but had left the church without finding another one.

"I'll call Zenón for soccer. He played in the third division of Racing when he was young and loves to train kids. Besides, he's amazingly fit considering he's in his sixty's," said Jorge, a lawyer who worked in the town's construction company.

"Did you know that Teresa paints on canvas, and that she studied Fine Arts?" Zulma was willing to suffer the momentary anger of Teresa, who was extremely shy, in exchange for the project she was so enthusiastic about.

"You're off my greeting list!" said Teresa, feigning anger but deep down delighted to feel useful.

"And I can talk to the school. I am a professor of Ethics and Law, and I could see how we could help in the area of art, perhaps combining it with the subject I teach," said Jorge. "What I would like to do is teach the basics about art, and then see how we can transmit the Christian message through this medium."

"What I think we have to do is find the people who know the most about art in the town and who like to explain it, call them, and offer them the church to give us free courses," suggested Juan.

"Clara Menéndez!" shouted Teresa.

"I thought the same thing!" added Horacio.

The project was set in motion. Juan called Zenón, who immediately came on board. They began by forming the church's soccer team, among the children of people who went or had gone to the church and kids from the neighborhood. They put up signs in the main stores of the town that said: "We are setting up the soccer team of the Church of the Open Word – Come and see us, Tuesday 12, 9 a.m." The week before, with a group of men who had appeared for this project, they worked on the lot next to the church, cleaning it and tidying it up.

282

Marcelo was a carpenter and made the goalposts, and Damián, who worked with cloth, made the net. Early on Tuesday, at 8:00 a.m., Juan met with the three men who were with him in this idea and they began to pray intensely. They wanted to put together a good soccer team, but more than anything they wanted to transmit the life of Christ to these boys and their families, and that the team, in some way, would transmit this life each time it played.

Juan didn't have good experiences with soccer in the church. He remembered competitions between church soccer teams where, in spite of all the players praying before starting the game, they ended up in fierce confrontations, with verbal and other exchanges. He also had in his mind how many believers were transformed when they entered the field, leaving all spirituality outside and putting all carnality inside. His question was: which were the true believers, those outside or those inside the field? What behavior was the faithful reflection of what they really were on the inside? Wasn't it that the true "I" came out the moment the ball started rolling? Wasn't this a reflection of the dualism that many believers handled, able to say the words or sing the most spiritual songs on Sunday morning and do the opposite on Monday morning?

Already before 9 a.m. a group of boys between 10 and 12 years old had come, and before long there were about twenty boys of different ages. Juan greeted them one by one, and then sat them down in a circle, with Zenón at his side. He explained to them the idea they had of forming one or more soccer teams that would not only play well but would be an example in other things, both on and off the field.

"What things?" asked Julián, with the bearing of a captain.

"For example, knowing how to lose. And knowing how to win. And I tell you that I like to win in everything I play, but if you think about it, someone always has to lose. There's only one champion. Today I can win and tomorrow I can lose. Is it okay to win a game and lose a friend?"

"I think the other thing is to accept the referee's decisions," added Zenón. "Look, I have almost fifty years of watching and playing soccer and I have never seen a referee change a ruling because the players protested. On the contrary, I have often seen players sent off and others who continue to play unfocused because they didn't accept the decisions. We need to accept that the referee can make mistakes."

"But then you want us to play like sissies," said a chubby kid, the typical goalie.

"No, not at all. I think it's more of a man to play hard and clean, knowing how to lose and to accept the referee's decisions, even if they are wrong, than one who is always fighting, arguing. Besides, thinking that we are working as a team, the player who only thinks about showing off, about always being right, is no good. He would be better off in another sport, like tennis.

They weren't too convinced, but with effort and perseverance, Juan and Zenón, with their assistants, managed to put together a team that not only played well but had its own personality. It began to be known as "the team that doesn't protest," and although at first the opponents thought it was a weakness and tried to take advantage of this and provoke them, they soon realized that it was a virtue. The Pure Soccer players—that was the name of the team—were always focused on the game and didn't waste time protesting or simulating. Everyone remembered that time when Zenón took little Arias off the team when he feigned a foul in the goal area. On another occasion, Julián—the team's leader, fully imbued with the principles—asked the referee to annul a goal scored by Ortes with the help of his hand. The other thing that attracted attention was the small ceremony they performed as soon as the final whistle went in all the games, whether they won, tied, or lost. They would shoot out into the middle of the field and greet the opposing team and the crowd, always in the same way.

For Juan, it was an experiment in what he thought the Christian influence on society should be. They had to show that things could be done differently. Not simply better, but in a radically different way. After all, Jesus was a revolutionary, who said and did things that puzzled those who were used to doing things the same way always. Faced with the traditional principle "eye for eye, and tooth for tooth," he told them, "do not resist an evil person. If anyone slaps you on the right cheek, turn to them the other cheek also." Unusual, crazy. But if they weren't capable of doing things like this, what would they bring to a society used to revenge, to respond with more violence to violence?

Moreover, Juan thought that if Christians couldn't contribute something to society simply by being Christians, it would be difficult to get them to listen to the message they had to give. It had to be natural, a byproduct of who they were, and not so much through words. And it worked. For the players, who were only dedicated to playing and didn't have the burden of imposing justice or twisting it, and also for the people who came to see them. At this point, he was content for them to take the message that things can be done differently.

On the other hand, and without even suggesting it to them, several of the players began to participate in the youth activities on Saturdays and some also participated in the other church meetings, along with friends and family.

Something similar had happened with the work with art. Mariela contacted Clara, who was surprised at first.

"I was under the impression that evangelicals were against art as such. They only liked it if it was evangelistic, if it had a religious message. And I warn you that I don't agree with that position," said Clara.

"Maybe you are right about the evangelical prejudice against art, and that's exactly why we want you to help us," Mariela said.

Clara went to work with all her enthusiasm. She obtained reproductions of paintings and sculptures from different periods and gave three classes on Art History in the church, although with a more engaging title. The posters they put up said: "We want to learn to see a work of art – Come to COW (Church of the Open Word), the first three Thursdays of August, at 6 p.m. - Professor Clara Menéndez." The classes grew in attendance and interest. Clara had the gift of infecting others with her enthusiasm for art. As she spoke, the works and the artists came alive, and people were able to get out of the monotony of a remote town and into the minds of people from other centuries, places and customs, but who shared the same longing for meaning and purpose in life, and who asked themselves the same questions as they did: Where do I come from? Where am I going? Why am I here? Pain and joy. Hopes and betrayals. Love. Violence. Passion. Beauty.

Juan had several conversations with Father Tomás in the following months. They covered different theological and practical issues, such as the baptism of infants, the role of the church in salvation, the different structures, the worship of Mary and the saints, the concept of what a cult is. There were no taboos, and based on mutual respect for each other and for each other's vocation, they knew that they were free to disagree, and that the other would first try to listen and understand before trying to refute something. Juan didn't remember having had this level of openness with other pastors or brothers and sisters in the evangelical churches. And that was logical, because the tendency was to group together by people who thought alike, or by people who didn't think and lined up blindly behind a pastor or leader. It was very uncommon to find healthy dissension within a church, or to have opportunities to dissent healthily with brothers from another church.

But the theme that they were most passionate about was that of unity among Christians. It appeared repeatedly, behind and underneath any conversation. Perhaps because their experience was so good, so natural, they wished it could be repeated in others.

"I have my position on the theme of unity. Rather, why it is difficult to achieve unity," Juan suggested.

"Let's see," asked Tomás. They had chosen to meet alternately in their respective churches. On the one hand, they understood that it would be a strong symbol of unity, and on the other hand, they didn't want anyone to interpret it as something clandestine. Today they were in Juan's remodeled office, with its light-colored walls and comfortable chairs removed from the desk, Mariela's decorative touches.

"I think it has a lot to do with the pyramidal structures that each of our churches have erected. Notice that the higher it is, the more levels it has, the more it tends to shelter members under that structure, like a chicken under a hen, while keeping them away from the neighboring structure."

"Yes, I understand. But a structure can also help to bring together a lot of people who would be scattered, if it didn't exist," said Tomás.

"But you're already putting a stamp of belonging on it. A Catholic, for example, is under the pope, so he belongs, in a figurative sense, to the pope. A Protestant, an evangelical, is usually under a pastor, or a structure or denomination. So he belongs to that person, or group."

"It is inevitable to have a structure, a leader, a person in charge," Tomás added.

"I don't know if it's inevitable. At the very least, it should be as small a structure as possible, with as few levels as possible. What happens is that human structures tend to grow, to reproduce, beyond their basic need. And the people who make up that structure tend to rely on those structures increasingly, rather than on the essence of the global organism, the body of Christ. What also happens is that people who are within the structure, especially those who are at the top, tend to look down, to what belongs to them, what they have achieved, what they have to maintain or grow. And if they look to the side, it is usually for comparison, or for criticism. But they can't feel part of a much larger and more encompassing whole. Your world ends in your church, denomination, group."

"I understand what you say, though I don't share everything. What I can share is that unity is easier and more natural the closer you are to the grassroots, and the more that unity is related to specific jobs and interests," Tomás said.

The point of coincidence would find its confirmation in the reality of Pueblo Manso. Both from one side and from the other came observations, first veiled and then more open and stronger, indicating they didn't agree with such ostensible displays of fellowship between the two churches. On Tomás' side, this approach to the "evangelists" was added to the questioning he was already suffering from the most traditional Catholic group of the town because of the charismatic meetings. Before he arrived in town, it had been a traditional town church, with its masses, baptisms, weddings, and funerals. The most popular masses were those of Good Friday and Midnight Mass, at Christmas, and for the great majority of the parishioners these were the only times they stepped foot in the church, apart from the traditional baptisms, first communions and weddings. There were some groups of women who gathered to do some handicrafts, and the weekly masses were attended predominantly by women. With the arrival of the new priest, the very concept of what the church was and what it meant to be part of the church changed radically. Father Tomás instituted weekly Bible studies, participatory prayer meetings, vigils, and charismatic worship services, with their signs and miracles, and greater involvement and commitment of young people and also men.

Naturally, the five traditional families that had run the church for the past thirty years felt threatened. While they didn't object much to the changes as a way of attracting young people, the friendship with the pastor of the "evangelist" church was more than they could tolerate. After all, it had never been done before, and they didn't know other towns where Catholics and evangelicals fraternized, which, after all, were only a sect that had drifted away from the mother church years ago, and had always been offered a hand to return. They wrote to Bishop Prátola and asked for an urgent meeting with him, after several meetings with Father Tomás, where he told them repeatedly that he was only fulfilling the biblical mandate to "be one so that the world may believe."

Something similar happened on Juan's side, although not from the town but from the Buenos Aires church. They had received news of the great growth of a church that they had considered dead, and Juan himself had called them several times on the phone, excited at the doors that were opening. He even told them that there were possibilities of doing similar work in the three towns that were within a fifty kilometer radius—Villa Norte, Balmaceda and Cinco Fortines—and where the Church of the Open Word of Pueblo Manso had begun a modest work years earlier. He hadn't concealed from them his contacts with the Catholic priest; he had simply written to them saying that he "maintained excellent relations and regular meetings with the leaders of the various Christian churches in the town." Nor did he consider that contact with Tomás had much to do with his work in the church but was more a personal and symbolic relationship.

Brother Francisco Gómez only came to visit them a year and a half after they were in the place, supposedly to learn about the evolution of the mission. Because of the previous lack of response, Juan had been under the impression that they didn't expect him to last that long, let alone to raise up that church. But perhaps they had realized the possibilities and how the Lord had blessed them, Juan thought. How nice it would be to be able to count on the support of the central church after the disagreements they had had! For them, at least, it would help heal many wounds. It was something he had talked about a lot with Mariela as soon as they heard about the scheduled visit.

When Francisco arrived, Juan received him with an affectionate hug.

"How are you, don Francisco? It's been some time! How nice to see you here!"

"Hello, Pastor Juan. It's good to see you again," without a shred of emotion. *Maybe it's because he's tired*, Juan thought.

After a fresh drink and some sandwiches that Mariela had prepared, Juan took Francisco on a tour of the remodeled church, the soccer field with its dressing rooms and the new room in the back where there was an exhibition of paintings by local artists and a couple of sculptures. What struck Francisco powerfully was the number of people everywhere. A study group in the church hall, kids playing on the field, a group of people in the... art room? In a church? It was very different from what he remembered on his last visit here in 1995, when they had made the decision to retire the previous pastor. Nor did it fit much with the atmosphere of the central church in Buenos Aires, with the same people always, less but good, less but predictable, who knew what a church was, who respected those who had been there for many years and had kept it during so many years and problems. Evidently this pastor was obsessed with changing things.

"I see that you have worked hard, pastor." Francisco recognized, once the tour was over, sitting in Juan's study.

"Yes, but I believe that the Lord has worked harder than us."

"I'm sure... And what about the relationship with the other churches? Specifically, I understand that you've had a very considerable and... visible approach with the Catholic priest. Is that so?" Francisco measured his words, as if he had been practicing them and thinking more of the report he had to give than of what he had just seen.

Juan didn't realize at that point that he was treading a minefield.

"Ah, yes! It was a real blessing to be able to get along with Father Tomás so well..."

"The Bible says not to call anyone 'father,' pastor."

That's when he realized what the reason for the trip was.

"I don't think that's what the passage refers to... but, as I was saying, I found a true believer who loves the Lord and the Word..."

"And the Virgin, and the saints, if I'm not mistaken."

"Maybe, but we have our things too..." He was digging his grave.

"Like what?"

"Traditions, customs. People we consider infallible... like Don Giovanni..." Giovanni Nucelli was the hero of the denomination, a Genoese who had come to the country from Italy in 1904 and who, like the country's heroes, had never made a single mistake, a single sin, if you went by the references to his life and words. Everything he had done was right. The usual phrase, for those who had known him, was: "There are no longer any brothers like don Giovanni..." accompanied by a sigh and a lost look.

"Maybe you'll find some of the popes better..."

"Look, Francisco, I understood that your visit was to see how the church is doing, and I think you have seen good things and a very encouraging future. And I would like nothing better than for you to participate in this moment..."

"I think you need to know your place, pastor. *We* have asked you to participate, and *we* have sent you. I don't think *you* are the one to invite us to participate."

Juan was left stiff by this man's words. He didn't know if the anger, disqualification and evident jealousy were his alone or were the message he had come to convey from the church in Buenos Aires, even without knowing what they had been able to achieve in such a short time. It seemed like a deaf dialogue, with one person excited about successes and the other trying to quench that enthusiasm.

"As I was saying, I think the reason for your trip is different, so I would like you to tell me why you came and how I can help you," Juan said directly.

"Of course. The problem is that your... ecumenical position isn't in line with the position that our church has had since its foundation. We have no problem with Catholics, but we believe they are wrong on key aspects of doctrine."

"What about the things we share? Don't we share much more than what divides us?"

"That's not for us to decide, pastor. Sometimes emotional outbursts can lead to serious mistakes, dragging everyone behind us."

"Excuse me, Francisco, but I think I have enough experience and knowledge to take care of myself and not drag anyone along." Juan felt that the discussion was pointless, that this man wasn't listening to him, so he asked him to be specific.

"May I ask you what you expect of me? What do you want me to do?"

"We want you to put an end to the contacts with the Catholic priest, for one thing."

"Impossible! Is there more?"

"Yes. We want to send a person from the central church to supervise how this... experiment is working, making sure especially of the doctrinal part."

"An intervention."

"That seems like too strong a word. We simply want to observe... and help."

"Is there a deadline?" Juan asked.

"We want you to break off contact with the priest immediately. As for the supervision, we have to designate the person, who will be coming every weekend, probably within a month at most."

"What if I don't agree?" Defiant.

"I'm afraid we won't be able to keep you as a pastor here. Nor would it be possible in another mission," clearing his throat. "Remember that you've had issues with us in the past."

Juan said nothing, but he had already made up his mind. A person who could strike a cheap shot like this, knowing all the suffering that the departure from the previous church had caused him and his family, didn't even deserve an answer. He would consult with Mariela, and they would see what to do. Of one thing he was certain. The work here was going to continue, with or without the church. Because it wasn't theirs; it was the Lord's.

Simultaneously, they began to encounter opposition from secular sectors of the town, for various reasons. On the one hand, the new church—rather the old renovated church— was disturbing the monotonous general peace of the town. The young people, accustomed to wandering aimlessly in groups killing time on street corners, in bars, and at the only dance hall, began to gather in larger groups with a more challenging goal: to win a soccer tournament. First within the town and then in the regional tournaments. Those who attended the youth activities or the other church meetings—Sunday service, Wednesday prayer meeting—found more serious discussion environments than the constant gossip they were used to.

There they realized that much of the tranquility they enjoyed was based on the absence of conflict, on the lack of alternatives, on the gray monotony of daily life. For example, during the practices of the church team, Pure Soccer, there were hidden grudges between the boys from the north of the town—the most elegant area, where the professionals and businessmen lived—and those from the south, the workers' sector. Previously, they barely met and had no dealings at all. Juan and Zenón found a way to bridge the differences by working hard as a team and with individual talks. When they entered the regional competition, they realized what others were saying about Pueblo Manso. They were the "losers," "the town where nothing happens," "the cemetery." Several times they nearly came to fists when their rivals hit them artfully to provoke them by using these kinds of phrases and even stronger ones. In this case, Zenón's iron discipline had an effect, and they ended up being respected for the quality of their game and the way they behaved in the face of provocation.

There was also opposition due to the classes and the art activity, basically because of the considerable participation of women. Pueblo Manso was quite chauvinist. Women were there to be wives and mothers, and their natural environments were the home and the church, always in submission to men. Apart from a few professionals, no woman occupied a position of any importance, either in the public administration or in private activity. That Clara's classes summoned some women into a church wasn't new, but that they should gather those numbers, and that men should begin to come, almost in the same number, was unheard of, and dangerous. And for women and men to have a common space where everyone participated equally, with common ideas, proposals, and projects, was extraordinary. Mariela's role, organizing this activity without the intervention of her husband, the pastor, became an unexpected symbol of women's liberation.

The third area where the church's activity altered the tranquility and balance of the people was in politics. Pueblo Manso had always been governed—nobody remembered a different situation—by a small local party, the Pueblo Manso Republican Party, the PMRP, which was in turn controlled by the three founding families of the town: the Ramírez's, the Costas Navas's and the Pelliteri's. Apparently, there had been a pact far back in history between these three families to take turns in the town hall, because there was always one of these families in that position. They also appointed the police chief, the justice of the peace, the school principals. It was, in short, one more fiefdom of the many that exist in the country at the municipal and provincial level. Juan and Mariela, logically, thought it was an atrocity, and they began to share it in whatever meeting or conversation they had, but people simply shrugged their shoulders and said, "That's how it works and it always did. Why change?" Until the accident happened.

One day, the 4x4 truck of Claudio Pelliteri, the mayor's son, crashed on the route to Buenos Aires, route 41. That was at dawn, at about 6 a.m., and by 7 a.m. the vehicle had been removed and all traces of the accident had been erased. To the point that some began to say that it was a false rumor, that it couldn't be true. But that's when Mario appeared. Mario Mansilla was one of the boys on the soccer team, and he had just passed through the crash scene on his way to the sausage factory where he worked. Although he didn't pay much attention to the crash, he clearly remembered both the green 4x4 that everyone knew and a wrecked red Renault 11 on the shoulder. He couldn't be sure, but he could almost swear he'd seen a body lying on the ground. There was also a police car and an ambulance.

The next day, when Mario shared during soccer practice what he had seen, no one believed him. Nothing had appeared in the local paper, El Independiente, and everyone told him that maybe he thought is happened, maybe it was somewhere else, or he had fallen asleep and dreamt it. But he was so insistent on what he had seen that Juan began to investigate discreetly. He remembered the story Saverio had told him the first day he arrived in the town, about the people who didn't accept disloyalty and lies. At the time, he had found it interesting, but hard to believe, especially in times like these, when everything in the country was corrupt. Maybe it was a legend, or maybe it was a situation that had happened a long time ago. Moreover, deep down he would have liked such a place to exist, to reject with its own antibodies, naturally, the infections of lies, deceit, and disloyalty.

So Juan went with Mario to the office of El Independiente. The director, Rafael Costas Navas, received him.

"What can I do for you, pastor? We were just thinking of doing a story on 'the team that doesn't protest' in our next issue." *What a coincidence,* thought Juan, *we started with this a year ago and right now he's going to publish a story.*

"Ah, that would be wonderful. We are also doing other things that we think can be useful for the Mansan society."

"For example?"

"The art room."

"Ah, yes. Where the women go. Yes, it's good that they have something to entertain themselves. So they don't get bored, right?" with a knowing smile towards both of them.

"It's not exactly the goal. We believe that all creative activities show that men and women have the image of God in us."

"Of course, of course. Well, we're traditional Catholics, and we're fine with people from other religions to come and do their work. Always within the customs and traditions of the town, it is understood."

"Yes, but also trying to improve it. Everything can be improved. Well, Mr. Costas Navas, I come to see you with this young man, Mario Mansilla, a member of the Pure Soccer team, because it seems strange to us that an accident he saw yesterday morning on Route 41 hasn't appeared in your newspaper."

The director's round face turned white and red in the space of five seconds, too late to hide that he knew something, and that he had been caught off-guard. Unforgivable for a journalist.

"An accident?" as if he had said he had seen a flying saucer. "Impossible! If there had been an accident, it would have appeared in El Independiente, don't you think, Pastor?". Circular reasoning at its best.

"Of course, and that's why it seems so strange to us. Besides, in the accident there was a car well known in the whole town, the green 4x4 of the mayor's son, Claudio. Oddly enough, I haven't seen it around."

At that moment, a large man entered. Costas Navas must have summoned him with some hidden button. He addressed him without even making the introductions.

"Resuello, we have a very serious matter here. This young man says he saw an accident on Route 41 yesterday. At what time?"

"That would be around six in the morning," Mario answered, his face transformed by fear.

Juan looked at Mario and then at Resuello. He really looked like a gangster, a thug. What was he doing in the office of El Independiente? Mario appeared to know him. But he wasn't going to be distracted by this. So he pressed further.

"Also, there was another car, a red Renault 11, and a body lying in the road," Juan added.

"Maybe the young man was drinking, or taking something else," Costas Navas suggested. "It wouldn't be the first time."

Juan saw that Mario was getting more and more uncomfortable. He would almost say he wanted to leave.

"You didn't hear anything about an accident like the one I just described?" Juan asked Costas Navas.

"Absolutely nothing. I repeat: if there had been anything, especially with such an important and well-known citizen, it would have appeared in our newspaper. Look, pastor, don't feel uncomfortable. You don't know the amount of false news we receive, by phone, by letter, personally... What we call "rotten fish." But thank you for your interest and for coming. It was nice to meet you personally, and I'll call you for the interview I told you about."

The editor stood up, shook Juan's hand alone, while the fat man put a hand on Mario's shoulder, who seemed to melt under its touch.

When they came out, Juan noticed that Mario was extremely nervous and looked over his shoulder constantly. He invited him in for coffee at La Ronde, chose a secluded table, and after he calmed down a bit, asked him:

"What's wrong with you, Mario?"

"Nothing, pastor. Well, what's wrong is that Resuello is a thug..."

"What do you mean by that? What's he up to?"

Mario lowered his voice to the point that he could hardly understand what he whispered to him.

"Drugs."

The startled look on Juan's face scared Mario even more.

"What?" Now it was Juan who was looking all over the place. Could he be in danger because he was talking to Mario?

"No way! You wouldn't be imagining this too?"

He realized he was telling Mario the same thing as the editor of the newspaper, so he decided to ask him a few more questions.

"But he's not from here, is he?"

"No, he's from Tres Cruces. I know him from there." Juan remembered that Mario was from that town. "Now I'm surer than ever that there was an accident, and that they cleaned everything up, covered everything up, because it was drug related."

"But the son of the mayor? So... and the Costas Navas' are involved too?" Juan realized again that his face would be giving them away, so he tried to hide it.

"I'm scared, pastor. When I saw the fat guy, I realized they were telling me to shut up. If I had known it had something to do with drugs, I would have kept my mouth shut. Now it's too late. I'm going to have to leave town..."

Juan had a hunch, an inner voice, which dictated the best move, and he had to play it now.

"Let's go and see Father Tomás."

"Father Tomás? Why?"

"Come, and I'll explain."

They didn't take the most direct route, pretending to go in the direction of Juan's church, but after two blocks they turned left and, hurrying up, ended up at the bottom of the Catholic church. Through the window they could see Tomás in his study, and they knocked on the back door.

He was surprised to see them and ran to open the door.

"What's wrong, Juan? Hi, Mario."

"Can we talk?" Juan closed the door quickly and went inside the chapel. Tomás didn't understand anything. But when Juan told him about the strange accident that was nowhere to be seen and the even stranger interview with the newspaper director, he didn't seem too surprised.

"You don't seem so surprised," Juan said.

"Not really. It was always said that there were strange things in the municipality. Well, you don't have to be a genius to be suspicious, when the same people have been pulling all the strings in the town for so many years. It's textbook. Permanence in power equals impunity, corruption, more permanence in power, more impunity, more corruption. A vicious circle, in every sense of the word."

"And the whole question of the collective unconscious not tolerating lies?" asked Juan.

"Ah, did they tell you the legend? They always tell it to newcomers."

"But isn't it true?"

"Half and half. It comes from a time of great honesty and transparency that no longer exists, except on the surface, *'pour la galerie.'* The thing is, it's a pretty perverse arrangement. They arranged to keep Pueblo Manso clean, mostly to have a place to flee to..."

"A kind of hide-out."

"Exactly. But it's clear now that something happened here, an accident, and they were able to cover it up quickly, except for what Mario saw." The kid still had that look of terror. "But you don't have to be afraid, Mario. They won't dare do anything here, and you can stay with me as long as you want."

"Let's go and pray," said Tomás, with determination. Juan nodded, and they began to pray and cry out for Mario's protection and against the corruption and drugs that were in and around Pueblo Manso. Mario had never seen anything like it. The two men had knelt as if driven by an outside force and alternated in words, cries, tears, and songs of praise to God. They were pouring themselves out before a being who was as real or more real to them than he was. It was as if they knew him intimately, and spoke to him as to a father, but also as the owner and creator of everything. It was strange, but at the same time tremendously reassuring. If it was possible to get in touch with God himself, and he listened and could protect you, then there was no need to fear.

At one point, they invited him to kneel with them and they took each other by the arms in a solid block of intercession for the people of Pueblo Manso and against the web of evil that was in the shadows. At one point, Juan took a Bible that was in a pew, looked for a passage, and began to read, while Tomás accompanied it with several "Amen's."

"'I am sending you out like sheep among wolves. Therefore be as shrewd as snakes and as innocent as doves. Be on your guard; you will be handed over to the local councils and be flogged in the synagogues. On my account you will be brought before governors and kings as witnesses to them and to the Gentiles. But when they arrest you, do not worry about what to say or how to say it. At that time you will be given what to say, for it will not be you speaking, but the Spirit of your Father speaking through you.'"[54]

"Do you want to continue, Tomás? Let's jump to here..." He handed him the Bible and the priest continued reading, "'So do not be afraid of them, for there is nothing concealed that will not be disclosed, or hidden that will not be made known. What I tell you in the dark, speak in the daylight; what is whispered in your ear, proclaim from the roofs. Do not be afraid of those who kill the body but cannot kill the soul. Rather, be afraid of the One who can destroy both soul and body in hell.'"[55] Tomás closed the Bible and set it aside.

The spontaneous prayer session ended with the three men strengthened and ready to face anything that came their way. This was an opportunity to show true unity among Christians to face lies and hypocrisy. Mario stayed that night in the church, and Juan and Tomás arranged to meet the next day to agree on a plan of action.

Both realized how important this moment was in their lives and in the lives of the communities they were leading. They also found themselves facing the *kairos*, God's timing, again. Why was it at this very moment that a reality that had been hidden for so many years came to light? Was it not because they were now able to face the forces

---

[54] Mt 10:16-20

[55] Mt 10:26-28

of evil using the unity they had begun to forge among themselves? "There is nothing concealed that will not be disclosed, or hidden that will not be made known. What I tell you in the dark, speak in the daylight; what is whispered in your ear, proclaim from the roofs."[56]

They also realized the downside. If they overlooked this opportunity, they could ensure a more comfortable time with those in power and save themselves a lot of trouble, but they would deal a fatal blow to the testimony, to the essence of their message. "Do not be afraid of those who kill the body but cannot kill the soul." Christian history, even from the very pages of the Bible, said that "the blood of the martyrs is the seed of the Church," as Tertullian had said. Here they were talking about confronting one of the most powerful forces on earth, the power of drugs. Juan thought, *Would he be willing to take the risk? What about his family? Wasn't this more of a police matter?'*

With all these questions in their minds, but with the conviction that they would do the right thing, whatever it took, Tomás and Juan met the next day in the Catholic church. Don Francisco Gómez was still in town.

"And? What did Mariela say?" Tomás asked him.

"Imagine. It was quite a shock. To think that in a place so far from Buenos Aires, so supposedly idyllic, there are drugs and corruption, cover-up, isn't a pleasant thing to say the least. But we've been praying, and the choice is clear," Juan said.

"What is it?"

"To continue or to compromise. There is no middle way."

"I thought so too. If we are in this for real, we can't be less than those who preceded us and risked everything for the truth. To be half-Christian is not to be Christian. And let it be what God wants," said Tomás.

---

[56] Mt 10:26-27

"Then let's go on!" Juan said firmly.

They got to work. The first thing they agreed on was to set up a team between the two churches and give the campaign a name. The same phrase came to both as like lightning: "The truth will set you free." They agreed to meet in two days in the Catholic church.

Juan had one pending issue: Don Francisco. They hadn't remained on good terms, but Francisco had stayed that week, and they had got to know each other a better during the time they had shared. It was evident that the first contact had been more influenced by the pressure and directives of the central church than by his own convictions. In time, they began to see the more human face of Francisco. As a young man, and even after his marriage, he had preached in plazas every Sunday afternoon. The so-called Happy Hours allowed children to be reached through songs and Bible stories. He loved children, but they hadn't been able to have any of their own. He was a great uncle, and he always had a nephew staying in his big colonial-style house. When he showed us pictures of his seven nephews and his wife, Clara, his face was transformed. He was another man. Juan didn't remember having known as much of that man in the more than two years they shared in Buenos Aires as in these few days in Pueblo Manso. His anti-Catholic stance was partly due to the position of the denomination, and partly a product of the mistrust that hung in the air in Argentina from years of disagreements between Catholics and Evangelicals. But, in reality, he had never had any significant contact with a priest or a committed Catholic layman.

So, when Juan decided to raise the issue and the challenge to him, he wasn't sure how he would react. But it was quite a surprise.

"It's outrageous! They can't get away with it! They're scoundrels! They think they can handle us like puppets!"

It turned out that Francisco had been an old unionist and had great passion and experience in the struggle for workers' rights. He had participated in countless marches and pickets in his youth and during the time we worked. He knew all the twists and turns of organizing a protest, including the different times, pressure tactics, diversionary maneuvers, intimidations, and threats. So there was no need to even suggest an action plan when he had already designed it in his mind. Against all odds, don Francisco Gómez was one of the members of the evangelical group in the protest "The truth will set you free," when they met in the Catholic church. They met with Father Tomás and in that initial handshake years of prejudice and estrangement collapsed, united by the common cause in favor of the truth.

The evangelical group brought ten people, and the Catholics nine. A few knew each other, but most did not, so the idea was that the first few minutes would be spent in an informal time of getting to know each other. Between the coffee and the *facturas*, the time went on to almost an hour, but no one dared to interrupt it. Finally, Tomás took the floor, as the house owner.

"Well, I see we're getting to know each other, and that's always good. I would like to read a short passage from the Word of God. It is in Ephesians 5. It says, 'you were once darkness, but now you are light in the Lord. Live as children of light...[57] Have nothing to do with the fruitless deeds of darkness, but rather expose them. It is shameful even to mention what the disobedient do in secret. But everything exposed by the light becomes visible—and everything that is illuminated becomes a light.'"[58]

If anything was lacking to motivate the group and to increase their conviction that they were doing God's will, it was this passage. After a brief prayer, led by Juan, they began to plan the protest.

"I'm told that Don Francisco is an old unionist and labor rights activist, so I ask him to speak to us from experience," said Tomás, looking at Francisco. "What things should we do, or know? What things should we not do?"

"First of all, I thank you all, but especially Pastor Juan and also Father Tomás—using the "F word" naturally— for this opportunity to be with such a varied and rich group of brothers and sisters in the faith. Few know," looking at Juan, "the miracle behind me being here, with you, today." He was deeply moved. "But let's get to the point..."

---

[57] Eph 5:8
[58] Eph 5:11-13

Francisco told them about several experiences in his life as a trade unionist and activist, but he told them especially how he had felt that the Lord cared for him and protected him even in the worst moments. He exhorted and challenged them. He told them that it wouldn't be easy. That the powerful, those who are used to doing what they want, using public money and resources as if they were their own, weren't going to stand still. For example, he would't be surprised if they invented a homosexual relationship between Tomás and Juan or fabricated some shady business of some of the group, especially if they had the support of the town newspaper. There would be calls in the middle of the night, shadowing, mafia-like messages. Someone who had a position in the public administration could lose it suddenly.

The question was: Were they willing to take this risk?

The answer was unanimous: "Yes."

11

THE NON-CHURCH

Rejected by others accepted by many
How can we build on what looks like remains?

When we decided with Mercedes to leave Pedro's church and I called Juan, Mariela answered. She told me that he had gone to a place in the interior of the province called Pueblo Manso. We knew that they had had problems at the previous church, and we were very sorry. The two of them were a couple that we respected very much, especially for their integrity and their search for a deep spiritual life. In fact, what I regretted most was that, in retrospect, the church was the main culprit in separating us during these fifteen years.

When they decided to leave the Church of Fellowship in La Plata and join an informal group that wasn't even a church, we told them that it would be dangerous, that they could end up in who knows what. But they told us about the spiritual experiences they had, the beautiful and simple time they shared, and we realized that this was what they were looking for and needed. We, in turn, told them about the incredible advances in numbers in our church, and we realized that they didn't share our enthusiasm. They never told us why, but I suspect they saw where this search for numbers and quantity would lead. Each one was able to predict what would happen to the other, but neither was able to listen to the other. And each thought that what they had was the best and the other was second rate.

305

When they left the group in Pueblo Santo, we didn't know what to do. We didn't want to appear as saying, "We told you so" kicking them when they were down, so we avoided the subject. It was a big mistake, because from then on, the subject of the church became taboo in our meetings. Although we saw each other occasionally in family events we avoided talking about our churches.

We couldn't even share our common concern for our friend Pedro. I felt a kind of false loyalty that prevented me from saying anything bad about my pastor, and Juan felt something similar, that if he said something bad he would be criticizing another pastor, or my pastor. I couldn't even share the first talk I had with Pedro, when I felt so misunderstood.

Everything was kept hidden, and we avoided the subjects, knowing, but pretending not to know. As in so many cases that I knew in these years, the differences of practice or style between the churches that one chose put a wedge between family and friends. The other side of the coin was that many of us thought that attending the same church, sharing activities, working together, made us friends, a great lie that became evident the moment one chose to leave that common ground.

It was a subject that concerned me and I felt that someone should do something about it. But what? The first thing we had to do was try to rebuild the relationships that had been broken or were dying of starvation. We invited Mariela to dinner with the kids. It was funny, but even though they were second cousins, our children hardly knew each other. As soon as we finished dinner, they went off to play. The three of us caught up with our lives over coffee in the living room.

"How long has it been since we got together outside of a family meeting!" Mariela said.

"And just when Juan isn't here. How is he doing?" I asked.

"I talked to him today. He was very happy about an experience he had with the town priest..." Mariela cut herself short. She didn't know if we'd agree to something like that.

"Tell us, please." It was Mercedes, with a sincere attitude. The years had changed us, and we were wanting to get out of the exclusivism we had been stuck in all these years.

"No, I stopped myself because I realize that sometimes we can seem... I don't know... like we always want to get out of the ordinary. You once told me, Raúl, that we were unconventional."

"I remember, but it wasn't in a bad way. Actually, I was always a little envious of you guys in that. You don't have trouble relating to people, and you're always looking for new things. I really felt this, although I may have said it sometime in a disqualifying way."

"Don't think it's so easy because we have a hard time finding what we want. Maybe what we do know best is what we don't want, what we don't like."

"Yes. Let me guess. You don't like crowds, big organizations, great characters, noise, show." These were things that had started to displease me more and more, so I had no trouble listing them.

"May I?" It was Mercedes. "Nor do you like two-faced people, those who confuse religion or service with politics, those who always want the limelight..."

"Yes, you're both right. But we understand that others like it, or at least don't mind it as much as we do. What happens is that we see that these things have hurt many people. For example, Pedro."

With that phrase we entered one of the subjects that had been taboo until now. And we touched it maturely, with love, from the perspective of those who wanted to help a whole family, and not just one person. I told them about the two interviews I had with Pedro, the one at seven in the morning and the one late at night, what Mercedes was doing for Virginia with Camila and Sabrina, and Mariela began to tell how much they had prayed with Juan for Pedro and for his church.

I spoke of my concern for the people who had been left out of our church, and many others, because of the mistakes of the leaders. Mariela shared with us the work that Juan had begun when they left Christ the King Church, and how he too had a heart for those who were left behind. She told them also what they had suffered when they left the Church of the Open Word in Buenos Aires, and how everyone had ignored them, as if they were the plague.

"Sometimes it seems to me that we're all in a wheel that spins without stopping, and no one dares to stop it," I contributed. "Some go up, others come down, but 'the show must go on.' I wonder if anyone cares about those who are being left out of the system."

"I don't think so. I remember a family in the cult, the Porvioso's, a beautiful family." Mariela was remembering with nostalgia and sorrow, and using the word "cult" freely, recognizing the reality of their experience. "They were both professionals, doctors, and came from sad stories, of much deprivation and hatred against everything religious. Both had been staunch atheists, anti-priests, anti-churches. She had even begun to write a book challenging the main Christian doctrines. I think it was called 'In the beginning was deception... or lie,' I don't remember well. They had a strong conversion when they almost lost their lives in a boat on the river and to this day they don't know what or who brought them to the shore without a single scratch. When they came to the Lord, they got into it with everything they had. They were so grateful that they were always helping people, participating in the meetings. When the project in Pueblo Santo came out, they moved immediately to the community and seemed to be touching heaven with their hands. Many people came because of them, and they made generous contributions. They gave up their vacation two years in a row to spend more time with the brothers. They were considered an example of consecration and dedication..." Obviously, the second part of the story wouldn't be easy to tell.

"Let me guess. Today they don't want to set foot in a church." I tried to help.

"Alberto is in an extremist political group with Nazi-like ideas and Adriana turned to ecology, both with the same fervor as before. As you say, none of them want to have anything to do with their former brothers and sisters."

"What happened?" asked Mercedes.

"They became suspicious when they saw that several of the leaders were buying new cars and had their houses decorated with the latest stuff, when none of them had a job that justified it and they hadn't had any change of jobs while they were in Pueblo Santo. The change coincided with a series of prophecies by Sister Violeta that spoke of God beginning to show the abundance in the leaders, as a sign of his blessing. In addition, they were traveling to the United States and pastors were also coming from there. Alberto tried to find out for the first time how money was handled, since it had never even occurred to him to distrust or find out about such a worldly subject. No one could give him an answer. In fact, there were two of the leaders who had kept their lifestyle simple, so he asked one of them why there was such a difference with the others, and between those and the rest of the community. Do you know what they answered? You won't believe it..."

"Some spirit..." I suggested.

"Precisely! They told him that he had a spirit of envy, and that it was something Satan had sent him. That it was even preventing them from prospering. That he had to repent and try to be more like those leaders he was criticizing."

"No way!" said Mercedes, incredulously.

"They left. And they left badly. None of those they had helped—medically, financially, humanly—even called them. Not even us... We thought they had done something wrong, that the leaders were dealing with them, that it was not for us to interfere. When we learned the truth, we felt it was too late. Once Juan called them and they refused to take his call."

"How terrible!" It was the only thing I could think to say to cover the silence. Then I remembered Carlitos Cecchi and looked at Mercedes. "And the Carlitos case?"

"Yes, I was just thinking about him," she answered.

"Carlitos was around seventeen..." I started.

"Nineteen, do you remember he repeated the grade?" said Mercedes.

"OK, nineteen. He came from drugs, from a destroyed family, and was converted in a church work camp in the summer. When he returned, he came to the front to give his testimony. Everyone was in tears. It was a miracle what the Lord had done. His life really showed that change was possible." I had it vividly in my mind.

"I know what happened," said Mariela. "They put him on a discipleship course under a responsible person who helped him to correct bad habits, to sort himself out, to see why he had fallen into drugs. They surrounded him with a group of supporters, without demanding important commitments..."

I realized the irony, and I also realized that Carlitos's wasn't the only case.

"No, he was immediately put in charge of a group of teenagers! Don't laugh, it's a crying matter. And to think that I believed at that moment that it was a daring but wise decision of Pedro, to take advantage of the initial enthusiasm and not let it decline... How could I have been so stupid?" I exclaimed.

"I'm remembering the parable of the sower. The seed that fell among the stones, grew fast, and dried up quickly. Is that what happened?" It was Mariela.

"Exactly. In the beginning he was unstoppable, he lived in the church, devoured his Bible studies, talked to everyone, testified even to the walls... To top it all off, Pedro and the leaders used him as an example for the older believers. The message was, more or less: 'This kid just converted and is doing all this, and you, who have been believers for years, aren't doing half of what he is doing. You should be ashamed of yourselves.' The kids became attached to him, because he took care of them, called them, told them about his experience and what God was telling him. Until, as Mariela says..."

"As the Word says," corrected Mariela.

"Yes, the Word, the parable... he dried up. He stopped coming from one day to the next. Nobody explained what had happened. The children were left adrift."

"Did you know what happened to Carlitos, in the end?" Mariela asked.

"A few months ago, I ran into him on the subway. He greeted me very well, but he looked terrible. I asked him if he went to any church and he said, 'No, I don't want anything to do with those people. They are all hypocrites.' What could I say to him?"

"Wow! And who's to blame? Surely not Carlitos," said Mariela.

"Of course not!" I said.

"Since you're remembering cases, I can't get the Barzak family out of my mind. Raúl, do you remember?" It was Mercedes, again.

"Yes..."

"They were the ideal family for Pedro. The parents always agreed with everything he said or did. They sat in the first pews and said their 'Amen's' in the right places in the sermon, laughed at all his jokes and were the first to volunteer for everything. They were also the first to arrive at the church, and the last to leave, after the pastor. They took all the courses, tithed religiously, had perfect attendance. They didn't tolerate anyone saying anything negative about the pastor or simply disagreeing with something he had said or done. They said it was rebellious, it was questioning authority, that the pastor would know why he was doing things. They were content to obey, and they were convinced that they would be blessed if they did."

"Don't say anything... They're in another church, distanced, angry with Pedro," Mariela suggested.

"More or less. When Pedro started having problems, they turned on him completely. As if trying to make a good impression on the one who would be his successor, ahead of time. They began to say all kinds of offensive things. It did Pedro a lot of harm, but he should have realized that the previous attitude wasn't healthy either. Nor was it reasonable."

"We need healthier, more stable relationships. Beyond fascination or rejection. That allow recovery. Recovery mechanisms..." Mercedes was thinking out loud.

⚓

Suddenly, there was a silence. All you could hear in the background was the noise of the kids playing.

Mariela kept running through her mind people they knew and didn't even know where they were anymore. The Rosas's, with their Down baby girl... what faith they had shown in the face of the test!

311

Hugo and Celina, when they lost their jobs and helped build the temple of Pueblo Santo. Andrés Humada and his warnings! "Gerry" Hans, with his impressive voice, always taking the kids around in his truck, also German. What happened to Ángeles, a real angel for her when she lost her baby? And Yamila, Pastor Samarián's niece?

Mercedes especially remembered the children, and the children's parents. The Loreto twins and their mischiefs, but with impressive potential. She had had them for three years in Sunday School, and now they would be her boys' age. Pablo... always fighting with everyone, but the most loyal, the most trustworthy. Leader material, for good or for bad. What happened to Rosita, in that abusive family? So many talks with the mother, but it's been a while since she's heard from them.

People came to mind who I hadn't treated well in all these years. Convinced that I was absolutely right, more so at the beginning than at the end of my time at the New Church of Blessing, I didn't give them a chance to give their opinion, and I had helped to show them the door, unconsciously. I remembered Fabián, when he started the relationship with F&G, saying to me, "But this is all *yankee* marketing. What does this have to do with a Christian church?" I had felt very superior when I said, "It's not a question of prejudice here. I don't think Pedro would let himself be tricked by a salesman." When he left the church soon after, I thought, "What a prejudiced guy! He's going to miss the blessing just because the program comes from the States. Silvio was the first to alert me to the personalistic path Pedro was taking, and I never recognized he was right. When I realized, he was gone with his whole family. I also remembered the beautiful group of men that we had formed and that became dismembered one by one, almost in every case because of the men's problems with Pedro, and I had done nothing.

The three of us had the impression that something had to be done. But what? How could we stop the bleeding of valuable people who were leaving the church because of disagreements with the leaders or with other members, many of which were easily solvable? Could we recover people who had become disenchanted, not only with the church but with the faith in general? Was it possible to dream of a future church with those "healthy and stable relationships" that Mercedes had mentioned?

Suddenly, the idea came to me as a flash.

"I got it!"

Mariela and Mercedes looked at me.

"I'm sorry I scared you. But I think I know what we must do. And it's something that's never been done before. Something original."

"What is it?" said Mercedes.

"A members' union," I said, triumphant.

"What?" exclaimed Mariela.

"The name doesn't matter, I can't think of anything better, but what matters is the concept. Notice that in all these cases we have been seeing, what was missing was someone to defend the rights of the common people who had had some problem with the church, with the leaders, with the pastor. Except in some churches that have this type of mechanism, in the great majority of churches that I know the common member, the person that attends, works, contributes, gives, as much and often more than the leaders, the pastors, doesn't have any type of protection, no rights."

"Keep going. I'm beginning to see your point." It was Mercedes.

"We've talked it over many times, Mercedes, but we don't do anything. People go away badly and remain feeling bad. And they think they're the only ones. Powerless to do anything about the structures that exist for leaders, to protect them and help them. The members are birds of passage, useful while they are there, to be replaced when they leave."

"Disposable," Mariela said. It was the same awful word Juan had used.

"That's the word! Disposable members," I said.

"It doesn't sound too good," said Mariela, with a wry smile.

"Disposable sheep, disposable people, if you like. The important thing is the idea. I'm not clear on it, but I think it's a necessity, and I feel like doing something about it. What do you think?"

"Let's brainstorm," suggested Mercedes.

I brought a blackboard from the kids' room and wrote down the ideas that came to us, without too much order.

"You have to control the money... transparency, reports," suggested Mariela.

"Avoid manipulation, the concept of 'giving to receive,'" I added.

"Accountability," said Mercedes.

"Of money and theology," I clarified.

"Yes, I think that's right. Both," said Mariela.

"Remove politics from the church!" Mercedes practically shouted.

"Slow down, please!" I said, while trying to write as fast as possible, so as not to curb creativity and spontaneity.

"Guarantee the equality of all members, those who have money and those who don't, those who agree with the pastor and those who don't." My contribution.

"Impartial mediation between members and the pastor, or the leaders, when there are differences," said Mariela.

"The whole Bible for everyone... the Bible above all other books," a serious concern of mine.

"Openness to other churches, denominations, groups," said Mercedes.

"Equality of professions." Mariela saw that she wasn't clear. "That somehow the office of pastor isn't considered superior to that of an employee, worker, professional... Equality in the concept."

"Less dependence from outside," I said. I had my reasons.

"Integral adoration". Mariela also had hers.

"Acceptance... no, I would say promotion of diversity. Rejection of uniformity." This was Mercedes.

"Protection of the family," said Mariela.

"Enough of disposable members!" said Mercedes, emphatically.

As I wrote the words on the board, I couldn't help but think why we hadn't used such a simple, powerful, unrestricted, and participatory method in the church all these years. So many methods and systems were used, but all to limit, control, pigeonhole, manipulate, standardize, lay the line. The three of us were amazed at each other's contributions, both at the things we agreed on, without knowing it, and at the things we would never have thought the other would think. Mariela, for example, thought, *What does Raúl mean by this dependence on the outside world?* I was amazed at the equality of professions Mariela had proposed, especially coming from a "pastor's wife," even though they didn't fall into the category of typical evangelical pastors. Mercedes was one hundred percent in agreement with Mariela about the control of money. In her experience, "the love of money was the root of all evil" not only in the lives of people in general and believers in particular, but also in the life of churches. "And charities," she had added, recalling her experience at Casa de Esperanza.

In less than five minutes we had filled the board, and we had shared fifteen years of our lives. I sat down, and we stared for a while at what was written. I had numbered it for clarity:

1. Money control
2. Transparency
3. Reports
4. No manipulation - No "giving to receive"
5. Accountability - Money, Theology
6. Non-Political - Inside, Outside Church
7. Equal membership – money, no money / agree, not agree
8. Mediation - members, leaders/pastor
9. The whole Bible for all - Bible above all books
10. Openness - churches, denominations, groups
11. Equality of professions
12. Less outside dependence
13. Integral Worship
14. Acceptance, Promotion of Diversity - Rejection of Uniformity
15. Family protection
16. Disposable non-members

There would probably be a lot more, but the list, as it stood, was pretty impressive for a five-minute job. Some points needed further explanation. For example, almost at the end, point 13, "Integral worship," proposed by Mercedes.

She had participated fully in one of the last phenomena of the "evangelical scene," the worship ministry. Initiated as a healthy renewal of the music that was sung in the churches, it ended up being a complete change in the proportion between music and the Word, creating as a by-product a "priestly" class that handled a large part of the worship services of a growing group of churches. Drawing on the spontaneity and expressiveness of Pentecostal churches, it made use of the American concept of a spectacle or show. Mercedes' evaluation, not entirely negative, emerged from her own experience.

During the first stage of growth of the New Church of Blessing, F&G recommended a renewal of the music, adding electric guitar, electric bass, drums and a conductor apart from the pastor to handle this part of the worship. The goal was to "prepare the audience" for the message as well as for the time of the offering. The idea was that people, in general, didn't come to church prepared for the service, so the time of singing and worship would function as a bridge between before and after, between the world and the kingdom. The recommendation was to start with very lively, optimistic, joyful songs. This part was called "praise." Then came the second part, "worship," which was slower, more reflective, and intimate.

This first stage began with David Ontiveros, an excellent musician, with a clear and strong voice, and deeply spiritual. He followed the guidelines of the program he was given, but one could see that he cared more about being in tune with the Spirit and the people. He had the ability to perceive any indication from both and immediately change the programmed song to fit the new situation. Once, he upset the applecart completely, and didn't get off lightly. We were in the middle of "praise" time, with the people motivated, clapping their hands, and in a positive spirit when he waved to the musicians and the congregation and stopped the song in the middle.

"Excuse me, brothers, but I understand that the Lord is telling me that among the people who are singing and clapping there is a young man who should be crying and lamenting. I propose that we sit down and seek the Lord in silence. Then we can continue celebrating and praising in complete freedom."

The impact was strong, and everyone still remembers the event. But David didn't lead the singing again because he hadn't followed the program, and there was never again an interruption of the "spirit of the meeting." He was one of many who had to go out the back door without anyone looking for them later. No one noticed either the young man who left in silence that day, deeply moved by the word he had just received.

I found out several years later, in another church, at a leadership conference. I approached one of the speakers whose face was familiar to me and asked him if he had ever been to my church.

"Yes, several years ago. I don't know if you remember a meeting where the praise leader stopped everything and made us sit down..."

"How could I not remember? Were you there?"

"I was the person the leader stopped the singing for... David, right?"

"Yes, David Ontiveros."

"You don't know how the Lord touched me that night. It was exactly like David said, I was singing and clapping while I had gotten my girlfriend pregnant and had disappeared. When I received the word, I went to find her and, making a long story short, we got married and now we have three little kids. You can imagine I never disappeared again, to avoid the Lord stopping the praise again... There she is... Silvia!" waving to a girl with a baby in her arms and two beautiful boys next to her. "The brother is from the Church of the New Blessing, remember?"

"Hi. How wonderful to meet you," she said with beautiful smile.

"I'm so glad..." I managed to say to them.

"And David? I never thanked him for having the courage to do what he did. If you see him, will you send him my regards and our thanks? A true man of God..."

"Of course." I didn't dare tell him what had happened. I felt vicarious embarrassment.

After David, there were several boys and girls who took turns leading the worship. Everyone had their own style, and people preferred one or the other. Then there was the support group, a group that sang the songs from the stage with a microphone, supposedly to help and motivate people. The next step was to integrate the praise directors, the support group, and the band of musicians into what was called the "worship ministry." The final step was to elevate the worship ministry to the most important place in the church, second only to the pastor.

But why had Mercedes spoken of "integral worship"? She had personally seen the change that people underwent from the time they entered the ministry, as simple believers eager to serve the Lord, until they became, almost invariably, a kind of star. She didn't know if it was because they were always in front, on stage, and this led them to perform, to be attentive to their image, or if it was because the pastor made them feel special, a kind of modern priestly caste. The concept of worship had also been distorted in the sense that, instead of being something that we all did equally directed towards God, it was now something that needed to be directed, stimulated, shaped (controlled?) by a group of people, supposedly a step higher in spirituality. There were levels, degrees, qualities of worship, and this worship didn't depend on the person's whole life during the week, but on what they did during that hour in worship.

Mercedes had the clear example of Rebeca, with whom she had begun serving in the worship group. It had been a beautiful experience at first, when there were only four young people who wanted to offer their voices to praise the Lord. Mercedes wasn't thrilled to have to do it from the front, on stage. She didn't understand why, but she was told that it would help transmit the spirit of worship. She took it as one of many things that needed to be done, but it didn't change her inner or outer attitude. But standing in front of so many people began to affect Rebeca. First, she noticed that she made a special effort to dress and put on makeup in a striking way, bordering on the seductive. Then she began to show exaggerated gestures of worship and seemed to be in pose most of the time. The third stage was when she started to notice her place in the group, showing off in the songs and assuming a role of diva when she had to sing parts alone.

The spirit in the rehearsals, which were held on Friday nights, also changed. Initially it had been a beautiful time. The rehearsals of the worship group began with a time of sharing experiences and of free and spontaneous prayer. The suggestions for songs, the way they were sung, and the corrections all came freely and in a spirit of humility and teamwork. But later the spirit of the rehearsal itself changed, with less time for prayer, more time for discussion and more time for showing off, both from the praise leader and Rebeca and some of the band members.

Mercedes finally left the worship ministry, with all the pain of losing a place of service that she enjoyed and where she felt she could be of help. Knowing how some of the worship ministry members were in their intimacy and in the rehearsals themselves, she couldn't accept that they implicitly or explicitly appeared as role models. Even less so when she understood that worship wasn't limited to one hour a week or to songs and music. You worshiped when you worked, when you admired God's creation, when you were grateful for life, when you helped your neighbor. In that sense, having a worship ministry made as little sense as having a life ministry.

We talked for a while about the different topics, among them the importance of recovering the reading and reflection of the whole Bible for all believers—a long struggle of the Reformation, which I had made my own—and not to leave it exclusively in the hands of professionals who tell them which passages to read and how to interpret them.

There was still room for improvement.

"I think we can group together some themes that go together," Mariela proposed.

"Let's see... which ones?" coming back to the board.

"One, two, three... and five can go together. Check it out."

"Yes, and 11 and 7 have to do with equality," added Mercedes.

"15 and 16 are about protection, don't you think?" My contribution.

"That could go with 8, since we're talking about protection," Mariela said.

"And 9 and 13 have to do with practices... correct practices in the church," I added. Let's see how I can group them. The list finally came up as follows:

1. Money control
2. Transparency
3. Reports
5. Accountability - Money, Theology

4. No manipulation - No "giving to receive"

6. Non-Political - Inside, Outside Church

7. Equal membership - money, no money / agree, not agree
11. Equality of professions

9. The whole Bible for all - Bible above all books
13. Integral Worship

10. Openness - churches, denominations, groups
12. Less dependence on the outside world
14. Acceptance, Promotion of Diversity - Rejection of Uniformity

8. Mediation - members, leaders/pastor
15. Family protection
16. Disposable members

We were excited about what had come up in such a short time and without prior preparation. How much more could be achieved with more time and more people, even from different extractions and with different experiences from theirs! And this only at the level of diagnosis. Proposals still had to be made and implemented.

"We don't know why they left," said Mariela, after a few minutes.

"It's true. Only in very few cases do we have any information, and in the rest, we don't know anything, or we just assume the reasons," I said.

"And I can assure you that in most of these cases we assume wrongly," said Mariela.

The three of us were silent again. The feeling was that we had to do something beyond words. That we could do something. And we had to do it now, riding on the impulse of ideas. At least, we had to start it.

"It seems to me that the member defense organization we were talking about has to start from the truth, from what really happened to those who left," said Mariela.

"Come on, keep going," I said.

"So we have to find a way to find out why they left..."

"...instead of guessing." It was Mercedes. "But how?"

Silence again. If they had left, if many didn't want to have anything to do with the church, they would hardly want to tell the reasons. To strangers. And after the time that had passed.

"What if we invited them to a meeting of people who had been in churches and had left?" Mariela proposed.

"But why would they go? Remember that many are sick and tired of the church and everything that smacks of church," said Mercedes.

"We can add a touch of mystery. Arouse their curiosity. With some creativity, you can do a lot," I proposed.

"Let's see." Mariela took a paper and pencil and began to write: "We are a group of Christians who are concerned about other Christians who have stopped attending church because of problems... with whom?" she started.

"With the leaders, pastors, other members..."

"Yes, I like it. But you must put on a positive vibe, else they're going to see it as another problem," suggested Mercedes.

"It could go on like this: 'And we understand that an isolated Christian... makes no sense. We want to help each other correct this... serious problem that is bleeding dry the church of the Lord," I said.

"Yes. I like that 'bleeding' concept. So graphic. And true. We have to make it clear that we are not a church and we don't want to put them back in a church," said Mariela.

"Let's see what you think." It was Mariela. 'We are not a church and we don't want to get you back into a church. We just want to create a space for you to meet again with other brothers and sisters who perhaps share many of your experiences."

"I like it. It needs a hook still," I said, "and who is sending the invitation."

"What do you think of the title 'A Second Chance'?" jumped Mercedes.

"Yes, that's exactly what we're looking for... A second chance for those who left... A second chance for the church... A second chance for the pastors, the leaders..." Mariela had taken up the idea of Mercedes.

"I like it too," I said. "But who's inviting them?"

After a while, I came up with a name.

"We are."

"What?" they both said.

"Yes. The name is 'We Are.' The idea is that you can be outside the official church, you may have had problems, disagreements, but as long as you keep the faith, you still are."

After several corrections and modifications, the invitation was as follows:

A Second Chance

Dear _____

We are a group of Christians concerned about other Christians who have stopped attending church because of problems with leaders, pastors, or other Christians.

We understand that an isolated Christian makes no sense.

We want to help each other correct this serious problem that is bleeding dry the Lord's church.

We are not a church and we don't want to get you back into a church. We just want to create a space for you to meet again with other brothers and sisters who perhaps share many of your experiences.

We will be waiting for you on Saturday, October 21, 2000, at 4 p.m., in the Social Hall of San Jorge Sports Club, Saavedra.

Raúl, Mercedes and Mariela
We Are Group

Mariela couldn't be there that day because she traveled to Pueblo Manso, but by then we had managed to incorporate three more people into the team who joined with tremendous enthusiasm. Fernando and Priscila Tormada were a married couple who had worked all their lives in the church and were now adrift, visiting one church or another, but hurt and needing to channel all their passion for the Lord's work into something.

"That's just what we were looking for! You don't know how many people are like us, feeling that the church, as an institution, and much less the pastors, don't care about us. It is as if they were telling us, silently, 'First come back, get into the system, and then we will consider you. Outside you are nothing. You don't exist.'" Fernando's pain was just below the surface, ready to explode. They had met in the supermarket and the We Are project immediately came out.

"And didn't you try calling people on the phone?" suggested Priscila, immediately offering to do the job. The first time we heard her doing the calls from our house we realized that she had an incredible gift, quite different from the cold and manipulative style of telemarketers.

"Hello? Néstor Franco? This is Priscila Tormada, a colleague in exile... From the church. Yes, I was also left out of the system, but not out of the church. We still belong to the body, you know... We are

323

coming together, no strings attached, in a positive vein, to help each other... No, I'm not from any church, rest easy... No, I'm not calling from any pastor... No, there won't be any pastor present... Noooo, there won't be any offering, I promise!" laughing. "I'll give you the details by phone, but you'll get an invitation in the mail. Can you think of anyone else who would like to be at this first meeting?"

The third person to join the team was Camila Reyes, from the Virginia support group. She had been very shaken by the conversation with Sara about how many people needed someone to just care about them inside the church, and how many more who had left the church without anyone knowing who they really were, what was going on in their minds, or in their lives. She was very straightforward, no fuss, and believed in getting right to the point.

The five of us—we continued to include Mariela, and in a sense Juan as well—had a mission, a church mission that hadn't emerged from the church. How strange! But at the same time, how exciting to be on something that had emerged from a real need, involving people, families. That had to do with the kingdom, and not with any institution. Would we end up creating another institution, with all the vices we knew? God forbid!

When the day came, we had no idea what the response to the invitation would be. We had spoken to many people, and the response was almost always positive, and usually each person in turn knew one or more people who were going through the same situation and offered to invite them. As we made our contacts, interest began to emerge also within the churches. Individuals, families, who were attending churches but weren't comfortable. Who were more outside than inside. And they were asking us if they could come. We didn't know what to tell them, since that wasn't the original goal. But it certainly pointed to another need that we hadn't anticipated. Would there be more?

We had arrived early at the neighborhood club that had lent us their main hall out of a contact of mine at the agency. We could hear the shouts of a soccer game at the far end of the club but knew they would be no problem for us. We put thirty chairs in a circle from those that were stacked at the end of the club room and spent some time praying about what was about to happen. Around starting time, a man came to the door.

"Is this the meeting of..." looking at the card, "A Second Chance"?

"Yes, come on in." I approached him with an outstretched hand. "You're the first one."

Camila and Mariela went to the door, with some welcome sheets we had prepared. When they arrived, they saw a couple in their fifties, and another slightly younger couple. After a while, two older men entered, a mid-age woman, three young people, two other couples...

We couldn't believe it. First, we added another circle of chairs, but we hadn't finished putting the last chair in when we had to start the next row. People were collaborating and seemed surprised too. Some of them knew each other and started chatting. We had set a limit to start at 4.15 p.m., but that was the time more people were coming in. We had made a hundred sheets because we got a promotional price. They now appeared to be insufficient.

"You're the pastor in charge?" asked a man in his sixties, who might as well have been a pastor himself, according to my first impression.

"No, there is no pastor in charge here. We are all lay people, ordinary people," I said with a smile.

"Ah, then I am more at ease," he answered, with a wink. I think he was checking to see if he had been cheated.

At about 4.30 p.m. the flow stopped, although not completely. We had used up all the sheets as well as the chairs. There was a group of young people who were left standing. We looked at each other in amazement. Mercedes was touched and somewhat overwhelmed by the responsibility of leading the icebreaker we had devised. Camila said that perhaps we should think of another activity. But we weren't going to let a good response, a miraculous response, intimidate us, we said. It was my turn to give the introductory words.

"Good afternoon, brothers and sisters. I think I speak for all of us when I say that we are surprised, pleasantly surprised, by the response to our invitation." We had all stood in front of the group and I took the microphone. "Only a month ago we were three people exchanging ideas about a problem that affected us very much, directly and indirectly: yours truly, Raúl Encinas, my wife Mercedes"— pointing to my left— "and Mariela Cristante, who is in Pueblo Manso, Buenos Aires, at this moment. A few days later, Fernando and Priscila Tormada appeared"—pointing to my right— "and Camila Reyes" —looking at her, next to Mercedes. "Today there are more than a hundred of us..." —the spontaneous and heartfelt applause touched us and gave me time to recover— "along with many more who couldn't come and many more who I'm sure would have come if they had known. The invitation you received" —raising it in the air— "speaks of 'A Second Chance.' And that is what we want to offer you this afternoon. A second chance for you, a second chance for the church, a second chance for the pastors" —there were some whistles at the back— "I know..." —I waited for the small murmur to die down— "I know... that there are many here who are, including us, very hurt by the attitudes of churches where we have been, where we have served with all our hearts for many, many years. Our proposal this afternoon is, on the one hand, to see how we can give ourselves a second chance... and give the church a second chance."

"But you will also have seen that the card is signed 'We Are Group'" —raising it up and indicating the place of the signature— "What does that name mean? Can anyone think of it?" I understood that I had to open the game, since this wasn't a passive audience that came just to hear nice words.

"To be what we are and not what we are not!" said a woman in the front row.

"Seems very philosophical, but I think I understood it. You're saying, sister..."

"Jimena."

"Sister Jimena, let me get this straight. You say that when you leave the church, you lose something of your identity, and you start thinking more about what you lost than about what you are, regardless of the church?"

"Yes, you give up part of your life, and then it's very difficult to get it back," she answered, with obvious pain.

"How many can identify with these words here today?" I thought I would ask.

Practically all hands were raised. I could sense that people were surprised and relieved that so many others had the same feelings.

"Very good. Any other interpretation of the name We Are?" I asked.

"We are part of the church, even though we are outside the structure, the system," proposed the man who looked like a pastor.

"Could you explain it further?" I asked. I realized that he had more to say and I had the impression that he would do it well.

"Of course," as he stood up. "I think one of the worst things that's happened to me—and I feel I can be a little more personal in this environment—is to feel that because I don't go to church, because I don't agree with a lot of things that are done in his name, I'm not part of the Lord's church. In reality, every church has always done the same thing: 'the one who is not with us, the one who does not comply with what we say, with our interpretation, our way of doing things, is an alien, not from outer space but to the inner space." Many smiled at the clever wordplay he had used. "And even more so if the person doesn't go to any church. That person doesn't exist." He sat down when he finished speaking.

"Even if he was right to leave, even if those who were wrong are inside, as if nothing had happened," added a man at the back, who I would say had been a youth leader.

"Exactly," replied the 'pastor,' turning round in his seat to speak. "You not only feel helpless but cheapened."

"I discovered a rather shady handling of finances in my church, and not only everything remained unclear, but I had to leave, and everything was swept under the doormat. Everyone who had anything to do with the 'sloppiness'" —stressing the word— "is still there and the subject was never discussed again," said a man on my right.

"Besides, the problem is that pastors cover up for each other," shouted a woman.

"They function like a corporation!" shouted another.

I felt that the moment of catharsis could become dangerous, but I didn't want to quash it either.

"Let's see if we can get some things from this first meeting," I said. "I'm going to ask Camila to help us by writing down some things that came up on the board. Mercedes, I see you've been writing some things already, right?"

"Yes, for example, two interpretations of the group's name 'We Are' came out. One: To be by one's own identity and not by negation." Camila quickly wrote the phrase. "and Two: To be part of the church even though we are outside the structure or system." Camila wrote it down as well. "I also see that the issue of helplessness..." —noted on the board— "cheapened..." —noted— "and what I would call a corporate attitude, or corporate behavior by the pastors," Mercedes concluded.

"Are we good?" Signs of approval. "Well, I think there's a lot of interest in participating from everyone, and that's wonderful. This is just the beginning. So I'm going to let Mercedes continue."

Mercedes came to the front, feeling much more assured than at the beginning. She already had a first impression and a lot of material to work with. Her initial terror was that this would be like so many church groups she knew, where no one participated, afraid to disagree, to think differently, to risk saying something. Obviously, this wasn't the case.

"I am going to ask you to do one thing that I think will be very useful to all of us," Mercedes continued. "Take ten minutes to talk to someone else you don't know and try to find out what were the reasons that led him or her to leave the church, and write them down in the sheets we are going to give you, from the most important to the least important. It can be one, two or three people. Then we're going to reverse the pairs. Now, the important thing here is not to ask the other person the reasons and write them down mechanically, but to do it as if it were an interview and then write down the reasons that you deduce, you understand, that were the real ones. And don't show it to the other person. Do you understand? This is because sometimes we think we did something for a reason and there are other reasons in the background that don't come out right away."

We handed out the sheets and pencils and the five of us gathered in the front. We were like in a haze. So much had happened in that last hour, with the people that had come, the things that surfaced, the spirit that could be breathed. We were only asking the Lord to help us handle so much emotional charge, so much life, so much pain. The participation of the people was amazing. I looked around and then I decided to walk around the room. I was surprised to see this group of people, very few of whom knew each other previously, united by a common theme. As if to disprove the cliché that was often heard inside churches when someone left: "What happened was that he was not in the spirit... she was not interested." Although it wasn't my strong point, I tried to listen to two or three conversations at a time secretly.

"But what was the real reason you were taken out of all the activities?"

"I think it was jealousy, but I never knew."

"And you never brought it up?"

"I had nowhere to do it..."

.....

"The same thing happened to me... but let's go back to the interview" —reacting unconsciously when she saw me nearby— "What was it that bothered you the most?"

"Well... I'd say... the hypocrisy. Yes."

"And what else?" in the role of a psychologist.

"The lack of interest. Especially on the part of a pastor."

"Why?"

"Because they're supposed to have a special interest in people. It's their vocation, isn't it?"

.....

"And you think it was all the pastor's fault?"

"No, I think the people are largely to blame. In general, one has the pastor that one deserves."

"I'll write it down, but I don't agree."

"Why?"

"Because I think many people deserve better pastors, but there's no possibility of improving them. Many stay at a very low level."

.....

Mercedes made them reverse roles, and the interest was even greater in this round. Finally, we decided to pick up the sheets with what they had written down.

"Well, we're going to take a break, and when we come back, we're going to give you the results of the surveys you've done."

We had prepared some thermoses of coffee and cookies, calculating a maximum of thirty people. We had to go out and buy more, but we did so gladly. We had thought of a ten-minute break, but half an hour had gone by and everyone was still talking excitedly. We noticed that no one had remained isolated, no one had left, and people tended to move from one group to another freely. Three characteristics that weren't usually found in church groups.

In the meantime, the five of us began to sort through the survey material, which logically didn't lend itself to easy systematization. But we wanted them to have a useful feedback from their effort that very day. We felt that we owed it to them, that they deserved respect for having come. We couldn't feel that we were treating them in a way that they had suffered in a church. So, in a mixture of professionalism and consideration, we made a great effort to sort through the more than one hundred pages in half an hour.

"Well, who wants to know the results of the surveys?" I shouted. The people went back to their seats.

Camila went to the blackboard, chalk in hand.

"The results are extremely rich and valuable, and they are good for much further study, but we decided to organize the answers into some basic categories, which we simplified. Are you OK with it?"

Murmur of approval. Camila came forward and started writing on the board.

"The first reason is lack of interest... care... attention from pastors or leaders. Thirty-four responses. The second, authoritarianism... not accepting questioning, blind obedience. Twenty-five answers. Then comes inability, lack of knowledge, need to update. Sixteen. Those would be the first three reasons, always taking the first reason you put on the lists. Actually we would have to take into account the second and third option, to weigh them... There is a lot to do, and we are going to continue working with all this material after we leave."

"The question is how to go on from here," I said. "Any suggestions?"

"I think it has been very positive to meet among us and to know that there are others who are going through similar situations," said a man who hadn't spoken until now. Why don't we meet to continue talking about it? At least we are doing something, and we can think about it."

"And why not have a time of prayer, of singing, of some words?" said a girl.

"A church?" I said.

"Noooo," said several, in chorus.

"So, it would be like a pre-church?" I ventured.

"I can think of the image of a place of recovery, a church rehabilitation center," suggested Camila.

"A field hospital," said the 'pastor,' "where the wounded can recover and return to the battle."

"I like the image of the pastor." He has already earned the nickname from others.

"I am not a pastor!" he said, pretending to be offended. "But I think such a place would be as much a church as the church itself... fulfilling functions that it isn't fulfilling at the moment, even with those who are inside."

The exchange continued for another half hour. No one seemed to want to leave. Finally, we agreed to expand the "committee" by adding five more people from among the attendees and to call for a second meeting in a place with more space. The idea that came up repeatedly was to create a "non-church"—in the words of the "youth leader"—with free meetings that would allow us to meet more people who were "on the loose" and that would allow us to minister to each other while waiting for a general change in the churches or in a specific church that could be the final destination of these people. Although it would have "church" activities—prayer, reading and Bible study—it was forbidden for anyone to even think that this would ever evolve into a new church or that a hierarchical structure would form that would begin to reproduce its vices. In addition, it was crucial that it be a transitory place, of transit, for the people who were part of it.

In this sense, the committee that had been formed, whose members were to be temporary and rotating, was critical. In other words, no one was to be perpetuated and everyone was to have a limited time on the committee, after which they should "return to the plain." Many other ideas came up in the final exchange, and all were written down and considered. In general, what was perceived was that people were very clear about what they didn't want from this fledgling group, which was the same thing they didn't want for the church: rigid structure, division between leaders and led, limitation of participation, hidden decisions, etc. There were also other aspects that they considered should be present: seeking out those who weren't there, care for those who were there, dialogue, real and practical fellowship, etc.

The meeting ended with a very deep and heartfelt prayer that I asked the "pastor" to make with the somewhat invented excuse that he was the oldest person in the room. I did this because I felt inside that he had something special. I wasn't wrong. He asked that we all hold hands and suddenly the collection of people, sadness and frustration became one body, throbbing, pulsing in unison and with one purpose. Perhaps what struck us most were his first words, clearly inspired:

"Just as we are... united to the brother or sister next to us... parts of one body that doesn't end in this room... let us take a few minutes to give thanks in silence... in complete silence... for this new opportunity, this second chance, that the Lord is giving us."

There was magic in those seconds, minutes, that seemed like hours or days. Each of those present experienced, alone and in union with the rest, a profound healing of the deepest pains that they had brought. There was a presence, a spirit that could only come from God. It was a group of people who were in the precise time and place for him to do his work in them. It was as simple as that. That deep. Like the edge of a knife striking at the place of the cut, so they were cutting ties, resentments, bitterness, burdens. Tears were flowing freely in men and women alike, with no one bothering to dry them. I saw clearly, almost personified, the anger that had built up over the years against Pedro. It became almost bodily, huge, dark, and then faded away and left me with a lightness and peace that I hadn't had for a long time. Then there appeared, almost as enormous and ominous as the previous burden, the accumulated pain of all those who had been affected by Pedro's ministry, for whom I had done nothing, out of comfort or cowardice. It was like a succession of images of people, one after another, with faces of pain and sadness. But after a while all that disappeared too, and peace returned, even more profound.

After a while—no one can say how much time passed on the clock of earthly things—someone began to sing, spontaneously, low and soft voice, a very simple song that repeated a single word, "Hallelujah." People were joining in as they finished their "silent treatment," no hurry, no pressure. When everyone had finished their inner process and had joined the improvised choir, the "pastor" said these simple words, above the singing:

"Now, Lord, send us off in peace, so that we may do your work. Thank you."

We ended by embracing each other and wishing each other the Lord's blessing.

When the last of the guests left, the five of us who had started that day stayed. We realized that something important had begun that afternoon. For us, for those people, and for many others who hadn't been there too.

We were amazed. Emotionally drained but spiritually renewed.

We needed to call Mariela to tell her everything that had happened. She and Juan were sure to share the same joy at a distance with us.

From then on, things happened at a dizzying pace. The following week, we of the ProRot — as we had been called because of its provisional and rotational nature—met. Apart from Fernando and Priscila, Camila, Mercedes and myself, the group had chosen the "pastor," the "youth leader," two women and a man, the latter between forty and fifty years old.

The "pastor" was Zacarías Montes and wasn't a pastor. But he had been involved in every church activity since he was a child. He had attended Sunday School and was a Sunday School teacher, had been in the youth group and had ended up being a youth leader. Then he ran the Bible School for young adults. He had been on countless committees within the church and in his denomination. He had preached in his church and in plazas. He had worked in hospitals and prisons. He knew the slums from the inside as well as all the wheeling and dealing. But he hated public exposure. Every time he had had a chance to get to a position of importance in an area or field, he had resigned. In his words, he was a "professional quitter." And not out of cowardice or to pass the buck, but out of conviction. For him, Christianity was renunciation, as opposed to the system of the world which was accumulation. Moreover, he jokingly said that with his renunciations he was anticipating the Lord, who would make him renounce if he didn't do it first.

The so-called "youth leader" was not such, but a highly capable private consultant who worked with first-rate enterprises. He was a specialist in motivation, teamwork, leadership, and change. Ariel Cernadas had worked with young people in the church, although not as a leader, trying to incorporate successful techniques from the business world into the church, but without sacrificing the essence of what the church was to him: a community of love.

The other two men who joined were Virgilio Montes and

Martín Soto. They had shared several years in the same church, in different areas. Virgilio was a born administrator, with no academic background but with a privileged mind in his ability to quickly see the priorities, the areas of danger and how to solve problems in the most efficient way. He had collided with the disorder camouflaged as spirituality that had shattered a flourishing church, also peppered with several financial scandals that were never cleared up. Martín had been in charge of the men's group. With a very enticing manner, he broke through any barriers and reached the essence of the person in a short time. I remember how I felt naked when he greeted me saying, "God is about to take away the anxiety you have now."

Verónica Graziani was the woman who joined the team. Separated, in the process of divorce, she was burdened with a history of infidelity and mistreatment by her ex-husband, who held a high position in a major church. Unable to defend herself or make herself heard impartially, she had opted for what she would never have imagined in a believer, especially to safeguard her three teenage children: to sue him. She was concerned with finding a group of her healthy children's age where they would really listen and practice the principles she believed in, without hypocrisy and duplicity.

The "non-church" movement spread like wildfire. We held the second gathering in a conditioned shed that we were lent. Around five hundred people came! After explaining the basic concepts that were being affirmed of the "non-church," the provisional and rotating character of the team that had appeared, we did an exercise that was more appropriate to the number, this time in charge of Ariel. Mercedes was in charge of organizing a very simple time of music and Zacarias ended with a brief reflection on Psalm 23, emphasizing the fact that our true Pastor was Jesus, and if the other pastors had failed us, he would never let us down.

The closing was different from the previous one, but just as moving, profound and healing as it was then. An implicit motto of the team was not to repeat ourselves, not to quench the spontaneity, not to create elements that repeat themselves over time out of comfort, laziness, or simply because they had worked before.

The movement continued to spread and reproduce itself throughout the country. As of today, we have reports of more than two hundred "non-churches," coordinated by a general ProRot with the same characteristics as the local ones.

In these two years we have had several satisfactions. In the first place, the great number of families healed and rescued from loneliness. Secondly, many, after some time in the "non-church," have returned to their own church or to another church, although this was never an explicit objective of the movement. Furthermore, all left on good terms and sometimes return, bringing another "wounded soldier" or simply out of nostalgia, to visit.

Many were saying, inside and outside the churches, that many of these "non-churches" had more church characteristics than the churches themselves. A tongue twister, perhaps. Or a curious reality.

12

Till we found there were ways of coming together
And ending the lies we had told ourselves ever

Each had received a blue envelope with their name on it, but no return address. When they had opened it, they found a sheet, also blue, with the following sentence written in gold:

A Second Chance

That was it. At least, in writing. Because the following day each received a phone call as mysterious as the envelope.

"Hello? Is this Pastor Julio Maciel?"

"Yes. Who is this?"

"You don't know me, pastor. My name is Miriam. I'm calling about the blue envelope you must have received yesterday."

"Ah, yes... I don't understand. Who sent it? What are you selling?"

"No, we aren't selling anything. Did you open the envelope?"

"Of course."

"And what did it say, please?"

"Look, I warn you that if it's a joke or a rib, I have no time to waste..."

"I assure you it's neither one thing nor the other. Please, pastor, what did it say inside?"

"A Second Chance," reluctantly.

"Exactly. A Second Chance."

"And what does that mean? Again, who sent the envelope, and why?"

"I just want to tell you that we've selected you for an intensive course for pastors called 'A Second Chance.' I can't tell you more details at this point, unfortunately."

"But how do you expect me to accept without knowing what it's about, who you are...? Besides, I'm swamped with activities, responsibilities, commitments... How do you expect me to leave everything overnight?"

"We understand perfectly. I just ask you to pray about it and let the Spirit guide you. I'll call you this time tomorrow. If you agree, the training will start right then, and it will end six days later. Of course, all expenses are covered, and we will implement ways for you to be contacted in cases of extreme urgency."

"And where is this... course going to be?"

"I'm sorry. I can't tell you that either."

"Look, it all seems very strange to me... but call me tomorrow."

"All right. I'll do that. Until tomorrow, pastor."

Julio Maciel was stunned. He had shown the envelope and the note to his wife, Roxana, who had told him it must be a joke of the young people of his church. It wouldn't be the first time. Now he had to tell her that he was going to disappear for six days in the hands of some strangers, in a mysterious place. It would only reinforce her theory. What about the preaching on Sunday, the interviews during the week, the preparation for the conference, the leaders' meeting? He couldn't deny that he was intrigued by the subject, or that he could use a retreat. He was exhausted, not so much physically, but emotionally, or rather spiritually. In fact, as he prepared to pray, he remembered that several times over the past year he had toyed with the idea of leaving the ministry and going into something with fewer personal problems. He had always loved computers, and perhaps he could serve the Lord in that way...

"I'll be praying, dear, so hold my calls for the next hour, please!" he shouted at his wife.

"Any special reason?" she asked, approaching him.

"Guidance... guidance..." Roxana remembered how many times they had both prayed, separately and together, seeking guidance in the difficult times in Rwanda, and the even more difficult times when they came back. Both were still open to God's will, but some of the romanticism and idealism of youth had been erased in the face of the harshness of daily reality.

As soon as he closed the door of his study and knelt by the chair, Julio had a strong conviction that he should go to the retreat. It was irrational, illogical. He found no argument, no logical reason to abandon everything he was doing and embark on an adventure into the unknown. But he knew that somehow the letter and call came from the Lord, or from someone the Lord had sent. At that precise time in his life. *God's kairos*, he thought. To top it off, when he opened the Bible at random to help him in his meditation, he came across the last chapter of the Gospel of John, when Jesus meets Simon Peter, who had denied him three times, and three times asks him if he loved him. He read up to verse 17 of chapter 21:

> The third time he said to him,
> "Simon son of John, do you love me?"
> Peter was hurt because Jesus asked him the third time,
> "Do you love me?"
> He said, "Lord, you know all things; you know that I
> love you."
> Jesus said, "Feed my sheep."

He was deeply moved. It was as if Jesus himself was saying "Feed my sheep" to him, a pastor! But if that was his job, his vocation, his reason for being. He reread the phrase again aloud, slowly, several times: "Feed my sheep... Feed my sheep... Then he tried emphasizing one word at a time, a technique that was always effective: "*Feed* my sheep... Feed *my* sheep... Feed my *sheep*."

Clearly, he knew he wasn't feeding them properly, at least not at this time. He had been losing enthusiasm, passion. And now, to be honest, he was just going through the motions. The expression "work by the book" came to mind, and he smiled unwillingly. How many times had he been jealous when his sheep had gone to other churches, even for isolated activities, and how much more so when they had decided to stay! He had felt betrayed, undermined, rejected. But they weren't his... they were His... and then, they were sheep. They needed a pastor, a shepherd, and many didn't have one. How little he knew about many sheep, and how much, in contrast, of the few he liked best!

The final confirmation that he should go to the retreat was that, when he told his wife about Miriam's call and what he had felt in his time of prayer, she took it as naturally as if he were telling her he was going to church.

"I think you have to go, too. Don't ask me why, but I'm sure it comes from the Lord."

So when Miriam called the next day, he confirmed that he would go.

"I'm so glad, pastor. I'm sure you won't regret it. Tomorrow morning, at 5 p.m. sharp, a blue car will pick you up..." and she continued giving him some instructions—not too many—about what would happen next.

Marcelo Rosales received the envelope and the call at his home in Resistencia, Chaco. He had been involved in politics in recent years and, although it had been a lifelong dream, convinced that it was a natural and necessary field of action for the Christian, he was deeply disappointed. The corruption he had seen was so great that he had practically lost hope of achieving any significant change through political participation. In addition, he had become isolated from other pastors when he began to engage in partisan politics— "politics is not for believers," "everything is rotten, and you will become corrupt," "we have a spiritual, superior message," "our message is not for this world." But after he was elected as a town councilman, many pastors sought him out for their own benefit, including some who had criticized him. When he proved to be inflexible in his impartiality, they accused him of betraying his people, but when they saw that there was no change in his lifestyle, either financially or personally, during his entire eight-year term, they ended up respecting him and using him as an example of what a Christian in politics should be. What inconsistency!

His confirmation to agree to this "madness"—words of his wife, Daniela—was through a time of very deep prayer and a call from a member of his church who simply said, "I have a word for you. I don't know what it means, but I'm telling you anyway: 'second chance.'"

Rosa Hoyts had abandoned any idea of working in the pastoral area many years ago when the envelope arrived. She had married a very capable Christian businessman, Gonzalo Freites, who was active in the church and other Christian and secular organizations, but she had been overshadowed by her husband's personality and the upbringing of her five children. She commented to Gonzalo, in passing, the strange envelope with the mysterious note, and he gave it no importance. "There are so many nuts on the loose these days..." he had said. But when Rosa said she would receive a phone call the next day he was alarmed and wanted to call the police. How did they know her phone number, her address and that she had studied at a seminary?

Rosa began to pray, and felt the conviction, but it was crazy to leave him and the five kids... if it hadn't been for the vivid dream Gonzalo had that very night. He saw himself at seventy, brimming with health, surrounded by his five children, all successful, strong, radiant, with his grandchildren. At the back of the room, there was Rosa, his Rosa, hunched over, sad, pale. The contrast was so dreadful that he felt ashamed and insisted that she take this opportunity. When she said "yes" to Miriam, the miracle had already started.

In Mabel Duverges' case it was almost the other way around. She had accumulated titles like someone who collects furniture. After graduating from the Seminary, she studied Medicine, specialized in Pediatrics, did a postgraduate course in infectious diseases and then, nobody knows why, started studying Business Administration. She had married Miguel Ángel Pérez, a faithful believer and excellent musician, but without the determination and discipline to keep up with her. If ever there was an odd couple, this was it. Their marriage had aged to the point that they barely spoke to each other, not even to argue. When the envelope arrived and she received Miriam's phone call, her first instinct was to accept, as one of the many courses that had kept her away from home over the years. Her only daughter, Claribel, was now fifteen years old and very attached to her father. They didn't have a good mother-daughter relationship, at least not as good as the one Claribel had with Cristina, who shared the worship ministry with her father.

When she began to pray, almost mechanically, she felt like a dark cloud that enveloped her and left her feeling naked before God. Suddenly she found she had no title or activity to cover herself with. She was simply Mabel Duverges de Pérez, brilliant professional, bad mother, bad wife... former student pastor. The cloud pushed her to the ground to the point that she couldn't get up for what seemed like an eternity. When she was able to do so, she realized that this wouldn't be just another activity. It was serious. She hesitated, until she felt the desire to embrace Miguel Ángel desperately. She told him about the envelope and the call. He simply said, "Mabel, I don't know if this is a second chance or the last one, but I'm asking you for our marriage, for Claribel and for me. This is from God. If you miss this opportunity, I don't think there will be another."

Marcos Suárez and Nora Maluf had married as soon as they finished the Seminary and had both gone into the Lord's work full-time. They had managed to build a beautiful independent church, which they had called Centro de Encuentro Cristiano (CEC). It operated with a cellular structure in the homes during the week and with general meetings on Sundays in a very simple building that was used during the week for various community activities. The church had multiplied steadily over the years because they had focused their work on preparing leaders. They had achieved a solid group of men and women younger than themselves that allowed them to think of a church without them, the ideal they had always set themselves: to organize things in such a way that if something happened to them or they decided to leave, it would go practically unnoticed.

But in its best moment a powerful Central American cell movement appeared that got into the church and captured half of the leaders with promises of progress and growth, appointing them pastors, ministers and whatever title and position was available. They were left with a church that was split in half, not only in numbers but in soul and heart.

In the middle of the period of pain, each one received a blue envelope. They wondered what it was about and began to pray at that very moment. Nothing special happened. They didn't mention the subject to their two children, Ariel and Silvana, but just as they entered the kitchen the TV was on and the title of the episode of the series the children were watching appeared: The Second Chance. They looked at each other, smiled and told the kids. They, of course, were delighted to be alone for a few days, but they also thought it would do the "old ones" good to take a break from the stress they had shared over the past month.

Ernesto Saccardi had just returned from Miami, USA, with his wife, Diana and their three children. With his spectacular natural voice, he had studied voice over and had worked in radio broadcasting. He was convinced that he could reach many more people through this medium, people who were otherwise inaccessible. He had managed to put together a respected radio program with a small budget and two other people, while maintaining his job at one of the country's major banks, and Diana continued to teach history in high school. Until he was offered to do the same in the States, where there would be many more resources, audience, and possibilities. They had moved five years ago, and while he had made material progress and in the scope of his ministry, none of the family had settled down, and he soon realized that there was little he could accomplish in a culture saturated with Christian media. Especially with so much need elsewhere. It was difficult not to count the last five years as a loss.

When the envelope arrived, he didn't know why he held on to it like a plank in the middle of the sea. It was something "spiritual," albeit incomprehensible. So different from everything material that he had breathed in the last few years in everything he did. The call with his indication to pray, led him to do it like a child, asking for forgiveness and light... forgiveness for the past and light for the future... time after time, until he fell asleep on the couch. In fact, in the case of the Saccardi's, there was no need for confirmation, because since they had decided to return to the country, they had insistently asked the Lord for a "second chance" literally.

When Pedro received the envelope, he was going through one of the best times of his life—individually, in his marriage, and in his family. His year or so in Faith and Progress hadn't been at all what he imagined. There were responsibilities and duties to fulfil, but the decisions and recognitions belonged to others, and rightly so. After all, this project hadn't been his idea and he had only come on board when everything had been decided already. Now that he thought about it, all the time since his first interview with Tony Vidal and his previous seventeen years with Fullness and Growth had been carefully choreographed by others. There also he had his part cut out for him. Yes, he certainly had enjoyed the fame, the lights, his name on the marquees, but in a strange and disturbing analogy, when he got off the train it was as if he had sold his soul to... No, that's impossible. Look at all the people who got to know the Lord through him and who knows how many he wouldn't ever know about? When he went back in time to their first two years after the Seminary, in the living room and the shed, it seemed that it was the only genuine time of service for the Kingdom, both for him and Virginia. The times of prayer, the visits after working in the dealership, the dreams that were theirs alone and not from another country or culture!

That morning he had been meditating on Isaiah 55. Yes, he had recovered this precious time in the morning. How beautiful to just let the Spirit and his spirit flow freely without any precooked, second-hand materials that were just as harmful as the junk-food he had stopped eating. He had started to recover his physical condition through a healthy diet and plenty of exercise, now that the time he had belonged to nobody else. Virginia had also recovered her figure and her smile together with him. "Come, all you who are thirsty... come to the waters... come.... come...Why spend your labor on what does not satisfy?"[59] Only now he understood this. "For my thoughts are not your thoughts, neither are your ways my ways..."[60] He was coming in from his daily walk during which he had been meditating on this passage when he saw the man with the blue envelope in his hand. For a second, he had a vision of other encounters with strangers in the past.

"Pastor Terrero?" he asked.

"Yes, who's this for?" as he took the envelope.

"For you sir. Have a nice day."

Pedro felt this was something special, related to the Lord's ways. He entered the house, called Virginia and opened it in front of her. When she saw what it said, she said, "Pedro, I don't know why, but I feel this is something good from the Lord."

When Miriam called the next day, Pedro accepted immediately.

Juan's two years in Pueblo Manso were the easily the best of his life. Especially when he contrasted the way he had arrived and how he felt now. To think that after all those years looking for a place to simply serve and grow in the Lord he was now in a place that he had helped take from near-death to vibrant life and where he was in a certain way one of the leaders made it all the more remarkable. He and Mariela had never looked to be in the limelight and were content to find someone to follow and help. Maybe all those years of simply being part of something — including his time in the army — were the

[59] Isa 55:1-2
[60] Isa 55:8

345

necessary training to be a good leader. Even the negative experience in the first Church of the Open Word where his leadership was never acknowledged was part and parcel of his formation. But more than being a leader he was proud of the team he had been able to form. Each had a function and each had contributed to define the church and all its areas. And their team had been able to construct something and work together with the Catholic church to unmask and then bring down strongholds that enslaved the people of the town. Mariela was also a fulfilled person in her own right and they both knew their three children were growing in a much healthier environment than two years ago.

When Juan received the blue envelope, he had just returned from the "meteorite" site. The block of stone found originally in the Costas Navas field had been examined by scientists a few months ago and had been shown to be a true meteorite. Thanks to the insistence of the group they had managed to give access to the public and small space center had been constructed beside it. With help from the University of La Plata who provided financial help and a couple of professors who gave lectures and classes on stars, planets and meteorites, star-gazing experiences and a series of activities the place was transformed from a pagan worship site into a scientific center and tourism site. The truth was setting the people free in this too. He felt the need to share this experience and all that had happened in this last year with other pastors, so he took the cryptic message and the phone call the following day as something strangely related to this need and accepted the invitation.

The blue envelope reached others who decided to reject the invitation for various reasons. For example, Zacarías Pimentel was an itinerant preacher who was always travelling, both in and out of the country. When he received the envelope during his five-day tour in Lima, Peru, he left it unopened and when he answered Miriam's call at night, at his hotel, he told her that he would see what the envelope had when he returned to Argentina. Too late. Santiago Vilches, from Formosa, had left the ministry and the church, after a very unpleasant situation where he had been unjustly accused of embezzlement. Instead of relying on other brothers, many of whom still believed in him, he chose to cut ties, curse the church and break with everything that reminded him of it. He did the same with the envelope as soon as he saw that it was addressed to "Pastor Vilches" and saw what it contained. When Miriam called, he treated her very curtly, even though she insisted that the training would do him good. Leo Nuccetelli, from Trelew, on the other hand, had entered an ultra-closed group that had no contact with any other church, so when he saw something that didn't belong to his group, he threw it into the trash bin immediately, without opening it. When Veronica Schmidt received the envelope with the title *pastora* the past came over her. She immediately thought of Hugo and how he had handled the situation so bravely, trying to protect her, even though he knew the son wasn't his. But she also thought of Leo, who preferred to go along with the lie and was an absent father to Benjamin, that precious boy the Lord had given her. She prayed about it and wept bitterly when she realized that she wouldn't be able to face so many who had let her down.

The procedure for all those who accepted the invitation was the same. The next day, punctually at the indicated time, a blue car arrived to pick up the guest and take them to the meeting place, an old ranch eighty kilometers south from Buenos Aires. In Marcelo's case, it included the trip by plane from Resistencia. At the entrance it had the sign "Welcome to Camp Poimén"[61] freshly painted at the entrance, with a shepherd's staff crossing the text. After driving through a long entrance bordered by cypress trees, the car stopped at a roundabout around a fountain, where it was welcomed by a young man, also in blue, who took them to their room inside the large single-story

---

[61] In Greek, *poimén* means shepherd

building. In the room there was a blue envelope, like the first one they had received, and inside it said, simply

Welcome to Camp Poimén
Please don't leave the room
until we pick you up,
at 8:00 p.m. sharp
Thank you

By now, no one was concerned by the intrigue and they were willing to follow the instructions, at least until the mystery was cleared up. The rooms were large and simple, with built-in bathrooms, and they overlooked a lovely garden with freshly cut grass, beautiful flower beds, and a pergola in the distance, but no one ventured into it until they were picked up.

Exactly at 8 p.m., each of them received a gentle knock at the door and found a young lad in blue who led them through darkened corridors into an inner room, completely dark, depositing them on a chair. Everyone knew at this point that there were others—they didn't know how many—participating in this "game," but, except for Marcos and Nora, who shared the room, they had no idea who the others would be. Miriam's call had suggested an intensive course, a pastors' retreat, but she hadn't said who it was for. The dim light filtering through a skylight in the ceiling revealed several figures sitting in front of what appeared to be a table with chairs. The soft music of an old hymn, "Nearer, My God, to Thee," helped reduce the anxiety of the moment.

Suddenly, when all the chairs were occupied, the music stopped, and a voice came over the sound system:

"Welcome to Camp Poimén. Please greet the brother or sister next to you."

The lights came on and the surprise couldn't have been greater.

"Juan!"

"Pedro!"

"Mabel!"

"Hugo?"

.....

They were all classmates from the 1980 class of the Pastoral Bible Seminary (SeBiPa), many of whom hadn't seen each other in over twenty years. The hugs and greetings seemed to go and on. Until the voice took over again.

"I hope you enjoyed the first of the many surprises we have prepared for you these days."

At that moment, a tall, athletic, balding man in his fifties, dressed impeccably in a blue sports suit, entered. He stood in front of the group and, with a wide smile and evident command of the scene, said:

"Hi." It was the voice they had heard before. "My name is Honorio Ayala. I am one of those responsible for this intrigue. The others will remain anonymous for now. To begin with, I think you all know each other, don't you? Juan, Pedro, Hugo, Julio, Marcelo, Rosa, Mabel, Marcos, Nora, Ernesto and Nacho. Eleven, in all. Did I forget any of you?"

He had everyone's full attention. The expectation was created.

"I want to give you some idea of what this retreat is about. The other details will be revealed as the days go by. You've all studied to be pastors. Some of you have had the possibility of putting it into practice, others haven't. Some of you have started and had to leave or are thinking of leaving. Most of you are going through a crisis now but all have had crises over these years. Crises are necessary and inevitable. They are neither good nor bad in themselves. But they can be either destructive or saving, depending on how we view them and make use of them. Am I doing well so far?" Honorio let his gaze rest on each one of them.

The silence was the best approval of what he was saying.

"We believe that this retreat is something that comes from the heart of the Lord, but we needed those who were coming to be really committed. That's why we didn't give you all the details and our assistant, Miriam, just asked you to pray. I understand that, if you are here, it is because the Lord confirmed to each one personally in one way or other that you should come. Otherwise, it is inexplicable that you would come to an unknown place with unknown people without further information. This also explains why the others who were invited, the rest of your SeBiPa fellow students, didn't come. We know that all of them are going through some kind of crisis too, but they didn't come because they didn't realize it, because they didn't pray or because they weren't willing to take risks to get out of the situation they were in."

Right then, the sign "A Second Chance" appeared on a screen, in gold letters on a blue background.

"We believe that God wants to give you a second chance. And it will be up to you to accept or reject it. What we are going to do in these five days of retreat, starting tomorrow, is a series of exercises, some individual and some in groups. The idea is to explore different facets of the pastor's life and to give you the opportunity to refresh concepts in a creative and updated way. The retreat is going to be intensive, demanding... I would even say rough. We believe that you have shortlisted yourselves for your interest in change and your willingness to believe in the Lord. But if anyone at this moment has doubts or decides not to continue, I ask you to say so now and we will take you back home immediately. All we ask is that, once committed to the idea of moving forward, you do your best to follow through for the sake of yourself and the entire group. Questions?"

"Yes." It was Pedro. "If you don't want to tell us who is organizing this, couldn't you at least tell us who is financing this? Or are you going to charge us?" with a knowing smile at his former companions, as in the old days.

"On the last day we will reveal to you all the information of all those who have organized this event, including who financed it. No, you won't have to pay anything."

Mabel appeared undecided, struggling with herself, and Honorio realized it.

"Mabel, if it's all right with you, we'll meet up later, okay?" he said.

"Ah yes, thank you," she replied.

"Well, you can use the facilities as you see fit. Dinner will be served at 9:00 p.m. sharp in the Koinonia Room."

The group was abuzz with conversations and banter. Meanwhile, Honorio went to see Mabel and they retired to the garden to chat. It was a beautiful autumn night, too perfect in every detail to be true.

They went to the pergola, lit by an old lantern, and sat down on an iron bench.

"Tell me what's wrong, Mabel."

"Look, this is all very strange... There's a part of me that says, 'go ahead,' and that's why I came, but there's another part that's extremely suspicious. Why can't we know what's behind all this? Why should I open up to you if I don't even know who you are? I've been to many intensive training courses like this one. And you always, in one way or another, end up realizing that you are being manipulated, that you are like a puppet... And I don't like it. I don't like it at all."

"I understand you perfectly. But we're all constantly subject to attempts at manipulation in life. Advertising, politicians, the media, people at work, spouse, children, relatives. We can't help it. We can only try not to be manipulated. It's like sin. It's everywhere, we know it is, even inside us. The solution is not to turn away toward a perfect world, which on the other hand doesn't exist, but to get along without being contaminated. I wouldn't be afraid if I were you. The one who should be afraid is the one who isn't aware of these attempts at manipulation."

"Yes, everything you say is true."

"Your salvation is the group, Mabel."

"How come?"

"Yes, your salvation is in the people you can trust. People you know. You lived with this group for three years, didn't you?"

"Yes, I did."

"Well, you know them a lot better than you know me. You know the good and the bad things about each of them. You even know who's more reliable than another. You know their weaknesses and strengths."

"I don't understand where you're going with this."

"I ask you to rely on the known to face the unknown, on the people you know and who know you to face what you don't know. Talk to them about your doubts. Much of the success of this experience is in the group, the people you know, the relationships that exist. And that's all I'm saying."

"Now I understand you a little better." Her attitude had changed. "I'm staying!"

Mabel returned to the group that had occupied the rest of the garden in small groups, and Honorio went to the house in the back, which he would call "the office" and the rest would call "the base" during the rest of the retreat.

"They're all staying," he said.

"Excellent," replied the man behind the computer. "So that's eleven."

"Yes. Counting you. Eight men, three women."

"What did you think of the atmosphere?"

"I think it's excellent. But I'll answer you after tomorrow's session," replied Honorio, with a sign of concern.

"Why?"

"I never agreed to put that session first. We could lose some of them."

The instruction at dinner on Tuesday night for the next day was to have a light breakfast and wear comfortable clothes. The meeting point and time would be the pergola, at 9 a.m. Everyone had already caught up with each other, and many had remained chatting at the table and even later after dinner. The tables were for three people each, leaving two people free to share the meal with Honorio. All the groups rotated, and a system of sanctions had been devised for those who broke this rule or any of the others throughout the camp.

Pedro and Juan had talked late into the night, and when they went to bed, they had much more to discuss than when they had begun. But it had done them good. The moment they saw each other in that unexpected and strange place, both had felt the futility of their estrangement, first because of church differences and then simply because they hadn't cultivated such a deep and strong relationship as they had had when they were younger.

They were all surprised to see Hugo, who had been publicly ousted, and equally embarrassed to learn of the injustice of the situation that had alienated him from the group and stopped him from finishing his studies at the Seminary. But it was clear that he didn't feel any resentment and that he was fully at ease in that place and with all of them.

After dinner, the tables were cleared and, between *maté* and *maté*, they remembered old anecdotes from the past.

"Remember Chiavetto?" said Nacho.

"The mentor! What a character!" replied Pedro.

"They tell me he's still there. Poor students!" Mabel's unmistakable voice.

"Ché, Pedro, where's Virginia?" Ernesto, the *riojano*, always told him he'd stand in for him.

"She's in good hands, so don't worry. And you, didn't you get married?"

"Of course. I was just kidding. Her name is Diana, and we have three kids. Here they are," taking a picture of the wallet. "We just got back from Miami. Quite an experience. I heard Virginia got into radio too. Is that true?"

"Yes, what a coincidence. Maybe someday you can do something together."

"I'd love to, but different from what I was doing over there. Something more authentic, more real... I don't know."

"Well, she started with a Christian radio station and left right away. Now she was in a secular radio, and although she had... we had some problems for taking the risk of going out on a limb, she saw it as much more interesting, a real challenge."

"Problems? What kind of problems?"

Pedro told Ernesto about the incident at Virginia's radio show, and while he was doing it, he realized that, thanks to that incident he was here. Because he wouldn't have accepted the invitation if he had stayed with the Faith and Progress group. When everything seemed to be going well, he was actually sinking deeper and deeper. When the world seemed to be falling apart, he was being saved. Ironies of the Christian life.

The conversation went on. Honorio watched and took notes, without anyone noticing. He was putting together a kind of sociogram, a graph of all the interrelationships that were taking place between the eleven participants. It was a subject that fascinated him: how relationships seemed to acquire an entity as real as people themselves. They were born, grew up and died. But they also got sick, they reproduced, they died of starvation. There were also relationships that looked more like monsters than people, frightening ones. There were always more relationships than people. Potentially, he knew that 11 people could produce 54 different relationships. 11 people, 54 relationships, 65 living entities before his eyes, which would vary over those five days, never the same, never static. Would he be able to handle such a pulsation of life? What would happen when one person got up badly, or when two people had disagreements, or if closed or confrontational groups formed? What if the group confronted him? What would he say to those who had hired him? Suddenly, he was overwhelmed by the task at hand and stopped writing and drawing. He retired to the garden and meditated and prayed as he walked in the light of the full moon.

But that Wednesday morning Honorio was in full swing. The burden of surprise had been lifted, and with the advantage of the good spirit that reigned among old friends, it was now his turn to begin the exercises that would constitute the "A Second Chance" retreat.

"I hope you have rested well and had a good breakfast, because you have a long, long walk ahead of you." He had assumed the posture of a military instructor, cap and scoreboard included. "Only one stop, when I tell you. And only one condition for this exercise and all the ones we are going to do in the next few days. You can leave at any time during the exercise, but that means you leave the entire program and you have to leave the venue. Understood?"

The timid response didn't satisfy him.

"Understood, pastors?" several decibels louder, with a tone between serious and humorous, as if he were a military instructor.

"Yes!" They all shouted compliantly.

"Then follow me," said Honorio, and he began to walk towards the bottom of the field, where some trees were visible.

The group starting walking. At first the pace was normal, almost slow, and everyone was together, chatting animatedly. The day and the scenery were beautiful. The first part was a path inside a grove of trees that gradually turned into a forest mostly of pine trees. After about fifteen minutes, they left the forest and opened up to an undulating plain, with no marked trails. At that moment Honorio decided to speed up his pace imperceptibly. Twenty minutes later they reached the edge of the mountains and it was all uphill, making their way through the vegetation in search of the least steep and dangerous path. The pace didn't slacken, so the effort was felt more and more. Within an hour, they were about three hundred meters high at a point from where they could see the house where they were staying.

The group had thinned over time. At the front, following in Honorio's footsteps, were Juan, Nacho and Julio. A little further back, Nora and Mabel were having a lively conversation. The last group was made up of the rest: Pedro, Hugo, Rosa, Marcos, Marcelo and Ernesto. Clearly, the strong point of the latter wasn't physical activity. Pedro had lost weight lately but still had to recover his physical condition and began to complain as soon as they left the forest. It was hard for him not to be ahead or to be the leader, as in the old days.

"What is this, the army?" he shouted at Honorio.

"I remember how you used to play soccer at the Seminary," Hugo reminded him. You wouldn't stop during the whole game."

"Yes, you don't know how I miss playing soccer. It would have been so good for so many things..."

Marcos and Nora had proposed endless times to go for a walk together, something that they liked very much, but they had rarely gone beyond the intention. Ernesto had maintained a regular exercise program before his trip to the United States, but since he arrived there, he had done nothing but accumulate weight and cholesterol, and the bad one, according to his latest tests.

Rosa walked alone, a little because of her proverbial shyness and another because it was a beautiful opportunity to be alone with her thoughts. And she needed it. Far from the pressure of home, far from the kids and even far from Gonzalo. Not because she didn't love them, but because she needed to recover her own identity. Rosa, the one who had dreamed of dedicating herself full time to the work of the Lord, the one who had studied so much, the one who had had so much to give. But now she was "the wife of," "the mother of." She felt that the environment invited her to think. The pines of the forest invited her to look up, as did the upward path out of the forest. The fresh air, the birds, the sun, the white clouds that were approaching, the silence... everything spoke to her of a creation that had always impacted her. It spoke to her of unity and diversity, of creativity, originality. No tree was the same as another, and in a tree no leaf was an exact replica of another. The clouds, the turning of the sun and the wind meant that no two skies were the same. Variety, movement, change. So different from her life, that had become monotonous looking after the children and her husband. Or was it she who had made it monotonous?

When the stragglers arrived at the rest point, Honorio told the whole group:

"Ten minutes rest and we're off!"

Among some complaints and protests, they all sat down in a circle. Some took the opportunity to drink water or eat something they had brought.

True to his habit, Juan had tried to make use of every moment to analyze the mysterious character of the mysterious place, Honorio. Even though he knew that he wouldn't tell him the whole truth, it would be impossible for the conversation not to reveal some personality traits. With a background in human resources, Honorio had been the manager of a multinational food company, based in Buenos Aires, but with responsibility for all Latin America. Five years ago, he had opened a consulting firm specialized in training top-level managers, for whom he organized retreats of different levels of demand.

"And how come you are in a training for pastors?" asked Juan.

"When I was converted five years ago, I began to study the church I was in, but also others that I got to know, with the elements I had to analyze any business, especially people, due to my personal formation... or deformation."

"And what was your impression?"

"Juan, I'll be honest with you. I was scared. I saw so many things done wrong that if any of these churches were a business, they would have gone bankrupt long ago. That's when I realized that the church is a miracle, that it can withstand all kinds of abuse. What we call resilience."

"But if things were being done badly, at least from your point of view, and the church was moving forward, wouldn't the church perhaps have ways of behaving differently from the companies? Other laws. And that's why it persists?" asked Nacho.

"That's the first thing I thought. Maybe the Bible has other principles that allow the church to grow and survive and that have kept it going all these years. But the more I read and researched, the more I realized that this wasn't the case. That what the Bible proposes is a quite simple, flat, communal... almost familiar structure."

"You're saying that pastors aren't necessary, then?" It was Julio.

"Many of today's pastors, doing what they do now, are not. Definitely not. They're more of an obstacle than a help."

"Are we an unnecessary profession, then?" Julio insisted.

"Quite the contrary. I think they are basic to leading any group, but they should be very different from the pastors that exist in almost every church today."

"What would you change?" asked Juan.

"Do you have five hours?" laughing. "There are many things, and we'll have a chance to talk about them in the rest of the retreat. But I would start with just one thing. Two questions. Choose one and answer it: One: What does the pastor exist for? Two: Whom does the pastor exist for?"

Just at that moment they had reached the break and the talk was interrupted, but the questions remained in Juan, Nacho and Julio's minds. What did they exist for? Were they superfluous, as Honorio suggested? Did they have a reason to exist, or were they an anachronism, an anomaly, in a world much more accelerated than that of the Bible? On the other hand, did the new versions of pastors that had emerged, supposedly up to date with the latest technologies, apply biblical principles or human principles, just like any company manager? The second question was even more incisive. For whom did they exist? The automatic answer was "the sheep," the people they pastored. So why had he raised the question? Wasn't it obvious? What had scared him about the churches?

They began the way back after exactly ten minutes. Everyone estimated an hour to return, like the hour it took them to get there, but Honorio chose another path, bordering a beautiful stream that demanded maximum attention at every step so as not to fall. When they were expecting to arrive soon, they suddenly found themselves at another high point in the mountain from where they could see the house from behind, almost the same distance as from the place where they had rested. They felt cheated and began to protest.

"But we are just like an hour ago!" shouted Mabel.

"No, we are at another point, and we have made a beautiful journey along the stream," replied Honorio.

"Why didn't you tell us we were going to make that journey?" Mabel was angry.

"Did anyone ask me?" said Honorio.

"Well, I'm dead tired, and I don't know if I can make it to the house," said Pedro.

"Yes, you're all going to make it, so stop complaining," and Honorio started to walk without looking back.

They had no choice but to follow him, although his level of popularity had fallen considerably. Honorio knew this. It was planned.

More than an hour later, the party arrived at the house. It was close to noon, and there was a pleasant smell of barbecue that made them forget about the fatigue, at least for a while. The meal met the expectations created and was enjoyed unanimously. The only instruction for after lunch was that they would meet again at 3 p.m. sharp in the small room where they had met the first night, the Ergos Room. Some took a nap in their room, others engaged in informal conversations in the dining room and in the garden.

"This second exercise of the day is about prayer, and it will have two parts," said Honorio when they met. "The first part will be spending a long time of individual prayer, in silence. I know that some will find it more difficult than others. All I ask is that you concentrate, that you don't let your mind wander or be distracted by things outside this place. I am going to ask you to focus all your prayer time on this place, in what you experienced yesterday, what we did this morning, with special emphasis on the sensations, what you have felt. I'm going to ask you to separate inside this room and start now."

Hugo took his chair and went to a corner. He felt uncomfortable at this point. So far everything had been fine, between meeting his old companions, the memories, and the jokes. The morning walk had been good too, and although he realized that smoking had affected him quite a bit in his resistance, he had liked being in contact with nature and not being locked up with everyone in Buenos Aires. But since he had received the envelope for "pastor Hugo Carvajal" and the call, he had thought it might have been a mistake by the organizer. After all, he had never been a pastor; he hadn't even finished the Seminary. How long had it been since he had set foot in a church? Technically, he was somebody who had "strayed," and he knew that the first step for somebody in his condition was to return to a church and participate in its activities. But there was something deep inside him that told him that it wasn't by chance that he met Pedro across Nacho's church, and seeing him in such a wrecked condition, he felt sorry for him. It had awakened the pastoral heart that he had had so far back in time, and which perhaps had always remained dormant, waiting for an opportunity to use it. He recognized that he had had the perverse satisfaction of rubbing in Pedro's face, first, and then the others, that he was innocent of the accusation that had ousted him from the Seminary. But that was wrong, and he wondered if deep down—as his therapist would say—he hadn't sought and found a good excuse to leave the Seminary.

A time in prayer. A long time. What would it be, half an hour, an hour? He supposed that these professionals were used to spending hours, just like that. And he hadn't prayed for years. Could it be that God was giving him a chance, a "second chance," more than twenty years later? Could it be that the Lord knew him better than he himself, and that he had been waiting for him all this time? He closed his eyes and began to walk through the time since his arrival to that moment and began to thank God for this opportunity. No doubt he was the one who deserved it the least, but perhaps that is why he would be the one to take advantage of it the most. He revisited one by one the encounters with his former companions. The embrace with Pedro, the genuine surprise of Nora and Mabel, the affectionate words of Juan. No one seemed to remember the incident that had estranged them. And if they did, it was evident that the joy of seeing him was even greater. They were interested in what he was doing, how he was doing, his family, and he found himself doing the same thing, naturally. Ah, if they could all turn back the pages of the calendar and the hands of the clock and start again! His technique for spending that long, indeterminate time was to think of each of his ten companions and ask God to bless them in the things they needed. There he remembered Veronica... and Leo, how he had taken the blow for them in silence. Perhaps that had been a loving, pastoral attitude after all. When he had finished his tour of the ten, and saw that Honorio was still standing impassive, he presented himself to God. His present, his past, his future. His plans, his projects, his frustrations, his fears. His body, his soul, his spirit. Mía, his current partner, his son Santiago, and even his ex-wife, Noelia. His family, his friends. He literally fell before God. Naked and shameless, with reverent fear. He had never had this experience before.

Each of the eleven went through different experiences, and

with different intensities. Pedro and Mabel, the most hyperactive, accustomed to action, finished first. Rosa continued her reflection on her walk in prayer, intensifying it. Marcos and Nora, although praying separately, felt a bond of prayer and had an idea of what the other would be praying. They would have liked to be together. Nacho continued to the end, fully concentrated and changing his position often: standing, sitting, kneeling. Juan also continued to pray until Honorio gave the new instruction:

"When everyone has finished, we will go to the second part of this prayer exercise."

After some minutes, he continued:

"In this second part I am going to ask you to do something very simple: to say, one after the other, the names of all the people you have met in your life, very slowly, expressing, for each one, a silent prayer, presenting them to the Lord. If you don't remember the name, you can simply bring the image of the person to mind. The Lord knows the name. No matter how long it takes, we are in no hurry here," he added, with a smile, with all the peace of the world. "As you finish, in complete silence, you can go out into the garden."

Marcelo had never done anything like that before. He had never been in a psychological therapy, no matter how many times it had been recommended to him. He had suffered a lot since he was a child from his parents, from his schoolmates, from women, who had always made fun of his scrawny, puny appearance. Even though in his adolescence and youth his body had been transformed, naturally and by his own efforts, into a full-fledged athlete, he felt that the wounds of the past were as strong and did as much harm as ever. He now had to add all the people he had met through his political activity, many of whom had hurt him considerably. As names and faces passed silently through his mind, he felt the wounds were going away, or at least they were getting better. He also felt that he was getting much of his life back, that he had tried to ignore or sink into oblivion. It was as if different pieces that had been left over from his life were coming together to reinforce his identity.

The comments of others showed similar experiences, although

not in all cases they were so significant, as they went out into the garden, where a snack had been served. What would come next? they wondered. Some were already restless, although curiosity and the desire to work on their lives in the company of these friends were superior.

When they had all finished, Honorio called them back into the room.

"The next exercise is quite simple, I think," said Honorio, showing a Bible. What I am going to ask you to do is to read aloud the Gospel of Mark, from beginning to end, without stopping. Some of you may have done it, but some of you probably haven't. To give you an idea, it will take you about an hour to read it slowly. Here you have different versions, so choose the one you like best.

"But that's too much!" protested Pedro. He thought Honorio was exaggerating, especially at this point in the day.

"You'll be surprised at how little it takes you...and you won't regret it," Honorio said enigmatically, unyielding.

Each one went to look for a version among those that were there: the Reina-Valera, the best known and most used in the evangelical environment, with the disadvantage of the use of the formal Spanish "vosotros" that nobody used in Latin America, the Popular Version, excellent for reading in a more everyday language, the Bible of the Americas, the Jerusalem Bible—Catholic—, the more recent New International Version...

All you could hear was a murmur and, from time to time, the tired look of some who were obviously not used to reading that long or out loud. But, after an hour and a half, everyone had completed the task. As they went through the various stages of Jesus' life, they relived those three dramatic and action-filled years in Mark's version.

But the greatest surprise would come at the end. When they were all tasting in advance a delicious and comforting supper as the culmination of such a demanding and mobilizing day, Honorio announced that the last exercise of the day was precisely the lack of supper—a fast! The next meal would be served early the next day, starting at five o'clock in the morning.

"But this is an abuse!" said Ernesto. "We didn't come here to starve."

"Why didn't you warn us, so we could eat better before?" said Marcelo.

"If this is the first day, what will the next ones be like? I'm leaving," threatened Pedro, with a tone that was somewhere between angry and humorous.

"You know the condition," Honorio reminded them. "You can leave at any time. All I ask is that you think it over calmly. Ah, I can assure you that I am on the same diet as you and I am not going to eat tonight. Good night."

And with that, he turned around and left toward the office, leaving the group alone.

On Thursday, the second day of the retreat, Juan rose early, as he always did, at five o'clock. He normally prepared a *maté*, read the Bible, meditated on what he had read and had a time of prayer. It was a practice he hadn't abandoned since he was converted. It was his wire to earth, and his wire to heaven. The times he couldn't do it, for one reason or another, he felt that something was missing. Not in the magical sense of being unprotected from evil but rather as not having been fed. Or being unprepared to face the daily barrage of pressures and surprises. Having such a time, every day, no matter what, was his first recommendation for all Christians, pastors or sheep.

When his devotional hour was over, he went out for a walk in the garden, which was at its most glorious moment. With the morning air still fresh and unpolluted, the dew still silvering the grass, the clarity peeping out from behind the trees. He was surprised to see a light in the dining room and approached it, curious. When he entered he was greeted by the smell of a delicious freshly brewed coffee and a table full of everything one could wish for: all kinds of fruit, bacon, scrambled eggs, fruit juices, cereals, cheeses, jams, *facturas*... At a table in the corner, reading, he saw Honorio.

"Good morning, Juan," he said, with a big smile, getting up to greet him. "I was waiting for you."

"What a… nice surprise! And I'm really hungry..."

"I wanted to surprise you, to earn some points after last night. Please help yourself. I was waiting for the first one to join me. I don't like to eat breakfast alone."

Neither did Juan, and he would have loved to have Mariela with him, but in a certain way they had shared that time in prayer, even if it was at different times. The Lord knew how to make the times compatible. He served himself what he knew would be the first dish, since at that moment he would have liked to eat everything at once.

When they began to talk, Juan realized that Honorio knew a lot about his life. At one point he said:

"And how did the Pueblo Manso uprising end?"

"Well, well." He didn't dare ask him how he knew so much about it.

"Well… that's all?"

"No, you're right. It was excellent... miraculous." Somehow, with simple questions, this man was helping him to appreciate something that had certainly been amazing. "The mayor had to resign, and the chief of police. And one of the judges. And for the first time those positions were filled by people who weren't from the families that had run the town for years, fifty years, the Ramirez's, the Costas Navas's and the Pelliteri's."

"What name had you given the movement?"

"The truth will set you free," answered Juan.

"And was it so?"

Juan thought for a while. He remembered the story/legend Saverio had told him when he had arrived in town and the last few days. What had been the evolution? From lie to truth, or from desire to reality? He thought about the relationship with Tomás and that of their respective churches. Wasn't that the truth liberating? And the participation of Francisco Gómez? Hadn't there been liberation in don Francisco and in Juan's relationship with him?

"Yes, of course... In many ways. Freedom from fear, from lies, from corruption... from useless and stupid division."

"And now, how are you?" The tone and the look indicated a genuine interest, pastoral rather than psychological.

"I find it hard to define myself. Expectant, surprised, enthusiastic. This here, meeting so many people after so many years..."

"Especially Pedro," added Honorio, completing the sentence he was about to say. *Who was this man?*

"How did you know what I was going to say?"

"They told me a lot about the friendship you had years ago. What happened to make that relationship go cold?" Only a couch separated the talk from a psychoanalysis session.

"You know I've asked myself that many times, and there's no answer. I would almost say..." He stopped abruptly.

"Keep going. I'm listening."

"It's just that what I was about to say sounds stupid."

"It doesn't matter, it's probably the truth."

"Don't tell me you know what I was going to say!" with a slightly annoying and frustrated air.

"No, I don't. But I can guarantee you were about to say a 'liberating truth,' to continue with the previous theme."

"What I was going to say was that it was as if the profession, the pastorate, the church had separated us. That simply because we went to different churches, with different practices, and because we had different styles of living our faith, that would have distanced us..."

"Exactly. It happens too often. There are often greater divisions between those who share the same faith than between these same people and those who don't."

"And why does that happen?"

"My theory is that because they don't confront the natural differences that exist between people and groups and prefer to cover them with the veneer of 'Christian love' or whatever, they keep widening until they explode, also with another veneer."

"What is that veneer?"

"Subjection or not to the pastor of the day, rebellion, seeking a church according to the will of the Lord… and I can give you a lot more rationalizations to cover up a simple untreated difference. But what was it that separated you initially?" Honorio insisted.

"I criticized him for his ambition to grow, for the numbers, for the programs, projects, people he knew. The church big time. And he criticized me for my lack of ambition. He said that we had to get rid of the mentality of the poor. There's an old song that talks about that, that we are a very happy little people." He started singing it.

"To many of us it just seemed simplistic, but Pedro hated it," Juan recalled. "On the other hand, I have to admit that many of us who participated in the renewal movement, in the home groups, considered ourselves several steps above, spiritually, from the rest. Something like 'less but better.' Our leaders, while they didn't have the characteristics that irritated me in the leaders of large groups that he admired, had another type of more subtle pride that ended up being as harmful as the other. Because they had the truth, and the unity they advocated had to be made by accepting their proposal. Just as we criticized the Catholic church. I remember that in the family meetings we felt a bit superior spiritually, and I'm sure the others perceived that."

"And today, with the distance of time… and in this place, what do you think?"

"That we lost a lot of time uselessly, that we should have enhanced and compensated each other. How many other similar cases must there be!"

At that moment Mabel arrived and, right behind her, Nacho, so they invited them to the table and the conversation was interrupted. But Juan had found it tremendously useful. Honorio noticed a certain coldness on the part of some of the arrivals.

After breakfast, they met in the living room. Honorio stood before a quite different group from the one he had met twenty-four hours earlier.

"Good morning, how did you get up today?" Without waiting for a reply, he continued. "Today we are going to spend the first part of the day evaluating yesterday's five exercises."

"What do you mean, five? There were four," said Hugo.

"Let's see, which were they for you?" asked Honorio.

"The morning walk, the two prayer meetings and the reading of Mark."

"You missed the fast," said Honorio.

"A forced fast, if anything!" said Pedro, seeking the approval of the rest.

"All right, a forced fast. And I am sure it was the exercise you will remember most, or at least the one you will remember me for the most..." The group relaxed somewhat, and some smiles appeared.

"I want to explain briefly what was behind yesterday's exercises, why we did them, and why we did them on the first day of this pastors' retreat," Honorio continued. "If I had to give a title to yesterday it would be 'Discipline.' Broadly speaking, in the morning we saw the need for bodily discipline, and in the afternoon the spiritual disciplines. In my experience, the two go together. The person who doesn't discipline the body, will find it difficult to discipline the soul and spirit, and vice versa. What I am talking about is the attitude of discipline. Of setting goals and accomplishing them. To deprive oneself of things in order to achieve others. Of setting aside time for useful activities and taking time away from those that are not useful. Of being willing to change habits for better ones. Something very basic, very elementary, which is the basis of all success: material, physical and spiritual. We can have physical fat, which prevents us from walking and enjoying God's creation, but we can also have spiritual fat, which prevents us from walking in the spiritual area and enjoying God's creation in the spiritual area.

The explanation of what they had done, and why they had done it, triggered an exchange of ideas and experiences that occupied the next hour. When he saw that he was no longer needed to lead the conversation, Honorio slowly walked away to the side, taking notes of what was said and working on his sociogram. He watched Pedro slowly regain his leadership role and the game of polemics with Juan that had been mentioned to him at the Seminary was repeated. Hugo was already one of the group. Mabel was a whirlwind of proposals and ideas, but she had found a balance in Rosa's shyness, the person she talked to most. Marcelo, Julio, Nacho, Marcos, Nora and Ernesto represented the traditional less committed majority in any group, who listened to the arguments of one side or the other, opting for one or the other alternately, even though the voice of the last speaker stood out above the rest constantly.

There were other themes that emerged from the experience of the previous day. Like, for example, the experience of people used to lead who had to follow the instructions of another. The pastor acting like a sheep. The proposal of the need to return to the plain periodically came up. That the person in authority should be able to be under authority. Whether it was convenient for someone to enter directly into the pastorate without having gone through the experience of working under authority, especially in the secular world. Or even whether it was convenient for a young person to enter directly into pastoral work without having known the "real world," as Hugo said. With a schedule, with a boss who mistreated him, with people pulling the rug from under, with the possibility of being fired, or of being out of work. From this also came the issue of the convenience of dedicating yourself full-time to a church or Christian organization as opposed to having a secular job while performing a spiritual service. And from there, another discussion about spiritual or secular work. One topic led to the other, freely, without a formal context. Honorio imagined them all twenty years younger. What would have been their views at that time on these same topics? He was especially interested in Pedro, and tried to pick out his contributions from among the others:

"I believe the church can function as a business, but you can't give all the power to the pastor. It's dangerous."

.....

"I like the idea of going back to the plain from time to time. What happens is that when one is up there is so much to do that, if it isn't established beforehand, no one will comply."

.....

"What happened to me when I was in trouble was that I didn't know how to do anything but pastor. I would have loved to have left everything behind and dedicated myself to something with less problems."

.....

"People are to blame too. I realized, deep down, that many of those who patted me on the back did it only out of interest... Actually, I was with them out of interest too."

.....

"There were two people, three, who helped me. A friend, who wan't a pastor, who sought me out. A pastor, who I looked for, and who is here" —looking at Nacho, without naming him— "and my wife. The rest only participated in the show I had put together."

The days and exercises of the "A Second Chance" retreat went as planned. After the surprise and some initial resistance on the tough initial day, it was easier on the second day, because bonds and relationships from years back had been reestablished.

On the second day in the morning they had to overcome several obstacles—crossing the stream, looking for something in a tall tree, getting food—and make decisions that could only be made together. The group split in two and set out as a kind of competition. The afternoon activity consisted of a time of reflection, also divided into two parts, where Honorio guided them to go through individually first and then in pairs, their life in the last twenty years and the instances in which they used the team's resource and those that didn't. The last session was a talk by Honorio on the basic principles of teamwork. Although he had wanted to limit this dynamic to the minimum, he realized that it was a necessity, since he saw that it was a very individualistic group, and that it had suffered—and made other suffer—a lot because of this. One thing he addressed in his talk was teamwork between leaders and led, a concept that few people knew, tending to see the concept of teamwork between leaders only. He ended with a role play to try to illustrate this concept. The theme of the day was clear: "Teamwork."

The third day, Friday, dawned rainy, and everyone took it for granted that they wouldn't go out in the morning. Wrong. Honorio showed up with rain gear for each one: hooded riders and boots, the right size. To the amazed and questioning looks of some, he reminded them of the theme of day one: discipline. Nobody said anything. Before leaving, Honorio gave each one an instruction, without the others knowing it. Juan had to ensure that the whole walk, which used to take about two and a half hours, was done in fifteen minutes less. Pedro, on the other hand, had to make it take fifteen minutes longer. Hugo had to be constantly positive about everything that was happening, including the rain. Julio had to be the eternal pessimist, criticizing everything, always negative. Marcelo would be Honorio's "bootlicker," the eternal obsequious and "snitch." Rosa, the rebel, the questioner. Mabel was to play the role of the fixer of all the problems and tensions that would arise. Marcos, on the other hand, had to fuel the confrontations. Nora was to take a negative attitude in general about the retreat, saying that she would leave the same day, once the walk was over. Ernesto had to advocate extending the retreat and making others; he was to be delighted with everything that had happened so far. Nacho had been assigned to support the different positions successively, to help create confusion. Ideally, he should represent the people in a group who don't have a fixed position and are constantly changing. In reality, they were the most difficult, and the most dangerous.

Honorio knew that he had planted a lot of mines in the group and that things could go wrong. But he preferred to take the risk than leave everyone with a false image of reality. "If it doesn't break, it means I can use it; if it breaks, I'm glad I didn't use it" was the philosophy he followed here. If the group didn't stand the test, there would still be time to work, but he had to be with the utmost attention, along with the infiltrator who would be helping him from the inside, as up to now. After all, he had done this exercise with so many groups of managers, why shouldn't it work with people who should be prepared to face situations of all kinds, by training and vocation?

The walk was rough, with moments of great tension. For example, during the first hour, when they had already left the forest, drenched and treading on mud, with several falls on their backs, Ernesto began to say:

"What a wonderful experience! Why don't we ask for it to be extended further? It would be good to go for a walk at night, wouldn't it? I am going to recommend this retreat to everyone I know."

Pedro, Rosa, and Julio, a little bit because of their roles but more because they represented the whole group, ran after him throwing everything they found at hand. That's where Marcelo came in:

"Guys, it seems to me that Honorio doesn't deserve this. With all he has done for us, and all he has to give us..."

"The only thing missing was a bootlicker!" Marcos, stoking the confrontation. "Don't you think your beloved Honorio gets something out of it?"

"It can't be that eleven guys let ourselves be driven by one! Why didn't anyone say anything about going out on a rainy day?" Rosa, the "rebel."

"Come on, guys, it's not that bad, we're nearly there." Mabel, the fixer.

"There's no point in all this." Nora, the pessimist. "When we get back, I'm going home."

"Well, well, Nora, don't be like that. I'm sure the sun will come out now and we'll be able to spend the rest of the day in the swimming pool. I think the sky is clearing up over there. You'll have to believe me." Hugo, pointing to a place that seemed to everyone to be darker than the rest of the sky.

"Of course, Nora is right and you who criticize, but this will also do us good and everything will be better in the afternoon. Honorio has his things but he's very capable." Nacho, the perfect nondescript.

While it was true that everyone was playing a role, the combination of functions began to exacerbate the mood, and they began to forget that it was a game, an exercise. Honorio knew that there would be a moment when he would have to stop the exercise so that it wouldn't cause any harm. It was one of the strongest criticisms he had for many apprentices of psychologists or sociologists, or recent graduates, or pastors and leaders who had learned some elements of these sciences, and who used the material in their churches for their experiments. He had seen real disasters in individuals, families, and groups as a result of incorrect or misused techniques.

The group endured the tensions until the resting place on the mountain, where the performance continued without interruption. Honorio suddenly realized that some were enjoying this performance, being able to do things they wouldn't normally do. It was there that the exercise was richer, when everyone realized that they were playing, and Honorio witnessed some exchanges that were almost more realistic than reality.

After lunch and a break, they met in the hall to discuss the topic of the day. Before that, each one tried to discover the role of the others and ended up revealing them. A spontaneous vote for the best actor fell unanimously on Marcelo, the obsequious to the point of irritation, but a faithful reflection of countless people they had all met throughout their life and ministry, for some of them. For Honorio, the exercise had been a success, and he smirked.

They were ready to address the topic of the day, Accountability, which began with a study of the concept in the secular world, the country's long tradition of politicians seizing power, reaping all the benefits, especially the economic ones, and then leaving the scene without being held accountable. He spoke of concepts that had emerged in the evangelical world that spoke of pastors not being accountable to people of flesh and blood here and now, but to God in the distant future. This was no different from enlightened rulers who wanted to be judged by "history." What was the error behind this reasoning?

"That we are all going to be judged by God in the future, so it doesn't add anything that God judges pastors," said Hugo.

"Right. It isn't a privilege of pastors or leaders. But the proof is that those who didn't submit themselves to a true, transparent, nonfiction accountability system ended up hopelessly in delusions of grandeur or sin. The history of the church says so. On the other hand, those who sought to have a system of control were able to avoid these excesses."

There Honorio proposed that each of them should have a control or accountability group, based on their own experience and that of others he knew. The idea was to meet once a week, a group of between three and five people of the same sex, systematically going through different areas of their lives before the others. He showed them on the screen a model of questions that allowed them to do this exercise. The first section dealt with the spiritual life, with questions about reading the Bible, prayer, temptation, confession, worship and witness. Then followed a section on home life (wife, children, finances), another on life at work, and the last was called "critical issues," with deep questions that went to the very core of personality and relationships:

Pedro was familiar with the concept. It was what Mercedes and the girls had done with Virginia. When Honorio asked if anyone knew the concept, only a couple raised their hand apart from Pedro. When he asked if anyone had ever practiced it, some said that it was partly what happened in home groups, but not in such a formal and transparent way.

The second part was a practical exercise. In two groups, everyone had to pretend to be a practicing pastor and go through the battery of questions that Honorio had handed out to them in a folder entitled "Accountability." Pedro remembered the material with the same title that Raúl had given him and that he had thrown away. How much good it would have done him, and how much suffering would have been avoided, for him, for Virginia, the children, and the church!

The exercise was constructive in both teams. The participants got into the roles perfectly and came out with a countless number of problems, their own or those of others, but all taken from real life, which Honorio was furiously writing down in his notebook. Something that emerged was how little the pastors read the Bible, outside of their "professional" responsibilities, often limiting themselves to known passages and thinking exclusively about their obligations, the Sunday sermon, and not to feed and change their own lives. The little time spent in intimate prayer or in a trusted group. In these two areas, it was as if their quota was covered by their professional task, and they didn't need to use them for their own edification. They didn't seem to need it. Or they were tired of them. When they touched on the temptations, between jokes and improvisations came the three usual themes: power, money, sex. There was little or no real confession in the presence of flesh and blood people. Questions about life in the home drew a negative balance. It seemed as if, for a pastor, the people and problems of the church took up much more time and were much more important than his wife and children.

The "critical issues" area was the most intense. How do you know if you're in the center of God's will? Maybe you were at the beginning, or years ago. And now? The "secret thoughts"... Here doubts, depression, inadequacy, loneliness arose. The question about integrity—is your moral and ethical behavior as it should be?—generated a very lively discussion in Pedro's group, with Marcelo, Ernesto, Nacho and Mabel. Especially in relation to political activity, where Pedro and Marcelo had been on opposite sides of the system. What was the area of high personal risk for each? Certainly money, power and sex, but also pride, manipulation, cowardice, accommodation, laziness. And so they continued to go through the questions, one by one, running through the entire life of each one and exposing it in this simulated exercise to others, as if they were really accountable to others.

Honorio organized the fourth day with a less emotionally engaged activity, basically dedicated to reflect during the whole day on a writing he gave them the night before to read called "Height, Depth, Direction."[62] In the article, the unknown author spoke of three aspects of the spiritual life that should be considered in order to move forward. Height, like birds, allowed us to have a wider vision, of another dimension, of reality. Depth, like icebergs, gave us the possibility to bear the onslaught of life with all serenity. Direction,

---

[62] Included at the end of the book

knowing where to go, allowed us to use our resources efficiently so as not to waste them in useless undertakings.

The supreme example of these three virtues was, for the author, Jesus. He had a vision "from above" that allowed him to have a more complete picture than the others, a depth that allowed him to withstand the pressures and betrayals of those who were closer to him but, above all, a sense of direction and opportunity to know at every moment what he should do, even when he had to leave aside fame and popularity to go to the scaffold of the cross. Of course, the message was very clear to all pastors: their example should be the supreme Pastor.

The morning walk, this time under a radiant sun and a perfectly blue sky, gave ample opportunity to illustrate from nature each of the three aspects of the article, and Honorio took the opportunity to share them at the time of the rest in the mountain. There they were at a high point, seeing their previous and future journey, and the house, from a particular perspective. The depth was illustrated by the invisible roots of the giant trees that had endured, for example, yesterday's rain. Direction was what had led them to that retreat, but it was also what directed them at that moment. They knew where they came from and they knew where they were going.

The afternoon was dedicated to various exercises aimed at investigating, in each, what things helped them to acquire height, what things gave them depth, and what helped them to have direction in the midst of so many confusing signs. It was, in a sense, a preparation for the last session, the one that Honorio thought would be the most difficult, and the most useful. For that reason, he let them have a free time after the snack, which was well used by everyone in the pool.

Sunday was the fifth and last day of the retreat, the day of unveiled mysteries and prepared surprises.

During the morning walk, always with the same route, they

had to think and meditate, or talk among themselves, the question: "What is my vocation today?" A little bit because of the theme itself, a little bit because it was the last walk, everyone made the most of it. Some preferred to reflect on the topic alone for a large part of the walk, others preferred to talk about it with one or two people, and others went around all of them, asking and wondering what their true vocation was. The talk continued over lunch.

They were now gathered in the hall.

"I see you've been thinking about this morning's question quite a bit. Would anyone like to share the answers?" Honorio asked.

"I shouldn't have been a pastor." The confession, the certainty with which he said it, but especially who said it, left everyone frozen.

"How's that, Pedro?" asked Honorio.

"I think I could have served the Lord and the church much better from somewhere else, but not as a pastor."

There was a silence that no one tried to break artificially. It was one of the lessons learned from the retreat. After a while, Honorio asked the obvious question:

"Then why did you become a pastor?" Honorio insisted.

"I don't think it was wrong to study at the Seminary, but I think my mistake, or the Seminary's mistake, was to make us believe that because we were interested in studying there and because we had finished studying there, we were automatically prepared to be pastors."

Another useful, powerful silence. Honorio knew that several were thinking deeply about every word that Pedro had said. He could almost tell who they were.

"And when did you realize that you shouldn't have been a pastor?" Honorio asked.

"When I did my practice in that little church, Light and Love, while I was still in the Seminary. There I realized that being a pastor, a real pastor, wasn't for me."

Third silence. As in music scores, it had to have the right length.

"Why didn't you leave earlier?" The instructor was cutting deep.

"I was thinking about it today. It's as if I had gotten on a train that was going faster and faster, with more and more people... When I realized it, twenty years had passed, and I was on the wrong train. Luckily, I was able to get off these five days and think about what I was doing... But I think if it's not too late..." His words had a deep sadness and sincerity.

"I, on the other hand, should have been a pastor." It was Hugo this time, as unexpected as Pedro's confession.

"How come?" asked Honorio.

"I think, like Jonah, I looked for the excuse of the incident in the Seminary to escape God's call." He was referring to the biblical character who, instead of fulfilling God's command to preach repentance in the city of Nineveh, took a boat to Spain and ended up inside a fish.

"I'm going to ask you the same questions I asked Pedro. When did you realize you should have been a pastor?"

"I always knew, even when I left the Seminary. And I think every day and every night since then. My way of avoiding the call was to criticize everything, avoiding anything that had to do with the church, but I always had that illusion hidden somewhere in my heart."

"Why didn't you try to come back sooner?"

"I think out of cowardice. Or because I thought... I think it's too late. Or because I never had a chance as precious as this, somebody who would believe in me, and meet all of you..." It had the same emotion and sincerity of Pedro.

"It's never too late," said Mabel, spontaneously.

"It's true. And I think of the envelope we received a week ago, and the name of this retreat, 'A Second Chance.' I think we have to take advantage of it." It was Ernesto's clear speaker voice.

"In my case, I think I was more of a pastor when I didn't have the title than when I did." It was Juan.

"Please explain," said Honorio.

"I think that with Mariela, we were always interested in spending time with people, their needs. Interestingly, when I ended up working as a pastor in the first church it was when I had the least freedom to do the work of a pastor. On the other hand, I know a lot of people who do the work of pastor without having the title, who aren't interested in the title or position, who have the vocation, the heart of a pastor. They pastor one by one, silently, anonymously."

"What Juan says is true," said Pedro, "because I, at the moment of my greatest 'success'—air quotes— "as a pastor, or at least according to my vision of the success of the pastor, was when I felt furthest away from the people. I had become something else, without realizing it. There were people who told me that silently, and others who liked that kind of pastor."

"It's as if people need a type of pastor and the system leads you to be something else." This was Marcelo. "The same thing happened to me when I got into politics, as a pastoral area, although it seems a contradiction in terms. The people want, need a person who takes care of their needs, but when you get to have a position the system molds you into what it is used to. It will file you down until all of your own edges are removed. It's like a monster that doesn't accept different, questioning people. It doesn't even expect you to be authentic. That is why the same people who encouraged me to be a light in the midst of darkness, the day I held office demanded benefits, perks. They saw me as another representative of the system, with the only difference or advantage that they knew me."

"I was thinking about the question Honorio asked me earlier: 'Why didn't I get out earlier.' I realized at one point that the only thing I knew how to do, which I had done all my life, was to work as a pastor. What was I going to do?" Pedro continued.

The spontaneous talk continued during the first hour of the afternoon time and each one felt free to be honest regarding their vocational situation before that group of friends and brothers who would understand and support them in everything they said. But there was a second part still to come.

At that moment Honorio told them the story of the We Are group. How it had emerged, the first meetings, and the tremendous growth they had had in recent months. He told them about the need it sought to cover for many people who had been left out of the system due to abuse, mistakes or simple neglect by pastors and leaders. Although only a few knew about the We Are group—among them, obviously, Juan—the topic was rich enough to generate another debate.

It was interesting because there were some who had been "on both sides of the counter," and knew the experience of leading and being led. The subject of different types of members, loyalty, accountability, loneliness of the leader, the demand for advice, difficult members, divisions, ingratitude, came up. And then Honorio asked them:

"Would you like to meet the brothers and sisters of the We Are group?", at the optimal time to cause maximum effect.

There and then Raúl, Mercedes, Mariela, Fernando, Priscila and Camila appeared through the door. The surprise was total, even for Juan, who didn't know Mariela was coming. She had come with Virginia, also a surprise for Pedro. After greeting each other, Honorio explained to them that he had thought of this possibility to try to bridge the gap that had arisen recently between pastors and members.

The last surprise was missing. Who were the people responsible for this retreat?

Honorio took the lead one last time.

"Now, what you asked me the first day and you haven't been able to discover these days, from what I see. I am going to ask the person responsible for this retreat to come forward and explain to us why and what for he did it," looking inexplicably at the group of pastors.

At that moment Nacho stood up and went to the microphone. After a few seconds of total surprise, a spontaneous applause of gratitude came from the group.

"Thank you very much...thank you very much, brothers and sisters." Nacho was visibly moved. "You don't know how much it means to me, first that you came and then that you participated with so much enthusiasm in this retreat."

Then he told them how he had maintained contact with each of the students of the Seminary throughout these years, even with those who weren't there today. He had made it a point to call each one at least once a year, wherever he or she was. The others nodded mechanically, remembering how many times Nacho had called home, or at work, just to see how they were doing. The reason for doing this was that he had had the deep conviction, a month before the end of the Seminary, that everyone would go down difficult roads and that a meeting like this would be necessary. He didn't know when or how, but he had relived much of what had happened these five days time and time again in prayer and in his imagination, to the point of being surprised at how many details were fulfilled exactly as he had imagined. For example, the rain on the third day. Or the number of people. He even knew with certainty that Hugo, the most unlikely, would come.

Honorio had gone to his church once and when Nacho learnt what he did for a living, the Spirit showed him that he was the person to lead the retreat. The final piece was when in a telephone conversation with Mariela she mentioned casually the name of Horacio Sosa, the retired manager of the Banco Nación in Pueblo Manso. When he heard the name, he had the conviction that he was the person the Lord had chosen to finance the retreat. He found out his number, and as soon as he called him, don Horacio told him that he had an amount set apart for a special use that he ignored so far. It turned out to be exactly what was required for the expenses of the retreat. It had taken him almost a year to organize the details. But the prayer that covered the entire event had taken more than twenty years.

The rest of that time and the evening, until dinner, was spent working together, pastors and lay people, a large team of seventeen, to find ways to bridge the gap between pastors and sheep. The mission had just begun.

FROM
THERE ON

(2003)

13

THE STORY GOES ON

Now we're free to be those we were meant to be
And release those we held to run and break free

Pedro left the pastorate for good and teamed up with Honorio and Ariel from the We Are group to form a training consultancy. Ernesto joined the Virginia radio team and they did so well that they were called to do a television program. Roque, the oldest of the Terrero's, returned home when he saw the settled parents. He's studying law but plays with the idea of becoming a pastor someday. The girls have never been happier.

Juan and Mariela are still in Pueblo Manso, where Hugo moved with his family to work in the church. Their son, Santiago, and the Cristante twins are great friends, and all three are members of the new Truth and Freedom Party. Mariela and Mía, Hugo's wife, are very close friends and work in the now Pueblo Manso Open Word Church, which ceased to be a mission in 2006, when the elders of the church in Buenos Aires came to give them all their support in this new phase.

We continue to work with the We Are group, going in and out of ProRot, but always collaborating. We have an office with a minimal structure; basically, a secretary and a telephone, and a room to interview the "wounded soldiers" and pray with them. Today the group has more than 9,000 members throughout the country, almost half of whom have joined different churches. In addition, we have joined a small church, but with many possibilities for healthy growth.

How can we conclude a story that continues, that is alive—in the protagonists of this story, but also in the readers who identify with their struggles and circumstances—and that is ultimately the product of the pen of the great Author of all? Perhaps the best way is to share the words scribbled on a sheet that appeared stuck to one of the columns of the pergola at the place of the retreat on the last day. Honorio read it as they were about to leave the place after asking who had written it, but no one answered. Knowing him, maybe he had written it himself... or who knows, it came from someone outside the group, but inside each of them... It went like this:

No

No
Not what I thought.
Not what I dreamed.
Far more difficult
Far more thankless
I was less strong
I am less pure

No
I couldn't win there.
I couldn't lose here
Far more difficult
Far more thankless
I was less strong
I am less pure

No
No more people to serve
No more people to hurt
Far more difficult

Far more thankless
I was less strong
I am less pure

But No
No and No
I can't accept I must lose
I can't accept I must quit
Although it's difficult
Although it's thankless
Because He is stronger
Because He is so pure

Camp Poimén, 2003

APPENDIX:
HEIGHT, DEPTH, DIRECTION

I like to watch the birds. Not only because of the beauty of their movements and their appearance, but especially because of their freedom to move and escape from the limitations in which we humans move. At one moment, a bird is in my garden, restricted to a relatively awkward movement on the ground, and at another it takes flight with tremendous ease and may be in another garden, in a tree, or in another city. I envy its ability to see things from a much broader and comprehensive perspective. Like when you look from an airplane at the same houses and roads you travel every day with a completely different aspect and proportion.

As I look at them and think about these things I cannot help but think about life in the spirit to which the Lord calls us, a life that must be able to transcend daily limitations in order to "take flight." Not only quantitatively, but qualitatively, with an additional dimension. We need to "fly" with our imagination to try to see our life or our mission as the Lord would see them, without the restrictions of the everyday or the known. Sometimes it does us good to close our eyes and try to imagine all that we could do in one year, or in five. Extending ourselves beyond our limitations and fears, beyond the "can't be done's" or "the never was done's" in order to "conquer the world." It is a very frequent technique in motivational talks or self-help books, and it can also help us in private or group prayer. The question is: Why don't we generally achieve what we visualize or imagine, or we achieve it and it is short-lived? Why isn't it enough with *height*?

We lack a second dimension: *depth*. Like icebergs, what our life shows—what can be seen—is only a very small proportion of who we are. In many ways, what is important is what is *not* seen. What gives sustenance to the outside, what allows us to resist attacks. One of the most important teachings Jesus gave is the so-called Parable of the Sower, although a more accurate name would be the Parable of the Seeds. It is found in Matthew 13:3-8, with Jesus' explanation immediately following in verses 18-23. Note the second case, the seed that falls on stony ground. It says that it "*sprang up quickly*, because the soil was shallow." The Master's explanation: "The seed falling on rocky ground refers to someone who hears the word and *at once* receives it with joy. But since they have no root, they last only a short time." A shooting star! The artist or the athlete of the moment! The fashionable character! They appear quickly... and disappear quickly.

Now, we all know people who have both great vision—height— and great inner life—depth—, but who don't manage to bear true and lasting fruit. They remain in projects and plans. They think but do not do. Or they do but do not achieve something valuable and lasting. Could there be another dimension missing? Definitely.

We need to have *direction*. We need to know where to direct our efforts and where to invest the little time we have. We also need to learn to say "no" when we understand that saying the opposite takes us away from the direction we have set. In reality, amid so many voices, pressures, noise and confusion, it is more important today to know where *not* to go than where to go. When we look back, any of us, isn't it true that at various crossroads in our lives we should have chosen the other path, that many things we did turned out to be a waste of time, that we heard the wrong voice in the crowd? We wish we hadn't made so many wrong choices in the past, and we would like not to waste our time and energy from now on.

So we need to simultaneously improve the three dimensions of our life to be truly productive: height, depth and direction. But how can we transcend the limitations of our daily lives, build a solid foundation and not mistake the road?

For the Christian, one of the main ways of getting used to seeing things as God sees them is through the *systematic, complete, and constant reading of the Bible.* The experience of those who have this healthy habit—as opposed to the habit of using loose pieces of written revelation to accommodate our previous ideas, the ideas of leaders or fashionable ideas—is that *our mind becomes aligned with the mind of God*, the ideas of the world disappear and we begin to see the same previous problems and situations in a different way. This gives us height, perspective.

As for depth, we associate it with *prayer and meditation*. I would clarify that it is not about the hurried prayer, the list of requests or thanks, or repeating the final prayer of the day's devotional. It is about *spending time with the Lord*, without rushing, letting the Holy Spirit show us how we really are and asking him to make us more and more like Jesus was and is in his innermost being, so that we can be like him in his actions.

It is more difficult to define the way to achieve direction in the life of the Christian. On the one hand, we know that the Bible gives us direction and the Holy Spirit in us speaks to us in different ways. We know that other Christians, especially those who are closer and more spiritual, can help us make decisions. We also learn from the past, from our mistakes and successes. Common sense does not stop working when we know the Lord, and we should use it without fear. But there is an especially important element in this area: *the actions of the enemy*. And the order of this list above reflects exactly what his greatest strength is: *not realizing his existence or his actions. Or his intentions.* What better for the one who came to "steal, kill and destroy" than a great venture, with vision and solid foundation, headed in the wrong direction! Plans, resources, people, structure, time, and even prayers... for something that is misdirected.

There are people who have the ability to see far and imagine great projects, and others who are very skilled at inspiring others to follow those projects, both outside and inside the church. They are always dreaming, always motivating, always optimistic. "Just imagine it, just say it, and it will come true!" "You can do it!" "Claim that word for yourself!" But the *vision without depth and direction* is not far from what we are offered shelf after shelf in the self-help section of today's bookstores.

There are others who have a deep devotional life, dedicating themselves to prayer and constant fasting. Their whole world revolves around them, their feelings, their experience with God, their "inner healing," what "God told them." They read and study the Bible, they spend hours in their "inner room," taking refuge in the only thing they know how to do as soon as they encounter problems in the turbulent and uncertain world of human relations outside. *Depth without height and direction*. Selfishness and isolation.

Both dimensions—height and depth—are necessary, together, to be a complete Christian, according to the model of Jesus. But even together they are not enough. *We need the right direction, the right course.* And this information can be difficult to obtain, and very easy to misrepresent. *Height and depth prepare us to set out on the path, but we want the path to be the right one, and the time dedicated to it to be used well.* We need to be trained in *obedience*, so as not to choose what seems best to us, what pleases us most, what looks good, what everyone does, and instead do the will of the Father.

As always, as in everything, *our example is Jesus.* Who, like him, had a clear vision of his life and the Father's purpose? Who surpassed him in the life of prayer, even after exhausting days of work, to the point that his disciples asked him, "Lord, teach us to pray?" But above all, *who like him was clear about the direction he should take at every moment of his life, in total obedience and even at the cost of his own life?* I am always impressed by the passage in Luke 9:51: "As the time approached for him to be taken up to heaven, Jesus *resolutely* set out for Jerusalem." Jesus was going through a time of great popularity and success in his ministry, but there came a key moment in his life (and in human history) when he turned his back on "success" to be "led like a lamb to the slaughter." I am struck by the fact that the above passage does not explicitly mention death or the cross, when Jesus clearly knew that "taken up to heaven" would come after the horrific death of the cross and "setting out to Jerusalem" was to enter territory where his enemies had sworn to kill him. It occurs to me that the reason for this omission is that, for the Christian who lives in height, depth, and direction, the "accidents" on the path laid out (problems, satisfactions, persecution, joys, death) are not as important as they are for those who live more according to the world's petty patterns.

Let us seek to be whole Christians, with the supreme example of Jesus. Let's always try to transcend the mediocrity and short-sightedness in which the world (and the world in the church) wants to confine us, but not by using the techniques of that same world, but by saturating our minds with the pure Word of God. Let's dedicate time to prayer, not just the hurried one, but especially the one that takes time and where the accelerated and hellish (adj. belonging or related to hell!) rhythm of the world does not enter. *And, above all, let us seek divine guidance at all times, to be productive and avoid the trap of the enemy, who doesn't care if we do many things, as long as they are not what God wants us to do.*

Alejandro Field

Printed in the United States
By Bookmasters